Shall We Dance?

SEASONS OF LOVE:
BOOK 2

CAROLINE FRANK

Copyright © 2023 by Caroline Frank

Edited by Jenn Lockwood

Cover by Ink&Laurel

All rights reserved.

No part of this book may be reproduced in any form or by any electronic or mechanical means, including information storage and retrieval systems, without written permission from the author, except for the use of brief quotations in a book review.

PRAISE FOR
Fall Into You

If When Harry Met Sally is the quintessential fall movie, Fall Into You is the quintessential fall book. So many quirky, funny episodes, romantic scenes and steamy, heart-racing moments.

AMAZON REVIEWER

I loved, loved, loved this book! It has spice, it has the brother's best friend trope, and it has the instalove, but done in a way that doesn't make me cringe. Liza and Matt's chemistry is over the top awesome, and I'm insanely excited to see that it is book one in a series!

@ROMANCEBOOKSFAN

If you're looking for a rom-com with a Fall feeling, look no further 🎃 I'm looking forward to the next installment in the series.

@LISSTHEBOOKLOVER

PRAISE FOR
Shall We Dance?

This book easily moved to my favorite rom com spot. Barbara and Theo are such a fun couple. I'm a sucker for enemies to lovers and Caroline Frank did a wonderful job nailing this with the perfect amount of banter, spice, and tension. I found myself thinking about this story constantly, and couldn't wait to finish it, but also wanted to savor every word.

@VICWITHTHEGOODBOOKS

This book is everything a romance novel should be. It had all the pieces for a perfect love story. Enemies to lovers, grump and sunshine, and a detrimental miss communication. What more could a romance lover want?? I loved the characters and how real and relatable they were. Shall We Dance is a 10/10.

AMAZON REVIEWER

I'm swooning over this book!

JENG

Where flowers bloom, so does hope

LADY BIRD JOHNSON

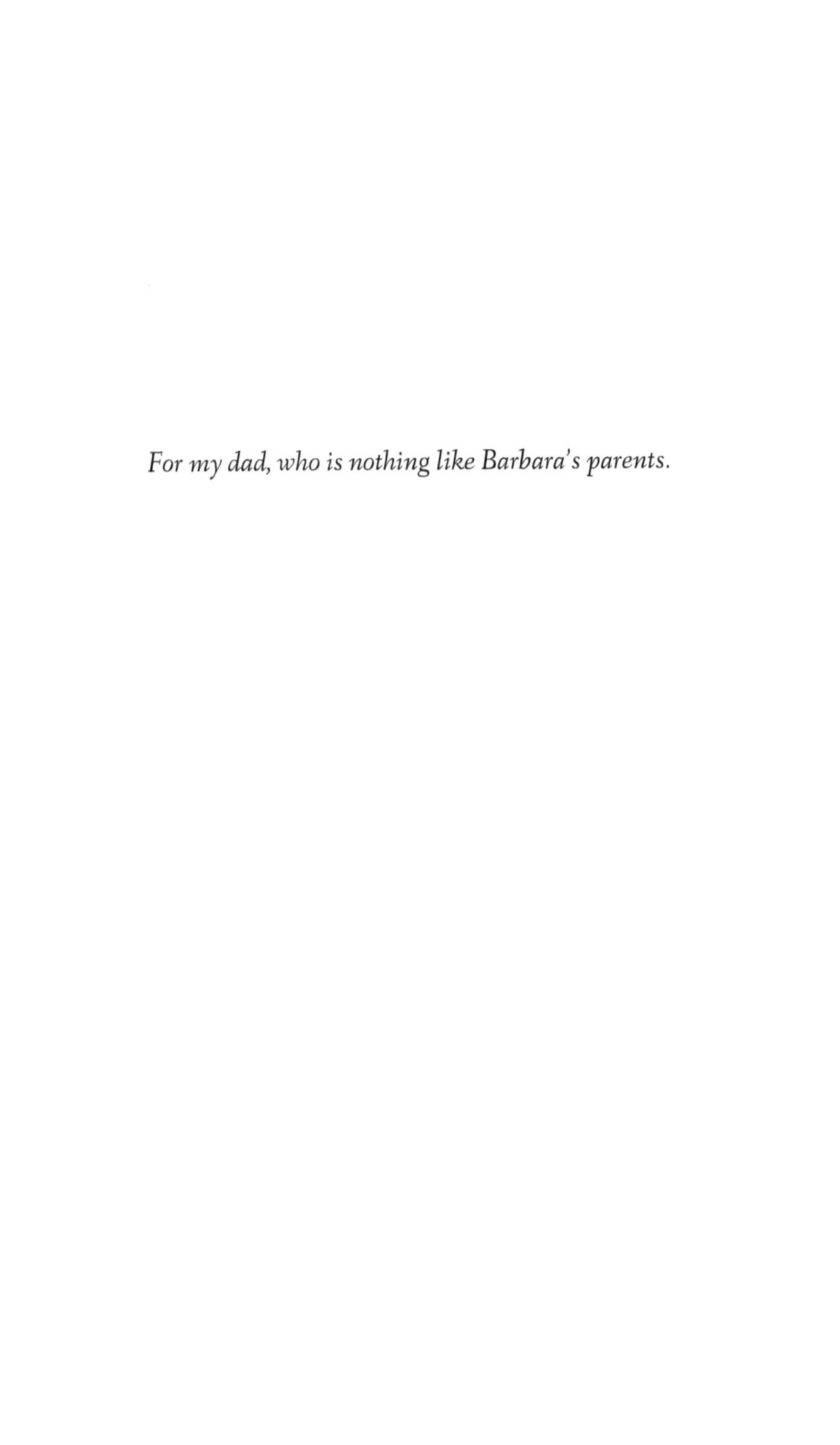

For my dad, who is nothing like Barbara's parents.

CONTENTS

Chapter One

BARBARA

THE DIRTY NEW YORK CITY RAINWATER CASCADES DOWN the subway steps. It's pouring outside—one of those early morning freezing March showers that flood stations and cause sick accidents. Dark-gray water sluices down the right side of the stairway, and I do my very best to dodge the likely bacteria-infested water. I press myself up against the opposite wall as I make my way back to civilization, but it's a dog-eat-dog world up in here. People keep shoving me aside, and I think longingly back to the days where I would have been able to just skip the crowded subways and afford an Uber.

I used to be somebody.

I know it's awful and obnoxious, but for half a second, I think it because, six months ago, I never would have had to take the subway during a torrential downpour. I would have checked the weather app on my phone and ordered a car to pick me up from the comfort of my 2,000-square-foot apartment on the Upper East Side. I would have walked out with my head held up high, not a care in the world.

But that was before I lost all of my money—or rather, before someone stole it.

I sigh and stop myself before tearing down this rabbit hole again.

It could have been worse. You still have your friends. You have a plan. You will survive.

It could have been worse. You still have your friends. You have a plan. You will survive.

I repeat the words—my mantra—over and over again in my head, holding onto them for dear life, pushing myself through the crowd. When I'm finally on street level, I take a deep breath through my mask, stretching my chest, my lungs, filling them with as much air as possible, holding it in for a few seconds before exhaling.

It will all be okay.

Thankfully, the entrance to the building where the dance studio is located is just at the end of the block, so my commute won't take much longer. The rain is so bad, though, that I still need my clear, bubble umbrella. I struggle to pop it open and set out to the next phase in my life—an unexpected, yet welcome one, considering the circumstances. So what if I lost all my money and I'm absolutely broke? A lot of people go through worse and recover. At least my old agent was able to get me a job last minute, even after not having worked in years. Sure, it's on one of those dance shows where D-list celebrities or washed-up former child actors (like yours truly) compete against each other. Where they take the opportunity to try and claw themselves back into the limelight in a super-obvious way.

So what if it's not very well-regarded in the acting community? A gig's a gig. And I desperately need one.

Celebrity Dance Battle is one of those guilty-pleasure shows you watch just to see how badly your favorite child actors have aged. Or how low reality stars will stoop to extend their fifteen minutes of fame.

When I stopped acting, I swore to myself I would never do anything like that—no celebrity cooking shows or sing-offs—especially since fame was never something I wanted. To me, it was a price I had to pay if I wanted to act (which, at the time, I did).

I used to watch trailers for those shows and snort derisively at them, making fun of the ridiculous things these "celebrities" would put themselves through. I'd feel sorry for them and wonder where their career went wrong.

Oh, God. Is that what people will think of when they see me out there doing the mambo on live television?

My stomach turns, the nerves finally hitting me. This never would have happened if—

I take a deep breath and close my eyes, stretching my arms up a bit, repeating the same mantra—out loud this time.

"It could have been worse. You still—"

"Watch it!" Someone runs into me, nearly knocking me over. "Jesus!" I hear a man yelp. "What the hell are you doing waving an umbrella around with your eyes closed on a crowded street like that?"

My eyes pop open, and I meet his gaze. He looks just about ready to kill me.

Stunned, I try to collect myself to apologize, but his eyes distract me. Half his face is covered by a black KN95 mask, so I can barely make out his features. But his eyes...*damn.* They're hypnotic—blue fire, blazing in frustration. I'm positively caught in them while he seems to be completely unaffected by my presence. I blush just imagining what I must look like—very damp. I wish I looked more like a glistening siren, and less like a wet dog.

"Do you have no sense of awareness whatsoever?"

Irritation finally breaks through the hypnotism.

"Are you going to get out of the way, or are you going to stand there all day?" he asks, his black hair wet from the rain. Ha! He doesn't have a super-cool, clear, bubble umbrella to protect him.

"Sorry!" I say. I mean, what's the big deal? "But there's really no need to get so worked up. It was just an accident." I roll my eyes, doing my best to keep my voice level. "I was just trying to *ground* myself." As soon as the words are out of my mouth, I regret them.

He frowns at me, giving me a once-over before shaking his head. "Yeah, well, try to not be *literally* grounded. You're blocking the sidewalk for the rest of us." He snorts, shaking his head disapprovingly at me. "I hate New Yorkers," he mutters under his breath before squeezing by me, bumping me in the side with his massive bright-blue gym bag. "You're all *so* weird."

My jaw drops. "Yeah, well, you're a—" I stutter. "You're like a—just plain rude! So, yeah!" I call after him in the world's worst comeback known to man. He looks over his shoulder at me with a smirk, and I want to die.

So embarrassing.

Grumpy Sexy Eyes guy keeps walking ahead, and I realize begrudgingly that we're headed into the same building. I see him disappear through the main entrance, behind the brass-colored doors, and decide to take a beat. The last thing I want is to be stuck in an elevator with that guy. I don't need his negativity affecting the rest of my day. Staying focused and calm is of the upmost importance for today. I can't let the stress of my situation affect my career's recovery, and I certainly cannot let it affect my *medical* recovery. I've had enough issues with my epilepsy in the past year, thank you very much. I'm supposed to be making strides to improve it, not make it worse.

I sigh, checking the time on my phone. It's only a couple of minutes until eight. Assuming the first day will probably just be about my partner and me getting to know each other and possibly strategizing about our first dance, I figure I can afford to be a few minutes late. We'll probably just be reviewing the basics.

Resolving to put a few minutes between myself and Grumpy Sexy Eyes, I stand a bit to the side of the sidewalk, clearing the way for other passersby, and shoot off a text to Liza, my best friend.

BARBARA

Got run over by ass with huge gym bag, but now OMW to first day of practice. Wish me luck!

LIZA

You got this girl! Send videos!

I hop on Instagram to browse what people have been up to, sharing a few memes here and there. I wouldn't consider myself to be a social media person, but I have a pretty decent following, considering I haven't acted in years. By the time I'm oversaturated with content, I realize fifteen minutes have gone by, and I am officially late.

"Shoot!" I pocket my phone and jog to the building entrance, pulling on the heavy brass doors before scrambling through my bag to show the security guard my ID. Once he has all my info, I rush to the nearest available elevator and press the button for the eleventh floor.

"Stupid Instagram," I mutter under my breath. That's the thing about social media: it's all fun and cat videos until it sucks you in and spits you the hell out. I don't know why I'm still on the thing.

THE FIRST THING I SEE WHEN I GET OFF THE ELEVATOR IS A buzz of people running around the hallways. Everyone seems to be operating on DEFCON 1, jogging from one room to another with dance shoes or heaps of fabric in their hands.

I sigh and resign myself to look for my contact, but the email I received from the network lacked any type of useful information. According to the message, I am supposed to, *"Look for the dancer who always frowns."* What type of info is that? I understand that many consider brevity to be the soul of wit, but sometimes brevity can be the soul of laziness. They couldn't even give me a first name? Nope, just a vague physical description—if you could even call it that.

"Okay, so we're looking for a guy who frowns a lot," I tell myself under my breath.

I adjust my bag over my shoulder and start checking every dance studio for a man matching that vague physical description, but they're either occupied by couples already practicing or empty.

Ugh.

Checking the time on my phone, I grow anxious. It's twenty-past, and I still have no idea where I'm supposed to be.

I try another door and find a shirtless man standing alone in the room by a stereo system. His, um...*physical attributes* momentarily distract me. The man's tan skin glistens under the harsh bright-white lighting overhead, and his dark-brown hair is wet with sweat and slightly disheveled. My eyes travel down his chest and—holy eight-pack, Batman!

I don't mean to objectify this man, but this moment right here calls for a two-syllable *daaaaaaa-yummmmm*.

Eight-Pack catches me ogling at him, and his brown eyes light up with mischief, throwing a smile in my direction.

Definitely doesn't look like a guy who frowns a lot.

"Can I help you?" he asks, his voice laced with a thick accent and intent.

"Um," I stammer briefly. "No, I'm good. I'm just looking for my dance partner."

Eight-Pack runs his fingers through his sweaty hair, casually flexing his muscles. I'd be really annoyed if I weren't so distracted.

"I could be your dance partner." He walks toward me, and I'm snapped out of my trance. "I could be whomever you want me to be." His sudden forwardness is completely off-putting, and I immediately regret ever having opened the door to this room.

Ew, gross.

Do women really fall for this stuff?

"Um, no thanks. I don't think you're the one I'm looking for." I quickly back out of the room, accidentally crashing into something.

"Oof!" I hear a high-pitched voice behind me say.

"Oh my God, I'm so sorry!" I apologize to the person I just turned into roadkill. Today is definitely not my day. It's like I'm a magnet for chaos.

The girl on the floor looks up at me, an explosion of pink, and blows her blush bangs off her face.

"It's okay," she squeaks. I extend my hand out to her, helping her up. "I'm Rosie. Rosie Castillo." She smiles.

Rosie adjusts the hem of her fuchsia dress before bending over to pick up some items that must've fallen from her arms during impact.

"I'm Barbara, and again, I'm so sorry," I say from underneath my mask. Am I allowed to remove it now? Can I dance without it? I mean, she's not wearing one and neither is Eight-Pack.

Sigh. I hate this post-Covid world. I never know what the right protocol is.

"I was just in there, and the guy, and his abs, and..." I trail off, waving my hand in the air.

"Oh—you just met Nico." She nods in understanding. "He's a charmer."

I laugh. "Not really. I was just *momentarily* distracted by his whole *thing*, you know?"

Rosie chuckles, totally understanding what I mean. "Fair warning, he is somewhat of a lady killer. Not the nicest guy in the bunch—unless you're looking for something casual," she adds quickly, no judgment in her voice.

"*God*, no. Not looking for *anything*." I snort. I need to sort out my personal life before I can even begin to consider reviving any sort of romantic life. And that's *if* I even decide to.

"Um, okay?" She laughs.

Desperately wanting to change the subject, I ask, "Actually, do you mind helping me out? I'm so late, and it's my first day. I have no idea what I'm doing or where I need to go, and you look like someone who knows her way around."

"I should! Been working here long enough. This is my sixth season on the show." She smiles, readjusting the heavy fabrics in her arms. "What do you need?"

"I'm actually meeting with my partner for the first time and don't even know his name. All the information the network gave me was that he frowned a lot." I snort.

"Oh, sure." She smiles immediately. The fact that she already knows who this person is by the identifier the network used cannot be a good sign. "You want Theodore." She frowns slightly, checking the time on her watch. "You'd better hurry, though. He won't like that you're late, and I'm pretty sure rehearsals were supposed to start a half hour ago. His studio is the last one down the hall," she says, throwing a thumb over her shoulder.

"Uh, thanks." I force a smile and hesitantly turn away from her.

"Good luck!" she calls enthusiastically. But as she walks away, I hear her mutter, "You're gonna need it," under her breath.

Oh, boy.

Positive thoughts, Babs. Keep it positive.

It can't really be all that bad. I'm sure that Rosie and the network execs are all exaggerating. Right? *Right???*

Determined to make the best out of this situation, I take a deep breath and open the door to the last studio down the hall. Three of the four walls of the studio are mirrored with a barre running across them, and the artificial lemony scent and the glossy wooden floor leads me to believe the room has recently been cleaned. I am fully braced to meet the wrath of my dancing partner, but the room's empty. No scary frowny man to be found. All I can see is a stereo system and, atop a bench pressed against the far back of the room, a large, bright-blue gym bag.

Perfect.

Chapter Two

BARBARA

"Of course," I wail as my brain processes where I've seen that gym bag before. *Of course* my dance partner for this season would end up being the jerk who almost knocked me over in the rain with it. *Of course* it's the guy who called me a weirdo.

I sigh deeply.

This is not good. I had hoped for us to make it to the finale—especially since we get paid by the episode, and I desperately need the cash. I had hoped to at least get along with my dance partner, but it's looking like it won't be an easy thing to do based on my previous experience with him. "*Of course* this is my life."

"Do you make it a habit of speaking to yourself, Miss Holt?" A frisson of electricity runs down my spine at the sound of his deep voice. I turn quickly to face him, but my pink light-up rain boots weigh me down, and I fall flat on my face.

Really, truly cannot believe this is my life.

I stop myself from going down a black hole again because things could definitely be worse than they are now.

I lie face-up on the floor, staring up at the ceiling. Theodore walks over to me, his feet by my face, and leans over to look hesitantly at me in the eye.

I'm left momentarily breathless, and it's not from the fall. His striking blue eyes bore into me as I take him in. His black, wavy hair is perfectly styled, if a little damp, and his angular jaw is grit in frustration. Now that he's not wearing a mask, I can tell there's not a bit of scruff on his face—he's perfectly clean-shaven. His broad shoulders and hard chest are on display under a slightly too-tight black t-shirt and I can't help but think that this rude man looks like an absolute *snack*. I gaze back at him, slightly taken aback because I don't remember him being this hot. Sure, I could tell his eyes were incredible, but the coat plus the mask he was wearing at the time definitely weren't doing him any justice.

Damn.

"You *are* Miss Holt, are you not?"

"You can call me Barbara." I blush.

"My name is Theodore Wallace," he says. Does he recognize me? "I'm your dance partner—and the man who ran into you this morning after you so rudely blocked off the entire sidewalk for your meditative purposes."

Well, that answers that.

"After *I*—?" I snort. I see he's not going to let this go. "Theo, I—"

"It's *Theodore*." He glares at me. My bad—how *dare* I give him a nickname? "You're late, and we have a lot for you to catch up on. Please tell me you brought another pair of shoes and are not planning on practicing in..."—he narrows his eyes at my boots—"whatever *those* are."

I sit up and glare at him. "I have shoes in my bag. And these are *rain boots*," I say, lifting my feet and tapping them against the floor so the multi-colored lights flash.

"They light up." He snorts. "They're ridiculous."

I sit up straighter and furrow my brows. No one questions my fashion choices—especially not a stranger and someone who looks so...*basic*. I give him a once-over, just like he gave me earlier, and take in his black sneakers, black track pants, and black performance tee. Is he trying to be the athletic version of Steve Jobs or something? "I will have you know that I got these in Tokyo for *six dollars* two years ago, and the lights still work."

Theo—*Theodore*—shakes his head and pinches the bridge of his nose. "Why would *anyone* past the age of five buy *light-up footwear*?"

I choose not to mention that the boots are actually part of a whole matching set, including a handbag that *also* lights up when you swing it. "Are you kidding me?" I say, struggling to get up from where I had lain face-up on the floor. "They look so cool when you go puddle-hopping in the rain!" I say excitedly, pointing at my feet.

Theodore opens his eyes, widened in shock. "'Puddle hop—?" His brows pull together, and he shakes his head at me again. "Enough. Enough. You're late, and we're already a week behind everyone else. We need to practice," he says gruffly.

"What do you mean?" I raise an eyebrow at him in confusion.

"You're a late entry, and we can't afford to waste a single minute of practice over trivial matters such as your awful taste in footwear."

"Awful taste in foot—?!" Those are fighting words, and I won't have them! But his statement on my participation in the show distracts me. Theodore folds his arms across his chest before rolling his eyes, walking toward the music system in the corner of the room.

I honestly don't know what to address first: his attack on my shoes or what he said about my position in the show. Since *I know* I don't need to defend my awesome fashion sense, I go for the latter.

"Late entry?" I ask, taking my coat off, hanging it on a hook by the door. "What do you mean, '*late entry*'?"

Theodore turns to look at me, frowning. "Didn't you find it a bit odd that you were offered this opportunity just a couple of days ago and filming starts next week?"

I take a seat on the bench and slide off my boots, frowning. "Well, I..." My voice trails off. It's true. I guess I did find it a bit odd that I received the final contract on Friday and was asked to start training the following Monday. Plus, I did notice that the filming schedule for the promo reels was insane. They had put me down for two hours tomorrow and Wednesday. I guess I did think it was fast, but I just figured, *Hey, it's showbiz. It's always demanding.*

"My previous partner quit last week," Theodore tells me, jaw tightening, his striking blue eyes darkening. "Apparently, there were some things about the show she couldn't handle," he says, his voice laced with resentment.

You mean she couldn't handle you?

Immediately, my mind races through all the possible things he could've done that led to her quitting. "I'm sure she had her reasons," I say, putting on my favorite heels—three-inch Manolo Blahnik leopard sandals that I got on a crazy sale before I lost all my money.

"She couldn't commit, and I don't tolerate flakes. Dance is about discipline and commitment—*not* about negligence or frivolity."

I snort at his statement.

His back straightens, and he turns back to look at me. "Do you have anything to say?"

"Well, yeah. I thought this thing was also about having fun. I get it's a competition, but shouldn't there be at least a little room in there for it?"

He crosses his arms across his chest again. "No," he says simply. "Not when it comes to ballroom dancing."

I snort. "Wow, way to make me look forward to this experience."

He sighs. "That's the difference here, isn't it? You see this as a fun experience, whereas you don't realize that this is my *job*. This is serious for me. This isn't something fun that I do on the side because I'm a bored actress with nothing better going on in my life."

I take a step back, as if he'd pushed me in the chest. "You think that I'm just some bored actress with nothing better to do?"

"Why else would you be here? You retired from acting years ago, and it's not like you have a movie or show to promote by being here." He turns back to the stereo and picks out a song by Sinatra. He lowers the volume slightly and walks toward me with a determined look in his eyes.

I honestly don't know what to say at this point. I want to tell him how committed I am to this, to tell him just how high the stakes are for me. I could tell him how I owe $183,572.14 just in medical bills. I could tell him how I owe even more in back taxes. I could tell him how my financial manager royally screwed me over, neglected to pay my insurance, my bills, and stole all my cash before disappearing to an island in the Caribbean or something. But I definitely don't want or need any of his pity. Even if I *didn't* desperately need this job to cover most of my expenses, I would be committed. I've always been extremely professional in my work—even as a child. Sure, it was difficult to balance my epilepsy and my career when I was first diagnosed, but even then, I managed to get it together *and* keep my diagnosis from most people.

As far as his approval is concerned, I need it like I need a shot in the head—meaning, not at all. All I need from this guy is for him to have the ability to work with me in a professional manner so that we can kick everyone's butt and win.

God, I desperately need a win.

"You don't need to worry about my professionalism," I say curtly.

"Good." He nods once with finality. "Now, how much experience do you have with ballroom dancing or just dance in general?"

"I'm trained in musical theater and was in a musical for eight months on Broadway. I played Fanny Brice in *Funny Girl*," I say proudly with a grin. Starring in a Broadway musical has been the highlight of my career. It was the most demanding role I've ever played in my life—and also the most fun. I got to play one of Barbra Streisand's most legendary roles—a dream come true.

"So no experience whatsoever, then," he deadpans.

I scoff. "I wouldn't say—"

"Believe me, you have no experience." He sighs deeply.

Who does this guy think he is? He doesn't know my life *or* my abilities. "I can follow an eight count just as well as any other—"

"What are those?" His eyes widen, horrified, as he points at my shoes.

"Huh? These? What do you think they look like?" This guy. I swear I'm gonna lose it.

"Those are *not* ballroom-regulation shoes," he says, his voice rising. "Didn't you do *any* research whatsoever before showing up here?"

The corners of my mouth twitch, and I try my hardest to suppress a smile by pressing my lips together. His irritation is hilarious. I look down at my shoes and tap my toes together, taunting him. "But these are my favorite shoes," I say, neglecting to inform him that I know these aren't the right shoes, but that the show hasn't provided me with the required ones yet.

"You can't dance in those! It's impossible. It's a wonder you can even *walk* in them."

"Oh, I can do a lot of things in them, Theo," I say suggestively, lowering my voice slightly. I don't even know what I could logically mean by it, but the blush that shows up on his cheeks gives me a thrill. If he's going to be an ass, then I'm entitled to tease him.

He grits his teeth. "It's *Theodore*. And I'd honestly almost prefer you dance in those ridiculous pink boots. You're less likely to break your neck in them," he says in a more reasonable tone.

I wave a hand in the air, dismissing him. "I'm *fine*, believe me. These are my most comfortable heels. Don't worry about it."

He takes a deep breath, settling himself again. "This is gonna be a long season." He turns back to the stereo.

"Or a very short one," I mutter under my breath, concerned that we're at the end of the line. This isn't good. I need to make it to the end of the season. We get paid per episode, plus a bonus if we win, and I really need to win that grand prize of $250,000.

Theodore's back straightens. "Let's just try and make the best of this, okay?"

"You got it, bud," I say, my enthusiasm strained.

He presses play, and "The Way You Look Tonight" blares through the speakers.

"Next week is foxtrot week. I don't have time to teach you the basics, so we're just going to have to jump headfirst into the choreography. I hope you can handle that." He walks over and stops six inches from me. His proximity surprises me, so I take a step back.

Theodore sighs and closes the distance again. "We can't dance without touching each other, Miss Holt," he says.

"*Barbara*," I say, my throat suddenly dry. He's so close I can smell his aftershave—citrus and lilac. "Call me Barbara."

"Barbara," he says, looking down at me. I force myself to look him in the eye, craning my neck. Damn, he's tall. "Our chests should be two fists' length apart." He fists his two hands, presses them together, and puts them between our chests like a measuring stick, his skin hovering just over mine. I inhale sharply because I really didn't think the part where dancing means touching the other person through. I'm such an idiot. Theo clears his throat and drops his hands to his sides.

"Here, put your right hand in mine and your left on my shoulder like so." He adjusts the fingers on my left hand and places it correctly on his right shoulder. I do my best to remain focused and not get distracted by things like how his muscles feel under the palm of my hand whenever his arm moves.

Theodore's right hand moves to my waist, and my breath catches. His left hand tightens around my right. Suddenly, it feels a little hard to breathe. Relieved, I realize belatedly that I'm still wearing my mask. I exhale. Yes. That's why I'm having trouble breathing.

"Hold on," I say, separating myself. Theodore frowns and drops his hands. "I need to take off my mask. Is that okay?" It should be since he's not wearing one.

"Yes—that's not a problem for me," he says, his voice serious and deep.

I want to laugh because asking for someone's consent on not wearing a mask in front of them nowadays feels so similar to asking a lover whether it's okay not to wear a condom. Like you're imparting this massive amount of trust that the other person isn't contagious, isn't going to hurt you. I remove my mask and set it on my bag as I laugh at my own observation.

When I turn back to him, he flinches slightly, his expression slipping briefly into one of surprise. Feeling self-conscious, my hand flies to my face. Maybe the mask smudged my lipstick? Wait, no, I'm not wearing lipstick.

"What?" I ask. "What's on my face?"

He shakes his head, controlling his features again. "Nothing. Nothing's wrong. Let's start."

Chapter Three

THEO

After five hours of non-stop practice, I give her permission to break for lunch. Now, don't go thinking it's because I feel sorry for her or anything—that's not who I am. It's mostly because it looks like she's about to pass out, and I really can't delay our rehearsals any further by her getting injured or something like that. We're behind enough as it is.

Plus, if I'm being honest, I want to give her the chance to admit that her shoes were a mistake.

"How are your feet now?" I smirk at her from behind my water bottle before taking a sip. She limps toward the bench, so obviously struggling to stay upright, and I do my best not to burst out laughing.

"Fine," she bites back, looking like she wants to wipe the smug look I know I have off my face. Because I was right. I'm always right.

I do my best not to focus too much on how her hair shines in the noon sunlight coming in from the windows—what is it about her hair? Is it made out of some ultra-reflective material or something? Does it also have an anti-gravity component? The way it floats in the air while I turn her and we sway in each other's arms is distracting. I might have to enact a new rule, ask her to tie it up for practice.

She leans over to prod the arch of her foot with her index finger, surreptitiously trying to massage it, and her hair falls over her face like a golden curtain. I sigh, frustrated. "Your feet aren't sore? No blisters?" She tries to hide the pain, but I notice. I notice everything. It's my attention to detail that makes me the best dancer on the show—even if I don't win every season.

She glares up at me, and I press my lips together tightly and stare into her hazel eyes. I want to laugh—just a bit maniacally. I feel like a kid in a playground, wanting to yell, "Nee-noo-nee-noo! Told you so!" She's been driving me crazy all damn day, but I still can't help making fun of her.

"*No*," she insists. "I feel like I'm wearing Ugg slippers; they're so comfortable. I can barely tell that I'm wearing heels. I could do jumping jacks in them, see?" She gets up, throws her arms in the air, and proceeds to struggle through three jumping jacks, her heels clicking on the glossy wooden floor. "Perfectly comfortable." Barbara drops back onto the bench, rather clumsily.

I scoff. "Right. It doesn't look like you want to chop your feet off *at all*." I shake my head at her. "Just know that you need to be ready tomorrow with the appropriate attire. I'm sure Rosie, our wardrobe assistant, can help you locate some shoes." Really, was it that hard to get the appropriate wardrobe? What if her feet hurt so much tomorrow she can't dance?

Barbara sighs heavily, running her hands through the ends of her hair. "Fine." She digs through her bag and pulls out a giant bag of peanut M&Ms.

"*That's* your lunch?" I ask, horrified.

She rolls her eyes at me. "Are you going to criticize my eating habits now, too? My choice in shoes wasn't enough?"

I smirk at her and pull out a large plastic bottle with some green juice. It sloshes as I take a drink. "'Eating' implies that what you're ingesting is food, and *that* is most assuredly poison." I take another swig of juice.

"Yeah, well, you go ahead and enjoy your green goop from that high horse over there," she says angrily. I can tell by the way Barbara unconsciously rolls her ankles that she's struggling. Her shoulders are tense, and her golden hair is a wild, hot mess. "Although, it looks like someone already enjoyed it and threw it back up for you."

I look down curiously at the contents in my bottle. She's so dramatic.

Sigh. Actresses.

"*...want to pour that goop over your head...stupid perfect hair...*" she says under her breath.

Does she realize just how often she talks to herself?

I open my mouth to reply, but she looks up, her hazel eyes boring into me. My words get stuck in my throat, so I do my best to clear it.

"*What?*" she snaps.

Whoa, I guess I pushed too hard.

"Is that really all you have for lunch? I have a protein bar in my bag." Surely she needs more nutrition than that?

She gags dramatically. "No, thanks. I have a PB&J sandwich in here somewhere." She turns to her bag in search of her sandwich. I stare in horror as she pulls random items from her purse. From the depths of her massive handbag come batteries, stamps, a phone charger, a flashlight, and more candy.

Honestly, how much sugar can one person eat?

"What—?"

"Found it!" she says with a grin, pulling out the flattened sandwich in a baggie. Setting it to one side, she throws everything back into the bag.

When she tosses her purse aside, I hear it rattle. "Why does your bag sound like a maraca?"

She freezes, and her eyes widen. "Uhh, it's candy. I have some Tic Tacs in there." She shifts in her seat, a little jumpy. Weird. "Don't be so nosy," she says softly as she takes the PB&J and practically inhales it in three bites. Once she's done, she struggles to get back on her feet and says, "Let's get back to work."

Not having to tell me twice, I extend my hand, offering to help her up. When her hand makes contact with my own, however, a strange sensation runs up my arm. Instinctively, I let go, and she falls to the floor on her knees.

"Fuck! Sorry! Let me help you!" It was my fault, but in all fairness, this wouldn't have happened if she had been wearing the right shoes.

"Don't," she whispers, swatting my hand away and squeezing her eyes shut. Okay, I deserve that.

"I didn't mean to—"

"I know," she says curtly. "It's fine. Back to business, right?"

I want to sigh, ask her if she's okay—her knees took most of the hit—but I keep myself in check.

I wince. That didn't feel right.

By the end of the day, we're both exhausted. I don't know if it's just the fact that we trained for a total of nine hours, or whether it's because I had to control myself from losing it on her. I couldn't quite put a finger on exactly why I found her so annoying, but it was affecting our performance. The entire time, our bodies remained tense, unable to relax. It frustrated me. I had to constantly remind myself to bring it down a notch. It's her first day, after all.

After giving her an important lecture on how she will have to change her eating habits, incorporate a workout routine, and other issues she probably tuned out, I feel sorry for over-whelming her with information. I decide to walk her out of the studio to the elevators and at least have a more human conversation. Unfortunately, someone has other plans that interfere with my own. Again.

"Ahhh, Miss Holt," I hear a deep, accented male voice come from behind us. Barbara and I both turn.

"Nicolás," I say in acknowledgment, my voice poisonous. I am too tired to deal with him right now.

"I see you found a partner. You're dancing with Theodore, then." He smirks at her, ignoring me. They know each other? When did they meet? He gives my partner a once-over before turning to me. Nico and I glare intensely at each other as I wonder how this guy could possibly move so freaking fast.

From the corner of my eye, I catch Barbara looking curiously at us.

"Just remember that my offer still stands." He winks at her. I feel fire coursing through my veins. Does this guy not understand what boundaries are? Is he seriously going to do this to me *again*? How desperate is he? We all want the win, but come on! "I'm available all day and night for you."

I hate the way he says it, the way he just *assumes* how Barbara—how any woman—will easily fall at his feet. This guy needs someone to write him a reality check, but I refuse to waste my time on him.

Barbara rolls her eyes at him—something I've been on the other end of at least twenty times today. I relax a little at her annoyance with him until I hear her laugh. What the—? Is she enjoying this?

"Bye, Nico," she says, shaking her head, dismissing him. He walks away, throwing a smile over his shoulder in her direction, and I feel my skin ignite.

I turn to look at her, my brows pulled together. I fist my hands at my sides. "You know each other?" I ask her, aware of the tightness in my voice.

"Uh, no," she says, narrowing her eyes at me. "I met him this morning before practice."

"Is that why you were late?" I ask, the volume in my voice rising. I need to get it together, but I can't have Nico sabotaging me again.

"What?" she stammers. "No. Not really."

I turn my body to face her head-on. "No or not really?"

"It wasn't on purpose." She throws her hands in the air in frustration. But I don't care. I need an answer. "I was looking for you, and I ran into him. He started talking to me, and—"

"This competition is not about sleeping with the other dancers or finding a new *boyfriend*," I spit out, and she takes a step back from me. Her eyes widen, and she shakes her head, mouth open.

"I didn't—"

"If you're not going to take this competition seriously, I ask you to please withdraw from it. I already told you—this is my job. This isn't some joke or little project to me." I can feel people poking their heads outside the other studios, wanting to see what the commotion is about. "I won't risk my career over someone who won't take things seriously, who's just a bored celebrity." Her eyes glaze over, mouth slack-jawed, and I know I've stepped *slightly* over the line. But honestly, I don't care.

Running a hand down my face, I take a steadying breath. "This is important to me. I've been burned before," I say in a lower volume.

"I—I—" she stutters. "This is important to me, too. I—"

Not like it is to me.

"Fine. It's fine," I grunt, turning on my heel toward my studio, not wanting to hear any excuses from her. "See you tomorrow. Don't be late!" I yell at her over my shoulder.

Another disappointment.

I run my fingers through my hair and walk back to my studio, where I take a seat on the bench. Putting my face in my hands, elbows on my knees, I exhale deeply to calm down.

I hate Nico.

He's there, wanting to sabotage me every chance he gets. It's exhausting, keeping up with him, trying to fight him off.

I used to be able to handle it, but I can't deal with this on top of everything else anymore. I have bigger things to worry about —like finding better care for Bubbe, making sure she's comfortable for however many years she has left on this earth. Not many, if I can't get the appropriate care for her.

Sure, she's upstate in a home right now where she can get 24/7 care, but she's not happy, and I can tell how it affects her rapidly declining health. She wants to spend her last days in her house, in the home she shared with my grandfather—the house I grew up in. But do you know how much at-home care costs? Because I do, and it is certainly not something I can afford. Just because I'm on TV, doesn't mean I'm making the big bucks. Dancers on the show don't make nearly as much as the celebrities do, obviously.

I check my watch and see that it's almost time for one of our daily talks. I make it a point to call her every day—even if it's just for five minutes—since I don't get to see her often. I know talking to me lifts her spirits up significantly, and it definitely gives me some peace of mind. I'll know, no matter what, that I did my best to help her in any way I could.

I just wish I could do more; wish I could make her more comfortable...

I take another deep breath and dig for my phone, dialing her direct line.

"Hello, darling," she picks up, the phone barely ringing once.

"Hey, Bubbe," I say, wincing at the sound of her voice. It sounds tired, rough. I can hear her struggling, her breathing getting worse with each day. That, combined with her Alzheimer's, scares the crap outta me.

"How are you?" she asks.

"Great, thanks. I had my first day today," I say.

"Ohhh, how exciting. Your first day of dance school! I'm so proud of you for getting into Julliard." I can practically feel her beaming from the other end of the line.

"No, Bubbe," I say, squeezing my eyes shut. "I already graduated from school, remember? I'm working on a TV show now. I've been working on it for a while."

Total of eight years, sixteen seasons.

There's silence on the other end of the line as she processes this information. "TV? I... Oh, yes. Mmhmm. I remember now." But we both know she doesn't.

I do my best to ignore the stinging behind my eyes and ask about her day. She proceeds to describe how she spent it outside in the pool, under the sun. How she met this man who she thinks is going to ask her out on a date. At first, this information makes me sit upright, until she mentions the guy's name is *Walter*—my grandfather. Also, it's the end of March, so there's no way she was outside sunbathing. And I realize...she's not here anymore. I caught her too late in the afternoon. She's already sundowning, her Alzheimer's symptoms getting worse like they do every afternoon. Soon she'll turn aggressive. My sweet Bubbe will turn mean, and I really don't think I can handle that today. I need to start calling her earlier in the day, before things go downhill.

"Bubbe, I need to go," I choke out, ashamed of myself for not being man enough to handle it today. "I need to work on a couple of things, but I'll come see you this weekend, okay?"

"Of course, darling," she says. Does she even know who she's talking to now?

"Love you, Bubbe."

"Love you, Teddy! Good luck with your new partner!" she says, my Bubbe coming back to me for a brief moment. I sit up straight. That's the way it is, isn't it? One second they're here, then they're gone—and vice versa. "See you soon. Take care!"

I hang up and stare down at the screen until it goes black.

She doesn't have much time left. Maybe I can take some time off. Take her out of the home and become her primary caregiver. I could watch her 24/7, and that way, we wouldn't need a nurse or anything. I could ask the network to let me take a sabbatical. I should have enough savings to pull it off. I could pull out now. They'd understand, and Miss Holt wouldn't care, really. She's no different than the other flaky celebrities I've had to perform with in the past—here for the attention, the extra cash she can live without, and the entertainment. The network would just have to find someone else to replace me—but that's easier than replacing a celebrity. No big deal. Plus, it's not like we're going to win, if today's rehearsal is any indication of our future performance. I can't see myself having a good partnership with this woman, and honestly, there are more important things in life than this season of *Celebrity Dance Battle.*

Family is more important, and if I don't have much time left with my Bubbe, then...

It's a hard choice to make, but I know exactly what I need to do now.

I unlock my phone again and immediately shoot off an email to the show's executive producer, asking to meet first thing tomorrow. The idea of not working for several months, not practicing every day, scares me a bit. As with any athlete, falling out of practice can destroy a career, and I hope to come back to one after my Bubbe... Well, I just hope I still have one. But I'd rather have extra time with the woman who sacrificed so much to raise me than live the rest of my life in regret. She's the woman who took over when both my parents passed. The one who taught me how to dance. My Bubbe and I are all we've got, and I'm gonna step up the same way she stepped up for me.

Yup, it's decided. I'm taking time off from *Celebrity Dance Battle.*

Chapter Four

BARBARA

I tap my key card to the reader, and the door to my hotel room unlocks with a beep. I leave a trail of clothes and boots behind me as I make it to the queen-sized bed, throwing myself face-down on the mattress. Happily, I close my eyes and sigh into the comforter.

Is there anything better than a hotel bed?

Before I pass out from exhaustion, I pull my phone out of my leggings pocket and FaceTime Liza. It barely rings once before she picks up, and I see her excited face in my screen.

"Oh my God, tell me *everything*!" Her grin is broad and eager. My heart warms at my chosen sister's excitement. I miss her, even though it's just been a couple weeks since I've seen her. "How was it?" she asks.

"Exhausting." I sigh. "But pretty good. I'm in the hotel room now. Wanna see?"

"Yes! Show me. Is it super glamorous?" she asks, flipping her long brown hair over her shoulder.

I chuckle, getting up from bed and flipping the camera so I can show her the room. "It's just a regular hotel room. But honestly, it wouldn't matter if it were a one-star motel on the side of the highway—at least it's my own space. For now." Liza winces. "Not that I'm not super grateful for your mom letting me stay with her all this time!" I add in a hurry.

Because I had to sell my apartment so quickly and was basically homeless, Catterina, Liza's mother, generously offered for me to stay at her house for as long as I want. It really wasn't an offer I could pass up, seeing as Liza and Matt, her husband, have a newborn, and there was no way I could deal with that. Sleep is too precious to me. I couldn't afford to be woken up in the wee hours of the night by a crying baby for fear of it affecting my health. I was incredibly thankful for Catterina's generosity, but was definitely excited that the network required all contestants to stay at the same hotel throughout the filming of the show. For the first time in several months, I finally have my own space and privacy. I can come and go as I please without feeling guilty. Plus, I'm in the city instead of all the way out in Long Island.

Liza chuckles. "Girl, I understand. I lived with her most of my life, remember? I know she's very traditional and can be a pain sometimes."

"She's not—" I sigh, feeling like the worst person alive. "She's great. It's just—you know. It would be nice to have my own space." I shrug.

Liza frowns. "Soon, Babsy. I promise. You're doing everything you can now, and that's all anyone can ask of you." I give her a weak smile. "How was practice?" she asks.

I grin, silently thanking her for changing the topic. "Fine," I say, playing with the arrangement of tulips on my nightstand.

"Just fine?" She rolls her eyes at me. "You gotta give me more than that."

"It was fine. Much more physically demanding than I expected, but nothing I can't handle." Sure, the physical part I could handle, but my partner, on the other hand... I thought back to Theo and how no-nonsense he was, how uptight. I wasn't excited about doing this show because of what it said about my career, but I was at least hoping for it to be fun. I thought dancing would actually help my mood, the silver lining in this whole thing. But today was definitely not fun. He made it kind of miserable.

Liza internalizes everything, though. And I really don't want her worrying about me. Plus, I've been trying to make a conscious effort not to dwell on the negative things in life. So, I try to focus on the positives: "I'm so sore—which is awesome, really, because it means it was a real workout. I have a date with a hot bath after I hang up with you that I'm really looking forward to."

She laughs and shakes her head. "Just with a bath? What about your partner?" She winks, and I roll my eyes at her.

"God, no. No way." I scoff. Who in their right mind would date someone as uptight as Theodore Wallace? Actually, now that I think about it, he's so short on patience I doubt he'd even *want* to go out with anyone. "Absolutely not."

"But all the dancers are so hot! Who did they assign as your partner?" she asks. Among the millions of reality shows that Liza watches, *Celebrity Dance Battle* is one of her favorites. When she heard I was going to compete in it, she completely freaked out. It was a total fangirl moment. "Is it the Texan guy? I bet it's him. Please tell me it's him. He looks like a sexy dancing cowboy."

"A sexy dancing—? What? No. I didn't really meet any of the other dancers. Except for some Spaniard," I say, laughing.

"Oh my God! You met *Nico*?" Liza squeals, sitting up. "Holy— Okay, you need to tell me everything."

"He was a total jerk. Hitting on me and being completely obvious about it. It bordered on sexual harassment." I pause. "Actually, I'm pretty sure it *was* sexual harassment."

"Oh, *ew*." She sits back, grimacing. "Yeah, the fan blogs have mentioned him being a bit of a man-whore." She wrinkles her nose. "So, if he's not your partner, who is?"

"Wait, hold up," I say, holding a hand up. "Can we go back to the fact that you just said '*fan blogs*'? How often are you on these? Please tell me the only reason you were on them was for my benefit and it's not, like, a regular thing you do."

"Don't worry about it," she says, blushing, her eyes flashing to the side. "Just tell me who your partner is.

I lie back on my bed and chuckle. "I have Theodore Wallace. Do you know him?"

"Oh my God," she says again. Liza almost hyperventilates, and I watch in horror. Not because I'm concerned she'll pass out, but because I've never seen my friend like this. "Babs, he's, like, an OG cast member. He's been there since season one."

"Okay?" I'm so confused. What's the big deal here?

"No, you don't get it. He's *incredible*. Granted, he's only won, like, twice, but he makes it to the final every season!" she says reverently. "Can you introduce me? He's a god."

"He's an ass," I say simply.

"What?" she asks, shoulders slumping. "He's an ass? But I love him!"

"Yup. I'm not gonna introduce him to you. Haven't you ever heard the expression 'Never meet your heroes'?" I tell her, adjusting my body to lie on my side.

She sighs heavily and shrugs. "I wouldn't say he's my hero, but...I guess you're right. I want to keep the illusion intact. Is he as hot as he looks, at least?"

"I don't know, Liza." I raise a shoulder. I think back to those blazing blue eyes, the hypnotic effect they had on me, his hard body, how it felt under my hands, his perfect posture, the way his hand felt on my waist... I shake my head quickly, trying to dispel these thoughts. He's the worst. "I mean, sure, I guess he's what you would objectively call '*attractive*'." I air quote with my free hand, but Liza narrows her eyes, seeing through me.

"Just *objectively* attractive, then?" She scoffs. "What's his celebrity comp?"

I squint at her. Seriously? We're playing this game? "You've seen him in pictures and on camera! Why do you need a celebrity comp?"

"Because the camera adds twenty pounds."

"If that's true, then doesn't that mean that whichever comp I give you would be irrelevant in this case? He could be his own celebrity comp."

"Seriously. Gimme a comp."

I sigh and think for a minute. "I guess he looks kind of like a grumpy, angry Prince Eric, but sexier and slightly more built," I say finally.

Liza's eyebrows pull together. "Prince Eric? Which country is he from? I don't—" She shakes her head, and then her eyes widen when she gets what I mean. "Are you kidding me, Barbara? From *The Little Mermaid*? You're comparing him to a *cartoon*?" Liza frowns at me through the camera. "Seriously?"

I shrug and sit up, setting my phone against the table lamp. "I don't know who else to compare him to! He genuinely does look like a grumpy and angry Prince Eric! Down to the hair."

She purses her lips and glares at me. After a beat, she says, "I guess that's kinda hot. Really hot, actually."

I suppose he does look like the type of guy who can throw you roughly around a mattress once or twice. I mean, the way he handled my body today during practice—

Ugh! Control yourself, Barb!

I roll my eyes (mostly at myself) and laugh at her. "He's alright." But we both know I'm full of shit.

Liza chuckles at me. "So typical of you to pick *The Little*

Mermaid, too, my little rebel. You used to be *obsessed* with that movie."

"I wasn't *obsessed*. I simply admired and craved Ariel's independence," I clarify.

"Independence?" Liza snorts. Oh boy, here we go again. "The movie wasn't about *independence*. It was about a spoiled brat! Ariel was sixteen, running around in a bra, leaving her family behind to be with a dude she didn't even know. She left her poor widowed dad just so she could be with this guy who she saw *once* and never even spoke to! I mean, what kind of message does that send to kids?"

"Jesus Christ." I hold a hand up to stop her. "I am *not* having this discussion again. I refuse to. We have it every time the topic of Disney movies comes up and you act like a total nutcase. If you really want to get into it, I can dig up my argument about how *Lion King* should not have been a kid's movie. The movie is based on *Hamlet*, for Christ's sake! That is *way* too heavy a subject matter for children."

Liza sets the phone against something and crosses her arms over her chest, leaning back in her chair. "Whatever. I just hope —*as my child's godmother*—you don't start telling Lucy that it's totally cool to run away from her parents to be with some random dude."

I laugh at her seriousness. "Liza, *chill*. I think we can both agree that *The Little Mermaid* doesn't precisely send the best message to girls out there. Plus, you don't need to worry about it. She's not going to abandon you over some dude with a title and a fancy boat. Your daughter is lucky enough to have two parents who love her and give a shit about her and won't let her do something so incredibly stupid. Not everyone has that," I mutter the last sentence bitterly under my breath.

There's a pause on the other end of the line, and I can practically feel the tension oozing from Liza. "Have you heard anything from them?" she asks quietly. I don't need to ask her who she's referring to.

I look down at my hands and fidget with my fingers, frowning. "Nah. My parents either haven't checked their voicemails or are too busy to call back. Either way, who doesn't check up on their kid after six months of not talking to them? I know they're *alive* and have access to internet because I've been following their social media. They constantly post about their archaeological digs and stuff." I shrug again, not meeting her eyes. I know what I'm gonna see in them, and I really don't think I can handle her pity right now. "It's fine. I never really expected them to help me. Maybe I expected them to at least call me back, offer *some* type of moral support. But I never would have even asked for financial help, you know? It's not like they could afford it, either."

"Still, though. They could have at least offered moral support or even just let you stay at their house—it's not like they're ever there," Liza says bitterly. I love how overprotective she is of me. It's nice to know I have someone in my corner.

After a minute of silence, I look at her, and she controls her features into a neutral expression. "At least I have you, right?" I ask.

"Abso-fucking-lutely." She grins broadly. "Always." My heart warms in my chest at the love I feel for my bestie, my sister.

"So, in conclusion, Theodore Wallace is an ass?" she asks.

I chuckle. "A bit, yeah. He thinks that I haven't worked in years because I haven't wanted to. He thinks I'm a bored former actress who doesn't care and isn't committed."

She snorts. "You're, like, the most committed-to-your-craft person I know."

"I know! Plus, I am aware it's been a minute since I've been on TV, but my role on Broadway finished up right before quarantine. It's not like the last time I worked was a decade ago!"

She waves a hand dismissively in the air. "Don't even worry about it. You and I both know why you haven't been working. You had to focus on your health. You don't owe him any sort of explanation. And you don't even have to like the guy. You just have to make it through eight episodes with him. How much do you get if you get to the finals?"

I sigh. "I get twenty-five grand per episode. So, if I make it to third place, I'd make two hundred thousand. Two hundred twenty-five if I get second place, and two-fifty if we win. I'm pretty sure we also get a bonus if we win, but I haven't been able to confirm that."

"Holy cannoli," she breathes.

"Yeah, but that's if I even make it past the first episode," I remind her.

"Regardless of what happens, you get paid twenty-five grand, right? That's huge!"

"No, I know," I say. "It's so much money. But the messed-up thing is, though, that twenty-five grand wouldn't even make a dent in what I owe, which is kind of ridiculous, when you think about it. But it definitely helps." I smile at her. "At least I get my next residual payment by the end of the month, so that will help chip away at more of the debt."

"Definitely." She nods. "If you need—" I hear the cry of a baby coming from her side of the call. She looks over her shoulder. "Sorry, Lucy just woke up. I need to go feed her."

"No worries," I say, slapping a smile on my face. "Give her my love!" Liza hesitates, grimacing. I laugh and wave her off. "Go, go! Go feed Lucy. I'm fine!"

"Okay. See ya, doll!" She blows a kiss at me and hangs up.

I throw my phone to the side and drop my head back on the bed. Closing my eyes and exhaling heavily, I try to remind myself that things are looking up, even though it doesn't seem like it sometimes.

I. Am. So. Tired.

I roll on my side and force myself out of bed and into the bathroom. I strip off the last of my clothes, tossing them haphazardly as I go, and turn on the tub's hot water. I dim the lights and am heavy-handed with the bubble bath, letting the lavender scent soothe my tired body and soul. As I sink into the hot, relaxing water, I bring my knees to my chest and notice two black bruises appearing on my kneecaps. Must be from when he dropped me. Suddenly, I wonder whether we'll be doing any lifts in our routines, and whether or not I can trust Theo to catch me when he so evidently doesn't like me.

There is no way I trust him enough to do some Dirty Dancing *level lifts right now.*

I poke at the bruise on my right knee from when he dropped me and wince before dipping completely under water. Popping back up after a few seconds, I do my best to take a minute and remind myself of all the things I should be grateful for.

I am grateful I have this job. I am grateful for my friend. I am grateful for this amazing bathtub.

Chapter Five

THEO

The next morning, I arrive to the network building half an hour before practice. With a protein shake in one hand and a cup of coffee in the other, I wait for Rob, the show's executive producer, just outside his office door.

I see him come in, and he rolls his eyes. "That coffee better be for me—especially since you basically forced me to come in so early in the morning."

"Come on, you know I don't drink caffeine." I happily hand him the scalding cup, noting the redness on the palm of my hand.

He hesitantly takes it, narrowing his eyes at me. "Did you at least get my order right?" he asks.

"I've known you for eight years—since you were a wee personal assistant. I know you." He's arguably my only friend.

Rob lifts the lid of the coffee cup and inhales. "Jesus, that's good. Like a drug." He takes a small sip, wincing as he burns his lip on the piping-hot liquid. Rob takes out a set of keys from his coat pocket and unlocks the door to his office, pushing it open for me.

I take a seat in front of his desk as he sets the cup down gently and takes off his coat, hanging it on the rack behind his chair. When he's put his things away and settled into his chair, he brings his hands together, elbows on the desk, and looks me straight in the eye.

"Okay, what's going on? Why'd you make me come in at this ungodly hour? What do you need to tell me in person that's so time sensitive?"

I bite the inside of my cheek and take a beat. Rob and I have been friends since the show's first season, but some parts of our relationship have changed as he's grown into his career. Sometimes, I need to remember that I'm no longer speaking to Rob Ortiz. Nope, it's Roberto Ortiz, *Celebrity Dance Battle*'s EP.

I need to be careful how I phrase this. I don't *think* he'll fight me on it, but I'm prepared to point out the leave of absence clause in my contract. In the event that a family member falls ill and needs medical care, I'm allowed to take some time off.

"I…really don't know exactly how to say this," I start. Rob leans closer and narrows his eyes at me. "But I, uh, need to withdraw from this season's competition. I need to take a leave of absence."

Rob pushes off the desk and leans back in his chair. "Leave of absence? What do you mean? I don't understand."

"Bubbe… She, uh… She's not doing well, Rob. And I can't afford to get her the care that she needs. She's miserable in that home, and I don't want her to spend her final days depressed and confused because she doesn't recognize her surroundings."

"But—"

"Plus, this season is already messed up for me. My dance partner quit, and now I have this…" I grunt and sigh, running a hand through my hair. *Barbara*. "I just—I need the time off. I need the time off to take care of her, and…I don't know. I'll come back after she…" My voice trails off, and I gulp.

Rob stares at me for a long pause, not knowing what to say. "Listen, I get it. Bubbe is amazing—I've met the woman. And I know how much she means to you. But there are problems associated with you taking a leave of absence. First would be the fact that she's not exactly immediate family—" I sit up, about to interrupt, but he raises a hand at me. "Which we'll overlook since she is basically your mother. That woman raised you, I know.

"The problem here, Theodore—and please don't take this the wrong way—is that we can only allow for a leave of absence for *one* season, as per your contract. If your grandmother doesn't...*you know*...by the time the new season comes along, and you still need to be her primary caregiver, then we can't promise that your job will be here when you get back." He frowns, his eyes kind. "I can try my best with the network, but they'd already be making a huge concession, given the fact that we're talking about your grandmother, not your mother."

"But she *is* my mother—for all intents and purposes."

Rob nods sympathetically. "I know that, Theodore. But *legally* the network will be able to fight you on it. They'll want to keep you on. Especially since you are one of our fan's favorite dancers. Although, who the hell knows why," he adds with a small, teasing smile.

I sigh deeply and lean back in my chair. "So, what are my options, then? Just let her rot in a home, or take care of her but essentially throw my career away? I need something to come back to after she—" I swallow. "I *need* this, Rob."

Rob puckers his lips thoughtfully. "I understand where you're coming from, but I have info that I think will change your mind. Info that we haven't released yet, so I'd appreciate it if you kept it to yourself for the time being."

I nod. "Tell me." What could he possibly say that would sway my decision?

"One of the judges—I can't tell you which yet—is retiring." I inhale sharply. "And the network is scouting for a new one."

"Wait, do you mean...?"

"They're looking to cast a new judge from within the existing dancers."

Holy...

Instantly, I tense up. I haven't won a season in several years, and I'm almost positive there's no way I'll win it with my current partner. Is it really worth sticking around for another season when the goal seems impossible?

But becoming a judge would be...

"You don't have to win to get the job, Theodore," Rob says, reading my mind. "The network will be looking at the top three dancers—the ones who make it to the finale. The reason for that being that it demonstrates how popular they are with the audience—not just their ability to dance. If you think about it, that's what this show is all about in the end, isn't it? You guys don't just win based on the judges' scores, but on the fans' votes as well." He takes a tentative sip of his coffee, testing the temperature. "It's a popularity contest." He blows on the hot beverage.

"So, if the audience likes me, and if the network thinks I'd make a good judge...?" I ask, tentatively.

"Then you'd get a much, *much* bigger salary, plus better benefits and some sponsorship deals, as well as a more flexible work schedule. Additionally, public exposure like that could mean the opening of doors for other streams of revenue for you. This would mean that, six months from now, you could be making significantly more than enough to offer your Bubbe the at-home care that she deserves."

The offer is tempting. Way too tempting. What it would do to my career is just the cherry on top. Getting my grandmother the appropriate care she wants and deserves is truly what's tilting my decision.

"I apologize for speaking so crassly, but...realistically, do you think your Bubbe could make it a couple of more months?"

I shake my head, unsure. "Yes? But it's like the place just speeds up her deterioration, you know? It's the reason why I want to pull her out. I feel like it will make her sicker faster if I don't. If I take her home, back to a place where she recognizes everything...I think it will help slow down the progression of her Alzheimer's, help her mood, and ultimately make her feel better."

Rob nods. "That makes sense. Unfortunately, though, these are the only options you have at the moment. If I were you, I would risk staying on this season. Frankly, do you really want to have Nico as your judge?"

I sit up in my seat. "*Shit.*"

"Exactly."

"Does he know?" I ask Rob. "Does he know about this whole thing?" Maybe I'm being paranoid, but my mind starts working over the events that have transpired in the past couple of weeks. How Nico could have probably had any of the other women on the show but went specifically for my partner. How he slept with her and dumped her after spending the entire weekend together. How he left her so heartbroken that she had to leave the show because she couldn't handle seeing him anymore.

Rob shoots me a warning with his eyes. "*Nope,* don't even think about it. There's no way he knew. We've been instructed not to announce it until tomorrow. And I highly doubt Nico is Machiavellian enough to think of a whole plan to sabotage you this season."

"I don't know, Rob. He's incredibly manipulative. The way he treated Alessandra... He spent the entire weekend with her, told her he loved her, and then dumped her. He destroyed her. Told her she was a joke—that her entire career was a joke." I shake my head. I remember Alessandra running out of his studio last week, crying her eyes out. Later that day, I received an email from her explaining what had happened and that she was leaving. I wasn't friends with Alessandra, so I felt no need to avenge her or anything like that. But human to human, I felt for her. "I don't know how you guys didn't fire him, honestly."

Rob frowns at me. "He was a complete ass; it's true. But there's no rule against sleeping with a member of the cast."

"There should be," I mutter bitterly.

Rob lifts a shoulder nonchalantly. "Listen, the fans *love* Nico"—I roll my eyes—"and TV romances always make for good television."

I scoff at him. "This was a one-sided romance that never even made it on TV! Whatever." I run my fingers through my hair. "You're always thinking about publicity opportunities."

He shoots me a grin. "Always. Especially nowadays, bro. Everything is about *branding* and about doing it right. You'd do well to remember that." He points at me threateningly.

"*Jesus.*" We chuckle.

"So, what's it gonna be, huh?" he asks finally.

"I don't know, man. My partner...she's...agh."

"She's '*agh*'?" he air-quotes. "What the hell does that mean?"

I take a deep breath before answering. How can I describe her? "She's like...ditzy. Flaky. She dresses weird and...I don't know. I'm wondering whether it's even worth it to stay here this season, because I doubt I'd even make it past the first round with her, you know? She doesn't seem to want to take it seriously." I think back to her leopard heels and peanut M&Ms and frown.

Rob's brows pull together. "Really? I find that incredibly surprising and hard to believe." He takes a sip from his coffee—apparently it's cool enough to drink now. "I've met her. I'm, uh... actually seeing her agent—*Sabrina.*" He wiggles his eyebrows suggestively at me. "She's the one who begged me to get her this job."

"She *wanted* this job?" I feel my eyes widen in shock.

"Well, I don't think it was *this* job, specifically. She just needed *a* job. Any job." Rob picks at some lint on his sweater. "She's in a tough spot financially, apparently. I doubt she'd throw this opportunity out the window when she's strapped for cash."

I scoff, crossing my arms in front of my chest. "She piss away her cash, then? Typical former child actor." I cluck my tongue.

"Man, you are not as sweet as you seem, you know that?" he says sarcastically. "No, her financial manager apparently ran away with all her money. He'd been pocketing everything she made for a while without her noticing and neglected to pay her bills. Then, one day, he disappeared, leaving her with nothing but an empty bank account and massive debt."

"Oh," I say, feeling like an ass. "Her agent told you all this? Seems like a little too heavy a topic for some casual hook-up." I smirk at him.

He smiles at me from behind his cup. "Let's just say it's not as casual as you'd think."

I smile, happy he seems to have found someone.

"So, what's the verdict, then?" Rob asks. "You gonna stay or what?"

I take a deep breath and run my fingers through my hair in frustration. On the one hand, I'd be sacrificing time with my grandmother by staying on another season. On the other, if I get selected to become a judge, I'll have the cash to get her at-home care, improve her quality of life, possibly delay the advancement of her Alzheimer's. The answer seems simple enough, except...

"You really think Barbara is up to this?" I ask. Yesterday, she seemed distracted. The way she carried herself felt like she thought it was a joke. Was it me? Did my experience with

Alessandra completely poison the waters and make me prejudiced against Barbara?

"Dude, she's a professional. We wouldn't have picked her as a replacement otherwise."

I neglect pointing out to Rob that he just admitted to picking her because the woman he's sleeping with asked that he help her out. To be fair, though, Rob is very good at his job, and he wouldn't have allowed for Barbara to come on the show without doing his due diligence.

"She's got this, bro," he assures me. "I saw her show on Broadway a couple of years ago. She was incredible."

I sigh, resigned, and nod. "Okay. I'll do it."

"Awesome!" Rob says, rising from his seat. I get up, too, and he extends his hand. I take it and shake it, but he doesn't release me. "I should warn you, Theodore. If you want to win this, you're going to have to step it up. We need a judge who can become a true celebrity. We need that brand appeal, so go find it."

I leave Rob's office a bit stunned.

What did he mean by stepping up my brand appeal? I'm a great dancer. I'm well-liked publicly... Do I have a million sponsorship deals? No. Do I consider myself to be a wellness influencer like some of the other dancers here do? No. But that's because it's *my* choice. My career goals are centered around succeeding in *dance* and not around being famous.

I sigh, heading to the elevators while I roll this over in my head.

Regardless of what Rob meant, it's clear to me that my relationship with my partner needs to improve. That we at least need to make it to the final episode of the season, something I know we can do with enough practice. But practice won't be enough—we'll need trust as well.

I think it's time I had a candid conversation with Barbara.

Chapter Six

THEO

When I make it to my studio fifteen minutes before practice, I don't expect to find Barbara there, sitting on the bench, looking pensively at her hands. I'm surprised, to say the least. I don't think anyone has ever beaten me to the studio—at least not in some time. Truthfully, after how strained and awkward our training went yesterday and how I practically yelled at her, I half expected her not to show up at all. I never would have imagined seeing her here this early.

Maybe she's here to tell me she's quitting? My stomach turns. Yesterday, I honestly wouldn't have minded. I would've welcomed the news, actually, taken the time off. But after my conversation with Rob... Well, there's just too much at stake now. I need to make this work with her. I can't let her quit.

She doesn't hear me approach, so I take a minute to examine her. She's wearing leggings and the appropriate ballroom dancing shoes, so I *assume* she's not planning on quitting. *At least, not today*, I think. There are bags under her eyes—I can tell even with her head ducked low—and she looks concerned. I think back to what Rob said about her financial situation, and I wonder if that's what kept her up last night. Or was it me? Was it how big of an ass I was?

Remorse courses through my body, but I shake it off. Maybe the delivery of the message was wrong, but I feel like what I said yesterday wasn't. This show *is* my job, and it *is* important to me —even more so after hearing Rob's news this morning. I'm not going to apologize for telling her she should take it seriously, for warning her about getting involved with Nico. He's a fucking menace and ruthless, and I don't need another partner falling for his crap. I need her to take this seriously.

I hear Barbara sniffle and see a tear fall to the glossy wooden floor. I inhale sharply in surprised and, she hears me, her head shooting up.

"Hey," she says, turning her face to the side, wiping the tear from her cheek, doing her best to hide it from me. Does she not realize that this room is covered by mirrors on three sides? "Good morning." She turns back to me, forcing a smile.

"Hey." I eye her suspiciously, walking toward the bench and dropping my bag next to her feet. "Are you alright?"

"What? Yeah, I'm good. Allergies, spring, et cetera, et cetera. You know." She waves a hand in the air, dismissing me.

"What are you doing here so early?"

"Oh, I—" She takes a deep breath. "I brought you something, actually." She turns to her massive bag and starts rifling through it. I consider timing her just to prove to her that she should consider getting a smaller bag—or at least one with compartments.

Her bag rattles, and I hear objects clink against each other until she pulls out a white pastry box and a bottle of green juice.

"What's this?" I ask.

"Breakfast." Her smile widens a little as she hands me the items. I take them both in my hands, cautiously.

"It's not poisoned." She rolls her eyes at me, frustrated,

and I have to say, I'm a little relieved a part of her is back. I'm going to take her annoyance at me to mean she's feeling better.

"Uh, thanks," I say, popping the lid open. Inside are two large almond croissants. They smell heavenly, like butter and sugar. To my embarrassment, my mouth literally waters—I actually have to swallow. I'm sure they're incredible, but I can't accept them.

"I stole those from the hotel breakfast." She shrugs apologetically. "But I bought you the juice." I look down at the logo on the bottle and recognize the brand. It's ridiculously expensive—each juice costs about twelve dollars—something someone struggling financially should never spend a dime on (though, frankly, why *anyone* would spend twelve dollars on a juice they can make themselves is beyond me). I realize she's extending an olive branch.

"I, uh, can't have these," I mutter, giving back the pastries as diplomatically as possible. "I train and have a special diet I need to follow," I say, feeling like a jerk.

"Oh." She looks down at the box in her hands, frowning. "I understand."

"But the juice," I say quickly, trying to salvage the situation. "I can have the juice. Thank you. This is really nice of you." I crack the bottle open and take a sip, even though I already had my protein shake this morning.

"Great." She smiles a little. "Yeah, I thought this looked better than that sludge you had yesterday." I wince at the sweetness of the drink and do my best not to take a look at the label. I'm sure it's drowning in sugar and carbohydrates. Everyone thinks packaged pressed juices are healthy, but do they ever check the labels? No.

Still, I appreciate the effort.

"Listen," I say after drinking what I consider to be a sufficient amount, "I wanted to talk about yesterday and about practices going forward."

"Me too." She stands, interrupting me. "I—" Barbara takes a deep breath. "I think we got off on the wrong foot. I hope I got the wrong impression from you, and I *know* you got the wrong impression from me. We're in this together, and I want you to understand that I do take this very seriously."

I frown at her, absorbing her words. It seems she came in today with the same intentions as me—to smooth this over, to get us to work well together. Does she truly mean it, or is this more about having to be liked by everyone? I sigh. Perhaps I'm being too hard on her.

"Yeah." I scratch the back of my head. "No, I agree with you. I think yesterday didn't go as planned. I was hoping to discuss things with you today, too. Like I said, this is important to me. In fact, since yesterday, I've discovered that there's a hell of a lot more riding on this for me than before. At this point, it's not just that it's my job."

Barbara's eyebrows pull together in confusion, crossing her arms in front of her chest. It distracts me because she's wearing a tank top, and the movement pushes her breasts together.

Agh.

"I don't think I understand what you mean," she says, and I look back at her face.

I clear my throat and close my eyes briefly, trying to keep my eyes from drifting below again. I don't want to be creepy, so I decide to take a seat and search through my gym bag for my water bottle while I answer her. "The network is treating this season as a competition for the other dancers. They're hoping to choose a new judge to join the panel from the cast."

"Oh," she says, surprised. "That's a huge deal."

I nod, taking a drink from my bottle. My stomach turns again at the thought of losing this opportunity to one of the other dancers—especially to Nico. "Missing out on this opportunity would be...devastating." I sigh, holding my head in my hands, elbows on my knees.

"So...we need to win this in order for you to get the job?" I look up to see her grimacing, understanding finally hitting her. She doesn't believe we can do it either.

"Not necessarily," I admit, trying to relieve some of the pressure I just put on her. "I need to make it to the finals and show the network that I'm a fan favorite."

"Are you?" she asks simply.

"Am I what?"

"A fan favorite."

I hesitate for a beat. "I'm well-liked enough that I've made it to the finals almost every season and I have a pretty solid fan base, I'd say." I shrug.

"That doesn't mean anything, though. You're competing against other dancers who have a stronger social media presence than you. Daniel, for example, isn't just a dancer on your show. I actually knew of him from before because of his baking videos on TikTok."

"Well, I—"

"And Alex, the guy from Texas? He plays up the whole cowboy thing on Insta. He often takes pictures in his cowboy boots and cowboy hat with a sunset in the background, but I highly doubt that's what he wears every day while living in New York." She takes a seat next to me and pulls out a wrap sweater from her bag. Thankfully, she puts it on and spares me having to focus on not looking at her.

"Not to mention Nico," she says cautiously. "I can tell you really dislike him, but his entire feed is a literal thirst trap."

"What the hell is a—"

"And he has more sponsorship deals than all of you combined. None of the celebrities have any type of dance background that I could find, but one of them is a basketball player, which means he has a natural talent for hand-eye coordination and his team's fans supporting him. Plus, I hear that he's extremely popular with the ladies."

I raise my brows, my mouth slack-jawed. Where the hell did she get all this info?

Barbara shrugs simply and shoots me a gentle smile. "You were right. I hadn't done my homework, so I spent last night doing some research on our competition."

"Wow. I'm impressed." And I mean it.

She sighs deeply. "What I want to say is this: this competition is important to me, too. And if what you say is true, I'm pretty sure we're going to have to fight twice as hard as you usually have to. That means working it off the dance floor as well. We're competing against people who have fan clubs and are pretty active on social. If they didn't have a fan base, they wouldn't be on here. So, what are you going to do to get more support?"

I stare open-mouthed at her. "I—I don't know. Just make sure our routines kick ass and make sure we impress the judges and the fans?"

Barbara is quiet for a moment, waiting for me to continue, I think. "Is that it?" she asks, a bit horrified. "You don't have, like, a marketing plan or something?"

"A marketing—? *No, I do not have a marketing plan.*" Since when did this turn so intense? "This show is about *dancing.*"

Barbara rolls her eyes at me with a snort and stands, walking toward the barre. "I've only seen a couple of episodes of this show, and even *I* know that's not true." She scoffs. "Now I know why you've never won."

Her words trigger something deep inside me, because I know I'm the better dancer, and every season, I'm left wondering why the hell I rarely win. "You're wrong," I say, my voice deep. "I've won in the past."

Barbara laughs at me, watching me through the reflection in the mirror as she lifts her leg onto the barre to stretch it. "Yeah, like, *one time*."

"I'm not going to reduce myself to become an influencer selling 'wellness' products that do absolutely nothing for people but empty their bank accounts and hand out false hope of a healthier lifestyle." I half-growl, fisting my hands at my sides, but do my best to control my temper. We need this to work.

"Listen..." I sigh as she dips into a plié in front of me, her long legs stretched out. It doesn't go over my head how flexible she is. "I—I don't want to fight or argue. We need to present a united front, be partners. This is a life-changing season. I *need* this."

"Well, it's life-changing for me, too!" she blurts out, clearly frustrated.

"Why?" I open the door for her to come clean, to tell me about her financial situation, but she still keeps it to herself. Knowing this piece of information without her having shared it feels a bit like an invasion of her privacy, making me half-wish I didn't know anything at all.

"Well, I—" she stammers. "Being on the show could help get me more roles, you know? *Exposure.* And I need that if I want to go back into acting."

I frown at her answer. Either Rob was wrong, or she just flat-out lied to me. Why would she do that? Is she ashamed? It's not like it's her fault she got screwed over.

Regardless, she says she's committed.

I exhale deeply as Barbara puts her leg down and reposi-tions her feet on the ground, looking down. I think I hear her say, "*...hope he would just mind his own business...*" but I can't be sure. My lips twitch. Does she know how often she talks to herself?

Eventually, she turns to face me with a pleading look in her eyes. "Okay, so we agree we're both serious about this. We don't particularly seem to like each other—or at least we can agree that we're...a little different." I snort. Understatement of the century. "But can we at least agree to be friends?"

I frown. "The thing is, Barbara—and please don't take this the wrong way—I'm not here to make friends. We don't *need* to be. We don't even have to be *friendly*. We just need to be able to have a good partnership. So, can we be partners?" I extend my hand out toward her, and she looks down at it, biting her lip. For a brief second, I feel bad, thinking I've hurt her feelings. But I push the guilt back down again because this is business, after all —it's not personal.

"Yeah, sure," she says in a low voice, shaking my hand.

I tense at her touch, the same feeling that ran through me right before I dropped her yesterday running up my arm. I clear my throat and drop Barbara's hand.

"Now that that's settled"—I start toward the stereo—"let's get to it. We need to take advantage of every minute of practice this morning. There's gonna be a camera crew coming in this afternoon to shoot promo reels of us practicing, remember?"

I search through my computer for our song when I hear her speak again. "Now that we're partners and everything," she says from behind me, "can we discuss the choreography?"

Two steps forward and one step back.

I turn quickly to face her, my eyes narrowing at her. "What *about* the choreography?"

"It just feels a bit...dated. Boring." Barbara winces, as if realizing immediately her mistake.

"*Boring*? And you know this from all of your ballroom dancing experience? Do you suddenly consider yourself a professional after seeing exactly, what? Three episodes of the show?"

God, she can be infuriating.

She bites her full lip before answering. "I'm just saying, in the past, it seems like your routines were less...um...you know, *out there* or exciting than the others?" She winces. "What I mean is...your routines are lovely, of course, but they're very traditional."

I cross my arms in front of my chest. "That's because I'm a purist. I don't do gimmicks."

"And I totally get that," Barbara says, waving her hands in front of her as if I were about to shoot her. "But I mean, the other teams are probably going to step it up even more this year, and I thought maybe we could make it a bit more exciting, you know?"

"And how exactly would you make the choreography more exciting?" I spit out.

"Well, I don't know." She shrugs. "Maybe adding influences from modern dances? Changing up the music? I have no idea. I'm not a choreographer."

"Exactly," I say. "My point pre-cise-ly. *I'm* the choreographer. I've been on this show for eight years. Prior to that, I competed internationally. I went to school for four years for this. I think I know more about this kind of stuff than you do."

Barbara frowns and swallows hard. She nods once and goes to stand in the middle of the room. "Fair enough," she says in a small voice. "I'm ready, then. Let's win this."

Chapter Seven

BARBARA

Promo reels are the bane of my existence. For two hours, I had to look cute and ready to take on the competition, all while having to pretend like everything was alright. I had to pretend like Theo's—ugh, *Theodore's*—request to just be partners, not having to even be friendly, didn't affect me. Am I really so repugnant? Is my personality that intense, or am I really that weird that he can't even muster up the ability to be *pleasant?* Nope. We can only be *partners.*

It's not like I was looking forward to braiding each other's hair and making friendship bracelets or whatever, but *damn*, I would have liked to have some sort of amicable relationship with the man I'm meant to spend almost every day with for the remainder of my time in this competition.

Whatever. I just need to focus on the task at hand. Dance my butt off onstage, sell the fact that *everything is great* during filming, and win this thing.

"Ouch!" I yelp when I feel Rosie accidentally poke me with a pin.

"Sorry!" She winces, holding the hem of my very short dress in her hands. She's been kneeling on that floor for an hour now, and I wonder how her knees can handle it. "It slipped."

"Don't worry about it." I smile. "It happens. If you don't get poked by a needle at least once per dress fitting, you're not doing it right."

Rosie laughs and nods with the measuring tape between her teeth. Her hair is bright fuchsia today, and she's wearing an all pastel-pink outfit, down to the vintage-looking Mary Janes and a pink, embellished denim jacket.

I look around at the other contestants in the room who are also getting measured. Their outfits are made of fun, vibrant colors, and all have sequins, rhinestones, or a combination of both throughout the fabric—even the men. I look down at my long-sleeved navy dress and frown. Sure, it's flowy and flawlessly follows my every movement, but it's boring in comparison. Standing next to everyone else, it will be easy to get overlooked, forgotten.

"Will we be adding any type of beading or something to this look?" I ask tentatively. I don't know if she designed it, so I don't want to hurt her feelings. Considering her bedazzled pink jacket, however, I highly doubt she'd be opposed to sprucing this look up a bit.

Rosie winces at my question. "I'm not allowed to," she says regretfully. "Theodore is...very traditional. He doesn't like it when outfits are too glitzy."

My eyes widen in disbelief. "But that's, like, half the reason why people watch this show. You guys do such an amazing job." I look over to a former Olympic medalist standing to my left and check out her dress—a green and yellow explosion of color, crystals placed strategically across her body to make her appear curvier. "Sure, they're not outfits I would wear out, but they're gorgeous."

"Thanks." She smiles sheepishly. "But Theodore thinks it's too much—gimmicky. He prefers to do things more old school, keep all outfits clean and minimal. He says it distracts from the dancing, which affects scores." Rosie shrugs and writes down another measurement on the notepad beside her knee.

"I wasn't aware that dancers got to pick wardrobe."

Rosie grimaces. "They don't. The producers discuss it with the wardrobe department, and they decide together. But Theodore has seniority here, so he has some say."

It looks to me like he has more than *some* say in the matter. I look down at my dress, playing with the unfinished hem. I guess I should try easing up on him a little bit. He's right when he says that he's done this for a long time, that he knows what it takes to win. The fact that Theo hasn't won in a while is just circumstantial, right?

"God, I hope so."

"What was that?" Rosie asks. I did it again. I said what I was thinking out loud.

"Sorry." I blush. "I, uh, tend to talk to myself sometimes."

She chuckles. "I get it." After a brief moment of silence, while she concentrates on pinning the fabric in the right places, Rosie looks up at me and meets my eyes. "Can I ask you something?"

I raise my brows at her. "Sure."

"How are you doing?"

"Uh, fine, thanks?" I laugh.

"No, seriously." She frowns. "How are you doing, *really*? I heard him yell at you yesterday."

"Oh," I say, feeling my cheeks heat. "You heard that, did you?"

"Pretty much everyone did, yeah." She winces. "I've heard he can be a bit tough," Rosie says sympathetically.

"It's...fine. I just don't get where all that anger came from.

And so suddenly, too. Sure, he wasn't in the best of moods all day, but then he just lost it, and I have no idea why."

"Yeah, it's Nico. He and Theodore have a super intense rivalry—in case you didn't notice." We chuckle.

"Well, what's up with that? They fight over a girl or something? Did he steal his toy?" I smirk, but Rosie grimaces.

"Kinda?" she squeaks. "There's a rumor going around that Nico slept with Theodore's partner." She says it like she's unsure she should be telling me the story. "Apparently, she and Nico had a fling, and then, after it was over, she mysteriously quit the show."

"Ah, that makes sense. And I guess that's also why you warned me about Nico the first day I met you?"

She smiles and shrugs. "You looked nice. I didn't want you to get hurt like she did." I smile back at the image in pink.

"On top of that, I guess they've *always* had a professional rivalry, you know?" she continues. "I think Theodore just thinks that Nico uses his good looks to get whatever he wants, and he hates that he abuses that. Theodore is definitely the better dancer, but Nico is adored by fans. Obviously not because he's a sweetheart, but because he's smoking. I mean, he even dated a Kardashian once."

"Who hasn't, though?" I snort, and Rosie laughs.

"So, I guess Theodore resents that—Nico's use of his good looks to get ahead. Which makes sense, because how annoying is that?"

I nod in agreement. "No, I totally get it. But it's just surprising. From the research I've done, there's nothing about rivalry between the dancers. The media just kinda focuses on the partners as a whole or just the celebrities participating in the competition. Outside of their own social media profiles, we don't really know much about them. And you can't really rely on social media for the truth nowadays."

Rosie laughs but agrees. "Totally. I guess the dancers hide it pretty well, but there hasn't really been a shortage of drama behind the scenes. Like, take Jess over there," she whispers, pointing her pencil in the direction of a tiny brunette dancer. "She used to date one of the dancers here. This guy Diego, from Mexico—smoking hot, by the way—but then he got eliminated in the second round last season, and she left him for Shawn, over there." She points to a tall, built man with shoulder-length dreadlocks. "Shawn won the season, and Diego decided not to come back."

I look over at both dancers as they're fitted and measured into their own outfits for next week's performance. The woman —Jess—is distracted by what the seamstress is doing to her dress, while Shawn, her boyfriend, looks busy flirting with someone else—another stylist.

"And then, one year, things got pretty ugly because one of the partners fell in love with each other—or so it seemed, at least," she mutters the last part. "And it was really tense for a while because no one really believed them."

"What do you mean?"

"Well, onstage, they sold it pretty well. Announced how the show had brought them together and they were ridiculously in love and stuff. The fans *ate. It. Up.* They were super invested in their relationship, and in the end, they beat the other two finalists that year by a landslide." She laughs, pinning another piece of fabric tight to my skin. "But a lot of the cast and crew here thought it was fake. The couple hardly interacted with each other while the cameras were off, and people noticed."

My eyes widen as the idea pops into my head. *Yes.*

"People are really competitive here," she says, misreading my expression.

"Uh-huh," I say, but I'm barely paying attention to her now, because now I know how we're going to get the audience to vote for us over Nico and everyone else. Sure, it will be difficult to convince Theo to do it, but honestly, what other choice do we have? He doesn't want to update his choreography, his outfits are boring, and he has virtually no social media presence. If we do this correctly—stage some posts, play it up during the promo reels, and fake being in love onstage—I think we can garner enough popularity to win the fan vote.

But there would have to be a progression... The audience needs to be able to see the tension onstage—the *good* kind of tension, not the awkward I-can't-stand-you-I-hate-that-you're-touching-me kind—and see us fall in love.

Yes!

Suddenly, I can't wait to get out of here and run to Theo's studio and tell him about it.

I start hopping slightly in excitement but stop when Rosie accidentally stabs me again. "Whoops, sorry!" I say. "I just really have to pee." I grin, so happy we have a plan.

Yes, it's immoral. Yes, it means lying to over a million people. But how is it any different than playing a part on a TV show or a movie? How is it any different than being in a play? It's a TV show, and we're both playing characters—just like on any other show. Sure, it crosses the line into a moral gray area, but just a toe—not completely. At most, it straddles the line.

I need this. I need to get out of this hole of debt. I need to pay my medical bills. I need to not worry whether I'll be able to cover my prescriptions next month! I already spent twelve bucks on that stupid juice I bought him as an olive branch!

All of a sudden, I can't wait for Rosie to finish up so I can run to Theo's studio and tell him all about my plan.

...and get shut down.

I frown at myself and my negative thoughts. *No, Barbara. Think positive. This could easily help us win—if we do it right. I'll just have to make him see reason.*

While Rosie wraps things up, I start thinking about what faking being in love with Theo would entail, how I need to sell it to him, and how we would have to sell it to the rest of the world.

It definitely won't be easy.

Chapter Eight

BARBARA

It's minutes before our first performance, and I feel like I'm going to pass out. My heart is beating so fast and so hard against my chest that I feel like, any second now, it'll rip through my dress and pop onto the floor.

Okay, so I'm being a bit dramatic.

But still. You would be, too, if you were minutes away from performing in front of millions of people.

As I stare out at the audience from backstage, I feel defeated. This is it. My first and final performance on *Celebrity Dance Battle*. We're not going to win—not by a long shot—not with Theo's dated, stiff routine and music. And certainly not when we don't have the fans eating out of the palms of our hands. Our dance is old, boring. There's no way we're going up against the other seven teams and beating them like this.

The first six performances were just incredible. It will take a miracle for Theo and me not to go home tonight. We need to bring excitement to the stage, a story...something we definitely don't have.

I look to my right and see Theo fidgeting with the sleeve of his shirt, making sure his hair is sleeked back before we have to go onstage. He doesn't look nervous, but he's probably done this hundreds of times. I admire his confidence, but I'm afraid that sometimes it borders on hubris.

I would be considerably less anxious right now if he had just listened to me.

When I went to see him after my fitting on Tuesday to tell him my idea, he absolutely lost it, immediately shutting it down.

"No way, are you crazy? What are you even thinking?!" he exploded.

"Theo—*Theodore*," I caught myself. "I'm telling you, it's going to work. The audience will eat it up. You're handsome and talented, and you've never had a relationship in the public eye. They'll be fascinated by it. They'll start to wonder what is so special about our relationship that made you finally decide to date—and in public.

"We'll sell them on our chemistry, smile lovingly at each other while we dance, flirt during the promo reels, and post a few silly things a week over social media to keep them engaged. That's it. There's really not much to it!"

His eyes widened, staring at me in shock. "It's a lie. We'd be tricking everyone. How can you just think about lying to people so easily like that?"

"We already kind of do when we dance! We smile at each other lovingly and pretend, so why not extend it to post-dance?" I pinched the bridge of my nose and closed my eyes in frustration. "Listen, I totally get the fact that you think this is a bit morally reprehensible—"

"Because it is," he interrupted.

"But we both really need this." *I need it more than you know*, I wanted to tell him. "We both need to succeed, right?"

He frowned at me, as if considering it for a split second. I jumped at the chance, at this one moment of weakness. "Don't you want to win? Don't you want to stick it to Nico? Would you really be okay with having him as a judge? We can win this, Theo. I know we can."

Theo frowned at me and shook his head. "No. Not like this. Not by lying and manipulating people. It wouldn't make me any better than him, and you know it."

I sighed, frustrated. I understood where he was coming from, but the disappointment was crushing all the same. I knew that if I pushed him too far, he'd truly lose it, and we'd destroy whatever it was we had managed to rebuild that morning.

But that was a week ago, and I can't let myself dwell too much on it now. I bring myself to focus back on the now, the present, because in less than three minutes, we will be performing a two-minute dance in front of an audience, and it will be transmitted to millions of people on live television. I've performed in front of live audiences before, and I've been seen by millions of people on TV before, but I've never done both at the same time.

I try to swallow the knot in my throat, but it doesn't budge. My hands are cold and clammy, and I blush lightly, thinking of how I'm about to dance with Theo and my hands will be gross. *God*, he's going to feel them and get freaked out. And what if I slip out there? That floor looks much shinier and smoother than the one in the studio. It didn't look that clean during dress rehearsals. Oh my God, I'm going to fall flat on my face in front of the entire world and embarrass myself, and I'll never find another job, and I won't be able to pay my bills, and—

"Barbara? Are you okay?" Theo asks, taking my hands in his. I quickly pull them back, hoping he doesn't notice how sweaty they are. He's taken aback by my response, though. I guess after spending the entire week in each other's arms, it is a little weird that I'd respond that way to his touch. I should be used to it by now, right? Especially considering the foxtrot requires near constant body contact with your partner.

"I—I think I'm freaking out." My chest constricts. I can barely get a word out. My breathing grows shallower, faster. "I *know* I'm freaking out. Oh my God," I wheeze.

"Stop. *Stop*. Look at me," he insists. My eyes meet his—navy, dark, blazing—and I realize how big of mistake that is. His eyes are distracting in the worst possible way. They pull me in, hypnotize me, make me even jumpier and anxious when he stares at me like that. I squeeze my eyes tightly shut, needing to break off the contact.

"I can't do this," I push out. "I—I'm going to embarrass myself. We're going to lose." I inhale a ragged breath. "Those other performances—"

I hear Theo sigh before he pulls me to the side, away from everyone else. We're the next to last performance of the night, and I have no idea how we're supposed to just follow all the amazing dances we just saw.

"Theo," I say shakily, and he doesn't correct me. "They were all so incredible. How are we supposed to compete against them?" I think back to the intensity and emotion our competitors just exhibited during their routines and wince. I don't know whether me being a participant has changed how I look at the performances or whether all the dancers have truly stepped things up this season in comparison to the others. I never saw performances like this in the few episodes I watched from the previous season. It's like they all collectively got together and decided to step their game up even further.

His eyes bounce between my own, and he frowns. "Barbara." My name on his lips sounds like a plea, but he quickly recovers. A glimpse into his vulnerability is enough to distract me momentarily from my anxiety, though. "I know it's intimidating, but it's going to be okay. We're going to be okay. Our routine is flawless. You're amazing, and we've got it down to a science. Don't worry about anyone else. Just worry about us."

I look back toward the sweaty couples who have already performed—all smiles. They look so self-satisfied, and I envy them. Theo shakes my hand to bring me back to him. "Listen, we have about forty-five seconds before we need to be on that stage. The only obstacle you need to overcome now is your mind, because *I know* you can do this. And I know *you* know you can do this."

"But we aren't going to win," I almost wail.

"That doesn't matter, Barbara." Theo's right hand cups my cheek, but he drops it immediately, almost as if my skin had burned him. "I need you to take one massively big breath, hold it in for a few seconds, and release it slowly. I need you to calm down. *You* need you to calm down. So, let's do it together—just like you did the first time I met you. Without the umbrella this time." A tiny smirk plays at his lips.

He takes hold of my hands again, and this time I let him. We inhale together, raising our arms all the way above our heads. With his eyes, he tells me to hold the breath. I begin to release it when he does as we lower our hands to our sides together.

"How are you feeling now?" Theo's brows are pulled together, and he looks so good in his white button-down and black tails.

"I'm..." I take another deep, steadying breath. "Good. Good." I don't sound convincing, but it will have to do. "Better, at least."

"Miss Holt? Mr. Wallace?" A PA with a headset and clipboard approaches us with caution. "You have fifteen seconds to take your place."

"Shit," I mutter under my breath, my wide eyes meeting his concerned gaze. He squeezes my hand briefly before we both run to take our spots onstage.

"Hey," he says from his spot. His navy eyes glitter under the low light of the stage. *How do they even do that?* Theo smiles encouragingly at me. "You've got this, Barbara. I know you do."

THE LIVE BAND STARTS PLAYING THE INTRO TO OUR SONG AT the same time as a spotlight is pointed at me and Theo. I thought for sure I was going to throw up in front of everyone or at least completely freeze up, but the second he takes my hands in his and we lock eyes, all the nerves disappear. It's like he said: I've got this—we've got this.

Theo and I start gliding down the dance floor, my dress flowing with us with every movement we make. We start with a basic slow-slow quick-quick step pattern, but then we're practically floating into pivots and quarter-turns, my hair flying, trailing behind us despite the copious amounts of hairspray that went into my half-do earlier today. His strong, firm hands lead me, showing me that he's there too. Suddenly, we're twirling, twirling, twirling fast, and I laugh. But not because it's funny—no. Because I'm *so happy*. My neck is arched back, and there's a smile plastered on my face, but it's not fake. Nope, I'm not putting on a show like I said I would. This is real. For the first time in a long time, I feel free, and—despite everything that Theo had said about ballroom dancing—I'm having fun.

Our outfits aren't glitzy, and we're not the audience's favorite couple by a long shot, but the dance is romantic and freeing, and being in front of an audience again is exhilarating. How I'm feeling now...I don't care if we don't make it past the first round.

Okay, so maybe I would care if we don't make it to the next

round, but still. The joy I feel as our bodies move together is incomparable, and I will treasure this moment forever.

After years of not being able to control my body, my seizures, being able to get it to move this way, to have it follow my commands in such a graceful and precise way, is empowering. I hadn't realized until now just how much I had been fighting a battle against myself and how badly it was affecting my state of mind.

This is incredible.

I laugh again as we take another turn, and I feel my hair hit Theo's chest. I know it secretly annoys him, so I smirk up at him when I'm back in his arms.

Theo smiles back down at me, surprised. But I can't help but wonder whether he's playing the part of dance partners, or whether he's feeling as incredible as I am.

The song starts drawing to a close, and I'm brought back down to earth. It's not a big finale like the other performers had —nope, not even close. But it's what we have, and we have to sell it.

We're meant to end with a quick turn and separation, but when it's time for him to release me, Theo pulls me a bit roughly into him, my back against his chest, and the song ends with his arms around me.

Chapter Nine

THEO

SHE GAZES UP AT ME, CONFUSED, BUT QUICKLY READJUSTS her features as I knew she would. For all I ragged on Barbara for her professional abilities, I knew she would be able to handle a small amount of improvisation. She did perform for several months on Broadway, after all, and that was live. I bet on the fact that she knew how to think quickly on her feet, that she could improvise, and won.

"What was that?" she whispers as the lights come back up and the crowd cheers—with noticeably less enthusiasm than they did for my cast-mates and their partners—which, of course, is exactly why I pulled her in at the last minute.

Barbara was right. We were going to lose otherwise. And though I am a purist, and I don't believe in gimmicks or lying to get ahead, I also believe that family should come first. And I need this for my Bubbe.

"You were right about all of it, okay? Just go with it," is all I manage to tell her before our mics are turned back on. We walk hand in hand over to where the show's host, Troy Bass, awaits us, right by the judges' table.

Judging is going to be brutal, that's for sure. I just hope she can take it.

"Wow! Wow! Wow!" Troy's overly enthusiastic voice comes over the cheering, which slowly comes to a stop. "Wow! Theodore and Barbara, everyone!" The crowd starts cheering again, but just barely.

My stomach turns.

Troy runs a hand through his frosted tips, which have enough product in them to perfectly defy gravity and stay up like blades of blond grass. "I gotta say, Theodore, it's good to have you back for yet another season, old timer."

I don't appreciate the joke about my age—I'm only thirty-three—but I know the deal by now. I know I have to be upbeat and fun. I should play along with his joke, say something charming, but this whole thing has me full of dread and completely tongue-tied.

"Yeah," I cough. "It's so good to be back for another season." I wrap my arm around Barbara and pull her close into my side, my hand on her lower back. I sense her tense briefly, but again, just like during the foxtrot, she effortlessly follows my lead. I move my thumb back and forth affectionately and try not to notice how smooth and soft her skin is.

"And Barbara—wow," Troy says, shaking his head. "It's so good to see you back on TV. I think the world has missed you!" More cheers. More bullshit. I want to sigh in frustration and get this over with, but I'm playing a part—*we're* playing a part.

"Thanks," Barbara says. She looks up at me and gives me a toothy grin. "Happy to be back and to have such a great partner!" I wink at her, wrap my arm around her waist, and squeeze her side.

"Well," Troy says with a sly grin. "Amazing, then! It looks like you two are getting along! Let's start our judging, shall we?" We all turn to look at the judges' table, and my smile falters for a second. I've worked with these people for years, stood in front of them to take their critique, watched them give it to other people. I can already read the judgment on their faces before they even open their mouths.

Disappointment.

Fuck.

"Let's start with Bex Smith, our favorite choreographer!" The crowd *woos!* in excitement.

"Wow. Okay. Barbara, Theodore. Where do I begin?" Bex purses her lips and flips her flaming red hair over her shoulder. She brings her hands together in front of her lips and looks at us intensely. "I gotta say... I'm a bit...disappointed." The crowd collectively gasps.

This isn't good. Normally, when the crowd disagrees, they *boo* the judge—they don't gasp. They don't let their favorite dancers take it. It's easy to see many agree with Bex.

"You know," Bex continues. "It's not a question of ability. Barbara, I think you did an incredible job. Your form was perfect, your footwork impeccable, and you truly looked like you were having a good time," she says sympathetically. Bex is right —she *did* look like she was having a good time. The best. "But the dance itself..." Bex shakes her head. "It was lacking." She leans back in her seat, apparently done. "Dated."

Ouch.

"Okay, thank you, Bex!" Troy says into his mic. "Let's move on to our favorite British grump—former ten-time international ballroom dancing champion Hugh Davies!" The crowd cheers for the head judge, and he waves at them, his gold watch catching in the stage lights.

"Barbara, I am happy to see you here, but I'm quite disappointed in this performance." Jesus, okay, I guess we're not sugarcoating anything today, are we? "The choreography was a bit stale. Executed perfectly, no doubt—but stale, nonetheless. It was not a great start. If I were you, I'd look into perhaps finding ways to bring us more excitement in your next routine. I was honestly quite bored watching it." I want to knock Hugh's white toupee off his head (I don't care what he says—it's definitely a wig).

I look down at Barbara and feel extremely guilty. Though it was my choreography, my costume and song choices, she's technically the one competing and therefore the one receiving all the criticism. I think back to just a few minutes ago when she seemed to be on the verge of losing it, looking so scared and fragile, and now here she stands, strong and graceful. She takes the harsh critiques with a smile, like the champ that she is, nodding at the judges' suggestions and comments. There is no hint of the scared woman I saw backstage less than ten minutes ago.

"Thank you, Mr. Davies," she says. "I appreciate your feedback."

"Now, I think we'd all love to hear from our favorite party girl, Mademoiselle Coraline Lyon!" The crowd goes wild for the seventy-year-old former burlesque dancer. She's a kook, and super fun, and by far the easiest judge to please. I breathe a sigh of relief because I know that she'll go easy on Barbara. I've always doubted whether she takes her job seriously or not. She practically gives away nines and tens during judging—something that used to irk me. Now, I couldn't be more grateful for it.

I squeeze Barbara encouragingly again and smile down at her. I want to tell her it will all be okay, but my mic is on. I do my best to communicate it with my eyes.

"Barbara, Theodore," Cora says in a thick French accent. I wait for a smile or a joke...but it never comes. "I, too, am so disappointed with your routine. Because that's what it was. It definitely was not a *performance*." There is a collective silence among the audience and the rest of the cast and crew. "Did you get a chance to see the other performances?" she asks.

I can't answer. Normally, she'll make a slightly inappropriate joke about the male dancer's look during judging and tell the woman that she's fabulous and move on. What fresh hell is this?

"Yes," Barbara answers her question. "I did. They were incredible."

"Correct," Cora nods. "Do you think your performance was anywhere near as good as the others?"

What?

I hear the catch in Barbara's breath. She hesitates before answering, but she seems to gather force from somewhere deep within her. "I think, for our first performance, we did pretty well. Theodore is a great teacher, and I'm sure, with more practice and his help, I'll do better." She takes Cora's harsh words and reflects them like a mirror with such grace that I stare down at her in awe. Minutes ago, she looked like she was about to pass out over dancing in front of a crowd, and here she is now, essentially being called inadequate and handling it like a damn queen. We may or may not be about to put on a show now with regards to the true nature of our relationship, but her thanking the judges like that, her taking the critique so gracefully...that's all her. That's not an act. I know now that Barbara is a true professional and stronger than she looks.

She may not be my favorite person, but I appreciate and respect the hell out of her now.

"I just hope I do better by Theo." She looks sweetly up at me, and I pull her tightly into me, squeezing her in reassurance.

"*If* you're still here next week," Cora adds venomously, "which I highly doubt, darling. If I were you, I would start packing my bags." She scoffs and looks down at her blood-red nails.

I don't miss the shocked and confused looks the other judges throw in Cora's direction.

There's an awkward silence for a bit until Troy finds himself.

"Uh, well, thank you, judges!" He turns to face us again. "So, Barbara, Theodore. While we wait for your scores, what do you think about the judges' comments? Do you think you'll be here next week to show them you've got it in you? You've never been eliminated this soon in the season, Theodore."

And there's my in. I hesitate for half a second but decide to go for broke.

Fuck it.

"You know, Troy," I say, staring into Barbara's eyes. "I would obviously love to win the competition with Barbara, but I can't say that I'd be devastated to see our time here end."

"Oh, no?" Troy raises an eyebrow at us, his eyes bouncing between our faces.

"Nope." I look back at him. "Because I know Barbara's and my story doesn't end here. This season has led me to the woman of my dreams, and she's standing right here in my arms."

Barbara's face snaps up to look at me, eyes widened in surprise.

"Wait, are you saying..." Troy wiggles his eyebrows at us, a wry smile on his face. "Did more than just a dance partnership blossom during practice between you two?"

"Yeah," I sigh, looking down at Barbara again, whose face and ears are now beet red. "I mean, I can't speak for Barbara, but it's safe to say that this guy is falling in love with the beautiful actress standing before us."

Barbara makes a weird choking sound.

I genuinely don't know how I'm doing this. I don't know how I'm pulling it off. Am I? Suddenly, I start to question whether I'm being convincing enough. I don't have any acting experience, I don't like to lie, and I've never been in love, really.

But this is how it goes, right? People get nauseatingly cute in public about their feelings toward another person.

Fuck, what if I'm making it worse?

Barbara hasn't said anything, and I start to doubt whether she actually knew where I was headed with me pulling her into my arms, acting all flirty.

"Barbara?" Troy turns to face her head-on. "You okay?"

"Me? Yes, of course!" She smiles at him and wraps an arm around my waist. "It's just all so surreal to me, you know? I fell so hard and so fast for Teddy."

Now *I'm* the one who's choking.

Teddy? On national television?

She's an evil mastermind, and I kind of like it.

"Well, then," Troy says, taken aback by our public confessions. "Why don't we, uh, take a look at the judges' scores. Bex?"

"Barbara, you did some amazing work, but your performance lacked shine. I'm going to have to go with a six." She throws her a sympathetic smile, and Barbara nods.

Harsh.

"Miss Holt, I did love you so very much on your TV show when you were younger! You brought so much life to the role. Unfortunately, this performance made me want to take a nap. It's a six for me as well."

I shake her a little in encouragement. She's doing so great, taking all of the heat when the judges know that this is all my fault. The choreography, music choice, and wardrobe were all my responsibility.

Cora is up next, and she doesn't seem her playful self. What is wrong with her tonight? Why is she being this way?

"I think this was a truly disappointing performance. It belongs on the dance floor of a small-town high school prom, like in one of those teen movies. It's a four for me—barely."

My jaw literally drops open. *Four?* It was a technically

perfect dance. Was it as exciting or glamorous as the others? No. But it sure as hell doesn't deserve a four out of ten.

Troy inhales sharply and pats me on the shoulder. "That was rough." He chuckles a little, and I wonder whether anyone has ever had the pleasure of punching Troy in the face. "Anything left to say, team?"

Barbara looks up at me with a sweet smile. "I just want to thank the show for introducing me to Teddy. This has been the most incredible week of my life." Her smile is beaming, and for a second, even I believe her. I have to remind myself all of this is fake—none of it is real—before I place a tender kiss on her temple, and she softly closes her eyes.

"Awww. Well, it's so nice to see this show bring love to people. Up next, we'll get to see former rock star Veronica 'Ronnie' Roberts take the stage with her partner, Daniel!"

The lights dim around Barbara and me, and we take it as our cue to leave the stage. She pushes my hand off her waist as soon as she confirms no one can see us and stalks off backstage.

Chapter Ten

BARBARA

"I don't understand why you're so upset," Theo says, following closely behind me as I stomp into one of the dressing rooms. "It was *your* idea, after all!"

I throw my hands up in frustration. "I know it was, but you should have discussed it with me before pulling something like that. We could've planned it out—executed it much better. This isn't how it was supposed to go. We were supposed to build up to it, make it more realistic. No one is going to believe this is real if it was so sudden. Plus, how could you catch me off guard like that? That wasn't okay."

He checks that the door is closed behind us, that no one can overhear us, before continuing. "Well, I panicked! I admit it was rather careless and a spur-of-the-moment thing, but you're such a good actress—so talented—I knew you would be able to catch on and improvise."

I glare at him, fisting my hands at my sides so I don't accidentally strangle him. "Don't patronize me, Theo. It's insulting and beneath you."

He turns to look away and runs a hand down his face. "Listen, I already apologized. And I meant it. I didn't know what to do. I thought I had a handle on it, but you were right. And it took me all of five seconds into our performance for me to realize it. I just started thinking about how my grandmother was going to see this, and—"

"Your *grandmother*? What the hell does your grandmother have to do with any of this?"

Theo frowns and scratches the back of his neck. "Actually, pretty much everything." He exhales and takes a seat on the nearest chair. "I wasn't completely honest about what winning this season means to me. It isn't important to me because of the judge role. I mean, yes, it is. But it's not about being a judge exactly. It's about what that would mean for me and my family. And my family is my grandmother—she's all I have left." He looks up at me to meet my eye. My hands are on my hips, and I eye him suspiciously as he speaks. "I need the extra cash I'd get from being a judge—and the hours—to be able to get my grandmother the care she needs. She's..." He exhales deeply. "She's not *well*."

There's a pause between us before I break the silence. "You better not be bullshitting me here." I cross my arms in front of my chest.

Theo shakes his head. "I'm not. I swear. I really want this so I can pay for twenty-four-seven, at-home care." His eyes are pleading, and suddenly, I can see the deep lines in his forehead brought on by stress. "I need this, Barbara. And...I know you need this, too," he says tentatively.

I straighten instinctively, on high alert. "What do you mean?"

"I heard about your financial situation." He winces, as if regretting the words as soon as they leave his mouth.

I feel my jaw fall open but don't say anything. How much

does he know? How did he find out? Does he know about the medical part of it all?

"Who told you?" I manage to eventually ask, my voice barely a whisper.

He shrugs sympathetically. "People talk."

I take a seat in the chair across from him and sigh, suddenly *exhausted*. I place my elbow on the armrest, my hand holding my face. I'm squishing my cheek, probably ruining the makeup the stylists so expertly applied.

"Is that why you were crying a couple of days ago? When I walked into the studio?"

"You saw that, huh?" I ask with a little dark laugh.

"How bad is it?" he asks quietly.

I lift a shoulder. "Not great. I paid most of my debts off by selling my apartment, but I still owe almost half a million dollars total."

Theo whistles and leans back in his chair. "How is that even possible?"

"Back taxes. Unpaid bills."

"That seems like a lot for a few unpaid credit card bills and back taxes," he says.

"Well..." I clear my throat, hesitating. Very few people know about my epilepsy, but since we're being brutally honest... "The shock and stress of the whole thing kind of triggered a seizure, which caused me to hit my head and landed me in the hospital for several days. So that added to the bills."

"Seizure?" Theo's eyes widen. "Are—are you okay?"

"Yeah, I'm fine," I shrug. "I have epilepsy. I've had it for quite some time, actually. I just don't tell *anyone*, really. People have used it against me in the past."

"Jesus." His eyebrows shoot up into his forehead in shock.

"It is what it is," I say. I try to play it off like it isn't a big deal, but it's cost me some jobs. Directors, for example, don't quite understand or like it when you can't show up to work because you had an aura or a seizure. I actually had a director once fire me because of it, claiming it was for my own good: "*If you can't handle the everyday pressures of working on a set due to health constraints, then perhaps it's best you look into other options and we look into other actresses,*" he had said.

"What did you do for cash before? I mean, I know you said you worked a little bit since your TV show ended, but it doesn't seem like you've had too active a career since then."

"Well, I did the odd commercial from time to time. And the show actually has a pretty solid fan base to this day, so I didn't really *need* to work thanks to all the residual payments I receive. I was living pretty comfortably until recently. I get a ton of money each month from all the reruns and licensing deals I still have with *Phantom Fighters*—at least in theory. It used to range anywhere between eighty to one-hundred thousand a month." Theo chokes slightly, and I see him do the math in his head. "Yeah, I was doing pretty well for a long time."

"I'm confused, though. How do you still owe money? If you make that much each month, shouldn't you have been able to pay it off quickly, then?" His brows furrow.

"Well, yes and no. I owed a ton more than I do now, so as soon as any money came in, it went out to pay people off. My financial manager hadn't paid taxes in *years* even though he said he had. So, I owed the government quite a lot of money. Then, there were the credit card companies and other miscellaneous bills. Plus, turned out he'd purchased cars and boats under my name, which hadn't been paid for. I got lawyers to help me argue against those, but some of them stuck, which added to my debt. And also, well, legal fees."

"*Jesus,*" he says, his eyes wide, bright navy.

"Yup." My lips pop as I nod, looking down at my dancing

shoes. "I don't know why I'm telling you all of this," I mutter, laughing once. "I must have lost my mind."

"Don't worry. I won't tell anyone. You can trust me." And oddly enough, despite us clearly not being each other's favorite people, I believe him.

He takes a deep breath before going on. "So, I guess there's a lot at stake for both of us here—more than we originally thought." He deserves an award for pointing out the obvious. Should I offer him a round of applause? "And you're right about tonight," he goes on. "What I did was wrong. I'm sorry. But I think you were right—this might be our only shot. So, let's set up a plan, because we desperately need one."

"That's if we even make it past this round," I mutter bitterly. "Judging was *brutal.*"

"You took it like a champ, though," he says with a small smile. "Seriously."

"Thanks." I feel myself blush. "I did my best, but it was tough. That Cora is merciless." I joke-shiver.

Theo frowns pensively. "Actually, she's not. That's what bothered me the most about this whole thing. She's usually the most lenient judge of the three of them." He shakes his head and runs his fingers through his no-longer-neat hair. I think I prefer it disheveled and messy, if I'm being honest. He looks sexy and unraveled; his usual neat and controlled self nowhere to be seen.

Okay, so he might be a little more than objectively attractive...

"That's so weird, then," I say, trying to shake off my wayward thoughts about Theo.

Definitely shouldn't be thinking about him like this.

"Now that I think about it, in the few episodes that I watched, she always did seem to be the comic relief." Where had this extreme dislike come from?

"Yup. I don't know what's up with her either, but I wouldn't worry about us getting to the next round," he says with the utmost confidence.

I scoff at him incredulously. "Are you kidding? Was I the only one paying attention during that whole ordeal, or was it so awful you blocked it out?"

Theo laughs—*a genuine laugh from Theo*—and I wonder whether hell has frozen over.

"No, I definitely remember that. But you didn't see what I saw as we left the stage, apparently." His eyes sparkle with a hint of mischief.

"What was that?" I eye him suspiciously.

"A very drunk Ronnie Roberts stumbling out of her dressing room, skirt tucked into the back of her underwear." Theo smirks. "There is no way she and Daniel were able to manage a halfway decent dance with her being so wasted. It's just not possible. I promise there's no way we're getting voted off this competition. At least not tonight."

THEO'S ARMS ARE WRAPPED AROUND ME, MY BACK AGAINST his chest, as we await the final results. We're in the bottom two couples along with Drunk Ronnie and her partner, which isn't really a surprise at this point. But still, I'm not used to failure, and from what I've heard, neither is Theo. It sucks, given how much these results can affect our lives so significantly. It's odd how people voting from home don't know exactly how life-changing this moment is for the both of us.

"Alright, then. We're down to our final two couples. One of you will get to stay and compete for another week, while the other will be going home tonight empty-handed," Troy says with the same joy in his voice that a child has when describing all the gifts he received over Christmas.

This guy...

"The couple moving on to compete next week is..." He opens the envelope and pulls out a piece of paper. Troy's eyes widen in mock-surprise. "Whew! It's a close one! *Barbara and Theodore!*"

"Wee!" I scream and turn to face Theo, who is grinning from ear to ear. I surprise him—and myself, to be honest—by jumping into his arms. It takes him half a second, but he reaches down to grasp my thighs to hold me to him and buries his face in my neck, laughing. I tell myself I'm just acting, just pretending—it's all part of the show—but I can't deny how freaking *amazing* it feels to have him hold me like this, completely over-joyed that we made it to the next round.

"I told you we'd get through this round," he says in my ear, his breath on my skin sending shivers up and down my spine. "I told you we've got this." I wrap myself tighter around him and smile goofily. "You were incredible."

After a few seconds, he sets me on my feet, eyes never leaving mine. He opens his mouth to say something else, but Troy interrupts us.

"I'm sorry, Ronnie and Daniel, but that means your time here has ended." Troy grins before turning to me, the losing couple pushed out of the way. "Barbara! That was a close one!"

I'm breathless with excitement, my heart is racing, skin tingling. *Damn*, it feels good to still be here. "Yeah," I say, trying to catch my breath, the adrenaline still coursing through my veins. "Theo and I are so happy to still be here." I grin up at him, feeling my cheeks get sore from smiling so big. "We're gonna take the judges' notes into consideration and kick butt next week!" Theo's fingers lace through mine, and he squeezes my hand in encouragement.

"Well, we can't wait to see what you've got in store for us!" Troy turns back to face the camera head-on. "And we'll see *you* next week for Eighties Night! Until then, from everyone here on *Celebrity Dance* Battle, we hope you have a lovely week!"

The lights come up, and the crowd starts to leave the theater. My hand is still in Theo's, which he pulls on for me to follow him backstage.

"That was incredible. You were incredible," he says, pulling me into a friendly hug. Because we're friends now, right?

God, he smells good. Like sweat and aftershave and citrus or something.

I push softly against his chest to put some space between us. I'm suddenly a bit overheated and in need of air. I'm sure it's just the stage lights, but still.

"Yes! I think we should meet up tomorrow morning and go through everything. We just need to remember not to tell anyone. Everyone needs to believe that we're actually together." I think back to what Rosie said about the couple who won a couple of years back. About how the crew and people on the show didn't believe it was real. "Every single dancer is competing for the new judge spot. I don't trust that one of them won't try to out us to get ahead."

Theo nods thoughtfully. "No, I agree. We need to make everyone believe that we're *together* together. Like, actually."

"Good. So, let's meet up tomorrow to discuss what we do next."

"Oh my God, Barbara! Theodore!" We turn to see Rosie barreling toward us with her arms open. "This is so freaking exciting!" She reaches us and throws her arms around us both. "I knew it! I *knew* it! I knew the whole fight because of Nico was because you were into her. I knew you guys had a spark. I could see it the second I saw you together."

I gently push her off us with a smile. My first instinct is to say, "Ew! Nuh-uh!" Because I disliked Theodore the first second I saw him. But of course, things have changed. It's showtime.

"I guess so!" I fake-giggle. "He hadn't told me he was attracted to me then, but of course that was only the first day." I look up at Theo and playfully bat my eyelashes at him. "Theo told me later that he fell for me then. He couldn't stand the idea of us not together, and I felt the same way. It was love at first sight." Theo's eyes narrow at the use of his shortened name, and I grin in satisfaction. I do love to push his buttons.

After remaining rather unresponsive, I elbow him in the side, and he grunts, snapping out of it. "Uh, yeah. I was taken by her the second I saw her standing in my dance studio." I take his hand and wrap his arm around my waist. He takes the cue and kisses me on my temple. I jump a little in reaction.

"Eeek!" Rosie squeals. "I am so happy for you, Theodore! You know, we've never really been friends, but I always saw you as the lovable, grumpy, older uncle type of the CDB family, and I hoped you would find someone, because you seemed so lonely, and now you have Barbara, and—eek!" It's like she can't get the words out fast enough. "So freaking excited!" Rosie sighs and bites her lip, looking between the two of us. "This is incredible. Well, I'll leave you two lovebirds alone."

Rosie runs off with a massive smile on her face, and my stomach turns out of guilt. "I feel bad for lying to her, but oh my God, she's so happy for you it's kind of sad. Until now, she felt bad for you. Poor Teddy," I tease him, clucking my tongue.

"Don't call me that," he snaps at me, but his eyes aren't filled with the initial disdain he served me during our first encounter. This time, there's a spark—his navy blue eyes shining in amusement, a hint of a smirk appearing on his angular face.

I roll my eyes at him, pretending I'm deeply annoyed by his behavior. "I forgot you're not into nicknames. Except, you're going to have to be, so get it together." Theodore glares back at me. Mr. Grump is back, and it's kind of thrilling. I bite my lip to hide my smile before continuing: "Let's meet up early tomorrow to hammer out the details. Your homework for tonight should be to figure out which pet name you actually are okay with." I chuckle. "See you *mañana, amigo*." I smile with a wink and leave him standing there.

Chapter Eleven

THEO

As I walk down the hallway toward my dance studio, I can't help but notice the curious glances thrown in my direction. I'd say I have no idea where they're coming from, but I have my suspicions. It could be the fact that I'm holding a paper bag from Dunkin' and these people have never seen me drink or eat anything that isn't green or from a bottle. Or it could also be the fact that Grumpy Theodore confessed his love on live television to former child-star Barbara Holt after keeping his personal life very private all these years (not like I had much of one to begin with, but still).

Though the smell coming from the white paper bag is quite pungent, and I swear it can travel through walls (seriously, how can Barbara eat this much crap and not have died yet?), my guess is that the curious glances are due in part to recent events.

I move my hand to adjust the strap of my gym bag on my shoulder and accidentally get a whiff of the sandwich. "*Gah!*"

Disgusting.

I can't believe I am contributing to this, but this morning, I figured we have a rough day ahead of us and thought it would be nice to bring something for her like she did for me last week.

I push open the door and find her sitting on the bench, fastening the buckles of her dance shoes. They're hot pink and covered in rhinestones, sparkling so much a helicopter could probably see them from the sky—but at least they're proper dance shoes.

Progress, Theodore. Progress.

"You don't need to do that."

Barbara gasps, and her hand flies to her chest. "You startled me!"

I apologize and walk toward her, nervous. Why am I so fucking nervous? Maybe because we told the entire world that we were dating, and now we have to act like a couple in love in order to convince them?

Calm down, man.

Barbara looks like she's about to say something, but her beautiful hazel eyes widen, her jaw drops, and she points at the bag in my hand. "What is *that*? Did you get yourself something from Dunkin'? And—oh my God, is that *coffee*?" She gasps, bringing a hand to her chest in mock horror. Realization dawns on her, and a smile spreads across her face. "Theo..." A thrill courses through me every fucking time she calls me that. It's... unnerving. I hate it. "Theo, is that for *me*?"

I roll my eyes at her. She's looking at me as if I am the love of her life and I'm down on one knee proposing to her. The greasy breakfast sandwich may as well be a twenty-carat diamond engagement ring. *Jeez.* Is Dunkin' really the way to her heart?

"I thought I'd pay back the favor from the other day. Plus, I thought you could use a treat. You must be exhausted after last night, and we do have a lot to talk about today." I pass her the bag and the coffee, and she looks like she could cry from happiness. I snort. "Really, Barbara, don't be ridiculous. It's just an iced coffee and a breakfast sandwich."

"A *breakfast sandwich?*" She sets the coffee gently beside her feet on the floor and practically tears through the bag. "Oh, sweet Jesus, *yes.*" She takes it out, unwraps it, and takes a massive bite with a moan, her eyes practically rolling to the back of her head. The image makes my lower stomach tighten and leads me to start imagining whether she makes the same noises when she—

"You got *two* of them?" she says with half a sandwich in her mouth.

I clear my throat—and my mind—and say, "They had a two-for-one promo going on."

"God bless you, Theodore Wallace," she says. I grimace as she takes another moan-inducing bite.

Jesus, she needs to stop doing that.

I clear my throat again. "Well, anyway, I figured you'd be dead tired, and this could be a good pick-me-up."

"Hit the nail on the bullseye," she says, her mouth full.

"That's definitely not the correct expression," I deadpan.

"Who *cares?* Just let me enjoy this moment, will you?" She smiles at me over a bite.

"Okay, then, Miss Holt," I laugh, shaking my head in disbelief. "Glad you enjoyed it." Barbara finishes off the first one and tosses the wrapper in the garbage can from a rather impressive distance. "So, let's get to it," I start, clapping my hands and rubbing them together. "I think—"

"I'm not done!" she says, taking a long sip from her iced coffee. "I still need to finish the second one!"

"What? You can eat *two* of those atrocities in one sitting? I thought you'd at least save the other one for later."

"Ew." She wrinkles her nose and stares at me like I've lost my mind. "A soggy sandwich? That's disgusting."

"*That's* disgusting? Are you sure it's not that artery-clogging *thing* you just mauled? Do you even know what that type of food does to your insides? It's all processed garbage."

She rolls her eyes at me—again. It drives me insane, makes me want to spank her for it.

Wait. What?

"I'm not eating a soggy sandwich. Are you insane?" Barbara shoots me a look, and I sigh as she unwraps it. I fake-gag when I see the cheese stick to the wax paper wrapping, but she ignores me, devouring the sandwich in three bites. With a huge grin, Barbara crumples the second wrapper and tosses it into the wastebasket again.

Damn, she's good.

"Thank you. That was incredible." She sighs longingly, and I shiver.

With a grumble, I tell her not to mention it. "Now," I start again, "we should discuss our strategy here. I think we should—"

"Yes! Okay!" she says enthusiastically, throwing herself at her purse. I sigh, pinching the bridge of my nose as I hear her bag rattle. What the hell is in that thing? "I had so much adrenaline coursing through my veins from last night that I couldn't sleep. So, I decided to jot down some ideas instead. I thought this would help save some time this morning."

She starts pulling items from her bag again, her tongue between her teeth. "One sec," she says, placing an open family-sized bag of peanut M&Ms on the bench beside her.

"You haven't finished those yet? They've been in your bag since last week!" I snort, teasing her.

She pulls out a Yankee Candle, a stapler, and a face towel from her bag—seriously, what is up with this woman?—and glares at me. "*Actually*, this is a new pack I bought this morning."

"And you already—?" I'm stunned. I shake my head in

disbelief. "There are just...so many questions I want to ask. Or maybe I shouldn't—I don't want to know." Doesn't she know she needs to take care of herself?

"Ah-ha!" Barbara holds a small pink Post-it above her head like a trophy. It's a wonder she found something so small underneath all that junk. "I've got it. Okay." Clearing her throat, she settles into her seat, leaning back against the wall. "We need to convince everyone we're dating, right? So, first thing we need to do is build out a social media calendar, you know? Like, what we're gonna post to show them we're together and when—just to stay organized. And then we need to set aside time to film videos and take pictures."

I can't stand the mess she's left beside her, so I start putting her things back in her bag. "Can you put this away first? You're a little bit of a walking disaster, aren't you? What *is* all this stuff, anyway? Who needs to take this much crap with them every day?" I ask, holding up an empty Tupperware container before shoving it back in.

She tears the purse from my hands with a glare. "Wish you'd mind your own business." She sighs and continues. "Now, can you please focus? I'm thinking we need to go on a date or something and post about it, you know? And maybe do a TikTok dance or something."

"What? A TikTok dance? Absolutely not." There is absolutely no way she's going to get me to do one of those. Nope. No way.

She raises a perfectly groomed eyebrow at me. "Are you seriously about to tell me you have a problem with *dancing*? Is it not your livelihood?" Again with the eye roll.

"I dance *ballroom* dance. Not viral choreographies fifteen-year-olds make up to popular songs. Also, you should probably stop rolling your eyes so much. It can't be good for you."

"Maybe if you were capable of not saying idiotic things, I'd be able to stop," she says like it's the most obvious solution. She snorts and continues. "Right, so we'll do a TikTok dance and maybe a live. Obviously, we're going to have to monitor our growth on social media and stuff. We were trending on Twitter last night for, like, five minutes, and it wasn't because of our performance."

"Wait, really?" I ask, surprised. "Are you sure it wasn't because judging was awful?"

Barbara shakes her head, her blonde hair shining in the early morning light. I *hate* it when her hair moves. It's bright and distracting, and the smell makes me think of caramel and sugar and—*ugh*! It's all so confusing.

"There were definitely some comments about how much our performance sucked and how savage the judges were, but mostly it was shock that you even had a girlfriend." She smirks and glances sideways in my direction. "We already talked about not telling anyone else, which is good, and keeping up appearances off camera as well—at least while we're surrounded by cast-mates and network people."

"Right," I agree. "But we should also talk about not over-doing it. I think calling me things like *Teddy*," I nearly spit out, "is just too obvious of an exaggeration."

"You don't think *Teddy* is a sexy nickname?" She smirks at me again, her hazel eyes almost green in the sunlight, her expression witchy. She's trying to provoke me again, and the look in her eyes makes my stomach tighten.

"No," I scoff, trying to pull myself together. "My grand-mother calls me Teddy." She grins widely and sits up eagerly. "Oh no," I groan, rubbing a hand down my face. I'm such an idiot. Why did I tell her that?

"She calls you *Teddy*? Awwww!" Barbara giggles, and I just know now that I'm fucked.

"No! No, '*Aw.*' Okay? This is not going to be a thing."

She reaches out with her right hand and pinches my cheek. "Poor Teddy, getting teased by his evil dance partner," she says in a mocking tone.

"Agh! Don't!" I push her hand off my face, but she keeps coming at me, going after my other cheek with her left hand now. "Stop!" I yell, but she's kneeling on the bench with the advantage. She pinches my cheek again, my side, and I'm about to lose it.

"I. Will. Not. Take. This. Ridicule!" Finally, I manage to grab her by the waist and pick her up with a laugh. Quickly—but carefully—I tackle her to the floor and start pinching her side and her cheeks as she squeals, and I tickle her. We're laughing, and I can't remember the last time I enjoyed myself this much.

"Stop! Stop!" Barbara begs between giggles, but I'm not done with my payback. I attack her right side and start tickling full speed ahead as her limbs flail. "You're really going to regret feeding me those two sandwiches if you keep at it," she struggles to say. "I'll throw up all over you," she threatens, but I keep going as we laugh and beam at each other.

Suddenly, something in the air, something between us, shifts. Watching her body buck beneath me while I'm on top of her, feeling her every curve of her body pressed to mine... My blood rushes to my dick, and we're panting. Our faces are inches apart, and I can taste the scent of her skin on my tongue. I want to lick it, see if my imagination does it justice—if it's really as sweet as I imagine it to be. I've got her hands pinned to the oak dance floor, straddling her, Barbara's hips arching below me just barely, when the door to the studio flies wide open.

Barbara immediately stops squirming beneath me, and I freeze in shock when I see my only friend walk in.

"Rob."

I'm stunned, my breath coming out in pants, so I barely notice when Barbara struggles to free herself from my grip and whispers, "Get off!" I quickly snap out of it and jump to my feet, helping Barbara to hers.

"Don't stop on my account, please! This is great. Although, I do wish you would have waited until the camera was rolling. The sexual tension would have made great television." Rob walks into the studio, followed by his PA, Lawrence, a redheaded man with a clipboard permanently attached to his hand. Behind them, a man holding a camera like a bazooka is ready to start recording at their general's orders. "But let's try to keep it PG."

I clear my throat and look over at Barbara, whose face is now beet red. I turn around to readjust myself slightly in my pants before facing Rob again. "So, what can we do for you?" I ask, my voice tight with frustration.

"We're here to shoot promo reels." He smirks at me.

"Promo reels? But it's not on the schedule. It's the first day of rehearsals for next week's show. I haven't even gotten to telling Barbara we're doing the samba to a Bowie song. What the hell are you planning on recording, exactly?" I *hate* promo reels. They're a disruption to practice and an absolute waste of time.

"We're not here to film your *dancing*." Rob rolls his eyes at me like I've just said the most ridiculous thing. I feel like he and

Barbara would get along well. "We're here to film your new relationship."

"What do you mean *you're here to film our new relationship*? You're just going to film us...I don't know...on dates and stuff?" I ask. Barbara and I talked about *faking* dates, and we hoped the network would buy into our relationship and give us some extra airtime. But I don't think either of us truly expected them to want to film us *together*-together. Even if we were actually dating, wouldn't that be a gross invasion of our privacy?

Rob scoffs. "Of course not! Just the occasional sweet, stolen moment and maybe a few outings, you know. But no *actual* dates—just a few seconds of footage."

"We also want to discuss your new filming schedule," Lawrence pipes in.

"New filming schedule?" I ask, really annoyed.

Barbara walks up to Rob and, in a low voice, says, "You know, Mr. Ortiz. It's always lovely to see you and your team, but today really isn't a good day. I'm not exactly camera-ready." It's obviously an excuse because she looks amazing in her hot-pink sweats and light-gray workout top. Sure, she's also wearing a sparkly pink cat ears headband (to match her shoes, no doubt), but she still looks incredible. "Can you please come back later this afternoon? Or tomorrow, preferably?" She bats her eyelashes at him with a heartbreaking smile—one that I'm sure I'd find hard to resist.

"No can do, doll. You guys started something last night, and now you're going to finish it." Rob shoots me a look. "Theodore has never gone public with a relationship before, and now he's doing so with one of his dance partners. The audience loved it, and we're going to give them what they want: a look at your relationship." Rob turns to the camera man and orders him to start filming.

"So, what are we supposed to do now, then?" Barbara asks quietly.

"Just...you know. Talk about last night. How it felt to reveal you were together. Act like we're not here."

"Uh...Rob, this really isn't—"

"Come here, Theo." Barbara pulls me by the hand to sit on the studio bench. "Don't think about it too much. Just pretend," she whispers so low only I can hear. Barbara takes both my hands in hers and smiles up at me.

"We're rolling!" the cameraman says.

"I can't believe we told everyone about us last night. It was amazing, but a real surprise. I thought we were going to wait." Barbara bites her lip, looking a little bashful.

Holy shit, she's a better actress than I thought she was. When I don't reply, she wraps her arms around my neck and brings her lips to my ear, hiding from the cameras. "Just go with it, Theo." Her breath on my ear makes me shiver and I can actually feel my face heat. "Act like you're into me." At this point, I don't think I'd have to try too hard, as is evidenced by what I'm currently feeling in my pants. What the hell is happening here?

Fuck.

It's just physical attraction, Theo. You were both rolling around on the ground not two minutes ago. Your dick is still half-hard, for Christ's sake! That's why you're being this way.

"Uh..." I softly push her back and scratch the back of my head, completely messing this up. "I know, sweetheart. But I just couldn't keep hiding it from everyone." I squeeze her hands and then reach out to put a stray strand of beautiful brass-colored hair that had fallen across her face behind her ear. I thought touching her like this would be awkward, weird. But it feels normal. More than normal. It feels *nice* to be able to touch her like this.

"That's great, you guys," Rob calls out. "Now, Theodore..."

Rob claps his hands together, forcing me to look back at him. "I want you to look into Barbara's eyes, tell her you love her and how happy you are to have met her or something like that. And then I want you to kiss."

Barbara makes a weird choking sound, clearly uncomfortable, and I drop her hands. During our whole discussion, we never talked about kissing. How the hell did we miss that?

"Rob, we're not really into the whole PDA thing. We'd much rather—"

Rob puts his hands on his hips and shakes his head. "Guys, you can't just announce to the world that you're together, get them interested, and then not deliver. Kiss her. It's not rocket science." He sighs.

I turn to Barbara and our eyes meet. Her hazel eyes shine bright with some hidden emotion. Is it anxiety? Nerves? She nods slightly at me, and I nod back. I take a deep breath, swallow the knot in my throat, and slowly lower my face to hers, hesitating just before, giving her an out. When she doesn't stop me, I bring my hand to cup her jaw, feeling her soft skin under my fingertips, and press my lips gently to hers. The kiss is brief —way too short—but *damn* does it feel good to have her soft lips on mine. They yield to mine as a small moan breaks from deep in Barbara's throat. When I gently break away, she follows my kiss with her eyes closed, falling forward a little—though only for a second. Slowly, she opens her eyes—a storm of greens, browns, and golds—and meets my gaze. My chest constricts and I suddenly find it very difficult to breathe.

That was incredible. Short, but incredible.

The room has gone so quiet, you could hear a freaking pin drop.

"*...so soft...*" she whispers to herself, looking up at me with wide, shocked eyes.

I quirk a smile at her, a nervous laugh bursting from my

chest, as I stare down at her and dig my fingers into her hair. "You're talking to yourself again, Miss Holt." She blushes a deep, crimson red.

Barbara looks almost as hypnotized by me as I am by her.

She tastes better than I imagined.

Rob clears his throat in the background. "Great. Now let's try to do that again. This time, though, try to make it look like that *wasn't* your first kiss, and you're not lying to everyone."

Chapter Twelve

BARBARA

Busted.

"Rob," Theo breathes, suddenly panicked. "It's not what you think." His hand drops from my face and he shifts in his seat. Meanwhile, my heart is still racing a million miles a minute from that kiss—so soft, so gentle, *but so fucking good.* I can feel the heat still coursing through my veins, and I press the back of my hand against my cheek to feel the flush on my face.

There's no hiding it.

Rob turns to his PA and cameraman, his hands on his hips. "Hey, guys, can you give us a minute?" Both men glance at each other before exiting the studio. They close the door behind them, leaving me, Theo, and Rob in an awkward silence.

Finally, I decide to break it. "Listen, I don't know what you're thinking, but—"

"Stop," he interrupts me, lifting a hand. "At this point, the less I know about this, the better. All I know is that, for the past couple of seasons, our ratings have gone down significantly. Unless it's a finale episode, we don't even trend on social anymore. But last night..." Rob runs his fingers through his hair.

"Last night, we had about half a million people stream the rerun on the network app—old viewers; viewers we'd lost."

Theo looks at Rob with a frown on his face. "And...?"

Rob runs a hand down his face. "It means people who had lost interest in the show and stopped watching are suddenly interested again. The network has suspected for a while that the dancing aspect of the show is no longer enough to keep viewers interested—and last night's stunt certainly proved that to be true. You've intrigued them, given them an added form of entertainment, and they're here for it."

"It wasn't a stunt. I swear. Theo and I—"

"Don't, Miss Holt. I've known Theodore for over eight years now. He has dated women in the past, of course, but I've never known him to have a girlfriend—much less one he would flaunt on national television. He is a *very* private person when it comes to his personal life. There is absolutely no way in hell he would have announced being in a relationship to the world in such a public manner." I blush and glance at Theo, who seems to be about four seconds away from completely chewing off the inside of his cheek.

"Rob, I—"

"Theodore, I get it, okay?" Rob sighs sympathetically. "I told you you had to step it up, and you are. It's not an uncommon thing to do. Actors do it all the time to promote their movies. I just didn't expect it from you." Theo flinches, guilt evident on his face. "Now, the higher-ups at the network don't know you like I do, so they don't suspect a thing. Also, they honestly don't really give a shit whether you two are really dating or not, if we're being honest. So, as long as no one finds out, and it doesn't create a scandal, you guys are fine."

Theo and I look at each other, and I can see the panic written clearly all over his face.

"For now," Rob continues in his official voice, "it would

appear that you've gotten your old fans to start watching again, and it's something they're really happy about. So"—he claps his hands together—"how about we work together on how best to showcase your relationship, yeah?"

Theo and I can only nod, absolutely stunned.

"Great, then." Rob opens the door and sticks his head out. "Lawrence? Pete? Come on in so we can discuss filming schedules."

"I DON'T UNDERSTAND. HOW THE HELL ARE WE SUPPOSED to get any practice time in here? When are we even going to be able to learn this dance? Half our calendar is scheduled for promo reels, Rob!" Theo is upset—and with good reason. Our whole schedule is off now. Having to film more means having less time to practice, which really isn't great when you're in a *dance competition*. But as Rob points out, "Your routine is only half the battle. Your *real* performance is everything combined." This does not comfort Theo, though.

"I told you," Rob says with an impatient sigh, "this is important. Now, Barbara"—he looks to me—"we need to film a segment with your family. Maybe you introducing your parents to Theodore, or maybe just have them bonding and pretending like they already love him and stuff."

"Uh, I—I don't have parents." My words are met with silence and confused stares. I stumble over my words: "I mean, I obviously have parents, but they're not here. They're not dead or anything. It's just they're not...*present*." I wince. How else would you describe the status of parents who never seemed to care about your existence?

Theo's eyebrows pull together, and he frowns, while Rob and his team try to control their expressions. God, I hate the looks on their faces.

"It's fine, okay? It's not a big deal." I roll my eyes and walk over to my bag in search of my water bottle—anything to keep me from having to look them in the eye right now.

"Okay. So, I guess we'll have to go with Theodore's family, then."

"What? No. I'm not involving Bubbe in this, Rob," Theo panics.

Bubbe? Oh my God, he calls his grandma Bubbe? My heart melts, and I have no idea why.

"You have to, Theodore. We need to show you two involved in each other's lives. We need to give audiences what we didn't know they wanted until now: a love story. And seeing you bonding in a familial situation...well, that's perfect."

"No, I'm not doing it," he practically growls.

"Do I need to remind you what's at stake here?" Rob narrows his eyes at him. "You're putting the network at risk, too, you know."

"How about we do family day if we make it past week four? It wouldn't make sense to introduce each other to our families after only a short while of dating, Rob," I try to reason with him. "It's not believable in the slightest. The audience will know we're shoving the relationship down their throats. This thing has to be gradual."

Theo looks hopefully at me, a small smile on his face. Rob narrows his eyes at me, taking my words into consideration. He knows I'm right.

"Week *three*." He points at me. "If you make it past week *three*, we're doing it for the promo reel of week four. Got it?"

Theo sighs in relief and puts his hands on his hips. He's still chewing on the inside of his cheek, though, thinking. After a beat, he says, "Fine. Family day at the home is on Saturdays. We can go then, but *only* if we make it past week three, and *only* if Bubbe agrees to it."

"Perfect." Rob grins.

"And it *has* to be early in the day. We can't film past three p.m. I won't allow it."

"Deal. Now let's talk about how we're going to help you make it until at least then."

After mapping out our promo reel film schedule for the next week, Rob and his team leave us so we can practice.

I watch Theo sigh heavily and walk toward the music system with a frown on his face. I can practically feel the tension rolling off his body. I've seen him anxious before, sure, but never like this, never looking like he has the weight of the world on his shoulders.

"Hey," I say, trying to distract him. "I didn't know you had friends."

He snorts, his eyes on the computer screen as he searches for our song. "Rob?"

I nod, but he doesn't see me.

"Yeah," he continues. "I've known him since season one. He was just starting out back then. His job mostly consisted of getting coffee for his boss and getting yelled at for things that weren't his fault." He chuckles a little. "I caught him having a panic attack in a broom closet one day, and I took him out for a beer because I felt so bad." He half-smiles and shrugs.

"That's...really nice of you," I say softly.

He looks back at me with a raised eyebrow. "You sound surprised."

I don't want to say that I actually *am* surprised, considering how standoffish and unapproachable he can be sometimes. He's usually reserved and unfriendly, and can often times be down-right *unpleasant* when you first meet him. But I've come to realize in the past couple of days that Theo is *kind*.

I think back to last night, when I was absolutely panicked, when I couldn't breathe, and how he managed to bring me down to earth. It *was* in his best interest for me to be calm in order to perform, but looking back on things now, I don't think that was his sole motivation. I could see the concern all over his face, the empathy there. He talked me off a ledge because he didn't like seeing me on the edge.

Could it be that Theodore Wallace has some humanity in him? Yes, he can be irritating, but I suspect that deep down inside, he's a good man.

"Barbara?"

I realize I've taken too long to answer, so I clear my throat and recover. "No, not surprised," I lie. "Just...happy. That you have someone. You know."

Theo's lips twitch, almost a smile. "No, I don't know."

"I just mean...I'm glad you have *people*, you know? It's important to have people. I thought you were more the loner type." I shrug and turn away. God, I sound like an absolute idiot.

"Yeah, I mean, I'm not the type of guy who has a million friends. But I feel like when you grow up with little to no family, it kind of forces you to find your own, right? If not, life can get a little lonely."

I turn to look at him, the look in his bright navy eyes—liquid, ocean blue—completely disarming me. The memory of gazing into them as he straddled me earlier floods my mind, and I briefly struggle to form a sentence. I shake my head, trying to clear it. "Yeah, I know what you mean. I—I have that. I'm lucky to have that with my best friend. Like I said, I'm not really in contact with my parents, and she's the closest thing to family I've ever had." I thank the universe every day that I found a sister in Liza.

"That's nice." He smiles at me, his eyes locked with mine.

My chest tightens and my skin heats under his gaze. "Yeah."

There's a silence between us, but it's not uncomfortable. We just look at each other, sharing this brief moment in time where I think I finally get to see a part of him I never knew he had.

"We should probably..." he breaks the silence, pointing toward the stereo system.

"Right. No, absolutely." I shake my hands at my sides as I walk toward the center of the floor. "Now, could you please explain to me how the hell we're going to dance the samba to a Bowie song? Is that even possible?"

Theo smirks with a glint of mischief in his eyes. "Oh, Miss Holt." An electric current runs down my spine. "You ain't seen nothing yet."

Chapter Thirteen

BARBARA

I wait for Theo to arrive at our meeting spot by the entrance of the Brooklyn Botanical Garden. Turning my face up toward the sky, I feel the light raindrops fall on my face and start to go over how things got so screwed up, how the hell I ended up here.

It's overcast, just barely drizzling, but so obviously going to start pouring any second now. A horrible day to film here, but ultimately, it's no longer our choice when and where Theo and I stage our fake dates. Not really, not after Rob inserted himself into our whole plan.

I feel a vibration in my raincoat pocket for what feels like the millionth time in forty-eight hours and sigh. I don't have to look at it to see who it is: *Liza*. I've been hardcore avoiding her calls since the night Theo and I went public with our "relationship" in front of the whole world. By the time I got home that night, I had four missed calls from her. Yesterday? *Twelve* missed calls and *four* voicemails.

I know that I have to pick up eventually. I have never gone this long without speaking to her, and she must already be suspicious. Knowing her, I wouldn't be surprised if she just randomly showed up at my hotel, looking for me. But Theo and I promised each other we wouldn't say anything to anyone, that we would keep it just between us (and I guess Rob, too, kind of?). So what am I supposed to do here? Lie to the person I'm closest to? Or break my promise and have her be disappointed in me?

I exhale in relief as I feel the phone stop vibrating, but I tense up again when I feel it start up once more.

"*Ugh!*" I fish it out of my pocket, frustrated with myself and this thing I've gotten myself into. Swiping my thumb over the screen, I answer the call. "You're killing me, Smalls!" I tell her.

"*I'm* killing you?! *I'm* the one doing the killing?!" she asks, her voice high and accusatory. "You're the one dodging my calls and hiding a relationship with a man you described as *angry and cantankerous.*"

"I'm positive I *never* used the word cantankerous. I'm not even sure I know what that means."

"Babs..." she sighs at my attempt to distract her. "What the hell is going on? I thought you hated the guy, and now you're both declaring yourselves to the whole world?"

"I—I—" I struggle to find the words. I don't want to lie to her; she's my best friend and the only person who has always been there for me no matter what. She doesn't deserve to be left out in the dark. Not after everything we've been through together. But what if she gets pissed because we're lying to everyone? I don't think I'd be able to live with myself if she hated me. Then again, I can't really live with myself now, knowing that I'm lying to her about something so major.

I squeeze my eyes shut and just push the words out. "I never said that I *hated* him. But I should tell you... Liza, it's not real."

There's a pause on the other end of the line. "What do you mean it's not real?"

"The relationship. Me and Theodore. It's not real. It's—it's all for the show."

Another pause—longer this time. "Was this the network's idea or something? Are they making you two do this? That is so messed up! You should—"

I shake my head even though she can't see me. "They didn't force us to do anything, Liza. We just...weren't going to win. So, we did it for the votes. And we both need this. I need it for obvious reasons, and he...well, he has his own reasons. We're just trying to gain popularity to get people to vote for us."

There. It's out there. I told her.

There's silence on the other end of the line as Liza processes this information. I can't imagine her being anything but disappointed, and it kills me. My stomach turns over as I wait for her to respond, biting so hard into my lip I feel the sting. I know I'm lying to everyone, and I know it's all for my own self-interest. But it's not like I'm hurting anyone with this lie, right? I'm actually *helping* someone besides myself—Theo's Bubbe.

"I'm sorry," I say, gripping the phone harder in my hand. "I didn't want to lie to you, so I was just avoiding your calls. I just... I know it's awful of me." I groan and kick the sidewalk, looking down at my feet.

"What's awful of you is that you thought I wouldn't be able to understand why you're doing this. Listen, I'm not sure how I feel about you lying to absolutely everyone else in the world, but I get it. And it's obviously not unheard of. Isn't Hollywood always pulling crap like this to boost sales for movies and stuff? I mean, I wouldn't tell my mother about this if I were you, because it is a morally gray area *at best* and she'll murder you, but I understand why you're doing it."

I lean back against the building wall in relief. "You don't know how happy I am to hear you say that. Seriously. Not telling you was killing me."

"I do have to say... I mean, you know you have to be careful, right?"

"Duh. I know we can't get caught." That's Theo's and my first priority. If anyone finds out that it's all for show, we're screwed.

"Yes, that too. But I mean more about protecting yourself and your feelings. I saw you guys the other night on TV, Barb. You have some serious chemistry going for you."

I snort. "You're insane. We're completely different people. I can barely stand him." I feel a pang of guilt in my stomach, because that's not exactly true anymore. Theo isn't as bad as I had originally thought. Still, it's not like he's my favorite person in the entire universe, but we're friendly-*ish*. "We were just acting."

"You did say he was really attractive."

"I said he was *objectively* attractive, not that I was *attracted* to him." Although, it's not like I'm not *not* attracted to him. Does it feel great to be pulled around the dance floor by him? Yes. Does the feeling of his fingertips on my skin sometimes give me the chills? Absolutely. But that's totally normal. You try not being attracted to a hot guy who spends most of the day with his hands on you. I'm not exactly made of stone, here. I'm human.

"I just think that—"

I spot Theo coming around the corner and cut her off. "Listen, I gotta go. I'll call you later, okay? I have to go meet the film crew to get these promo reels done and stuff."

"What? No, I still have to—"

"Bye!" I say before quickly hanging up and stuffing my phone back into my pocket.

I see Theo spot me, and a small smile makes an appearance on his face. He looks a bit disoriented, running his fingers through his hair as he looks around at the crowds of people.

"Hey," he says when he reaches me. "This place is packed."

"Cherry blossom season. Duh."

"Right," he chuckles. "How silly of me not to know that," he says sarcastically. "Is that what we're doing today?"

We walk together toward the entrance, and I hand him a ticket. "Yup. Rob wants us to walk through the trees and stuff, but I don't know how long the weather will hold up for. We're meeting the crew there."

"Jesus." He shakes his head in frustration. "A whole crew? Aren't they sick and tired of filming us? These past couple of days have been insane. We've barely had any time to practice."

"I know, but I don't really think we have a choice. If it helps, our strategy seems to be working. I definitely have had more activity on my social media platforms," I tell him proudly. "What about you?"

"I don't think I've been on Instagram for a year or so," he says, handing his ticket at the door. "So, I really have no idea."

I balk at him. "Theo, that's not gonna work. We need to take a picture of the two of us today and post it on your Insta. Plus, we need to post other random stuff—non-relationship pictures— so we don't make it too obvious that we're Insta-spamming people." I groan. "This is gonna be more difficult than I thought."

"Relax," he says, waving a hand, uncharacteristically nonchalant. "It'll be fine. It has to be."

EVENTUALLY, WE MAKE IT ALL THE WAY TO THE CHERRY Walk where Rob's PA, Lawrence, and the rest of the crew are waiting for us. As we get mic'ed in, I turn to glance at Theo, who looks about as comfortable with this scenario as a cat would be in a cold bath. I realize belatedly that, even though Theo has been working on a TV show for eight years, he's never had his privacy or personal life invaded like this before. I grew accustomed to it—though I never enjoyed it—while I was working on *Phantom Fighters*, but it wasn't easy when I first started. For someone like Theo, so set in his ways, I imagine it's nearly impossible.

"Are we ready?" Lawrence asks impatiently, looking up at the sky as if waiting for the rain to come down any second now.

Theo and I both reluctantly nod. "What exactly are we doing here, then? Just...walking around the garden?" he asks hesitantly.

"Just pretend like you're on a normal date. Ignore us and act like you normally would together."

Should we bicker and argue about absolutely everything, then? I snort at myself.

"Um...right. Okay. Should I...?" Theo points to my hand.

"You want to hold my hand?" I raise an eyebrow at him, the thought causing my heart to flip in my chest.

This is stupid. I literally spend all day touching him. I should not be reacting this way to handholding.

"I— Well, he just said—" He gives a frustrated sigh, his eyebrows pulled together. "I don't know. Sure?"

This is the most awkward thing that has ever existed ever in the history of the world.

I look at the crew and laugh. "Sorry about that, boys," I take Theo's hand and start pulling him forward, because we still need to sell this relationship thing. "Theo's not really big on PDA, are you, baby?" His eyes widen at the moniker, cheeks flushing, and I smirk. Boy, do I love to push his buttons. "Let's enjoy the afternoon and walk around. Maybe we can head to the Japanese Hill-and-Pond Garden later—if the weather holds a bit." I squeeze his hand in encouragement, the way he does to me when I need some reassurance. His eyes flash to mine, and one side of his mouth quirks up.

We start walking hand in hand down the path, under the canopies of a seemingly endless forest of cherry blossoms. I don't exactly know what the crew is hoping to get on camera here, but I'm not about to let them ruin my annual pilgrimage through these gardens. No way. I am going to enjoy today, even if it is about to start raining, there's a camera crew following us, and I'm with my fake boyfriend. Everything is pink and gorgeous and reminds me of different and less complicated times. I think back to my last visit and how different life was for me. How I would donate five-figure sums to the garden every year, and now, having to buy a day pass means skipping dinner.

"It's so beautiful here," I say, sighing happily. "I love cherry blossoms."

"Is that your favorite flower?" I look to see if there's some joke behind his question, but it looks like he's genuinely interested. It shocks me.

"No, actually," I say. "I love ranunculus flowers."

"Ra-what-culus?" He raises an eyebrow at me like I'm crazy, and I chuckle.

"They're these dainty and delicate flowers that bloom only during springtime. I used to fill my apartment with vases of them while they were in season. Every single room." I smile sadly, remembering how beautiful and cheerful it made my apartment look. "I felt like I was walking into a fairy garden every time I walked through my front door."

He laughs, and it's beautiful because it reaches his eyes.

God, those ocean blue eyes...I'd happily sail away in them, leaving my whole world behind.

My heart does another one of those weird flippy things, but I ignore it.

"Whoa." I pull us suddenly to a stop and stare at a

mammoth of a cherry tree. Reaching out to touch one of the flowers, I enjoy the feeling of the velvety softness of the petals under my fingertips.

Theo reaches out and plucks a flower from the tree, placing it in my hair with a smile on his face. "What are you doing? Are you insane? They're going to put us in the BBG jail!" My hand goes to the flower behind my ear, but I don't remove it.

Theo presses his lips together, trying not to laugh. "The botanical garden has a jail?"

"Probably!" I throw my hands in the air. "It's where they keep all the pluckers."

"*Pluckers?*" He bursts out laughing and shakes his head at me, taking my hands in his.

"Yes. People who pluck flowers from the plants!"

"You're crazy, you know that?" His laughter instantly relaxes me and makes me absolutely forget why I was upset with him in the first place. Kind of.

"You don't get it. This is a huge deal, and it's my favorite time of year to come to the BBG. I used to come to the Sakura Matsuri Cherry Blossom Festival every year and it was *the best*. But they canceled it this year due to Covid. Crowds and all that." I shrug.

"That sucks. I didn't know you were so into—"

"Hey, guys," Lawrence interrupts, reminding us that we're not alone. "Not to be a dick or anything, but we're losing light here. It's about to rain, and we haven't really gotten any romantic date scenes yet, you know?"

We both stare quizzically at Lawrence. "Getting to know one another is part of a date, Lawrence. And I think the whole point is to get the audience to connect with us, right?" Theo asks.

We're connecting, Lawrence. Leave us alone.

"Yeah, but we want some kissing or whatever with the backdrop of the flowers. That's like, the only reason we're here." Kissing? My cheeks flush at the thought of having to go through that again—something we still haven't dared to address. "I think this isn't working, though..." Lawrence starts rambling about all the different ways in which we can film a more "authentic" date, but I start to tune him out. Ever since the camera started rolling, everything seemed so forced and uncomfortable. And the second we relaxed and started acting like ourselves, the crew cut us off.

"God, Barbara," Theo says suddenly, frowning. "What are we even *doing*? This whole thing is insane," Theo whispers so only I can hear, obviously forgetting he's wearing a mic. "Do you think this is how the contestants of *The Bachelor* must feel?" I snort and look into his navy eyes, sparkling with mischief. "Like, do you think the producers go up to them on a date and are, like, 'You need to be more interesting'? Is that why they always seem to confess their childhood or relationship traumas on national television and then start crying before dancing in front of a band no one's ever heard of?" We laugh together as we think about the ridiculousness of this situation, at being coached through a date that's supposed to be real.

"How do you know that's what they do on dates, though? Do you regularly watch *The Bachelor*?" I raise an eyebrow at him and smirk.

Theo shrugs with a grin. "I will *sometimes* watch it with my grandmother."

"Sure, sure," I tease him. "*With your grandmother*. I totally believe that. Are you positive you've never watched it on your own?"

He chuckles and reaches out to fix the flower in my hair with a smile, his fingers accidentally grazing my cheek with the softest touch.

I bite my lip as a frisson runs through me at the contact,

looking up at him in surprise. His eyes lock on mine, and suddenly, I'm confused. Are the cameras on us or something? I turn to look over at the crew, but Lawrence is currently deep into a discussion with the cameraman on lighting and timing. No one from the network looks to be paying one bit of attention to us or their surroundings.

Suddenly, he looks like he knows exactly what to do. "Should we play hooky? Leave Lawrence and the team and just keep walking?"

I smirk at him and glance over my shoulder. "Leave them just like that? What about our mics?"

He shrugs. "Let's slip them off and leave them on top of his backpack there." He points to where Lawrence has dropped his bag against a tree. "It's going to start raining any second anyway. Not like we can film through this, you know?"

"Alright." We smile wickedly and carefully pull our mics off. He takes both of them and quickly jogs over to the backpack. He drops them carefully on top of it, trying not to get caught by Lawrence. As Theo jogs back to me, he wiggles his eyebrows with a glint in his eyes. "Let's go." He grabs me by the hand, and we power-walk down the path for a few seconds, trying to put as many feet between them and us without drawing too much attention.

Chapter Fourteen

THEO

We giggle as we put more and more space between the crew and ourselves, Barbara's purse bouncing slightly and her boots lighting up as we go. "I wonder how long it will be until they realize we're gone."

She chuckles, her laugh free and genuine. "I don't know, but can I just say how surprised I am at how much of a troublemaker you've turned out to be?"

I grin at Barbara, her hazel eyes locking with mine. "I learn from the best."

The light drizzle from before starts turning into something more, and I groan, trying to look up at the sky through the blossoms. The thick canopy of flowers should protect us from the rain for a few more minutes, but it's clear we should be heading for shelter soon.

I turn to look down at Barbara to tell her exactly that, but she's beaming at every tree we walk by. "*God*, don't you just love spring? Everything is so *beautiful*."

I scoff. "No, actually. It's a ridiculous season where the

weather makes absolutely no sense. It's as inconsistent as human nature."

She turns to look at me with wide eyes, shocked. "How *dare* you, sir? Spring makes everything beautiful. Just look at where you are!" She spreads her arms wide in showmanship.

I briefly look around, just to indulge Barbara, and smile. "Meh," I tease her. "It's alright. But it doesn't make up for nasty weather."

She shakes her head at me in disapproval with a half-smile on her face. "Of course you would hate on the one season that signifies pure optimism and resilience."

"*What?*" I laugh-yell, shaking my head at her. "And I don't *hate* it. It's just inconvenient, mostly. But I like things about it. Like...Passover, for example. And Spring Training."

This makes her stop mid-step, and her face lights up. "You like baseball?" Her grin is wide, hopeful. She bites into her full lip, distracting me for a second.

"*Yes,*" I say carefully after I bring my eyes back to hers. "Why? Do you?"

She scoffs. "*God,* no. I think it's quite possibly the most boring sport that has ever existed—and I'm including shuffle-board in there." She's smiling now, absolutely thrilled. "It's just so...*nice* to hear. That you like it, I mean. It's like...I just assumed you were all about dance and nothing else."

"I have hobbies," I say defensively. "I like other things."

"I know that now." She nods encouragingly. "You have friends, and hobbies, and a life, apparently." She squeezes my hand, and it's only then that I realize we never let go of each other. "You're *human.*"

"As opposed to what, exactly?" I ask, amused.

"A dance-obsessed cyborg?" She bites her lip, and I laugh.

"You're ridiculous," I say, but I chuckle. I pull her forward, and we keep walking down the winding path, tugging her to the side so she can avoid a puddle she didn't see coming.

"Ooh, look at that one!" She stops suddenly in front of a—shocker—cherry tree and starts jumping up and down in front of it. The lights in her boots start going off like crazy in soft, muted, pink tones.

Who is *this girl?*

"What?" I ask, completely confused. "You look like someone just handed you a certificate for a lifetime supply of candy or something."

"Oh my God, can you imagine?" She looks at me with hope in her eyes. "No, I mean look at this tree. It's *perfect*. Look at how full the branches are and the size of the flowers! It's incredible." She beams up at the its flowers and reaches out to touch its petals.

"It literally looks just like every other tree here," I deadpan.

"You're insane," she says simply. "Come here. Let's take a picture in front of this one. It'll be so cute."

I groan, but I let her pull me toward it all the same. "*It'll be so cute*," I try to mimic her voice, mocking her, and she pinches my arm. We stand directly underneath the tree, and she wraps an arm around my waist, burrowing herself into me. I'm hit with a wave of soft caramel as her hair brushes against me. I stiffen slightly, my breath catching in my throat, but I shake it off.

This feels like a date.

Duh, you idiot. It's supposed to feel like a date. Or look like a date. It's the whole damn point of today.

I take a breath and remind myself not to make more of this than I already am. She's acting. We're acting. None of this is real.

"My phone's dying. Use yours to take the picture," she commands.

See? She's—*you both*—are just doing it so you can get material for the show and your followers.

Relax, bro. Don't overthink.

"How do you not have at least *one* power bank for your phone in that humongous purse of yours?" I ask, shaking my head at her.

She rolls her eyes at me in frustration and tries to elbow me in the side, but I dodge it just in time. "Will you just do as you're told for once, please? Plus, if we do it on your phone, you can just easily post it onto your Instagram."

"Yes, ma'am," I mutter, slightly annoyed.

I pull out my phone and wrap my arm around her in turn. I raise my phone and adjust it so we're both in the frame with the cherry blossoms in the background. All of a sudden, raindrops land on my phone's screen, and I lose my grip on it a little, accidentally switching the camera to video mode. Before I'm able to fix it, I unintentionally click the record button just as a gust of wind rattles the branches above us, shaking the water accumulated by the flowers onto us.

Barbara and I stare at each other in shock for a few seconds, our hair soaked, bodies still dry, until we finally burst out laughing, completely in shock. We'd managed all this time to protect ourselves from the rain, thanks to the trees, and it completely backfired.

As I stare down at her, I can't help but notice just how pretty she looks today—despite the wet hair, odd boots, and the hot-pink raincoat that I hated at first. But I guess that's her style, and I guess I kind of love that she's so unique. There is no one like Barbara, that's for damn sure.

My gaze drops down to her lips and I wonder for the millionth time what it would feel like to kiss her again. Would she make the same little moan? Would she melt against me like she did before, pressing her chest into mine? Would she let me part her lips with my tongue and taste her deeper, better? Would she like it if I bit her bottom lip and tugged it?

God, I want to bite into it so bad it hurts.

I lean closer into her as I feel the blood rush down, and hear her breath catch in her throat. Her eyes widen and flicker to my lips for a half a second. She wants this too. I raise an eyebrow at her in question and she starts to rise up on her tiptoes, inching closer to—

Another gust of cold wind shakes the branches above, and I feel her shiver involuntarily. "*Jesus Christ,*" I say in frustration. I realize my phone is still recording, so I stop it and slip it back into my raincoat pocket. It's freezing and she's cold and today has been insane. "Let's get out of here, yeah? I'll buy you dinner or something."

She beams up at me. "*Really?*"

I laugh and roll my eyes at her just as my phone vibrates in my pocket. I pull it out just enough to barely see the screen:

> ROB
>
> Theodore, wtf man? Lawrence just told me you bailed? I thought we talked about this. Call me.

I'm tired of him bossing me around, and we still have some more filming to do scheduled for this week. He needs to relax— we both do. So, I wrap an arm around Barbara's waist and pull her quickly down the path before the rain gets even worse.

Chapter Fifteen

BARBARA

This week's performance turns out to be nothing like the one before. No disrespect to the previous one, but when Theo and I finish with him sliding on his knees to me and me kicking a leg over his head in the most amazing purple rhinestone-covered dress I've ever seen, it's absolutely obvious that we've moved about ten levels up. It is also evidenced, by the way, by how wild the crowd goes after our epic finale when Theo basically climbs his way up my body, his strong hands seemingly touching every inch of me, and pulls me into his arms in front of the everyone.

The audience loves us, and they love our story. When scenes of our training that week and flashes of our date came up on the screen before our dance, people whistled in excitement and *awwwwed* at us walking under the canopies of blossoms. We've succeeded in doing what we wanted. We didn't just get them invested in our relationship, though. Nope, we got them *hooked*.

"It's judging time!" Troy happily announces to everyone as the lights are brought back on. The crowd goes wild with excitement, and I'm pretty sure my face is paralyzed because I have not stopped smiling—don't know how I could even begin to. The dance was amazing, the costumes incredible, and the response epic. I know this week is gonna be our week. I can just feel it.

Theo and I worked our butts off, and it showed.

"Let's start off as we always do with the lovely Bex! Bex, tell us what you think." I feel Theo wrap his arm tightly around my waist, letting me know that he's here for me, that we're in this together, and the feeling of partnership is exquisite. I've never had it in any other role before—that sense that you can depend on your costar, that it's *two* of you taking on the challenges ahead of you as a team.

"Wow, you guys. Incredible job. It was like night and day in comparison to last week. There was excitement, there was passion, there was artistry! And those outfits! Brilliant!"

"Thank you," I say, running a hand over the bodice, admiring it. "Truly, the wardrobe department on the show is incredible. I'd love to give a shout out to the queen of bling, Rosie, if I may. She never disappoints!" The cleavage is quite deep, but Rosie added a stretchy sheer fabric that matches my skin tone to keep the girls in place and avoid any unfortunate incidents. I look up at Theo, expecting him to say something, but I just catch him staring down at my dress...a little appreciatively? I flush a bit but force myself to be brought back to the judging.

Bex claps her hands at us and grins widely. "I'm giving you both a nine. Really incredible improvement."

"Wow! Thanks so much!"

"Amazing!" Troy's over-enthusiastic voice causes me to flinch in annoyance. "Moving on to Hugh. What did you think about Theodore and Barbara's performance this week?"

"I thought it was truly incredible. Absolutely gripping. I mean, the chemistry you two have is just so *present* in your performances. I would just be a little careful with your footing. I know the samba is pretty fast, so that's okay. But the choreography was absolutely on point."

I look proudly at Theo because it was all him. He really tapped into his more creative side, and I know he really pushed himself to insert more modern moves into the Latin dance. "Honestly, Theo's choreography was incredible and so much fun to perform," I say, looking up at him. He beams down at me.

"I'm so happy you both are enjoying yourselves!" He smiles. "It's an eight for me!"

Troy waves his hands in the air in excitement, and I wonder how the hell he manages to keep this up every show. "Wow! Wow! Wow! Amazing stuff, Hugh. Cora?"

Theo and I turn expectantly toward her. I know he says she's usually the more relaxed of the three judges, but she was extremely tough on us last week. Hoping her extremely critical review of our previous performance was an outlier, I prepare myself for some more praise, similar to what we received from the other judges.

"Was it an improvement from last week? Absolutely," she says in her thick French accent with a raised drawn-on eyebrow. "But was it up to par with what I truly expect from the two of you? No. For me, it was another disappointing routine with a tacky costume and poor musical choice." She waves her hand dismissively and rolls her eyes at us. "A six, thank you."

My smile falters a little in disappointment. I thought for sure we would have been able to get through to her this week. I look up at Theo and shrug with a *Well, what can you do?* expression only to realize how anxious he looks. His brows are pulled together tightly, and his whole body is rigid. I can tell he's trying to figure something out—figure Cora out?

"Alright, well, that must be a little disheartening, but no worries! You still have the two other judges' scores and the viewers at home's vote to rely on." Troy turns to face another camera and says, "After our commercial break, we're going to come back to you with country star Nick Johnson and his partner, Jess! Get ready for more exciting dances from your favorite celebrities here on *Celebrity Dance Battle!*"

As soon as we make it backstage and away from the cameras, I run happily into Theo's arms, and he catches me, hands under my thighs. I try to ignore how incredible it feels to have his hands on my bare skin, how overheated I get, or the fact that he's between my legs right now. "See?" I whisper in his ear. "We did it! They loved us! Between your updated choreography, this outfit, and our fake relationship, we're going to win this. I promise!"

He holds me closer to him and laughs in my ear, relieved, I think. To my disappointment, he slowly puts me down and smiles back at me, his hair a mess. I reach over to comb it through with my fingers and say, "Even though we did the social media stuff and upped the ante in the costume department, it was mostly your choreography that got us those scores today, obviously."

He shakes his head, putting his hands on my waist. "No way. If it hadn't been for you pushing me to do more social media stuff, we wouldn't be going into next week, because I know the audience is going to give us great scores. You were right. Choreography isn't enough—not when everyone else is stepping it up this year, too."

"Well, if that is, in fact, true, then I'm happy I was able to put my grain of sand into what is a desert of everything that you do." He grins at me, both of us still riding that high of just having performed incredibly and having it pay off.

"Before I forget—and I fully know I'm about to be a Debbie Downer here—I just need to say that you can't let Cora's critiques bring you down like that. You need to try to not get upset. As performers, we both know that not everyone is going to like everything you put out there. It's just mathematically impossible."

He drops his hands and takes a step back. "I wasn't—"

I raise an eyebrow at him.

"Okay, I was a little upset. But not because of the critique itself. Mostly because it's so out of character for her. It kind of feels like she's singling us out or something. Because I really don't understand where all this—"

"*You cheating asshole!*" Theo and I immediately turn to look in the direction of the screaming. "*You lied to me! You told me you were having dinner with your* mother!" Jess is throwing makeup palettes and hairbrushes at Shawn, her boyfriend, whose arms are held up in front of his face as a shield.

"What are you talking about?" he yelps.

"What am I talking about?" She laughs humorlessly as black mascara streaks down her face. "*This*, Shawn." She waves her phone in his face. "This picture an anonymous number just sent me of you *fucking* Melissa, the other stylist, in the fitting room."

Shawn's face visibly pales. "I—I—I'm sorry. It was an accident," he says nervously, not even trying to deny the claims. I mean, how could he? There's a fucking *picture* of it. "I was thinking about you the whole time."

"*Oh no,*" I whisper under my breath. I see Jess practically bare her teeth and crouch back slightly, her posture reminding me of that of a lion about to attack a gazelle. Theo and I both react in the same way and quickly run over to her just as Jess jumps at Shawn and tackles him to the floor.

"*Aghhh!*" Shawn covers his face as Jess straddles him and starts swiping at him. "Babe, *stop!* I have a shoot with Power Protein Powder tomorrow!"

Jess releases a call like a banshee, and Theo carefully wraps his arms around her waist, trying to pull her off him. But Jess is a wild woman and not taking any prisoners.

"Jess! Stop!" A group of what look like three producers starts running toward us, and boy do they look angry.

"Come on, Jess," Theo whispers in her ear. "You don't want to lose your job, too, do you?" Jess breaks down into sobs and wails, going boneless in his arms. Theo picks her off of Shawn and carries her away from prying eyes. The producers and I follow them into one of the dressing rooms and watch as Theo carefully sets her down in a chair. The room has a strong smell of potpourri, and every wall is covered in vintage French posters. We must be in Cora's dressing room.

Jess puts her face in her hands and keeps sobbing into them. Theo starts rubbing her back in soothing motions, gently shushing her every so often.

"Jess," the first producer starts. "I think it's obvious at this point that—"

"W-w-we were talking ab-ab-about getting en-en-en-engaged!" she sobs. "We were going to e-e-e-elope after the season was *over*!"

"Jessica," another serious-looking man warns her. "You just attacked another dancer seconds before your performance. The network can get sued if—"

She drops her hands from her face and gives them a death stare. "*I don't care!* I just lost the l-l-l-love of my life! I left my previous boyfriend for him."

"Jess," Theo calmly tells her. "Listen to them. Don't give Shawn the satisfaction of losing your job over this. Come on. You're an amazing dancer with so much promise. Seriously. Don't let this ruin your career. There's so much more for you in the future, and how you act now can tarnish your reputation forever. You're better than this and certainly much better than him." He helps her sit up, and I take a step back, surprised, yet again, at how...how *not* of an asshole he is.

Jess looks up at him after a few seconds and sniffles. "You're right. Thank you." Theo briefly hugs her and gives her an encouraging smile. She takes a deep, steadying breath and shakily exhales it before turning to face the producers. "I don't know what to say," she says to them. "I'm so sorry." More tears stream down her cheeks. "It just...it broke me. And all the pressure from this season is just so intense. You guys seriously shouldn't have said anything about the judging position. It has us all freaking out and on the edge of breaking. I mean, Shawn and I can't even talk about it with each other!"

"We're sorry that the pressure for this season was too intense for you to handle, Jessica, but that doesn't excuse violent behavior. I think it's safe to say that you will no longer be performing this season or be considered for the judging position"—a sharp intake of breath, a trembling lip—"Additionally, your contract will be put into question. Now, I think you should go and apologize to your partner since he won't be able to compete tonight." He looks over his shoulder with a frown. "Although, to be fair, he looks absolutely thrilled that he no longer has to perform. Said something about finally being able to ask you out now, too," he mutters under his breath, and Jess's eyes widen. He turns to us with a stiff smile. "Theodore, Miss Holt. Would you mind leaving us alone so that we can discuss things further with Jessica here? Thank you."

Theo and I leave her in the dressing room with the three men, but not before I throw her a sympathetic smile over my shoulder. *"You've got this,"* I mouth at her.

When we make our way back to the backstage area, Theo shakes his head at me, his brows pulled in concern. "She's going to get fired, obviously. But she doesn't deserve that. She's a good dancer."

"I know. But it's hard to argue against. There's no way the network is going to keep her after violently attacking another member of the cast. Plus, he cheated with a stylist here. They're probably thinking, 'What's to stop her from doing it to *the other woman?*' You know?"

He runs a hand down his face and sighs. "Yeah. She just looked so destroyed. I mean, it's horrible luck that she received that picture just as she was about to go on, too. At least she would have been able to dance and maybe get away with it if she'd gotten it after. She caused such a big scene... Plus, the network probably had to extend commercial break and come up with an excuse as to why Jess and her partner aren't dancing tonight." He shakes his head again. "No way is she getting out of this one."

"That's horrible," I say softly. Over Theo's shoulder, I catch Nico laughing at Shawn, who's currently icing a bloody nose. He looks so self-satisfied, absolutely *thrilled* with the fact that Shawn is suffering. "Do they have beef, too?" I ask, lowering my voice to a whisper.

Theo turns to look at the other two dancers and frowns. "No. They're actually very close friends. Why does Nico look so pleased that Shawn was knocked on his ass?" He shakes his head in confusion. "None of this makes any sense."

"Maybe Nico has a thing for Jess and is happy he gets to hook up with her now?" I wonder aloud.

"Honestly, the Bro Code is not something that would've stopped Nico. If he had wanted to sleep with his friend's girlfriend, he would've."

I scoff, disgusted.

Is nothing sacred to that guy?

"I don't think so, no," Theo says thoughtfully. I guess I said that out loud.

I really need to stop doing that.

He turns back to look at me with a sad smile on his face. He takes one of my hands in both of his and says, "Well, Miss Holt"—that weird tingly feeling runs down my spine again—"I think it's safe to say that there will be no official elimination tonight, seeing as Jessica and her partner have officially taken themselves out of the competition. We're here for another week of crazy."

Chapter Sixteen

THEO

Did you know that there are a total of *FIVE* different types of tango? Three of them different versions of the Argentine, one official American ballroom tango, and one international ballroom tango? Each one with its particular nuances and defining characteristics. Some of them are characterized by dancing with an open embrace, for example, whereas others are characterized by having the partners dance pressed together at the hip level or chest to chest. Some tangos are more about kicking, whereas others glide more, or even consist of a more staccato rhythm. To the trained eye, every single one of them is incredibly different, but they all have one thing in common, of course: they're all trying to kill me.

I am going to die.

That is what I think every time I pull Barbara back into my body, every time we move to the rhythm of the song.

I tried to tone down the routine a little, without it becoming a snooze-fest, yet I'm still struggling. We have to do the tango—any type of tango—and it's clear that all five were created with the specific intention of being my absolute cause of death.

Someone call the coroner now, because I am not making it out of this practice alive.

It's killing me. *She's* killing me.

Every freaking time her hand slides up my chest to my shoulder. Or I have to drag my hands up her thighs and hold her leg against me when we glide from one end of the floor to the other. Every damn time she spins in my arms for the finale, her hair flying across my face, when her back ends up pressed against my chest, her hands supporting herself on my torso as she slides down...

Yeah, I'm pretty sure I'm gonna die.

I'm hoping to God it's just a temporary thing—a reaction to the Latin dance, which is very sensual by nature—but I think it's about time I admit to myself that I'm more than just a little bit attracted to her.

I just have to make it through tomorrow night's episode, and then we're done with this. If I make it out of here alive, and we make it to next week's episode, I pray to God we get something easier than this. Something where I touch her less.

"Bésame...bésame mucho como si fuera esta noche la última vez..."

Now, I don't know much Spanish, but I'm pretty sure I get the gist of this song, about how the woman with the deep, throaty voice wants to be kissed—a lot. And I curse myself for having picked it, because kissing Barbara? Yeah, that's all I've been able to think about this past week. I don't need an extra reminder when it's the only thing that's been running through my brain all day. If I'm being really, truly honest with myself, I've been wanting to kiss her again (*really* kiss her, not for the cameras) for a while now.

She moves into me as I flashback to her lips on mine—the way she tasted, how she melted against my chest—and my hands slip again, causing me to almost drop her leg and have her fall on her knees for the fifth time this afternoon. "Shit! I'm sorry," I grunt, running my fingers through my hair. We've been practicing the dance all day now, and it's been an absolute nightmare, a complete struggle.

"Are you okay?" she asks, her eyebrows pulled together, concern clear over her face. She walks over to me and takes my hand. "Are you feeling alright? You don't have Covid, do you? You look a little feverish." She places her soft palm over my cheek, and I have to focus all of my energy on not pulling away. "You don't feel warm..." She frowns.

"I—I'm fine." I take a step back, and she drops her hand. "Just a lot on my mind today. Sorry. I'll do better."

Barbara puts her hands on her hips, frowning. "So we didn't do too well during dress rehearsals today. Don't worry about it." She smiles softly. "You're so hard on yourself," she mutters. She looks like she wants to say more. Instead, Barbara just goes back to our starting positions, and I take it as my cue to restart the music.

We begin as we have all day, Barbara following the choreography to perfection, me trying hard not to focus too much on how smooth her skin feels under my fingertips (there's a special place in hell for whoever invented crop-tops and leggings, by the way), and then...the first leg wrap.

I stifle a groan.

Torture.

But I push through it because I am a goddamn professional, not a hormonal teenage boy freaking out because he gets to dance with the prom queen.

So what if she looks just as starved as I feel as her eyes lock with mine? It's the whole point of the tango! There's a lot of acting that needs to go into it because it's sensual and desperate and supposed to look like the dancers are incredibly into each other! So it's all fake. She's faking. Right?

Did I mention this is torture?

We reach the grand finale, where she doesn't just wrap her leg around me. No. I'm supposed to hold her against me and do a deep lunge, basically grinding together, and it's precisely there where I drop her every damn time. She comes into me with precision, her hair whipping in my face, and I release her instinctively. Barbara falls with a *clunk* and I wince for the millionth time.

"What? What did I do now?" she asks, anxiety clear in her voice.

"Your hair—it's distracting. I can't dance like this." I turn away from her, remembering the strong caramel scent of it, how it messed with my stability, nearly knocking me over. I hate that I just blamed her for my inability to perform the simplest of moves, but I'm not lying—her hair really is driving me crazy.

"My hair? What's wrong with my hair?" Barbara frowns, her hands gathering the ends of her golden-blonde tresses as I wonder whether they're as soft as they look.

Your golden hair, your hazel eyes, your fucking legs...

I squeeze my eyes shut and shake my head in frustration. "It's all over the place," I say, pinching the bridge of my nose. "I can't concentrate!" It smells too good. It makes me want to do irrational things, like bury my nose in it, inhale the scent of her until I can't breathe because my lungs are too full. Kiss up her neck, right below her ear. It makes me want to repeat our kiss, but keep going this time. A brief image of what she would look like under me—naked, wanting—flashes behind my eyes and I groan.

No. No. No. NO.

"You're going to have to put it up in a bun or something," I snap, immediately feeling like an asshole. It's not her fault I can't control myself.

Barbara flinches at my words but does her best to recover.

As she pulls her hair up into a bun, she bites her lip and avoids my gaze. I want to apologize, to tell her I didn't mean it that way, but what can I say? How can I explain myself when I don't even know what the hell is going on with me?

She's just so...

And I'm just so...

Sigh.

I hate this. I haven't been able to concentrate fully all day, which is terrifying, considering everything that's at stake.

I sigh deeply, closing my eyes. "I'm sorry. It's late. Maybe it's best if we just wrap it up for the night." I need space.

"But we still have to nail down the footwork for the turns. Hugh said I needed to work on that." She stares at me with those guileless eyes, and I feel something tighten in my chest. "Shouldn't we, I don't know, stay and practice *that* at least?"

I frown, taking her in. I was really wrong about her, wasn't I? She's not some bored, lazy actress. She's hardworking and dedicated, and even though she looks exhausted, she wants to keep going until things are perfect. I was way too hard on her.

"I know the performance is tomorrow, but I promise I'll do better then. I'm just too in my head right now," I say in a softer voice. "I'm tired. And I can tell you're tired, too. If we keep going, it will do us more harm than good. We'll be too sore tomorrow—trust me."

She smirks at me with that witchy smile of hers and my heart rate picks up. "You still get sore?"

I snort. "Well, no. I was just trying to make you feel better."

She smirks, prepping herself to say another one of her taunting remarks, but her face suddenly lights up, and she stands up straighter. "Oh my God, I know exactly what we should do."

"*Oh God*," I groan, rolling my eyes. "What?"

She bites her lip and starts actually jumping up and down in place, and it kills me. I try to glare at her, to pretend like I wouldn't do anything she asked me to right now, but ultimately chuckle at her desperation. "I'm not gonna tell you. But I *am* going to let you pay for my dinner."

"I feel so honored," I deadpan.

Chapter Seventeen

THEO

"Here, try the sweet *plátanos* with the grated cheese on top." Barbara pushes the plate toward me. "Ooh!" She jumps in her seat a little. "And these *tequeños* are amazing."

I eye both plates hesitantly. "Barbara. These are both fried. I can't eat these."

She rolls her eyes at me but grins. "Live a little, will you? It won't kill you to eat outside of your comfort zone for one night. I think that's what's been going on with you lately. You're too in your head." She taps her temple with her index finger. "Just enjoy the food and the music. I *love* this place."

The place in question is a Venezuelan restaurant in Chelsea —one that Rosie and Barbara apparently went to together last week. It's decorated with an array of trees and flowers, making you feel like you're inside a tropical rain forest. The lights are dimmed low, and the merengue music is turned up high. Couples dance together to the fast beat of the lively songs in the center of the restaurant while the tables surround the makeshift dance floor.

I can see why Barbara would like it. The whimsical pink

neon lights and decorations are unique enough to draw her in and fascinate her. She likes things like that, I've come to realize. Things like her. One of a kind, rare, *exciting*.

A waitress in a crop-top and high-waisted jeans drops two orange drinks in front of us. "*Guarapitas*," she says with a wicked smile on her face.

"This looks like a sugar bomb." I pick the glass up, which is already cold and wet from the condensation. As I bring the straw to my lips, Barbara wiggles her eyebrows at me in excitement. The drink is so sweet, yet strong, I can't help but pucker my lips. "Oh, man."

"I know, right?" She smiles, taking a long drag.

"This is awful." I take another sip of the fruity drink. "How much sugar is in this?" Another longer, deeper sip. "It's so bad." To my horror, I keep drinking it until it's gone. Barbara's eyes widen, and her jaw drops, her straw falling into the glass.

"Oh my God. Did you just finish that whole thing in less than a minute?"

"I, uh..." I look nervously down at my glass. It's all gone, and I hate to admit it, but it was delicious. Strong, but delicious. "What was in it?"

As she waves the waitress over, Barbara shakes her head at me and says, "You don't want to know, but you shouldn't drink it too fast. It's the sugar that gets you drunk. *Otra guarapita por favor*," she says in perfect Spanish. Barbara turns back to look at me and narrows her eyes. "I think I know what your problem is, *Theodore*." She dips a *tequeño* in a guava dipping sauce and takes a bite of it, a string of white, melted cheese hanging off the corner of her mouth. She drags her tongue over her lower lip, and I watch its trajectory from one side to the other quite intently.

Fuuuck.

I swallow the knot in my throat and bring myself to look her in the eye. "Oh yeah? What's that? What's my *problem*?" The waitress drops another *guarapita* in front of me, and I take a long sip.

"You think too much. Like, with your eating habits and our competition. I understand everything that's at stake here —*obviously*." She rolls her eyes. "But you can't let the pressure bring you down. It's why I have my mantras." She looks up at me as she takes a sip, her hazel eyes almost green under the lights.

"Uhh, your mantras?" I snort. "Like the one you kept reciting like a crazy person in the middle of the street when I met you?" I get a witchy glare from her, and I smirk.

"Your mantra should be to think less, act more. To enjoy life."

She has no idea what she's saying. If I were to think less and act more, we wouldn't be sitting in a restaurant right now, eating *arepas* and drinking what can only be referred to as the devil's sugar juice with burning alcohol (though it tastes out of this world). I would be kissing her crazy up against a wall somewhere, not giving a shit about the consequences.

"I do enjoy my life. I enjoy my work," I say before taking a bite of the *tequeño*. She raises her eyebrows, questioning me. "Seriously."

"Okay, but then, when was the last time you danced for fun, though? Or has it always been all about discipline and sport for you?"

I take another full sip of the drink until it's gone (it must be all ice, because there's no way I'm finishing these off so quickly, right?). "It's not that it's not *fun* anymore or that it never has been. It's that it's my *job*, so I put all my focus on that. It's not a hobby. I can't just suddenly go lax on it whenever I want. It takes discipline."

"Okay, but I think too much discipline is gonna eventually

kill all the love you have for it. Which is why I brought you here."

I look around as if it's the first time I'm seeing the place. She brought me here to dance?

"Now, I know it's not the tango or anything, and it's not regulation ballroom. But they dance salsa and merengue here, and *it looks like so much fun.*" I turn to see the couples dancing, pressed up closer together than what is technically allowed in competitions. They're not dancing to compete. They're dancing to feel closer to the other person and to connect with their own bodies—something I don't think I've ever really done.

"To be honest, I also asked you to come here a little selfishly. When Rosie and I came here the other night, we were dying to dance, but of course *I* couldn't dance with some rando if I'm supposed to be dating you." She shrugs. A wave of jealousy runs through me. What the fuck? She wanted to dance with other guys? "Obviously, I don't know how to dance the merengue, but you're great at leading, and I'm sure I can pick it up quickly with your help. It doesn't look too hard. So...are you down?" I stare intensely into her eager eyes for a beat. She looks hopeful but nervous, and I hate that she thinks I'm so difficult that I wouldn't be willing to dance at least one dance with her when I do it for a freaking living. Although, to be fair, I did veto the TikTok dances...

"Of course," I say, wiping my hands on a napkin before grabbing her hand and pulling her up. I pick up the rest of her drink and chug it back, even though I already feel the effects of the ones before it. Maybe that wasn't a good idea, but I think I need the liquid courage in order to be able to handle dancing with her like this—not ballroom distance, not ballroom rules.

As we reach the dance floor, I take her by the hand, and we move into the middle of the crowd. I turn and bring her toward me, my hands sliding down to her lower back. I pull her into me, and a small gasp leaves her mouth. I'm so attuned to her and her body at this point that I can hear it even over the loud music, feel her vibrate. Looking a little frazzled, Barbara lifts her hand and places it on my shoulder, warm and gentle. I take her other hand, and she dips her face into the crook of my neck.

And then we're moving, and fuck does it feel good. It's otherworldly, dancing with her—unlike any other partner I've ever had in my life. Barbara doesn't just follow my lead—it's like she already knows where I'm going and what we're doing before my body even tells her to. We're so connected to each other it's like she's reading my mind. I've never had this, never felt it, with anyone other than her.

I let Barbara go on a turn and spin her, pulling her back into my arms, her back to my chest. I hold her tight to me, burying my nose in her hair, inhaling her caramel scent, and she looks at me over her shoulder. I groan in her ear and hear a small gasp escape from her lips just before she pushes herself closer into me. Her hazel eyes lock with mine, and I can feel all my blood rushing to my dick. She's panting, looking at me half-scared and half-*starved*—just like me. Her warm, sweet breath falls on my parted lips, and I can basically taste her on my tongue. She's fucking *mouthwatering*.

Unacceptable. This can't happen.

I push her away into a sudden twirl, giving me a brief reprieve from how fucking incredible she feels pressed against me like that, and then pull her back in my arms, in a less intimate position. When the song finally ends and fades into a new one, we just stop and stare at each other, breathing heavily. We can barely catch our breath, and I don't think it's from the dance.

Her lips look so full and pink, her eyes so big and green under the muted lights... I cup her face just as I dip my head to press my lips to hers. The softest of touches, the lightest of pressures...

And then her tongue sweeps over my lips, pushing them open, and I'm fucking lost to her, wrapping my arms around her, pulling her closer to me than I ever thought I could. Her hands dig into my hair, and I start to feel dizzy from the feeling of her nails scratching through my scalp. Our breaths are coming in pants, and she presses her chest into me, my skin suddenly over-heated. I groan into her mouth as I cup her incredible ass with one hand, but lose my balance, forcing our mouths to separate.

"...*so good...*" she says under her breath, her eyes locked on mine, looking completely hypnotized. Her fingers go to her lips as if trying to hold the kiss there.

My hands go to her waist, trying to steady her—steady myself? I don't even know. All I know is that it was the hottest kiss of my life, and I want more.

"Barbara, I—"

But I stop mid-sentence, something over her shoulder catching my attention, my stomach dropping. "What the hell? Someone's filming us! I think someone's recognized us," I say, hearing the controlled anger in my voice. I want to half kill the person, half ask for the recording of one of the hottest kisses of my life to keep as a souvenir. Barbara turns to look at the brunette woman dressed in all white, pointing her phone at us with a smile on her face. Barbara hides her face in my neck and presses herself closer to me. I take the opportunity to tighten my arms protectively around her.

"I know who she is," she whispers in my ear, her breath tickling me slightly. "Her name's Mary Beth Taylor. She's a makeup blogger." Barbara's tone sounds defeated. She looks miserable, and I get where she's coming from. She brought us here to get away from the tension, the stress of the show. We were kissing, dancing, having an amazing time, leaving everything behind.

But it's like we can't run away from it. I'm tired of the cameras, of always having to be *on*—and it looks like so is she.

"Do you want me to go and ask her to stop?" I ask through gritted teeth, wanting more than anything to get back to what we were doing before.

"No," she sighs. "We don't need the bad press. Plus, we're supposed to be a couple, right? And she has a ton of followers, so this could actually be good for us. More exposure for the show." I feel a pang in my chest.

Everything for the show.

She starts to walk away, but I pull her by the hand back into me. She goes easily into my arms, fitting perfectly. Instinctively, I think, her hands lace together behind my neck. My hands move back to their original position, on her lower back.

Putting my lips to her ear, I say, "I'm sorry. I know you wanted a night without the crazy, and...well, so did I. And..." I sigh. Steeling myself but wanting desperately to talk about it, I say, "About that kiss... I—"

She holds a hand up to stop me. "Don't worry about it. I know you've had a couple of drinks already, and, you know, it was the heat of the moment. I'm not mad."

I take a step back, frowning at her.

Is she for real?

She's not mad? I may be a bit tipsy, but I did not imagine her pulling me tighter into her, or her taking our kiss to the next level. I did not imagine how the hunger I felt for her in that moment was only rivaled by the hunger she seemed to feel for me. And I *definitely* didn't imagine the tiny moan that escaped her lips when one of my hands made a grab for her ass.

She wants to play it like this? Like it was *my* fault?

"Let's just..." She sighs and lets go of me. "Let's just go back to the table and finish our dinner."

"Barbara—"

"Theo." She turns to look at me with a desperate, pleading look in her eyes. "*Please.*"

I'm shocked, my mouth slack-jawed. I watch her sad eyes for a beat and decide that if this is what she wants, then I guess it's what she gets. I understand that our relationship is complicated at best, but—

I sigh, giving in to her request. While I thought what we just did was amazing, I can understand that maintaining a fake relationship may become a bit harder to do if we start crossing lines we forgot to trace. "Okay. Okay. Let's get back to our dinner, then."

Chapter Eighteen

BARBARA

Last night was...

I don't even know.

And that kiss... Epic? A disaster? An epic disaster?

Don't get me wrong—it was incredible. I felt my skin burn to a thousand degrees, heat pool between my legs, my heart race so fast I could have sworn I was running a marathon, and I got so lightheaded I felt like I had taken a sleeping pill or something.

But it was also so, so incredibly stupid. He was drunk, wasn't he? And I was... I don't know what I was. Out of my mind? Having a mental breakdown?

God, it was so good, though.

Toe-curling, chill-inducing, breathtakingly incredible...

I'm not gonna lie and say I didn't think about it later that night, alone, in bed. But I'm so in my head I have no idea what's up or down, left or right. Do I like him? Or is it just because he's attractive?

I mean, Theo has his good qualities, obviously. He's not the monster I initially thought he was. He's sweet, often times misunderstood. And I love when he loses control and gets a little cheeky like he did at the BBG. I'm not so deep in denial anymore to say that the attraction I feel for him is purely physical. I'm a big girl. I can admit that I have a crush.

But still...

"How's the dress?" Rosie asks through the fitting room curtain, thankfully interrupting my thoughts.

I run my hands over the red number, admiring how it hugs my curves in the right places and flares perfectly right below my bottom. It's not even fully zipped up, and already I know it's perfect. It's short and has a slit, and *damn*, it's going to look great with our routine.

"It's *fire*, Rosie. Seriously. I'm so lucky that I get to have you do all my outfits." Everything she makes is insane—perfectly cut, sewn, designed.

As I finish zipping myself up into her latest masterpiece, I hear her chuckle. "Come out. Let me see you." I push through the curtain and walk toward the mirror with the better lighting.

"Perfect," she says. "I'm so sorry you weren't able to rehearse in it yesterday. I tried to finish it on time, but...well, with Melissa gone, the whole team had to haul-ass to finish all the costumes and pull an all-nighter." Melissa, the woman Shawn had cheated with, had quit last week. Too embarrassed to come back after that whole drama with Jess happened, she quit the next day.

To be honest, I would've found it impossible to stay as well. Being labeled as "the other woman" in my workplace would've sucked.

"I'm sorry you guys had to go through that. At least with every week the work will get easier. You know...because you'll have less people to dress."

She grimaces at me. "I don't like thinking about the possibility of you not being here next week. It makes me sad."

I scoff at her. "First of all, I'm not going to be eliminated this week. It's physically impossible. Our routine is going to kick everyone else's butt." I push the fact that Theo kept dropping me yesterday out of my mind. I'm banking on him being over whatever was going on in his head during practice yesterday. And I pray to God our whole thing last night doesn't distract him further, even if it's been driving me insane all day. "Second of all, it's not like you and I are gonna stop being friends after this. Are you insane?"

She smiles ruefully at me as she fixes the fabric over me. "Y'all say that, but it never happens. It's okay. You're celebrities. You get caught up in your world and forget about us little people."

I burst out in laughter. "Okay, well, first of all, I'm not a celebrity. Not really. I'm more like a D-lister. And second of all, you know I'm not like that. Don't dump me into a group of people you know I don't belong with."

"I guess you're right. You're really a nobody nowadays." She winks at me, but I grab a measuring tape from the table next to me and throw it at her. Rosie dodges it just in time and chuckles.

A deep voice behind me interrupts our laughter. "Hey." I turn to face Theo, his face vacant and difficult to read. "Rosie, do you mind giving us a few minutes?"

Rosie looks between the two of us. "Sure," she replies, leaving us alone, but not without shooting a meaningful glance in my direction. The tension is palpable.

"Hey," I say, feeling my face blush. The last time I saw him, things were pretty awkward between us, so I've been avoiding him all day. I know we *obviously* have to see each other since we are performing onstage together, but I've been doing my best to put some space between us. Last night, after the kiss, we barely spoke while we finished dinner, and the walk back to my hotel became essentially torturous. It was painfully awkward. "How are you feeling?" I ask, because he had two and a half *guarapitas* last night, and I'd stake my life that someone who doesn't usually drink would find it quite difficult to bounce back so quickly. Besides the dark circles under his eyes, though, he looks fresh as a daisy.

His lips quirk a little. "Not great, but not too bad, if I'm being honest. I had a lot of water at dinner and then when I got home."

Knowing him, he probably also drank some secret-weapon, green-juice hangover cure that revitalized him in just a couple of hours.

Health nut.

We chuckle, and I start to think how he's essentially just confirmed that he was, in fact, drunk. Which means that I shouldn't be taking the whole kiss thing seriously, right? He was probably horny or didn't know what he was doing. More importantly, he probably didn't even get a chance to think about who he was doing it with.

The thought that he could've easily done it with anyone is like a punch in the gut.

"You look...wow. You look great. Really." He scratches the back of his head as his eyes travel up and down my body.

I feel his gaze like laser beams over my skin, and my cheeks flush as I think back to how his hands had roamed all over my body last night. "Yeah, the dress is great," I say, looking down at myself. "Rosie is super talented."

"I don't mean the dress." He sighs, a little frustrated. "I meant *you*." He shakes his head. "Never mind. Are you ready?"

"I—" My hands go to my hair. "I still need to touch up my hair and makeup, but yeah."

"Okay, well..." *God*, this is so awkward. So painfully awkward. He looks like he wants to be anywhere else but here right now. Frankly, so do I. "Our call time is in twenty minutes. Shouldn't you be...I don't know...done?"

"It's fine. They'll probably just want to add another layer or ten of hairspray and make sure my eyeliner isn't smudged." I shrug as casually as possible. "It doesn't take much. It'll only be a sec."

He nods and looks down at his feet, hands in his pocket. "Right. You don't really need that much makeup because you already—"

"Theo," I interrupt him. "I—I just wanted to let you know that things don't have to be awkward. Like I said last night, you were drunk and...and caught up in the moment. I don't know. But it's fine. I can forget it. *We* can forget it. Pretend like it never happened." I bite my lip and fist my hands at my sides to keep them from shaking. Why am I so nervous?

He chews the inside of his cheek as he thinks over my words. "Is that really what you want?" he asks after a few moments of charged silence.

Do I want to pretend like last night never happened? Yes, absolutely. Because I *do not* want to think about how amazing that kiss was. And I *do not* want to think about it while his hands are all over me and we're dancing in front of all those people. Talking about it means acknowledging it far more than I'd like to. I just want it to stop existing, not even put it in the past. I want it gone from my memory. I don't want to think about him wrapping himself around me, or how he growled a version of my name in my ear, or how I felt just exactly how into it he was as he pressed my back closer into him.

"*Yes*," I finally say, closing my eyes, trying to shake the memories. "I want to pretend like it never happened. It would be better for the show, for us to..." I lower my voice and make sure no one's around. "For us to keep on with the fake-dating façade."

Even as the words leave my mouth, I know that they're absolute and total bullshit. Because what would make fake dating easier than real dating? Literally nothing, that's what. But I'm just not in a position to acknowledge these feelings now, thanks.

If I even had feelings. Which I don't.

Obviously.

"Right." He bobs his head, looking uncharacteristically self-conscious. "I can do that." He clears his throat and runs both hands through his perfectly combed hair, messing it up just the way I like it. "I'm just gonna..." He throws a thumb over his shoulder. "I'll see you in a bit, then."

When he turns and walks away, I exhale in relief and put my face in my hands.

THE LIGHTS DIM LOW, AND THEO AND I TAKE OUR SPOTS ON the dance floor.

I'm anxious, shaking, and I feel so cold my teeth are starting to chatter. I don't think I've ever felt this nervous before a performance in my entire career, and it all has to do with the man standing ten feet away from me.

The lights come up, and the music starts, and suddenly, he's there, across the dance floor, with that look in his eyes that's just...

God, the look in his eyes.

It's the same one he had last night after we finished kissing, before reality set in. That hungry, desperate one. The one that makes me feel like the only person in the room, the only one with his attention.

I'm supposed to wait here as he walks seductively toward me, but it's taking everything in me not to run into his arms.

He looks so incredibly good in his simple white shirt and

black pants. Plus, he never did fix his hair, so it's all disheveled and wild-looking. I want to run my hands through it, be the one to make it look even messier. His navy-blue eyes sparkle under the spotlight, and they lock with mine in the way they always do.

Theo finally reaches me, and I gasp as he pulls me against him. Even though I know what's coming, even though we've practiced it dozens of times, I can't help but feel a little helpless to the song, the dance, the way our bodies feel pressed together.

We start to move in unison across the floor, and I do my best to focus on my kicks, my steps, and my turns, trying not to think too much about how his hands feel on me, on how good he smells. I do my best to savor this moment, pushing away any doubts or confusion from my mind. During the tango, I can let go a little. I can let whatever it is I'm trying to suppress leak into my performance just due to the nature of the dance, the intensity.

Even though the song is just under two minutes, I'm still surprised as we reach the end of our performance. Saddened by the fast-approaching end, I mentally prepare for the final count —the one where Theo kept dropping me last night. Finally, he sinks into that deep lunge—our grand finale—and I go with him, my leg hooked on his hip, his hand running oh-so-slowly up my thigh. *It's just a dance, it's just a dance, it's just a dance,* I keep telling myself, but my skin is now covered in goosebumps and a very serious ache is starting to form in between my legs. Our hips are flush, and his eyes are locked with mine. We don't say anything, but even over the noise of the crowd and the clapping, I hear his sharp inhale as I instinctively press my hips closer to him, seeking friction. I blush in embarrassment at my own need and do my best to not topple over. We're being filmed on live television, for fuck's sake! And here I am, completely turned on by him.

What is wrong with me??

Theo's face dips, and I upturn my face to his. With no hesitation this time, his lips press to mine, parting them with his tongue. The kiss is short but fiery, and I fucking *melt* in his arms. I swear, had I not been held up by him completely, it would've made me fall to my knees with a happy sigh. I vaguely notice some *woos* in the audience as I place my right hand over his cheek and cup his face.

I break the kiss and drop my hand as Theo finally straightens, taking me with him, his hand squeezing my thigh once in acknowledgment right before setting my leg down slowly. The feel of his fingers grazing my skin...

God, why did they assign the tango? All I'm going to be able to think about is doing it with him over and over again—except horizontally this time.

The crowd is still going wild, loving our chemistry, as per usual. Except it's not pretend anymore—not for me. Theo pulls me into his arms and whispers, "You did incredible, Miss Holt." He's breathless, his voice low and gravelly. Does he mean the dance or the kiss? My stomach flips, my chest constricting at his words.

Which is it?

I finally muster up the courage to look in his eyes as the confetti starts to fall from the studio ceiling, glittering all around, and for the first time ever, I don't have a quippy remark or anything to say. I'm speechless.

Chapter Nineteen

THEO

DEAD PUPPIES, WATERFALLS, HUMAN RIGHTS VIOLATIONS, *slippers, inflation—FUCK, don't get a boner, don't get a boner, don't get a boner.*

You are on *live* national television. You *cannot* get a boner.

But holy shit *that kiss.* I can still taste her on my tongue, still feel her soft skin under my fingertips.

I squeeze my eyes shut and shake my head a little, willing my cock to stand down—*literally.*

Barbara's hand is still in mine, and I don't want to let go, but I also can't look her in the eye right now. We just went from agreeing to never speak about our kiss again to basically mauling each other on TV.

It was all for show.

I tell myself that it wasn't real.

"Wow, wow, wow, wow," Troy's voice breaks through the fog and brings me back to the present.

Right. Judging time.

I take mental stock of myself and exhale in relief as I feel the pressure no longer building in my crotch. I'm good. Safe. The network won't be getting an FCC violation for obscene content broadcast.

"Barbara, Theodore! Wow!" The crowd goes wild with another round of applause, and I run the fingers of my free hand through my hair. I finally grow a pair and manage to peek down at Barbara, who looks about as dazed as I felt a minute ago.

"Such fire! Such spice! Barbara, how are you feeling after that passionate dance? It was scorching!"

"Um..." Barbara clears her throat a little and smiles politely. "I just—*we* just got caught up in the moment toward the end."

I nod and squeeze her hand, hoping that simple gesture is enough to convey everything I want to say to her right now. That I'm sorry, that I didn't mean to, that we should *definitely* talk about it after this because I'm pretty sure this attraction we feel for each other is not going away anytime soon.

"I'll say." Troy smiles his toothy grin and wiggles his eyebrows at us. "I think I'd love to start hearing how the judges felt about your performance. Bex?"

"Oh my God, I think I need a popsicle to cool down or something! Is it even springtime? Because it feels like the hottest of days in August." Bex chuckles, and Barbara and I force out polite laughs. "That dance was something else, you guys. You took the tango—an already sensual dance—and brought your connection to it without cheapening the performance. Truly amazing. I'm giving you a ten."

Holy shit.

"Bex! I believe that's your first ten of the season!" Troy announces to the crowd.

"And it's well-deserved!" She smiles at Barbara and me.

"Hugh? What do you think about our favorite lovebirds?"

"Well"—he smiles—"I thought it was quite impressive. Miss Holt certainly took my feedback from last week into consideration and improved her footwork. Additionally, even *I* must admit that the dance had quite a lot of heat to it. *However*"—he raises a finger—"I still feel like there's more beneath the surface for you two. I feel like you can go all the way, but need to further tap into yourselves and what's beneath. For that reason, I'm giving this dance a nine and not a ten."

The crowd claps, and I wrap my arm around Barbara, smiling down at her.

We fucking killed it, and I don't think it's just because of the kiss. We really do make a good dance partnership.

I feel Barbara tense at my side and see Troy's fake smile drop just a bit as he turns to the last judge—Cora. I guess we all know by now what to expect from her, and it's not sunshine and daisies, is it?

"Cora, our favorite former burlesque dancer and our most glamorous judge. How do you feel about Barbara and Theo's dance?"

A scoff. "I thought it was pure showmanship—in a bad way. We understand you're in love, my friends, but there's no reason to flaunt it in such an exaggerated manner. Do you expect me to believe that's how you *actually* look at her? How you *actually* kiss her?"

I want to laugh at her questions, because if I could actually stop myself from doing both of those things, I would. It would certainly make our lives easier.

Barbara drops my hand and shrugs comically, trying to lighten the mood. Cora doesn't buy it, though. She narrows her eyes at Barbara, and the expression *if looks could kill* comes to mind.

"I'm knocking points down for your camp, performative behavior, and disingenuousness. *Seven.*"

Mother fucker.

I grit my teeth and fist my hands at my sides. Trying my hardest to play it cool, I look down at Barbara and give her a small smile. As she nervously chews on her bottom lip, she looks up at me with wide, hazel eyes, and I press my forehead to hers. "It's okay," I say to her, digging my fingers in her hair, cupping her face in my hand. "It's going to be okay." I honestly don't know if I'm referring to the whole thing with Cora or whether I mean our whole situation, but she looks so upset I'd say anything just to make her feel better. I softly press my lips to her forehead and pull her into me.

"*Adorable!*" Troy smiles into the camera and says. "We'll be back after this commercial break with TV chef Hayley Murdoch and Nico de Leon! They'll be dancing the Viennese waltz for us."

"We can't avoid talking about this any longer," I tell her after elimination. We've officially made it past week three into week four, which means at least another week of working together every day. Additionally, it means that one of the promo reels we film this week will be with my grandmother, and I'd rather we sort this whole thing out before we go visit her together. "Not if we want to win this thing."

We're essentially hiding behind a column, far enough away that no one can hear us. I briefly considered sneaking into one of the dressing rooms or a supply closet, but that just sounded like an absolute recipe for disaster, if we're being honest. The last thing we need is to hook up in a closet, making this whole situation far more uncomfortable than it already is.

Barbara leans against the column and sighs. "I know." She bites her lip and gathers all of her hair over one of her shoulders, playing with the ends. Once again, I do my best not to get distracted by it. "We're obviously attracted to each other, but I guess it was just an in-the-moment kind of thing. And we should just stop. Right now, with how things are, it's a little difficult for us—or at least for me—to pretend that we're a normal, stable couple, you know? I mean, I'm a good actress, but I think we can both agree that this is becoming a problem. Even Rosie could tell there was something going on—did you see? Granted, she probably thought we had gotten into a lover's quarrel or whatever, but still." She shrugs. "We need to be showing the audience that we're happy and in love, not going through an awkward morning-after phase. Which is precisely why I wanted to pretend it never happened. At least until you kissed me at the end of our performance."

Frustration courses through my veins, and I grit my teeth. "I agree with everything you just said, except for the last part. I won't have both kisses put all on me. Did I initiate the first one? Yes. But definitely not this last one. That was *both* of us, dammit."

She sighs, resigned. "I know. That wasn't fair of me to say." She hangs her head and looks down at her shoes, hands playing with the hem of her red dress.

"So, we agree, Miss Holt? We move past this. We continue to focus on winning the show."

She lifts her gaze back to mine and smiles softly. "We agree."

Though part of me is disappointed, I remind myself that it's for the best, really. No sense in complicating matters by adding feelings or attraction to the mix when our first priority should be winning this thing. I need to win this thing for Bubbe, and she needs to win it for herself.

Chapter Twenty

BARBARA

I SURVIVED THIS PAST WEEK—*BARELY*. YES, THEO AND I agreed not to speak about our kiss—*kisses*—again or act on our attraction for each other, but it's not an easy thing to put out of your mind when you spend almost every day with that one person that made your insides melt.

It's been a trip of a week, but we're doing well. We're performing the jive in a couple of days—which is significantly less sexually charged than the tango, obviously—so things could've been worse. All in all, we've managed to avoid talking about it and moved on with our lives, keeping our main focus on the competition.

So, as per our deal with Rob, our next promo reel will be of me meeting Theo's grandmother for the first time.

The home where Bubbe lives is a few miles east of Albany, which means a few hours' drive to upstate New York. Neither Theo nor I felt like riding in the cramped van the network film crew would be going in, so we decide to drive together in his late grandfather's car.

The car has style, that's for sure, but the sounds coming

from the engine and the brakes prove that it has definitely seen better days.

"This car is...interesting," I say as it jolts back to life after stalling in the middle of a traffic light.

Oh my God, we're gonna die.

"We're not gonna die." He rolls his eyes at me, shifting the car into gear. Fuck. I spoke my thoughts out loud again. "This car is unstoppable."

"Unstoppable? It literally just lagged in the middle of a turn! I don't think we should get back on the highway. It might happen again. Someone's gonna rear-end us and kill us."

Theodore laughs and shakes his head. "This car is a sixty-two Turbo Jetfire. Do you even know what that means?"

Now it's my turn to roll my eyes at him. "I honestly could not care less. It would be physically impossible, I'd say," I deadpan.

I see him smirk just the slightest bit. "This was the ultimate car in its day."

"Yeah, *in its day*. It's been sixty years since then, pal. Give the guy a break. Let it retire in peace and with dignity. For God's sake, the radio doesn't even work." I lean over to fidget with the knobs once again, hoping in vain that it has fixed itself since I last tried it. "The best part about a road trip is singing in the car, and we can't even do that! It's a miracle the heating system still works." Barely.

"Don't mess with the Jetfire. And you can still sing if you want. You just won't have musical back up."

I sigh and lean the side of my head on the cold passenger window, as I stare out at the trees. It's early April, and some of the foliage is starting to come back.

I love spring. Not because of the weather or anything. Nope. I like what it represents. That, every year, nature is put through the wringer—below-freezing temperatures, snow, rain—and it's still able to come out winning on the other side.

It doesn't take a genius to see why the concept appeals to me so much—especially nowadays. It's wishful thinking for me that I will be like those tulips one day, that I will suddenly pop up everywhere after being completely frosted over for months. That I want my life, my *April Showers,* to evolve into *May Flowers.*

I know it might take time, but I'll build myself back up. I'll pay off my debts. I'll get back into acting. I'll—hopefully—be able to manage my epilepsy. I mean, I've been doing better so far! I check the imaginary chalkboard in my brain that says, *"It's been 87 days since our last seizure!"* and smile. Because *progress.* When I get frustrated and feel myself slip, I look back at where I was and remind myself of it. Of how far I've come. How I've done it all by myself.

Though I can't help but wonder how much easier it would have been with someone by my side.

I turn to look at Theo's profile—at the shape of his sharp nose, his full lips, his strong jaw—as he looks ahead at the road in front of him. I can't help but wonder what would have happened if we actually had chosen to give this a shot.

My body certainly seemed to want to, at least. And I felt how his did too, for that matter. I felt it pressing into my stomach, just barely, even though millions of people were watching.

And then that stupid kiss... Agh! That stupid kiss that was ten times better than I thought it could ever be despite the fact that we were being filmed and everyone was watching. You'd think it would have sucked, right? Wrong. The only bad thing about it was that it had to end—and the obvious consequences.

All week, I've been so confused. Sure, we agreed to not *talk* about it anymore, but it doesn't mean I haven't been *thinking* about it. I mean, here is this guy—this totally rude, grumpy guy

—who I'm supposed to not like at all, but am suddenly thinking about kissing him? For real this time? *All* the time?

Sigh.

"What are you thinking about?" Theo asks after a moment.

I lift a shoulder and smile coyly at him—I can't help it. "Nothing much."

His head turns slightly to narrow his eyes at me. "You're lying to me, Miss Holt."

And there it is again. That weird feeling in my chest. I first noticed it during our tickle fight, but it's been happening more and more lately. *Especially* whenever he calls me *Miss Holt.* It just does something to me.

I lift my hand and absentmindedly rub the space over my heart—the one with the ache.

"Seriously, it's nothing. Just thinking about our social media posts," I lie, pulling my phone out of my coat pocket. "That TikTok dance we made was a great idea." It only took me a million hours of begging, but I finally wore him down enough to do one with me. "We must be doing something right, because you're almost up to five-hundred thousand followers from like, nine-hundred. And I'm almost at four million."

"Four *million?!*" Theo explodes, his eyes wide on the road. "Four million people see your pictures and comments and stories every day?! *Four million?!* How does that not scare you? Five-hundred thousand already *terrifies* me."

I laugh. "I mean, it says four million, but social media apps alter your algorithm based on your likes, so even if you *are* technically following someone, you might never get to see their posts on your feed." Seriously, why do I need to explain this to him? He's a millennial, not a boomer.

"*Jesus Christ.* That's not normal, Barbara." He shakes his head, frowning. "That can't be okay."

I shrug nonchalantly. "It might not be okay, but it *is* normal.

It's the world we live in, and honestly, I couldn't care less because our plan is already working. My agent already has a ton of great auditions lined up for me." I smile. "I was actually *asked* to audition for three roles already—she didn't even have to make a call. *They* called *her*." Apparently, I'm cool again—or at least on my way there. "I had no idea how big of a deal this freaking show is. How many people watch it."

"Wait, what do you mean you're auditioning? Does this mean you're going to have to go to LA? What about practice? And the show?" He turns to look at me, navy eyes wide.

"Relax," I laugh. "I'm obviously not dropping out of the show. I want to win this thing. The auditions I've been asked to go to are in New York. It just means adjusting our practice and film schedule a bit. But it's good. It proves that more doors are opening out there for me, and if this doesn't end well, there's still a shot for me to recover financially much sooner than I'd expected. It's what I wanted."

He turns back to the highway with a pensive frown. "Okay," he says after a few beats of silence. "Well, I guess congratulations are in order, then?"

"Yes." I grin. "This is really good news for me." I look back out my window and smile. My May flowers might just be getting here earlier than I thought. "Really good news."

"...I COULDN'T FIGURE OUT WHAT WAS HAPPENING TO ALL of our leftovers for weeks. And then, one day while I was putting away his laundry, I heard a little whimper from under his bed and saw three puppies wrapped in a blanket, chewing on chicken bones. Teddy had taken the rest of our rotisserie chicken and given it to them!" We laugh, and my heart warms at the thought of a young Theo rescuing all those puppies.

"What were you going to do once they grew into adult dogs? That's something I haven't been able to understand to this day!"

Theo laughs heartily and shakes his head. "Honestly, Bubbe, I have no idea. I was eleven. I think I genuinely thought I could hide three full-sized dogs in my room and pull it off."

I wipe my eyes and laugh again, loving all the ridiculous childhood stories Bubbe has been flooding us with. "Aww, Bubbe. You've given me so much ammo to work with this afternoon." I sigh happily as we sip tea in the home's sunroom. "I owe you."

"Darling, that's fine, but try not to tease him too much. He's sensitive." She smirks.

"Hey!" Theo protests, and I laugh again.

Theo's grandmother is the absolute best. Since the second we arrived at Blooming Field Assisted Living Home, she's been nothing but welcoming and a ray of sunshine. She gave us a tour of the facilities (which are clean and tidy, but mildly depressing) and proudly showed off her private room, which she had decorated with childhood pictures of Theo. Bubbe also introduced us to her friends, a group of lively women who had us in stitches all afternoon.

Theo's grandmother never once complained about the home, nor did she give me the impression that she was unhappy. However, it's not difficult to see that, underneath it all, she'd much rather be in her own home.

Honestly, who can blame her? I wouldn't want to spend my last days in a strange place.

Bubbe pats Theo's knee and smiles. "Shall we start the dance lesson?"

"Dance lesson?"

"Oh, yes. Teddy teaches a dance lesson here about once a

week. The girls in the home go crazy for him, you know. They were so jealous of you during last week's episode."

"But it was on at eight p.m. You were able to watch it live?" Theo asks, hope in his voice.

Bubbe grimaces. "No. I watched the rerun the next day."

"Oh." Theo shrinks a little in his seat.

"So, we're dancing, then? Is it something you enjoy as well?" I ask, pushing through the brief awkward silence.

"Pfft," Bubbe scoffs as she struggles to rise from the couch, her oxygen tank in tow. Theo gets quickly to his feet to help her. "Do I enjoy it? I taught him everything he knows. How else do you think he got into it?"

To be honest, I never even thought about it. Since the beginning, it's just seemed like something so integral to his personality. It seemed to be such a part of him that I never even thought to question where his interest in dance had come from.

"Bubbe was a dance teacher when I was growing up," Theo explains. "She worked all day at the studio, and since no one could watch me after school, I just joined her junior classes. After a couple of weeks, I was hooked."

"Ha!" she scoffs, leading us out of the room. The camera crew follows closely behind, and I realize that, for a moment, I had completely forgotten they were there. "I had to sign you up because you were getting yourself into all kinds of trouble after your parents passed away. I never even thought an eleven-year-old boy would be capable of lighting a coat closet on fire—*on purpose*. But here Teddy made me realize that child delinquency really was possible."

I throw my head back and laugh. "*What?*" I can't imagine my disciplined, perfect dance partner to be anything but that.

He rolls his eyes. "...wasn't a *whole* closet..." I hear him grumble under his breath.

"Oh, yeah. I didn't know what to do with him. He was out of control."

I imagine a misbehaved Theo, and think back to that look of mischief in his eyes from when we played hooky.

Theo scoffs. "I was not out of control! My parents had just died. I was working through some issues."

"Oh, we worked through them all right. I had him training like an old-school ballerina, several hours a day, seven days a week. By the end of the afternoon, he'd be so tired he wouldn't have been able to get into trouble even if he had wanted to."

"But I loved it."

"Yes, you did." Bubbe stops to pinch his cheek, and I grin stupidly at him. It's so nice to see him with someone who loves him this much. It makes him look...human.

We stop just outside a door marked *Multipurpose Room*, and Bubbe puts a hand on my shoulder. "I should warn you. Teddy has a bit of a fan club here. I was being serious before. You might not receive the warmest welcome from the other girls in class."

I laugh, but Bubbe looks me straight in the eye, any trace of humor gone. I look up at Theo to see whether she's joking, but he just stares back, looking bashful.

"Okay?"

How bad can it be?

"Okay."

Chapter Twenty-One

BARBARA

Bubbe was not kidding about not receiving a warm welcome. I don't even get a room temperature one! I walk into a room full of enemies I didn't even know I'd made, cringing at the number of death stares thrown in my direction.

"Uh, hi. I'm Barbara." I wave weakly at the group of ladies standing by a record player. The blue-haired mafia glares back at me, fire in their eyes, and I cower a little.

"Hey, don't be silly," Theo whispers. He places his hand on my lower back and pushes me farther into the room. "They're just mad because they wanted to set me up with their grand-daughters," he says, embarrassed. "It's ridiculous." He smiles encouragingly at me and drops his hand. "Hey, ladies," he says loudly. "It's so nice to see you again." They all turn in unison to look at him with big smiles on their faces, grinning like school-girls in love.

"Theodore, sweetheart!" The woman closest to him squeals with happiness. Theo bends down so she doesn't have to struggle too much to wrap her arms around his neck, while the others struggle to attack him, too. I understand now: she's the queen bee, and the others are her subjects.

"Mrs. Reynolds, it's so nice to see you again."

"Oh, sweetheart, how many times do I have to ask you to call me Bonnie? Mrs. Reynolds makes me sound so *old*. And married. I'm a widow, you know." She winks at him, and Theo blushes.

"Ha," he laughs awkwardly, gently pushing her away.

Theo moves on to greet the rest of the members of his fan club, and I turn to Bubbe. "You weren't kidding about the jealousy. They don't seem too happy that I'm here," I whisper.

Bubbe just shrugs as she watches her grandson be showered in affection. "He's hard not to love. But you know that."

I look back at Theo and think how, just a couple of weeks ago, I would have laughed at that statement. Today, I can absolutely see what Bubbe means. Theo isn't *horrible*. Plus, the way he acts around these women, who are so clearly in love with him, is adorable.

"Can you repeat that conversation a little louder, please?" I jump at the producer's voice. "The mic didn't really catch that."

Bubbe and I turn to glare at him, and he retreats. "You know what? It's fine. We just won't use it. Or we can add closed captions. No big deal."

I roll my eyes and turn back to the scene before me.

After a couple of minutes, Theo finishes catching up with his fan club, and claps his hands together to get their attention. "Okay, ladies. It's class time. Pick your partners, and go stand in the middle of the room."

"No men?" I ask Bubbe as we make our way to the middle of the "dance floor."

She shakes her head with a snort. "They wouldn't be caught dead here. Plus, I think they know they don't stand a chance against my Teddy."

I chuckle. "I can see that."

"We're gonna dance the waltz today, ladies. Are you ready?" The women smile enthusiastically as they pair up. Theo makes his way to a stereo system and scrolls through an iPod for a song.

"Would you like to be my partner?" I ask Bubbe.

"Oh, my dancing days are over, darling." She points to her tank. I'm such an idiot. "And even if I could, I want to see you dance with Teddy." She gently nudges me in his direction, and he turns just in time to face me.

He holds his hand out with a tiny bow. "May I have this dance?"

I don't know why, but the way he says it and the look in his eyes has me blushing like a girl.

"Um, yeah. Yes. Sure," I stutter, taking his hand. "But, I mean, I've never waltzed before, though."

"Good thing your partner is the teacher, then, isn't it?" He smirks, squeezing my hand gently, the way he's done so many other times before. He walks back to the iPod and presses play. The soft and familiar lyrics of one of my favorite songs floods the MPR, and I smile.

"Ed Sheeran?" I ask, surprised, as he takes my waist, and we start to move in unison. My hand glides over his muscular shoulder, hard and soft at the same time.

"What, you thought these women only listened to Sinatra?" he asks, amused, his lips at my ear. I shiver a little and inhale deeply, committing his scent to memory.

I've never danced the waltz, but with Theo, that doesn't seem to matter—it *never* seems to matter. Whatever we're thrown, we're able to face it together. After weeks of practice, my body naturally responds to his as he leads me through the steps, just like they did the night we danced merengue. The song is slower than what I expected a waltz could be danced to, but it's perfect for this moment, where I honestly just want to be held by him. In a turn, I take advantage of the inertia and settle my head in the crook of his neck, and he pulls me in tighter, my eyes sliding shut. Our dance has changed. We're no longer truly waltzing. It feels more like we're gliding together to the beat of the slow song, holding each other—and it's incredible.

"But she's doing it wrong! Her head has to be tilted slightly back!" I hear Bonnie hiss at someone.

"Shh! Leave them alone. Can't you see they're having a moment?" Bubbe comes to our defense in a hushed voice. I hide my smile in Theo's neck and continue to let him lead me across the floor.

I pull back, laughing a little, to see whether he heard Bonnie's comment. But when I meet his eyes, my breath catches. His gaze locks on mine, pupils blown. That feeling in my chest comes back with a mighty force when his hand lowers slightly down my back. There's a warmth there that starts spreading all over my body, and I don't hate it.

Theo doesn't smile. He doesn't say anything. His eyes flash down at my lips, and his head tilts. I inhale sharply and stare at his mouth as it grows closer and closer to mine. He hesitates just before, always giving me an out, an option to back out. But I'd rather die than miss out on kissing him again, so I meet him the rest of the way. Standing on my tiptoes, moving my hands up his arms and lacing them behind his neck, I press my lips against his.

So soft. Just like I remembered.

His lips move against mine, the barest hint of tongue playing at my lips. We're barely moving at this point, barely swaying to the song, as the tentative kiss turns into something more—something sweet but that grips my heart so tightly it knocks me breathless.

The kiss comes to a natural stop as the song ends, and Theo pulls back. My eyes are still closed when he presses his forehead against mine, his breath on my face. I press a palm over his chest, feeling his heart race just as quickly as mine is now. A low groan builds there, and I open my eyes to see his shut tightly. For a second, he pulls me in tighter into him.

"Theo," I whisper. "I—"

"Perfect!" I jump at the producer's voice. "That was incredible, guys, really. Perfect on-screen kiss."

On-screen kiss? Is that what it was?

Suddenly, I realize that that's exactly what it was, because we had definitely agreed to never do this again, right? *He* knew we were filming. *He* didn't forget like I did. I'm the professional actress here, and I can't seem to remember when the cameras are even on. Stupid Barbara. Did you forget you're putting on a show? None of it is real. He's just a better actor than you thought.

I'm mortified. I had one of the best kisses of my life in front of a room of cameras and octogenarians.

I turn away from Theo, my fingers on my lips. There's a stinging behind my eyes—where did that come from?

"What?" Theo asks the producer, a little dazed.

He comes closer to us, speaking in a low voice so as not to be overheard. "I said it was a great kiss—really believable. But we're losing light, and we need to film individual interviews now, so how about you wrap up your dance class? I think we have enough romance on tape to make something out of it."

"Oh, uh, yeah." I can feel Theo's eyes on the back of my head. "That's fine."

"Barbara?"

I turn to face them, calling on my best acting skills, and smile enthusiastically. "Of course. So happy we could deliver! Let's get these interviews out of the way so we can all go home."

Chapter Twenty-Two

BARBARA

We stay for a few hours after the camera crew leaves. Theo wants to spend some more time with his grandmother without them intruding, which I totally understand. It also works out well for me because I'm starved for more information on him, and Bubbe is all too willing to give it to me. We spend the afternoon flipping through photo albums and the stories behind them. I run my fingers over the first-place ribbons and school recital programs so carefully glued and taped to the scrapbooks, wondering what it would have been like to grow up with a parental figure who cared enough to keep track of my achievements.

I doubt my parents have any type of memorabilia from my acting days.

It makes me wonder...if we're the direct result of our upbringing, of our experiences, would I have become a different person? If I had had present parents—parents who actually cared about me—who would I be today?

I ponder that while Bubbe and Theo debate which performance was more fun to watch and ultimately decide that I like who I am, so maybe I'm just better off.

Theo asks if I mind staying for dinner so he can spend more time with his grandmother, and of course I agree. He looks so happy as he tells his Bubbe about our dance for this week over Jell-O.

"You know I usually don't like to go over the top with choreography or costumes, opting for a more traditional performance, but you should see what we've got prepared for this week." He grins broadly, his leg jiggling impatiently like he can't wait to tell her all about it.

It's so sweet.

Bubbe smiles at Theo and pats his hand. "I think it's good you're stepping out of your comfort zone." Her eyes flash briefly to me. "Now tell me about it."

"Well, like I said, we're doing the jive, and I thought maybe if we incorporated some—"

Bubbe frowns, and confusion floods her eyes. "What are you talking about? We're not doing the jive for the competition. Richard and I prepared a rumba."

"What are—" Theo starts to ask, eyebrows pulled together. Suddenly, I see him pale and slouch. "Bubbe?"

Bubbe looks uncomfortably around the room, biting her lip. "Where am I? And who are you?" I can see the panic settling into her features, and my stomach drops.

"Bubbe. It's me. It's Theodore—"

"What? No! I don't know who you are." She starts to get up, and a nurse runs over to us.

Theo slouches in his seat, defeated, looking down at his hands on the table.

"Esther," the nurse calmly says, taking Bubbe's hand and helping her up. "Esther, why don't we take you back to your room, okay?" Theo looks up, and the nurse flashes him a sad smile. "It's late for her."

Theo nods silently. "I'll try to come by next week, Erika. Thanks for your help."

"Sure, sweetie," she says, walking out with Bubbe. "I'll make sure she's okay."

I watch Theo pick his coat up and quietly get up. Following his lead, I put mine on and take my purse with me as we quietly walk out to the car and head home.

After an hour of driving in absolute silence, I can't bear it any longer.

"Theo," I start, but he shakes his head. I can practically *hear* everything he's thinking right now, his concern for his Bubbe. Guilt is clear on his face, because I know he blames himself. I can tell he thinks he's failing her, not doing enough.

I want to distract him, pull him from whatever dark hole he's dug himself into, but I don't know how.

The car wheezes and jerks a little, and suddenly, I know what to do. "Do you think we'll be able to make it back into the city without dying?" I smirk, trying to provoke him.

His expression is stony. "Barbara," he warns me.

"No, seriously. It's a real concern for me. Scout's honor," I say, holding two fingers in front of me.

"I know what you're doing. You're trying to distract me."

"Yes and no. I'm trying to distract you, but dying in this car is a real fear of mine right now." The universe decides to work with me, and it starts to drizzle. "Shit, look at that. It's gonna start pouring. Now we're really gonna die," I deadpan.

Theo shifts nervously in his seat and leans forward a little, laser-focused on the road ahead. "Shh, I need to concentrate."

Under the car's headlights, the wet asphalt glistens like black glitter. "Concentrate?" I tease. "On what? There's no traffic. We're literally the only ones on this highway."

"Yeah, well, what about deer? A deer can run in front of us, and we could get into a pretty serious accident—especially now that it's raining. Do you know what happens to the roads when it rains? Do you know what it means when they're slick and wet?"

"That the highway's turned on and she's ready to go? No foreplay needed." I smirk.

Theo tries to hold it in, but suddenly, he's bursting with laughter. My eyes widen in surprise. He's glorious when he laughs, his navy eyes liquid, and crinkling at the sides. It's like he briefly lets go of every single thing weighing him down and is able to feel free for a few seconds.

"That was a horrible joke," he says, but he's still laughing. "So gross."

"It was amazing, and you know it," I say. My cheeks hurt from how big I'm grinning, feeling victorious because I managed to make him laugh and relieved that he's out from the dark cloud he was under—at least, for a little bit.

"I'm sorry," he says, more serious now. "I shut down back there, I know. That was shitty of me."

My heart aches for him, thinking how difficult it must be to be Theo, how he just takes everything on himself—he doesn't have anyone else. "Are you kidding? You're absolutely entitled to shut down for a bit. What you're going through isn't easy."

"She was sundowning. I knew we shouldn't have stayed that late."

"Sundowning?"

"Sundown Syndrome," he shakes his head. "It's this weird

phenomenon that happens to people with dementia or Alzheimer's or other diseases where they get confused or violent in the late afternoon and into the night. It's been happening more and more to her lately." His mouth is twisted in pain.

"Is that why you told Rob they were only allowed to film early in the day?"

"Yeah." He runs the fingers of his right hand through his hair. "We should have left earlier." His brows are pulled together, mouth distorted into the deepest frown I've seen on his face yet. I haven't known him for long, but I've known him long enough to know what he looks like when he's drowning in guilt.

"You need to stop," I say. "Stop feeling guilty. I know my life is a mess, which doesn't make me the best person to be getting advice from." I pause briefly and think about that for a second. "Or maybe it's the opposite. Maybe you should listen to me *because* my life is a mess, and I know what I'm talking about. But take it from me: you *need* to keep going and do your hardest not to dwell. I'm not saying you should repress what you're feeling, because that's the opposite of helpful, but what you're doing right now? Doing everything in your power to change your situation by fake dating me and stuff? Being useful? That's much more important than just being sad and taking things how they are. You're doing your best, and that's all that anyone can ask of you."

Theo quietly stares out at the road ahead, biting the inside of his cheek. After a beat, he gives me a slight nod.

"Thank you," he says softly. "I think I needed to hear that."

"You're—"

A sudden jolt has my hands flying to the dash and passenger door for support. Theo tries to recover the car, but it slips, and the engines stalls, brakes squealing, struggling to bring it to a halt.

We finally stop skidding and end up parked diagonally across the road, completely blocking off the highway.

"Jesus Christ!" I yell. "I told you this car was gonna kill us!"

"I'm sorry, I'm sorry! Let me start the car up again, and we can get out of here." Theo turns the key, but the car remains unresponsive. He jiggles the key again with a grunt, but the engine still doesn't start.

I'm rattled, but very aware of how precarious our situation is. "Theo, oh my God, we need to *move*. We can't stay in the car —not when it's parked like this. What if someone speeds down the highway and hits us while we're in it? We need to get out and call a tow truck from the side of the road." I unbuckle my seatbelt and push the heavy car door open, taking my purse with me. "Let's *go!*" I walk over to his side of the car and open the door, tugging on his jacket. The rain is really starting to come down now, and I already feel myself getting soaked.

With one last failed attempt at starting his grandfather's car, Theo heaves a big sigh, unbuckles his seatbelt, and gets out of the car.

"Time to call a tow truck."

"Oh my God, Theo. I don't have any bars." I panic and start walking around in circles, my eyes never leaving my phone screen. "I don't have any bars, Theo. I can't get a signal!"

"*Fuuuuck*. Neither can I!" He runs his fingers through his now damp hair with one hand while clicking away at his phone with the other. "We're going to have to walk to a gas station or something. There's one a couple of miles down this road."

"Oh, fantastic. I've always wanted to be murdered and buried in the middle of nowhere in upstate New York. I hope someone starts a true crime podcast based on our deaths," I deadpan.

He rolls his eyes at me and runs a hand down his face. "Will you relax? I'll just put up some cones and triangles, and we can head out. It won't take us very long. I grew up in the area and drive up every weekend. I know this place."

I sigh and put my face in my hands, feeling the ice-cold rain drip onto my neck, under my coat. I shiver and pull up my hood and glare at him.

"Next time, we rent a car."

"THERE'S NOTHING I CAN DO FOR YOU TONIGHT, PAL," a grease-stained man called Geoff tells Theo. "I can tow your car for you and bring it here, but I definitely don't have the parts or the expertise to fix a sixty-two Turbo Jetfire. I'm gonna have to call one of the folks that organize the antique car show here every spring to see if they have anything."

I snort. "Hear that, Theo? *Antique* car show. As in *old*." I'm being a little bit of a bitch, I know, but you would be, too, if you were soaked head to toe from having walked twenty minutes in the freezing, pouring rain.

I shift from one foot to the other, and my boots make a weird *sloosh* sound. I look down at them and grimace.

They're ruined. My beautiful hot-pink rhinestone booties are completely ruined, covered in mud.

Theo glares at me and looks back at Geoff. "Okay, cool. Let's do that, then. We want to get back on the road as soon as possible, so I'm willing to pay a little extra for rush."

Geoff snorts. "Sorry, man, but do you know how old the people who run the antique car show are? It's nine p.m. They've probably been asleep for two hours already. I won't be able to get in touch with them until tomorrow morning."

"Oh. My. God."

Theo groans and looks at me. "I'm sorry." He looks so absolutely apologetic and miserable that I decide to let it go right then and there. He doesn't need the added pressure of my attitude right now. It's not helping the situation, and he's already been through enough today.

I sigh. "It's not your fault—I think. Let's just go get the car and find a place to sleep. There's nothing we can do now."

"I can find you a train? Drop you off at the station? It'll take you all the way to Grand Central."

I roll my eyes at him. "I'm not going to leave you, you idiot. Plus, I don't want to be on one of those late trains full of weirdos and drunk people." I turn to look at Geoff with my flirtiest smile, placing my hand on his arm. "Geoff? Do you think you could also tell us where we could find a hotel or something in the area?"

"My friend owns an inn in Red Hook."

"Awesome!" I bat my eyelashes at him and Theo scoffs, annoyed. "We just need to figure out how to get there, then..." I look innocently up at Geoff.

"I'd *love* to give you a ride." He grins wickedly at me, and I don't miss the double entendre. But I stifle a gag because we do need his help.

"You mean, give us *both* a ride." Theo stands in front of me, narrowing his eyes at Geoff, not seeming to care about the fact that he's antagonizing the six-foot-five man who resembles a bodybuilder more than he does a mechanic and is responsible for getting us to shelter and fixing our car. I smile shyly at him. Where did this protectiveness come from? *Jeez.*

"Right. Both of you. And then I can get started on the car first thing tomorrow morning."

Chapter Twenty-Three

THEO

"You know, it's really not that funny. I don't get why you're laughing," I say, peeling my drenched coat off and kicking my wet shoes off by the bedroom door. Barbara and I have been at each other's throats since the car broke down, and it's driving me crazy. I'm wet, my jeans are sticking uncomfortably to parts of my body that just *should not* have denim stuck to them, and she's laughing. Laughing like she finds this whole thing fucking hilarious.

"What would you prefer I do, then?" She giggles again, throwing her soaked coat on the radiator. "Should I cry? Should I yell at you some more? Should I tell you, '*I told you so*'? Don't get me wrong, I'd love nothing more than to do so, because *of course* I was right. I'm *always* right. But what exactly is that going to solve?" She walks into the bathroom and starts to wring her hair out over the sink.

I sigh. "I don't know. You could at least agree with me that the situation sucks. You can join me here in the dark side, and we can talk about how *of course* the cherry on top of this entire fucking day is that a random inn in a small town in the *middle of nowhere,* as you say, only has *one room available.* How is that even possible? Who would want to come here so much to have the place sell out? No offense to this town—I'm sure it's lovely in its own way."

She snorts. "We're already in agreement that the situation sucks, okay? And the lady at the front desk told us why the place is full," she says from the bathroom as I hear her kick off her boots on the tile floor. "This weekend is Parents' Weekend at the college in the next town over. It's a miracle they even had any rooms left to begin with."

"The Holiday Inn thirty minutes away must be booked solid, because I can't imagine anyone picking this place as their first choice. It looks like it's right out of a Stephen King novel." I grunt, taking in the creepy red wallpaper, the smell of humidity and mothballs, and the nineteenth-century furniture that has definitely seen better days. "Maybe this *will* be the night we die, and you'll get your wish of having a true crime podcast based on your death: *Skinned Alive: The Barbara Holt and Theodore Wallace Story.*"

"I find it extremely disturbing that the first cause of death you could think of was *skinning,* but I appreciate getting first credit."

"Don't flatter yourself. I was going in alphabetical order." I shrug, but she doesn't see me. I continue to examine the room and gasp. "There's a massive brown stain on the white rug! Maybe someone already *did* die in here. Gah!"

Barbara giggles from the bathroom. "I've missed Grumpy Theo. I was starting to think I imagined the whole thing, and you were actually a nice guy. Yet, here you are, going on a full-on rant about how much you hate everything." She sighs happily.

"You're so weird."

"You might have mentioned that once or twice before," she says a little curtly.

It was a joke—kind of—but I wince just the same, remembering how big of a dick I was to her when we first met.

She didn't deserve it.

"I'm sorry about that," I say, still standing in the middle of the room, uncomfortably damp. "I can be a real jerk sometimes and I was really stressed about having to start from scratch with another dance partner after the whole Alessandra thing. Although that's no excuse." I sigh, disappointed on how the energy between us has shifted now.

She pokes her head out from the bathroom to look me in the eye, pursing her lips. "Yes, you can definitely be a real jerk sometimes," she says after a beat. "But you can also be really kind when you want to be." She shoots me a small smile and relief crashes over me. "Here." Barbara tosses a white towel in my direction. "I'm gonna take a shower now, because *ladies first* and all that, but you can wear that so you don't have to stay in your wet clothes while you wait until I'm done." She shuts the door, and I hear the shower turn on.

I start stripping down, placing my wet clothes on the radiator as I go, but I stop at my boxers. We're sharing a bed. And our clothes are wet. What exactly are we supposed to do? I can't sleep in a towel, can I? Holy shit, is *she* going to sleep in a towel? There's no way it'll stay *on* all night, right? Won't it slip off? Jesus, what if I see her naked?

She's naked now. In the shower. While I'm out here.

Yeah, there's no way I'm going to be able to hide any type of morning wood from her, especially if she's going to be sleeping naked next to me. Not possible. Nope.

This whole sleeping arrangement is a mess.

I glance at the small armchair in the corner of the room and groan. That looks to be about my only other option. Or maybe the floor? Not on the brown stain, of course. Maybe right next to it?

Shit.

I guess I'm not sleeping tonight.

I finish stripping, placing my boxers on the radiator, hoping to God they dry quickly so that I can at least wear them to bed, and wrap the towel around my waist.

I lie back on the bed and run my fingers through my hair, exhausted. It was a hell of a long day. I just need to close my eyes for a second—just a minute, maybe. Just rest my eyes while Barbara wraps up her shower. Yup, just a few...

"Oh my God!" I hear Barbara squeal.

"What?!" I gasp, sitting up so quickly I get a head rush. "Ow. What? What happened?"

Barbara's in a robe, hair up in one of those makeshift towel-turbans women wear, her back to me, but I can tell she's covering her eyes with both hands. "Your—your...*penis,*" she chokes out.

I look down at myself and feel my entire body heat in embarrassment. "*Fuck.*" As hypothesized, you cannot fall asleep in a towel without it slipping off and *your dick* popping out and making an appearance. Mortified, I stand and wrap myself up again. "Jesus, I'm sorry. I—I fell asleep and—"

"It's fine. It's fine," Barbara tells me, her voice high and frantic. "Are you—? Is it safe?" I see her ears redden and her back tense.

"*Safe?*" I laugh in surprise. "I didn't know my dick was dangerous."

"Please don't say that," she groans, her back still to me.

"Don't say *dick?*" I laugh again, finding her nervousness adorable—and completely unexpected.

"Ugh! Is it safe to turn around or not?"

"Yes, it's *safe,*" I chuckle as Barbara steels herself by taking a deep breath before turning around to face me. She flushes beet red as soon as she makes eye contact with me, eyes widening. "I don't know why you think my dick is dangerous, though. It's not like it's a gun, locked and loaded, ready to shoot you at any moment."

She blushes again and mutters something about having to make room on top of the radiator to dry her clothes.

"I'm gonna go take a shower, then," I say, throwing a thumb over my shoulder. "That okay?"

She grunts in assent but still won't face me.

I turn around and make my way into the bathroom once I realize she won't be looking me in the eye anytime soon. Why is she so embarrassed? Shouldn't I be the one freaking out here? I was the one accidentally flashing her.

Unless...maybe she liked what she saw?

When I get out of the shower, I'm relieved to find a second bathrobe folded next to another set of towels. Breathing a sigh of relief, I put it on and tie it—*quite tightly*—around my waist. Don't need any further slip-ups tonight or tomorrow morning, especially if she's going to react the same way she did earlier.

It's quiet out in the room, so I hesitate before opening the door, just in case she's already asleep. I peek into the bedroom and see her lying on her side, still in her bathrobe, her back to me. Her damp hair is out of the turban now, spread across the pillow like caramel-colored seaweed. The lamp next to my side of the bed is on, but all the other lights are off.

I do my best to lift the covers on my side of the bed without waking her, sliding awkwardly under the comforter, wincing every time I make the slightest sound. When I'm finally comfortable, I hear her giggle. "You know I'm awake, right?"

I sigh heavily, annoyed. "And you just let me go through that?"

Barbara turns on her other side to face me, both hands folded under her face. "It was entertaining," she says, raising a shoulder.

She's so close I'm scared of turning to face her. Instead, I keep my eyes on the ceiling. "Why aren't you asleep yet?"

"I was about to be, but I forgot to take my meds, actually." She gets up and walks to her purse—the massive one that looks more like a fancy duffel than anything else, if we're being honest. It rattles as she rifles through it, and suddenly, I realize why it comes with its own personal soundtrack, why it always sounds like a maraca every time she moves it. Because she keeps her pills with her.

Her robe slips off her shoulder a little, giving me a glimpse of her collarbone before she quickly puts it back in place.

"You travel with your meds?" I ask, trying to get my mind off the fact that she's still naked under the robe, that I could easily take her all the way there by just lightly tugging on the belt. I try, but suddenly find myself remembering what I feels like to run my fingertips over the smooth skin of her thighs and shoulders, and wonder whether the rest of her skin is as soft. I start to imagine what her breasts would feel like in my hands, the sounds she'd make if I were to place my mouth just—

I shaked my head and suppress a groan.

Stop.

She pulls out two different orange bottles from her bag, popping a pill from each into the palm of her hand. "Yup. I don't ever want to be without them, in case of an emergency like this one." She smiles shyly at me and walks toward the bathroom, where I hear her turn the faucet on and then quickly off. "There," she says, coming out, wiping her mouth with the back of her hand. "*Now* I can go to sleep."

"Do you have to take those every night?"

She purses her lips and slides into bed under the covers right next to me. Her body is close—*so close*—I can feel the heat coming off it. "I forget sometimes," she says in a small voice.

"And...what happens when you forget?" I ask tentatively.

"Nothing good." She turns on her side, her back to me, essentially ending this conversation. "Can you get the light?"

I reach over to the nightstand and flick the light off. I settle back in bed and make sure that my robe is in place before I fall asleep again. For a moment, I swear there's no way I'm going to be able to fall asleep with her next to me. Eventually, though, exhaustion takes over and I start to slip under. Right as I'm on the edge, that moment where you're not really asleep but also not fully awake, I hear her whisper, "This is a very small bed." Without hesitating, I make to get out of it and head toward the chair. Immediately, Barbara reaches out, putting a hand on my shoulder. "Where are you going?" I don't miss the slight panic in her voice.

"It's fine. I can sleep on that chair. It's not a big deal." I look over at it and do my best to control my grimace. "You should sleep comfortably. I don't want to be the reason why you can't do so."

"*You're* not the reason. The fact that this bed is too small for the both of us is the reason. And I won't be able to sleep knowing that you exiled yourself to that small chair. Nope, absolutely not. I was just making a comment, pointing out the obvious. Something I thoroughly excel at."

I look down at her, supporting all my weight on my hands, and lower myself back down next to her. "Okay. I'll stay. I wasn't exactly looking forward to sleeping there anyway." I smile.

Even in the dark, I can see her smirk. Barbara lays her head down on the pillow next to me, facing me again, and makes herself comfortable. "But you really would have slept there, wouldn't you have? If I'd asked you?"

"How can you even question that? If it made you feel uncomfortable, of course I would've. What type of man would I be otherwise?"

"A normal one. One who would be very excited to be sleeping next to a more-than-half-naked girl in a full-sized bed next to him. A guy who would be thinking about trying something." She smirks again, but this time it's that witchy one, the one that she uses whenever she wants to taunt me.

I turn onto my side to face her, our lips just inches apart. "I'm not the kind of guy to just try something with the girl I like unless I know she is into me, too. And I certainly wouldn't sleep with a random girl just because she's in my bed—half-naked or otherwise."

"So, you wouldn't want to ever try anything with me?" She raises an eyebrow at me, pressing her lips together, trying her hardest not to laugh. She's teasing me, but she doesn't know the half of it. She doesn't know how many times I've thought about being with her. She doesn't know all the different things I wish I could do to her. My dick stirs at the thought of having her right here, right now.

I catch her eyes flicker briefly to my lips and then back up to meet my gaze. Suddenly, I'm tired of this goddamn game—especially after today and that fucking kiss and the way I catch her looking at me sometimes.

"I never said that, Barbara," I say a little roughly, my breathing coming in a little faster. "First off, you're definitely not some random girl. I just admitted to liking you, in case you didn't notice. And second...well, that one's up to you. But I never said I wouldn't try anything with you if I didn't think you returned the interest."

She stares back at me, wide-eyed. "Oh," she says softly, finally understanding that I'm not fucking around anymore. I'd bet my life that if I pressed a hand against her chest, her heart would be racing just as fast as mine.

"Yeah. Oh." My eyes roam all over her face, and then down her body.

I want her I want her I want her.

There's a pause before she inches closer to me, lips barely an inch apart. It takes a Herculean effort not to pull her closer to me right now and kiss her crazy, like I've been wanting to do for so long now. I want to reach out and grab her by the waist, roll her onto her back and—

"And what if I told you I wanted it, too?" Her breathing speeds up, just like mine, and I can feel the blood rush to my dick.

She wants this? For real this time?

"That I've been thinking about it a lot lately." She reaches a hand out and places it on my cheek. I roughly grab her wrist and hold her hand there, turning my face to kiss her palm, but keeping our eyes locked. I hear her sharp intake of breath in the dark and stifle a groan. My hips move involuntarily toward her. "That every time we dance, every time I feel your hand go up my thigh..." She sighs. "I think about what it would feel like if you didn't stop there. If you just kept going."

Holy shit.

"What would you do then?" she asks, her voice shaking slightly.

I FUCKING WANT HER.

I kiss her wrist, kiss slowly up her arm, carefully shifting us both so that she's on her back and I'm half-hovering over her body, staring down into her hazel eyes. I can see the hunger in them as her lips part and she releases a low whimper. I decide to go for broke and press my hip into her thigh, letting her feel just how hard the thought of being with her gets me. "I'd say it's pretty fucking obvious what I'd do."

Chapter Twenty-Four

BARBARA

I GASP, FEELING HIM HEAVY AND HARD AGAINST ME. Though he pulls back slightly almost immediately after, the ache and desire that was pooling in between my legs doesn't dissipate—it only seems to intensify.

His hardware is impressive—something I already know after having accidentally seen it not half an hour ago. But now that it's there, hard, wanting me just as much as I want it, it's even more shocking.

We stare at each other, his eyes low-lidded, and the air begins to get heavier with want. His face is *just* there, just half an inch away, but he doesn't come closer than that. Theo's eyes flash briefly down to my lips, his chest pressing down on mine, knee between my legs.

"Well? You gonna kiss me or what?" I ask, suddenly feeling brazen, completely forgetting about the conversation we had after elimination about not pursuing this. Suddenly, I can't think of a single reason why this is a bad idea.

He half-growls, half-smiles. "So fucking impatient," he says, and then his lips are on mine, hard and desperate—like he's been starved all this time. He shifts, his entire body now between my legs, and roughly grabs my thighs to wrap them around his torso with a grunt. Tightly cupping my face with his left hand, Theo tugs the belt of my robe with his right. He slowly slides his hand under the fabric, teasing, grazing my stomach with his fingertips, pushing it wide open. His touch raises goosebumps over my skin, sending shivers down my spine. He pushes his hips slightly into me, and I clench involuntarily, moaning into his mouth.

Theo looks down at me and groans. "*Fuck—*your *sounds.*" He dips his head and starts kissing down my chest, biting, licking. "Fuck," he groans again against my skin. "You're so fucking beautiful I can't stand it." He lavishes one nipple with his tongue, biting gently, tugging it between his teeth, while his other hand rolls and tweaks the other. I inhale sharply at a rough tug, and he smiles wickedly against my breast.

So fucking hot.

"Thanks." He smirks before kissing me, sucking my skin. I blush, realizing that, once again, I've said exactly what I was thinking out loud. He lifts off and kneels between my legs, tearing my robe open, pushing it off my shoulders, helping me take it completely off. "*Jesus Christ.*" He blows a gust of air out as he runs both hands slowly up my body, cupping and squeezing my breasts.

"No, the name's Barbara," I joke breathlessly.

"No jokes," Theo growls, throwing himself at me again. "No fucking jokes. Not when you're with me like this." He hitches my leg on his hip, bracing himself, his dick *right there*, rubbing my clit just right without ever entering me. The friction is *glorious* and makes my already intense ache for him unbearable. I gasp as I feel a jolt and he growls against my mouth. "Is this what you like? You like it when I grab you like this?" He squeezes my thigh and thrusts, his hard dick sliding over my clit.

"Oh God, yes. Right—" I inhale against his lips on another

thrust. "Right there." My skin feels heated and icy at the same time.

"Now you're gonna remember that..." he says in my ear, voice gravelly. *Thrust.* "Every time we dance..." *Thrust.* "Every time I run my hands over your body..." *Thrust.* "I want you to remember what I can do to you..." *Thrust.* "What I'm thinking about doing to you even while millions of people watch us on live TV."

"Oh fuck," I moan.

His lips crash down on mine again, tongue pressing in between my lips, pushing my mouth open to greet him in desperation—one that I match wholeheartedly. I've wanted him for so long, needed this for so long. Admittedly, I've imagined being with him like this since our first performance on live TV. It's like meeting one of your heroes but *not* being disappointed by them this time. Because being with Theo, kissing Theo...it's surreal. Better than I ever imagined it could be.

Theo crawls down my body, and I immediately miss his weight over me. But his tongue drags down my abdomen, all the way down to just below my navel, as he swings one of my legs over his shoulder, holding it tightly to him. I struggle to sit up so I can look him in the eye. "Come back," I plead, but his hand clamps down on my leg, gripping it even tighter to him.

"Keep your leg here," he growls me, his navy eyes blazing. "If you move it, I'm gonna have to punish you, Miss Holt." My eyes roll to the back of my head in pleasure because Grumpy Theo is back—in bed this time—and I'm totally here for it.

I feel his tongue slowly—torturously—part me, and I whimper, arching my neck back. I'm panting loudly—too loudly. I start to panic, worrying that he might think I'm a complete lunatic because I can't seem to catch my breath, and he's barely even started.

My God, if this is what it's like now, would I ever even survive actual sex with him?

I feel his tongue again, moving slowly all the way to my clit. This time, he doesn't stop. This time, he starts to circle it slowly, methodically. I cry a version of his name on a moan and my back lifts off the mattress. One hand fists into the sheets below us and the other flies to my mouth. I bite down on my fist to keep myself from making any more embarrassing noises. His eyes fly to my face, and he reaches out to knock my hand out of my mouth. "Don't do that," he orders. "I want to know what it sounds like when you *really* unravel, Miss Holt."

He's commanding and possessive and—"*Oh God*," I cry again as I feel his tongue flatten against me, adding more pressure right where I need it.

Theo presses his lips briefly to the inside of my thigh with a low chuckle. "Yeah. Exactly like that." He ducks back and sucks my clit into his mouth as my hips buck off the bed, but he uses his grip on my leg to keep me down, keep me where he wants me. He flicks his tongue at the same time as I feel him push a finger, then another, into me. His tongue and mouth and fingers and hands are all a masterful choreography created exclusively to pleasure me. And he pleasures me just like he does everything else in his life—with precision, and accuracy, and thoroughness, and passion.

"Theo—" My breath hitches at a particularly delicious pull.

"Hold on." His lips vibrate against me. I raise my head to look down at him and notice his hips rocking against the mattress for the first time, like he can't help but seek his own pleasure. Knowing I make him feel even a small percentage of how he makes me feel brings me closer to the edge.

"*Theo—*" I warn again. I'm so close. So damn close.

"*...pussy tastes so fucking good*," he groans against me, the vibrations from his voice causing my toes to curl. "*...wanna taste this every day.*"

That does it. The sound of his voice, desperate and hungry for me. With one more flick of his tongue, I'm pushed off the cliff and falling, falling, falling over the edge, screaming out his name.

By the time I open my eyes, I'm a puddle of Jell-O and lava, unable to move. "Holy shit," I croak.

Theo crawls back up me, kissing me on his way back to my neck. My skin is so sensitive from the orgasm he gave me, it's only then that I notice he's still wearing his robe. "What the hell?" I ask, tugging the robe off his shoulders. "Take this off. Right now."

He kneels, straddling one of my legs, and throws his robe off with a laugh. I drag my eyes—slowly—down Theo's body, and my jaw drops. I saw him naked less than an hour ago when he wasn't as...*excited.* And I was already impressed. And now? Now that he's...ready for action?

Daayum.

"You good?" he asks with a smirk.

"I'm...yeah. *Yes.*" I puff a gust of air through my lips, exhausted, boneless. "You have quite a mouth on you, by the way."

"Why, thank you." He smiles wickedly.

I laugh and shake my head. "I meant your dirty talk. But yeah, that too." We chuckle, and it feels nice to be able to laugh after that intensity. Still, I surprise myself by missing his closeness, wanting him over me again. "Get over here." I pull him down by the arm and lift my knees to his ribs, wrapping my legs around him. I bite his bottom lip and kiss him, tasting myself on his mouth, wanting to never have to leave this room again.

"Want to fuck you so bad," he breathes against my lips.

"Yes. Okay. *Do.*" I can barely breathe, still recovering from him going down on me.

"Yeah? You want to?" he asks, his eyes bouncing between mine in excitement.

I want to say a lot of not-nice things right now. Like, for example, I'd love to ask him whether he's stupid. Because I'm pretty sure I've made it obvious that I am into this whole thing. But I decide to be nice, and instead of calling him an idiot, I go with, "*God,* yes."

He ducks to kiss my neck once and pulls back again to ask, "Condom?"

I stare at him, wide-eyed. "Are you kidding me? You don't have a condom?"

"No." He looks just as panicked as I feel. "Please tell me you have a condom in that bag of yours."

"Why would I have a condom in my bag, Theo?" I ask, annoyed.

"Really, Barbara? You want to have this conversation right now? First of all, why not? Second, you have a *stapler* in there, of all things, but asking you whether you have a condom is a crazy assumption?"

I roll my eyes at him. We can't even stop arguing long enough to have sex. "I am more likely to use that stapler than I am to use a condom."

"Evidently not. I've never once seen you need to use a stapler in front of me, whereas we could really use a condom—or six—right now."

"Six?" I scoff, completely side-tracked.

Theo's eyes narrow and darken with a wicked smile on his lips. "Oh, yeah. If we had condoms, you can bet your ass I'd fuck you all night. I have a feeling that once definitely wouldn't be enough." I gasp slightly, and he presses his lips to mine. He has a surprisingly dirty mouth for how in control he usually seems to be. "I love those fucking sounds. I'm gonna replay them in my head over and over again all day tomorrow when I'm at home alone thinking about how much I want to fuck you." He licks the spot under my ear and pulls my leg over his hip again—hard.

"I HAVE AN IUD!" I scream it so loud I may as well be volunteering as tribute. "I—I haven't had sex in over a year, and I have an IUD."

He pushes back slightly to look down at me, an eyebrow raised. "You want to go without a condom?"

"I'm clean and..." I sigh, feeling my skin heat. I haven't had sex in what feels like ages—definitely not since my last check-up. "Anyway, if you're good, I'm good. That's what I mean."

His arms tighten around me, hesitating a bit. He looks down into my eyes, searching for something. Eventually, he finds whatever it is he is looking for and nods before dipping his face back to mine.

I run my hands up his strong arms, feeling every inch of his strong muscles. I'm not a stranger to them, but I've never felt them bare like this, never felt them under my fingertips. My heart starts beating so loudly, I wonder whether he can hear it. I want to tell him how much I've wanted this and for how long, but the words dry up in my mouth. They get caught in my throat, and I swallow them back down. Plus, I'm pretty sure he'd make an accurate assumption. Right now, though, I can't focus on anything other than his mouth and how it feels when he kisses my collarbone, on how his knees widen, spreading my legs farther apart to accommodate him as he settles in between them. I can't think of anything else when I look into his navy-blue eyes, and he looks into mine as he of-so-fucking-slowly enters me.

He's not even fully inside me, and my breath still catches at the feeling, the stretch. He's bigger than anyone I've ever been with, and it's been a while since I've been with anyone else.

"You okay?" His voice is choked, restrained. I can tell it's taking everything in him not to push all the way in. "You're so tight," he groans, his head dropping to my shoulder. I can feel his breath on my skin, warm and damp.

"Yes, I'm...it's been a while and—" A small thrust from him, a gasp from me. "And I just need a second."

"Okay," he rasps, kissing up my neck, nipping at the skin under my ear. "*God*, I love how you smell." He inhales. "Every time your hair hits my face on a twirl when we dance, I get so pissed, and I've never understood why. And now I know it's because you smell infuriatingly good, and it drives me crazy. It's addictive." He inhales deeply, his chest stretching over me.

I laugh a little, breathlessly, and lift my legs higher up his torso. I feel the cords of his back muscles tense under the palms of my hands in self-restraint, see how his hands shake as he runs them over my body. I dig my fingers into his hair, cupping his face, bringing his lips to mine, and cant my hips up to him in invitation.

He groans a, "*Fuuuck*," in my mouth and carefully pushes the rest of the way in. We both groan in satisfaction.

My God.

Nothing has ever felt this good.

He starts off with slow, deep thrusts, holding himself back, letting me get used to him—careful. Not soon enough, though, he starts to lose control, taking up a faster rhythm—desperate, fast, mind-blowing. On a particularly delicious thrust where he circles his hips a few times, my head snaps back against the pillow, and a sound that could have honestly come from either one of us bounces off the walls of the dark hotel room. For a split second, I worry about the neighboring rooms, the thin walls, and how everyone can probably hear the rocking of the bed, the sounds he draws from my body, and the dirty words he grunts against the shell of my ear—things like *so wet* and *want to live inside you.* But then the pleasure becomes too much to bear, and he makes me come, and come, and come, and I simply could not care less about anyone else. I smile a little at the thought, actually, of how anyone who heard us could not be anything but jealous, because that was the most mind-numbing, heel-digging, toe-curling orgasm I have ever had in my life—and I'm pretty sure everyone in a five-mile radius could tell.

Theodore Wallace is an absolute sex god.

"*Jesus.* I'm going to hear the sound of you coming in my head for *days.*" He kisses me deeply. "Fucking weeks." I'm practically shaking, and we're both panting heavily, struggling to control ourselves, wanting more but trying to savor every second we're together. "You have no idea how long I've wanted to do this," he whispers against my lips, his fingers sliding into my hair. "I can't stop thinking about you." *Kiss.* "Can't stop wanting you." *Kiss.* "You drive me *crazy.*" *Deep, plundering kiss.* "God, Barbara. You're incredible."

"*Theo.*"

"Don't," he growls. "Don't call me that. Not while I'm inside of you. You'll make me come."

"You—" I inhale sharply at another circling of his hips. "You can. We can do it together," I say because I'm already on the precipice again and don't know how much longer I'll be able to last. With a groan, his speed increases, grows more insistent, control pouring out of him. Still, he never loses focus on me—it's so utterly him I could die. "*Theo,* oh my God."

Theo holds both my thighs to his chest, his face in my neck, while I dig my nails into his damp back, holding him tighter to me still. "M'coming. So hard." *A gasp.* "So fucking hard."

Just his words and knowing that being with me made him lose control pushes me over the edge at the last second. I feel the pressure build below again, clenching around him, and I come, biting his shoulder to muffle my cry.

Chapter Twenty-Five

THEO

I'M AN EARLY RISER BY NATURE, WHICH IS WHY I'VE NEVER really felt the need to set alarms in order to wake up on time for anything, really. I'm up every morning at 5 a.m., ready to take on the day, and I honestly really like that about myself. There's a sense of peace that comes from waking up before everyone else. It's like being in a meditative state, or a bubble, where no one and nothing can touch you because most of the world is still asleep.

I love waking up early.

This morning, however, I feel prepared to kill anything and anyone who intends for me to get out of this bed before I absolutely have to. I don't care that the guy from the garage has already called me three times since seven a.m. to talk about my car's repair. And I don't care that we should probably get moving so we can be on time for dress rehearsals before tomorrow night. I'm in bed with a naked Barbara sprawled across my chest, drooling all over me after a night of the best sex I've ever had in my life. And I've never been happier.

There's no way I'm moving from here.

Barbara shifts a little, snuggling closer into me, and my chest constricts, a goofy grin spreading across my face, and I'm taken aback by how much I like her. I tighten my arms around her and kiss her hair, gold and brass in the early morning light.

She sighs softly, something she apparently does, I've discovered, every so often in her sleep. I do my best to control myself, but I can't help running my fingers through her wild, golden hair, which falls naturally over her sexy back.

God, she's so perfect.

I graze my fingers up and down her spine, counting the freckles on her shoulders, her skin so soft beneath my fingertips. I think back to last night, and smirk again. She must be exhausted after everything we did and how many times we did it. I can't blame her for being knocked out cold. If it weren't for the fact that I want to soak up every single perfect moment with her, I would be sleeping now, too. Every muscle in my body aches, and my lips are chapped and swollen from kissing her so much, but my God, I've never felt better.

I'm so fucking giddy, though, I have to actively keep myself from waking her up just to tell her how happy I am that we finally got together, that we can actually have a real relationship now, that I don't have to hide my feelings, because she feels them, too.

Except...

I frown, looking down at her peaceful face.

She never really said she had *feelings* for me, though. She only said she wanted me.

Shit.

My heart starts to race, beating so loudly against my chest I'm scared it will wake Barbara up. Suddenly, it's hard to breathe because I just gave her a huge part of myself, thinking my feelings were being reciprocated, when she never—not once —told me she cares for me like I do her.

Then, I start to wonder...did *I* ever really tell her how I feel? I definitely told her how crazy I am about her, how I can't stop thinking about her...but I don't think that I ever told her once all last night how I actually feel about her. I never told her I have true, deep feelings for her—even if they are fairly new.

What if she thinks this is a one-night stand thing for me? I run my free hand down my face and, before I can help myself, let out a deep groan in frustration, causing her to stir in my arms.

"Shit. I'm sorry. I didn't mean to wake you."

Barbara lifts her face to rest her chin on my chest and groggily blinks up at me, looking slightly disoriented. I can see the realization of what happened last night hit her like a truck as her eyes widen suddenly, and she pulls back slightly. I tense under her stare, waiting for her to say something. Half an hour ago, I would have welcomed her wakefulness with glee, eager to talk to her about last night and make plans for the near future. Now, I just want to go back to that blissful moment in time where she was asleep and I had managed to delude myself into thinking that one night of sex meant she is as into me as I am of her.

"Hey," she says shyly, blushing. She puts her lips to my chest, her eyes never leaving mine. After everything we did together last night, she's still shy?

She's adorable.

"Hey," I chuckle, reaching out to dig my fingers into her maddening hair. "Good morning," I finally say.

She runs her hand up my chest until she's met with her own saliva. "Oh my God, ew! Was that me? I can't believe you let me drool all over you!" She sits up, skin flushing red in embarrassment, wiping the drool off me with her hand. I don't really notice, though, since she's completely uncovered now, and my attention has been dragged elsewhere. To my disappointment, she pulls the comforter up to cover her breasts and admonishes me with a raised eyebrow. "*Theo.*" And there it is—that maddening, sexy way in which she says my name. I used to hate it, but it's so unique to her that I wouldn't want it any other way. It makes me feel like I belong to her.

And in many ways, I'm starting to see that I do. I so fucking do.

"What?" I laugh, trying my hardest not to smile, but I just can't help it.

"I was *drooling* on you, and you didn't stop me."

"It was cute." I shrug, grinning at her. "You were all peaceful and not arguing with me, for once. I didn't want to ruin the moment."

She bites her lip and takes a pillow in her hands, playfully whacking me in the face with it, accidentally dropping the comforter—and ultimately flashing me again.

"Hey!" I complain, wrapping my arms around her (naked) waist and tackling her down against the mattress. I grab both her hands into one of mine and press them above her head while I support myself over her with my other arm. I dip my face and start kissing down her neck to her collarbone. Barbara releases a soft moan next to my ear that I feel shoot straight to my dick, and she arches into me. And I want her again. And again. And again.

I spread her legs with my knee in a practiced movement and settle comfortably in between her legs—a place that, after last night, I'm quite familiar with. I hear her sigh when I swirl my tongue around her nipple, and I swear I've died and gone to heaven.

She's fucking perfect.

All of a sudden, I feel her tense underneath me. "Wait," she pleads, voice all breathy. "Just...wait." Barbara tries to break her hands free from my grip, so I release her immediately, climbing off her, wanting to give her the space she seems to be asking for with her anxious eyes. "We should probably talk about this first." She sits up and puts her face in her hands, hunched over.

"Yeah, no. Last night was..." I blow out a puff of air. "It was incredible, but yeah, we should probably talk about it."

I really don't want to talk about it right now, though. Can we go back to naked time, please?

She looks up into my eyes and gnaws on her lower lip, covering herself with her hands. "Hold on," I say. As much as I'd like to put a pin in this moment and go back to kissing her, I want her to feel comfortable as we address the topic of our relationship. So, I jump out of bed toward the radiator where we left our clothes to dry, and slip on my boxers. They're warm and oddly comforting around my junk, but I don't let that distract me. I consider bringing Barbara her clothes, but I'd much rather see her wearing my black Henley. "Here," I say. "I—So you're more comfortable."

She smiles at me as she takes the warm shirt and pulls it over her head, covering herself with it. My stomach clenches a little at seeing her in bed wearing my shirt. It's kind of caveman-y, but I'm definitely into it, into having something of mine on her. I take a chance and lean forward to release her hair from under the collar of the shirt, letting it fall naturally over her shoulders, down her back. "Beautiful," I say.

"Thanks," she says in a low voice, blushing.

There's a pause while we just look at each other, not saying anything, until she breaks the silence. "I really don't know what to say. Can you start?"

I've never seen her like this. She's usually either a ball of positivity or busting my balls, but never this. I don't want her to be nervous, but I have to admit, I kind of like seeing a more vulnerable side of her.

I take a deep breath and start with the obvious. "Well, I think last night was amazing." She smiles shyly at me, blushing again.

God, she's killing me.

"Yeah, it was," she whispers. "All four times."

I snort. "I think it was more like four and a half. We just kind of collapsed by the fifth time. Not quite six like I promised, but..." We laugh, relieved to know the ice has been cracked, if not broken. "So, it's a given we enjoyed ourselves, and...I'd personally like to enjoy myself more."

Her face falls, looking gutted. "Oh." She frowns. "I... The thing is, Theo... I don't really do the casual thing. I don't know what came over me last night, but...it's not something I do. It was very out of character. So...I guess we want different things."

"Huh?" I frown at her.

"I—I just think it's best if we go back to being friends, you know? I'm not the type of girl to do the whole friends-with-benefits thing."

"Wait, that's not what I was— Barbara..." I shake my head with a little laugh. Does she think I mean she doesn't mean anything to me or something? Did she not understand what I was saying? "Jesus, I suck at this. I'm sorry." I run my fingers through my hair.

Fuck it. I'm laying my cards out on the table. Carpe diem and all that.

"I don't do one-night stands or friends-with-benefits either." I shake my head adamantly. "I think you know by now what type of man I am, Barbara. Casual sex can complicate things, and I wouldn't waste my time—or a part of myself, for that matter—on someone who doesn't mean much to me, someone who I don't care about.

"I don't want a friends-with-benefits thing with you. I want to *be* with you. Like, for real. Not fake dating. Not fake anything."

Shit, was that too intense? That was too intense, wasn't it?

"Oh." She stares back at me, wide-eyed, genuine shock plastered across her face.

"Oh?" Suddenly, my confidence starts to waver. Is this really all one-sided? Am I really that big of a moron?

No. There's no way she doesn't feel anything. Not after yesterday's kiss, and definitely not after last night. It's not all physical. It's not all in my head. It can't be.

Can it?

"You like me, then?" she asks, in a small voice.

"Yes. I, uh... Yes. I very much like you." An understatement, really. *Adore you* would be a more accurate statement. "I couldn't stop thinking about that first kiss, even if it was for the cameras. And then dancing with you at that club, the way you felt... I've never had so much fun dancing," I laugh, surprised at myself. "I've never looked forward to anything in my life the way I look forward to holding you in my arms every day for hours on end. I want to feel *every single part of you* when we dance," I confess, suddenly losing a grip on myself. I dig my fingers into her hair at the nape of her head and press my lips briefly to hers. "It's like...you *consume* me. Every thought I have, every action I take. Everything is about you," I say against the corner of her mouth.

She pulls back slightly to look me in the eye. "I thought you said dancing wasn't supposed to be fun." She smirks, hazel eyes bright.

"I know what I said," I chuckle. "But I was an idiot whose world got turned upside-down by you." She gives me one of her witchy smiles, and I practically shake, doing my best to restrain myself. "And then yesterday... *Fuck*," I groan. "That kiss was just..."

"Epic. It was epic," she says, a hint of a smile. Because it was.

"Yes. *Epic*. Even better than the ones before, and I thought that would be impossible." I laugh, relieved that she seems to agree, and reach out to hold one of her hands. I squeeze it lightly before looking back up at her. "But was it real? Because it was real for me. It's *always* been real for me, even when I didn't realize it. I didn't kiss you for any other reason than because I wanted to, because I felt it. I need to know—please. Are you feeling the same things I'm feeling, or is this thing one-sided?" I realize that I'm practically begging, but I'm too far gone to give a shit at this point.

"I—" She sits up a little, pushing her hair out of her face. She can't seem to look at me. My stomach turns. *Fuck*. "It's...not. One-sided, I mean. It's definitely been real for me, too."

I'm smiling so hard my cheeks hurt. My other hand moves to cup Barbara's jaw, and I lean in to kiss her, and—

"Wait," she says, pressing my hands lightly against my chest, my lips less than half an inch from hers.

I lean back, trying not to crowd her, giving her the space to think. "I'm really sorry. I probably shouldn't have done that." I feel like a complete asshole, just throwing myself at her before we actually figure anything out.

"What? *No*," she says quickly. "It's not that I don't want it. I really, really do. Believe me," she insists, getting up from the bed, walking back and forth in front of it. The hem of my shirt barely covers her cheeks, making it difficult to concentrate—but not impossible. "But—but I don't know if any of this is a good idea, you know? I don't do the whole casual thing—I never have. I don't like it. And if it's something serious you want... I mean, look at me." She waves her hands over her body in a sweeping motion, and I can't help but appreciate it, despite the knowledge that she meant I do it metaphorically. "I can't do serious. I—I'm a fucking mess. I struggle to put one foot in front of the other every day, you know?" My stomach drops, and Barbara turns to face me. I can see the look of disappointment on my face reflected in her eyes. Suddenly, I wish I could take back absolutely everything I said. Maybe things would have been better if I had repressed my feelings. "It's not that I don't...*like* you, that I don't want you. It's that I like you too much," she whispers as if in a confessional. My head snaps up to look her in the eye, my anxiety causing my chest to constrict. "What if we do this and fuck it up and then just ruin our chances at getting Bubbe the care she needs? Or me paying off my debts? What if we realize we actually are way too different and end up going our separate ways? I don't want to lose you. I don't want you out of my life. I've grown accustomed to your grouchiness and making fun of your crazy healthy-eating habits. I really think I'd miss it." I smile softly at her, at her attempt to introduce some levity into this conversation.

She is just so utterly beautiful, with the sun behind her, her messy hair glowing like a sexed-out halo. The fact that her first thought was of my Bubbe and not herself... It's proof I don't deserve her. But that doesn't mean it will stop me from wanting to be with her.

I get out of bed and walk over to Barbara, tentatively taking both her hands in mine. "Barbara," I say, squeezing them lightly, letting her know that I'm here for her. "I think..." An exhale. "I think we can admit that we are both quite different, can we not?"

She nods. "Exactly! That's my point. We're so different. I mean, down to the way in which we talk. Why are you suddenly so formal?"

I smile softly. "Can I finish?" She nods again, grimacing

slightly. "We don't eat the same things—I mean, your diet is truly *appalling*. It's a wonder you don't have heart disease or something. I am *genuinely* afraid for your health." She narrows her eyes at me, and I smirk. "I enjoy discipline, and you're most definitely a free spirit. I prefer to dress in more...*conventional* clothing. And my first impression of your style was that of a six-year-old-girl-trapped-in-a-woman's-body aesthetic. I mean, who wears light-up rain boots?" She rolls her eyes at me. "And that! That right there drives me *insane*. Every time you roll your eyes at me, I want to..." *Kiss you. Fuck you. Spank you.* But I control myself. "You drive me insane, Barbara. In the best and worst ways imaginable. You're all I think about these days. And I'm a coward because I can't seem to build up the courage to kiss you unless there are cameras around or I've had a couple of drinks, afraid that you might not be feeling the same things I'm feeling.

"But I'm done. I can't do this anymore. We've been dancing more than the tango these past couple of weeks, if you know what I mean. We've been dancing around these feelings, too. And I'm tired. Tired of not knowing what's real and what we're doing for the show, for the audience at home."

"But we fight all the time," she whines, her brows pulling together.

"We bicker. It's different." I kiss her hands. "And it makes for amazing foreplay, if I do say so myself."

She almost smiles. "We're like oil and vinegar or water or whatever."

"Which, when beaten together, oil and vinegar make a delicious salad dressing." I smirk.

"What's a salad?" she teases.

I chuckle a little and kiss her forehead but steer us back to our original topic. "Barbara, I need to know once and for all if we're in this together. Do you feel this, too? Do you want this, too?"

A beat that lasts a lifetime.

"Yes," she breathes. "To both."

I smile, sliding my hands into her hair. "That's all I really needed to hear. I can work with the rest." I lean down and kiss her, making the ones we've shared in the past feel like a joke in comparison.

Chapter Twenty-Six

BARBARA

"I'M HERE! I'M HERE!" I SHUFFLE QUICKLY INTO THE dressing room, tossing my bag onto the nearest chair.

Rosie crosses her arms in front of her chest and smirks at me, shaking her head. "Girl, you're late."

"I'm so sorry," I tell Rosie. "I was at an audition, and—" Damn, it feels good to say that. I'm dying, though, so I bend over, hands on my knees, trying to catch my breath. "Wow, you'd think that after weeks of dancing nearly every day, I'd be in better shape than this."

"Sore?" she asks.

I nod and have to bite my lip to keep from smiling like an idiot. Because I'm *definitely* sore—in the best possible way. She doesn't know that, though.

Rosie chuckles and helps me with my coat. "Come on. I have a fitting room prepped for you. Theodore warned me you might be a few minutes behind today."

"*Thank you*," I say. "You look great today, by the way. I'm very into this hot-pink, fifties-housewife-with-cleavage vibe you're rocking right now."

She snorts as she pushes me into the fitting room. "Don't try to butter me up with compliments—even though I know how amazing I look right now, thanks." I laugh but stop short when I see a gorgeous sparkly silver dress hanging from a hook inside the door.

"Change into that. It's a little *on the nose* for your dance—you know, flapper and all that—but damn, it's some of my best work."

I laugh as I strip and toss my clothes in the corner. "Right," I snort. But when I pull the dress over my thighs, feel how it fits perfectly, snuggly over my body, and see the intricate beading, I start to think she's being serious. I put my arms through the sleeves and zip it up before turning toward the mirror.

It really is incredible.

I gasp. I literally gasp. "*Rosie,*" I say, coming out of the fitting room. "This is..." I run my hands over the beaded fringe bodice and skirt. The cut on the top gives the illusion that I have more up there than I actually do, and the different lengths in fringe create an effect that emphasizes my hips—in a good way. The hem is a high-low and makes my legs look incredibly long.

"*Holy shit.*"

We both turn to look at Theo, eyes wide, staring at me, completely slack-jawed. I smirk at the expression on his face until he clears his throat and recovers. "You look beautiful."

"I know, right?" Rosie sighs. "I think it's my masterpiece."

He looks incredible, too, in his tuxedo. The jacket and pants are made from a special breathable material made for dancing, but the suit is still impeccably cut to his body. It's been less than twelve hours since we got back from our adventure in upstate New York, since we last had sex, and I'm dying to have him again.

He's absolutely edible. My new addiction.

"The dress is nice." Theo shrugs, walking over to me, a soft smile on his face. "But I think the woman in it makes it look better—not the other way around. No offense, Rosie."

I melt on the spot because I'm such a sucker for him. I catch a glimpse of my goofy side-grin as he wraps his arms around me from behind, locking his gaze with mine in the mirror. I'm surprised by how easily we've been able to fall into this new thing and how affectionate Theo has turned out to be.

Rosie fake gags behinds us, but I catch her smiling in the reflection. "You guys are disgustingly cute." Hiding his smile in my neck, Theo's navy ocean eyes shine with amusement. "I'm gonna need you to leave, though. I need to finish making final adjustments."

"Absolutely not," he scoffs. "I haven't seen my girlfriend in *hours.* I'm gonna stay right here while you poke and prod her." My skin raises in goosebumps. *Girlfriend.* I know we've been faking it for a couple of weeks, but now that it's real, hearing the term out loud sounds completely insane. He pulls out a chair and takes a seat, a smile on his face.

I watch him while Rosie makes some final adjustments to the dress, and I think about everything it took for us to get here.

"Okay, I'm done," she announces after only ten minutes. "Not a lot of changes to make, actually, so you're good to rehearse in this tonight." She smiles triumphantly, hands on her hips.

"This dress is killer, Rosie. Really." I shake my hips in front of the mirror, watching the fringe move with me.

"I know. I'm the queen of sparkle. You're lucky you're my favorite couple." She laughs. "I'll leave you guys to it, then. Don't have sex in my fitting room, though. You guys have that look about you."

I laugh and turn to Theo but, to my surprise, catch a disappointed expression on his face. "Were you really planning on...*you know*...in the fitting room?" I whisper as he gets up to wrap his arms around me. Theo nips at my lower lip, tugging a little, and it's like a surge of electricity.

"Can you blame me?" He kisses under my ear. "I mean, *look* at you." His hands move to my hips, and he turns me in his arms toward the mirror, pressing his hips into my back. "You look incredible." Theo starts kissing down my neck, arms wrapping around my waist again, and I smirk. "Though, you always look incredible."

He makes me feel...everything.

He kisses down my neck again, completely unconcerned about PDA—very unlike him—and my eyes slide shut. I let him hold me tightly against him since my knees go weak. My breathing gets shallower, and I lean my head back, resting it on his shoulder. I know that if he keeps going, I'm either going to have to rip his clothes off right here, right now, or I will spontaneously combust.

We desperately need to change the topic and distract him.

"Aren't you—" A nibble from him, a gasp from me. I feel a wave of heat start rolling onto me. "Aren't you going to ask how it went today?"

"Mmm?" His hands tighten around me, and I feel him hard behind me. "What?" he asks breathlessly, pushing the beaded sleeve off my shoulder to kiss the skin there. "*God,* you're driving me crazy," he whispers against my skin.

"My audition?" I breathe, trying to pull us out of this lust cloud.

It works perfectly. Theo tenses and releases me from his hold, clearing his throat. "Right. Yeah. How'd it go?" His voice sounds off, so I turn to face him, raising an eyebrow at him. He runs his fingers through his hair, and I see him as he starts to shut down, his eyes staring off somewhere in the distance.

"I got a call-back, actually." I grin proudly up at him.

"That's—that's great." He smiles, albeit a little tightly.

What's up with him? I got the same reaction from him earlier this morning while on the train back into the city (Theo's car is kaput, and repairing it will take weeks). We were cuddled in our seats, talking about nothing and everything at the same time, when my agent called. Turns out, a famous Broadway director had seen my performance on TV and was interested in seeing me later that afternoon. The supporting actress's contract for his musical was about to be up, and they needed someone to take over soon.

I was incredibly excited when my agent called for this once-in-a-lifetime opportunity—but Theo seemed unsettled. The audition was totally last minute and nerve-wracking, but I kicked ass. It bothered me that he didn't seem to share my excitement. At the time, I just chalked it up to sleep deprivation. Now, though? I can tell something's up.

"What's wrong? What's with the face? You don't seem happy for me."

"No, I am," he says much too quickly. "I just—" A heavy sigh. "I don't want to sound like an asshole, but...didn't you say they wanted someone to start rehearsals soon?"

"Yes? So?" I frown, not getting it.

"Well, it's just that I... What about us?" He lowers his voice slightly, looking around to make sure no one overhears us. "What about the show? I thought we were in this together. If you get this part, are you just going to quit the competition?"

I take a step back—I feel like he's pushed me in the chest. "You really think I'd do that? Because if you think that, you're not just questioning my commitment to you, but my professionalism as well. And that's something I take very seriously." My voice is cold, hard, but him questioning my integrity? Unacceptable.

He stares wide-eyed at me for a beat until guilt washes over his face, and he drags both hands down his face with a groan. "I'm sorry, I'm just..."

"An ass?"

"I..." He looks up at me, his brows pulled together. "Yes. A complete ass. You're right."

I exhale and walk toward him, wrapping my arms around his waist. Theo hugs me tightly and presses his forehead against mine. "I would never do anything like that, Theo."

"I know that. I'm an idiot for even thinking that you—" He sighs. I roll my eyes at him, and a corner of his mouth quirks up, embarrassed. "I've never felt this way before and—" he groans. "I just don't want to lose you."

"I don't know where your abandonment issues stem from," I say, my tone light, "but you need to build a bridge and get over them."

"Maybe because I'm an orphan?" He raises an eyebrow at me like I'm crazy, but there's a hint of a smile tugging at his lips.

"Yes, but your parents didn't leave you by choice, Theo. From what I've heard from you and Bubbe, they loved you very much." For a second, his jaw tightens and his eyes flash with some unnamed emotion. I put my hand against his cheek, and he leans into me, his eyes sad. "Plus, when they were gone, Bubbe stepped up and took care of you. So, you're not allowed to be insecure. You are lovable, and incredible, and I'm not gonna bail." I cup his face and smoosh his cheeks together, trying to lighten the mood. "I'm the one who should have the abandonment issues—duh." I jokingly roll my eyes. "My parents barely even acknowledge my existence."

He takes my wrists in his hands and wraps my arms around him. He kisses me hard, claiming. "You're *much* stronger than me."

I free my hands from his grip and run them up his back and into his hair until I bring his face back down to mine for one of his deep kisses. I pull back before I forget to ask him something incredibly important.

"Would you like to spend Easter with me? I'm not particularly religious, but my friend Liza's family is, and their Easters are always amazing. I don't think I've missed one since I was twelve." I laugh. "The food is great, and they're all incredible people. They're the closest thing I have to family, and I know they're dying to meet you. Would you..." I swallow hard. "Would you like to come? No cameras this time? Just us? They'll probably be an Easter egg hunt, too, if that appeals to you in any way."

He smiles his heartbreaking smile—the one that used to be so rare, the one I've gotten to see more in the past twenty-four hours than I have in the five weeks I've known him. "I'd love to meet your family." And Liza *is* my family—or the closest thing to it.

We kiss until I feel lightheaded, my knees weak, brain foggy. His breathing is heavy, and he looks at me like I'm the juiciest burger he's ever seen—or I guess, in his case, the tastiest kale salad?

"You are so beautiful," he says, pressing his forehead to mine again. I push him away, needing the distance to get some air, breathe. It's something I seem to struggle with around him. He groans in frustration and I laugh, kissing him on the cheek.

I turn to look in the mirror and shake a little in front of it, the overhead lighting reflecting off the beaded fringe, throwing rainbows everywhere.

"Come here." I wave him over. "Let's do a boomerang and post it. Like a sneak preview of our outfits for tomorrow and stuff."

He sighs dramatically. "I hate this social media shit."

"Just come here." I pull him by the hand. "Give me your phone. You can post it on your account."

"What an honor, thanks. I love it when you make me do this," he deadpans, and I elbow him playfully in the side. "How do you do this again?" I give him a tutorial and a kiss on the cheek, and we stand in front of the mirror. I decide on a twirl to highlight the beaded fringe, whereas Theo just refuses to do anything but smile and hold the record button (which, honestly, is progress). When I'm done spinning for the camera, though, my vision blurs, and I feel the all-too-familiar cold current run through my head. I lose my balance, but I feel someone catch me —Theo. We fall to the ground, and I sit on the floor, using the wall as a backrest.

I try to look up at him, but I can't make my eyes focus or understand what he's saying. My hands move up to my head, and I squeeze my eyes shut, praying to God the aura passes, and it's not followed by a seizure.

"Barbara? *Barbara?*" His anxious voice finally breaks through the fog, distant. I want to reply, ask him to let me ride it out—that it'll pass—but I can't seem to make the words come out of my mouth. I focus on my breathing, on calming down. I think he reads my mind, though, because Theo pulls me into his arms and holds me to his chest.

When I feel better, more stable, I open my eyes and lean my head against his shoulder. "Sorry," I whisper.

"Don't. What was that?" he asks, his voice tight.

"I—I had an aura. It's like a foreshadowing of a seizure." Theo tenses and slides his hands behind my knees, making to scoop me up. "No! Please don't move me," I beg.

"I need to take you home—or to a doctor."

"I don't need a doctor. I just—" I take a deep breath, trying to settle myself. "I just need to sit here a little bit and rest." I burrow my face into his neck, inhaling his scent, letting it reach every corner of my body.

He stretches out his legs underneath us, getting more

comfortable. After a few minutes, he asks, "What brought this on?"

"Probably sleep-deprivation. It's one of my triggers, and we had a long night last night." I try my best to smirk at him, but I'm weak. I can't play it off like I want to.

"Are you serious? Why didn't you tell me?" He's upset, angry.

"I was too distracted by all the sex," I chuckle, closing my eyes, burrowing against him again.

"That's not funny. You need to take care of yourself. And I need to know these things so I can take care of you, too!"

I frown. "Theo, it's not your responsibility to take care of me."

"I know it's not, but I want to take care of you. At least the basics. *Jesus!* I—I need to know the things that trigger your seizures."

Not having the energy to argue with him right now, I turn my face into his shoulder and kiss him through his shirt. He cups my chin and brings it up to him, ducking to kiss me—

"Practicing for the cameras?" We turn to look at a smirking Nico, staring down at us on the floor, leaning against the doorway.

"I don't know what you're talking about," Theo says through gritted teeth.

Nico snorts and nods. "Right. It's just a coincidence, then, that after all these years of keeping your private life private, you suddenly have a very public relationship the same year the network started looking for someone to replace one of the judges."

"Going public comes with the territory when you're dating a celebrity." Theo shrugs nonchalantly.

"Celebrity," Nico scoffs. "Right. Sure. People barely know who Barbara is. She's just another washed-up actress."

Theo's arms tighten, and he makes to get up, but I start laughing. "I think you're right. Barely anyone remembers me anymore. But you know what?" I shakily get to my feet and walk over to him, keeping a hand in Theo's for support. "They'll sure as hell remember my name when we wipe the floor with you and win this entire competition."

Nico laughs once and turns on his heel back from wherever the hell he came from.

"Ugh! I hate that guy."

"That was incredible. You're incredible." Theo shakes his head at me in wonder. He kisses me lightly on the lips and takes both my hands in his. "Let me take you home. You need sleep."

"What about rehearsal? We haven't practiced yet."

He shrugs like it's nothing. "We can probably do it tomorrow before the show. I'll tell Rob there were extenuating circumstances. I'm sure he'll give me permission."

"Seriously?"

"We've got this in the bag, babe."

Chapter Twenty-Seven

THEO

Barbara fidgets with her low bun, tugging at it a little from side to side.

"What are you doing?" I ask curiously. Leave it to her to try and ruin her hair two minutes before we have to perform.

"This bun—ugh! It's so uncomfortable. It's like they added ten pounds of hairspray and a million bobby pins to keep it absolutely immobile. And it *hurts*."

I frown, a pang of guilt in my stomach. "That's my fault. I asked them to make sure your hair didn't move around while we dance."

She looks at me like I've completely gone insane, which, to her credit, isn't far off. "Your hair, it...it was *distracting* me. I couldn't focus well enough when we'd dance. So, I asked the hair and makeup team to help out."

"It was *distracting* you?" She quirks an eyebrow at me, struggling not to laugh.

"It smells really good," I mumble, feeling my cheeks heat. "And it's shiny, and I couldn't focus."

She bursts out in laughter, and I swear it's the most incredible thing I've heard in the past twenty-four hours. I've been so worried about her, making sure that she's well-rested after last night's ordeal, that nothing else has mattered, really.

"That's kind of creepy, Theo." She smiles at me.

"A little," I say, pulling her into my arms, kissing her neck, inhaling her. "See? Now you just smell like hairspray and less like yourself. I can focus on the dance and not on how amazing you feel or how seductive your scent is."

Barbara snorts, but she wraps her arms tightly around me. "My scent? You sound like a vampire."

"Aren't girls supposed to be into all that vampire-romance stuff?" I ask, playfully biting her neck. She squeals a little, but I know she enjoyed it.

Barbara laughs, a little breathlessly, as her fingers dig into my hair. I don't even care if she messes it up. I can barely keep my hands off of her enough to notice.

"*Ahem.*" We turn to see Lawrence, Rob's PA, tapping on his clipboard. Barbara pushes me off her, but I bring her back into my side. I've never been one for public displays of affection, but I can't help it with her. I feel like it's never enough. "You're on in forty-five seconds, guys," he says before walking away.

I release a heavy sigh, because I'd much rather be in bed with my girlfriend right now, taking care of her, than performing in front of millions of people and getting judged for it. "Are you sure you're okay to perform?"

"For the millionth time, *yes*. I told you. I'm still a little tired, but I'm okay. Nothing happened yesterday. It was just a small aura. A seizure would have been a completely different story, okay?"

"Fine," I grunt, and we start walking toward the stage. "But if we make it through next week, we're taking the next few days off for you to rest. I don't give a damn whether we win or lose."

She smiles at me, pressing her palm against my cheek. "You do care, but it's sweet of you to say just the same."

I roll my eyes at her, and we take our places on the dark stage.

THE MUSIC STARTS, AND BARBARA AND I START TO KILL OUR routine. Normally, I'm not a fan of the jive. Between all the kicking and flipping, it can be quite messy with the wrong partner. With the right one, though... I only recently realized that it can be a blast.

Our routine is mostly face to face, so I get the chance to see her bright smile as we dance, but we do have quite a lot of side-to-side choreography as well. I turn to look at Barbara and see her dress sparkle with every move she makes—every controlled kick, flip, and turn. I can't hold her close to me during this dance or run my hands down her body in a way that I now know drives her crazy, but I love how much fun she's having. Barbara looks luminous—her eyes bright, cheeks red and glowing—like she never felt weak or sick to begin with. She's such a pro performer in everything that she does, and I respect her so much for it.

We're about four counts from the big finale when strobe lights come on, which I find odd since we didn't have them during dress rehearsal this morning. I don't think much of it until Barbara slips after a slight jump and falls. I quickly pick her up, and we recover ourselves, but I find that her eyes are closed.

"Keep going," she says, the music so loud only I can hear her.

Through a fake smile, I ask her, "What's wrong?"

"Strobes are triggers. Just a few more seconds." Her eyes are squeezed shut tight, and I can't fucking believe we're still doing the routine (barely), that she's pushing herself like this, and that she's doing it blind. I can't stand it any longer and stop the dance just one beat short of the music ending.

The last half-minute of our dance is going to hurt our scores, that's for sure, but I honestly could not care less at this point.

The stage lights turn down on the dance floor, and Barbara collapses in my arms. I catch her just in time, but her head lolls backward, and she goes limp.

"Barbara!" I shake her a little. "Wake up!" She mumbles something about being awake, asking to take her away. I swing her into my arms and practically run backstage as I hear Troy's voice over the speakers, telling the audience at home that the show would be back with our judgment and scores after a commercial break.

Screw that. I have only one focus now, and that's to get her to a safe space and make sure she's okay.

Followed by a team of producers and assistants, I run to the nearest chair I can find and settle Barbara there. Taking her face in both my hands, I nervously search her face, slapping her cheeks (very) lightly, trying to get her to open her eyes.

"M' fine," she mumbles.

I scoff. "Yes, totally fine. You only just passed out onstage."

"Didn't *pass out*." She slaps my hand away with as much force as she can muster. "Strobes. Really bad aura. Trigger for seizures." She sighs and leans her head back as if saying those seven words took enough energy out of her to knock her unconscious.

I feel a PA hovering uncomfortably close to me and feel the fire burning in my chest. "Why don't you do something useful with your time and go find a doctor, huh?" I snap, practically growling at him.

Barbara makes a sound—a weak laugh?—and smiles softly as the PA scurries off. "Grump."

I pick up both her hands and put them to my lips.

"What happened?" I hear Rob's voice as he runs up behind me.

"She got sick. The strobes... They—" I stop short and remember what Barbara had told me about not wanting people to find out about her condition. I don't know how to proceed here. "They made her dizzy. And she hasn't been feeling well these past couple of days. The combination of the two..."

Rob places his hands on his hips and stares down at Barbara's nearly unconscious body. "Right." He nods. "But here's the thing. We need you guys for judging. We're about to go live again in about a minute, so..."

I stand to my feet and glare at him. "You've got to be fucking kidding me. Are you serious? *Look* at her. What part of that makes you believe she's capable of standing in front of judges, getting critiqued, while millions of people watch?"

Rob chews on the inside of his cheek for a minute, considering his options. "Then, you'll just have to do it alone."

I scoff. "I'm not leaving her." There's no way.

"This isn't a request, Theodore." He glares at me. This right here is why it's problematic to become friends with your coworkers. There's always the chance of an ugly power struggle. "Someone needs to stand there to receive the critiques and scores from the judges. Obviously, she can't do it, so you will."

"What about Barbara?" I ask through gritted teeth.

"I'll make sure the doctor on site sees her. She can rest here."

"Go. I'll be fine," Barbara says weakly, her eyes still closed.

It tears me up to leave her, but I do this for her because I know she needs this in the end. And I would have wanted her to do the same if the situation were reversed.

"*Aaaand we're back!*" Troy says to the audience at home. "Unfortunately, we've just been notified that Barbara Holt is not feeling too well at the moment. For this reason, Theodore Wallace, her dance partner, will represent them both during judging." He turns to look at me with the fakest smile plastered across his face. "Are you ready, Theodore?"

This guy is the worst.

"Yes," I grunt.

"*Oooh*, feeling taciturn, are we? Ha ha," he fake laughs. "All right, let's get right to it and start off our judging with Bex. Bex?"

"Wow, Theodore." She flips her red hair over her shoulder. "I just want to say that you and Barbara have made me so happy. Every week, your routines continue to get better and better. It's a true sign that you're communicating, and I'm sure being in love doesn't hurt the matter either." She winks at me and smiles.

Love?

I feel my eyes widen in realization.

"Everything seemed to be going great until she slipped. Was that when she first started feeling sick?" Bex asks, genuine concern on her face.

"Actually, she's been feeling sick with a...*stomach bug* for the past couple of days. She was feeling better but then almost collapsed in my arms..." My voice trails off, and I look down at my hands.

"I'm so sorry to hear that. Hopefully she recovers quickly. She's a pleasure to watch perform."

"Thanks." I smile genuinely. She really *is* amazing.

"Let's turn to Hugh Davies and see what he has to say about

your routine!" Troy wraps an arm around my shoulders as if we're best buddies and pulls me in. I shake him off.

"Theodore. When you next see your lovely girlfriend, I want you to kiss her deeply, because recovering after a fall like that while ill is not as easy as she made it look. Despite her situation, you both managed to present an entertaining and beautiful jive. I must say, I tip my hat to Miss Holt's resilience if, in fact, she's been ill for some time."

The crowd starts to clap, and my chest swells with pride. I love knowing that other people see her the way I do—dedicated to her craft, hardworking. I can't believe I ever thought she would be a spoiled former child actor with no work ethic, when she's the one who could easily teach me a lesson on resilience and hard work.

When the crowd dies down, Troy announces Cora and requests her comments on the dance. I tense and try to mentally prepare myself for whatever crap she's about to spout. Excluding our first one, every single one of our performances have been near-perfect, and yet she still manages to tear them down. I know she's not going to go easy on us this time around.

"I can't believe what I'm hearing from you, Hugh," she says in that thick French accent of hers. "You're excusing a poor performance—not even a mediocre one—and setting a horrible precedent on this show. What? The next time someone's performance isn't up to par, they're just going to blame it on a fake illness and ask us for leniency?"

The judges blanche at her comment, and I grit my teeth so hard I can actually hear them rubbing together, even over the crowd.

Cora leans forward in her seat and stares at me straight in the eye. "When I was a professional dancer, *I* was always able to deliver an amazing performance every single time—even when I was sick. Not like your Barbara."

I lose it. Something in me snaps, and I just lose it. I'm sick and fucking tired of this woman talking like that about Barbara, and I'm not gonna take it anymore.

"To be fair, Cora, being hungover, drunk, or high isn't the same thing as being sick. Just to clarify the differences between you and Barbara."

The crowd gasps and *ooohs,* and I can even hear an, "Oh, snap," in the background.

Cora's nostrils flare, and her eyes widen in rage. I realize I might have just lost my job, but I'm done with this bullshit. Not really caring about that or the fact that we're on live television, I turn on my heel and walk offstage to go check on my girlfriend.

Chapter Twenty-Eight

BARBARA

"Where is she?" I hear his voice through the fog and struggle to open my eyes. "Where the hell is she?" He sounds panicked. But more than that, he sounds *pissed*.

"We helped move her to Bex's dressing room," I hear Rosie's concerned voice from outside the door. "She has a couch where we thought she could rest for a bit." The door swings open, and Theo comes to kneel beside me.

"Hey," he says softly, his voice a contrast to how he was barking at people around him not fifteen seconds ago. "How are you feeling?"

"Tired," I say. "Dizzy and weird. My brain feels mushy. What happened with the judging?"

"Don't worry about it. Let's take you home." He helps me sit up and swings me easily back into his arms again. He makes it seem easy, as if I weighed five pounds. When we turn for the door, however, we realize Rob is blocking our exit.

"What the fuck, Theodore? Do you want to get fired? I can't keep defending your ass, man."

"Get out of my way, Rob," Theo says, his voice venomous. I

stare up at him but am only able to see his jaw lock in tension. If I'm being honest, I'm half-scared, half-turned on by his alpha-male behavior right now.

"You can't just insult a judge and expect there not to be any repercussions, Theodore. We need to talk about this." He insulted a judge? What the hell is he talking about? Theo would *never* do that. He's so poised and controlled.

"Rosie, do you know where Barbara's bag is? We need to head out, and she needs her stuff." I can tell he's having to restrain the tone of his voice.

"Yes, I'll run and get it now. I saw it in the dancers' dressing rooms." I hear her dash out of the room.

Theo readjusts me in his arms—seriously, how strong is this guy?

"*Theodore.*" There's a serious warning in Rob's voice. "This is truly unacceptable, and you know it. I don't know what the hell you were thinking, but this just isn't something we can gloss over. The network isn't happy. *I'm* not happy."

Theo manages to settle himself with a deep breath. "I know, okay? But I have more important things on my list of priorities right now. We can talk tomorrow. I promise."

Rob frowns at Theo and looks down at me. "You feeling better?" he asks as if suddenly realizing I'm there.

"No," I answer simply because it's the truth.

Rob opens his mouth to say something but is interrupted by Rosie's arrival. "Here. I also brought your coat and hers. I couldn't find either of your clothes, though."

"It's fine," he replies. "Can you walk with us while we get a cab? I can't carry her and that stuff at the same time."

"I can walk," I say.

"Sure, I can manage to slip out." They both ignore me. Theo holds me tighter as we walk past a frowning Rob.

"Tomorrow, Theodore! I want you in my office tomorrow at nine a.m. Or else."

"We're here," Theo says in my ear, softly pressing a kiss to my temple. I open my eyes and look out the Uber window.

"This is not my hotel." I look around the neighborhood, feeling completely disoriented. "This is actually not Manhattan. Did you bring me to a secret location to harvest my organs?"

He rolls his eyes as he steps out of the car, walking around it to open my door. "You have a weird obsession with true crime. It's disturbing. Is it, like, a fetish of yours? Because I can tell you now that I'm not into that, nor will I ever be. I'm also starting to think that this is more than an unhealthy obsession. Should I be worried that *you're* going to end up killing *me*?"

I snort and let him help me out of the car, wrapping an arm around my waist. "Come on. Of the two of us, I'm pretty sure you're more likely to commit murder than I am."

Leaning down to pick up my bag, he laughs and says good-night to the driver before slamming the door shut. "Jesus, this bag. You know what it makes me think of? You know in *Harry Potter* where Hermione has that bag that's spelled to look small but actually contains, like, a tent and food and books and stuff? That's what your bag is. It's full of just random stuff." I stare up at him, open-mouthed. Did he just use a *Harry Potter* reference? I think my uterus just freaked out a little. "What was it called?" He snaps his fingers a couple of times, frowning. "Ah! Undetectable Extension Charm. That's what it was."

He knows the names of the charms? Is he a book or movie fan? Both?

Holy shit. This is vital information, but a topic for another time.

"Is it weird that I'm suddenly really turned on by you? If I weren't really weak right now, I'd jump your bones. Wait, no. I still want to jump your bones." He snorts and walks us to the entrance of a two-story brownstone, pulling out some keys.

He snorts. "Nice to know my knowledge of Harry Potter trivia is a turn-on."

"Oh, yeah. Big time." I sigh. "Where are we, by the way?"

"Astoria. My place. Your hotel room is paid for by the network, so they know where you live, and I honestly don't trust them enough to not let you rest after what happened tonight. So, I brought you here to give you some space from them."

"To Queens?"

"I told you I hated Manhattan. Astoria is more chill. Plus, real estate is much more affordable here." Theo unlocks the door and pushes it open with his hip.

"It's...nice," I say, looking around at his place, absolutely fascinated.

"Nice?" He raises an eyebrow, amused. "Oh, wow. You hate it." He laughs awkwardly and takes off his coat.

"No, no! I really like it. I promise." I walk deeper into the living room—wood floors and exposed brick on three walls—my heart constricting, for some reason. The brown leather couch looks worn and well-loved but like it still has decades of good use in it. I'd bet my life that the cream cable-knit blanket atop the arm was handmade by Bubbe, and that the accent chair in the corner by the fireplace (*a fireplace!*) is one of a kind. I can absolutely see him sitting there at night, maybe with a book.

The two trunks pressed together that double as a coffee table look like they were actually used at one point in time for their original purpose and are not just something he picked up in a flea market in Brooklyn because he thought they would look cool. As my eyes travel through it, taking it all in, my suspicions are confirmed when I see '*T. Wallace*' written in black marker on the lower right corner in a child's handwriting. In a world full of phonies, I can happily say with absolute certainty that Theodore Wallace is a genuine guy.

I scan the room for other details, and though I can't see properly in the dim light from far away, I'm pretty sure I spot actual tchotchkes and pictures on the mantel. I make it my mission to examine those further tomorrow morning. Tchotchkes say so much about a person...

Everything about his living room makes me happy, gives me further insight into the type of guy Theo is and who he isn't. I don't know what I expected exactly—maybe an all-white apartment with modern furniture and barren walls, clean lines and zero personal touches. But I remind myself that Theo has surprised me at every corner, knocking down every single preconceived notion in my head of who I thought he was when I first met him. "I just expected something different. Don't take this the wrong way, but...I kind of thought your place would be cold. Whereas this is so..."—I sigh happily—"*cozy.*"

He quirks an eyebrow at me. "Cold? Is that what you think of me?"

I stare into his eyes, inky blue, and shake my head. "No. Not anymore," I say softly.

We stare at each other for a beat, neither of us saying anything. Eventually, he sticks out his hand and pulls me closer, pushing my coat off my shoulders and hanging it on a hook by the door next to his.

"Can you make it upstairs?" he asks, cupping my face, kissing me on the forehead. "I can carry you again, if you'd like." His voice is gentle, warm.

"Nah, I've got it. I can use the handrail."

My head is on his chest, his arm around me, as we binge *Phantom Fighters*. Theo thought it would be hilarious to download all of the first season and watch sixteen-year-old me act in the role that made me (briefly) famous. I have to admit, it *is* pretty entertaining to watch a bunch of teenagers fight demons and ghosts—especially when the CGI is terrible.

"What's up with the outfits?" he asks in a low voice in one episode. "Is that how girls used to dress back then? Layered tops, leggings under jean skirts, and furry boots? I don't remember that."

"Yes, unfortunately. But the true torture was how many hair extensions they'd make us wear on the show. I'm sure normal girls didn't have pounds and pounds of someone else's hair glued to their skull. It gave me the worst headaches. I hated it."

Theo snorts at a funny scene I'm in, where I trip and fall headfirst into a cake. "That looks like fun."

"It was! I loved working on that show. I used to have so much fun—at first, at least."

"What happened?" he asks, popping a peanut M&M into my mouth. He's been feeding me food all night, and it absolutely thrills me.

"You know," I say, avoiding his question, crunching on the chocolate. "I'm like a cat. If you keep feeding me like this, I'm gonna keep coming back. You're never gonna be able to get rid of me."

He smiles down and kisses me on the nose. "Ah, but see, I don't *want* to get rid of you. My plan is to lure you in with this poison, get you to keep coming back, and then pull a bait-and-switch and start popping carrot sticks in your mouth instead."

"Ew." I make a face and push off him, but he wraps his arms around my chest and pulls me back down again with a laugh.

"I want you around for a long time, Barbara." He takes a deep breath, as if inhaling my hair. "You'll see. I'll get you to start liking green juice soon enough." I fake gag but smile against his chest at his concern.

"Peanut M&Ms make me happy. And I compromised tonight. I let you swap out regular potato chips for Veggie Sticks." I look down at the green bag and grimace, though I have to admit they really aren't that bad—semi-tasteless crunchy puff sticks that pretend to be healthier than other snack foods.

Theo scoffs and shakes his head, giving up, I think. For a second, I think I've succeeded in sidetracking him, but he seems to remember his original question. Realizing I never answered, he tears his eyes from the TV and looks down at me with those intense eyes. "Why'd you quit acting?"

I shrug and reach for the Veggie Sticks. "A multitude of reasons..." When it looks like he's not going to let it go, I roll my eyes and go for it. "I first started getting seizures while filming the last season of *Phantom Fighters,* and it was an absolute nightmare. After I was diagnosed, I went through a trial-and-error process with my meds and was foggy, had memory problems, and my hair was falling out. I felt like absolute crap *all the time.* They had to keep rescheduling shoots because I would take sick days, and the producers started saying I was difficult to work with. On top of that, they were also pissed because I didn't have that *look* anymore—I wasn't a size zero. The meds...they made me gain at least twenty pounds in just a few months, and I... well, I didn't look like the type of girl they wanted on their TV show anymore. But of course they would never admit to that.

"When the show ended, I decided to take a break from

acting—at least until I managed to stabilize my seizures and stuff. But by the time I was ready to go back to work, I had lost momentum in my career, and my poor performance on the show that final year gave me a really bad reputation in the industry. No one knew it was because I was struggling with my health, so they just assumed I was this spoiled actress who didn't want to work. Sound familiar?" I lift an eyebrow at Theo, and guilt washes over his face.

I catch my breath and continue. "Eventually, I realized three things. First, I *hated* the fame aspect of acting. I really did. I enjoyed acting itself and the independence it gave me, but I did not like being in the tabloids or anything—especially when articles with false information are spread worldwide.

"Second, I was told that, given the cult following my show had, I was pretty much set for life financially—if I was smart about it. Though—spoiler alert—I wasn't, because I trusted the wrong man and lost all my money.

"And third, I tried out Broadway and loved it a million times more. So, I put whatever energy and focus I had into pursuing a career there. But it's tough and competitive—more so than Hollywood, I think—and I was very picky about roles because I had the luxury to be at the time."

"You should still be picky about roles. You're incredibly talented and have an amazing work ethic. I think you owe it to yourself to find the right roles for you and not just whatever you can get." His eyes are earnest, intense. "I'm sorry I was just another asshole who judged you before I had even met you," he says after a beat.

"It happens." I shrug. I'd already forgiven him without him even saying it, but it feels great to hear just the same. "I did the same to you."

He chews the inside of his cheek. "What about your parents?"

"What about them?"

"Did they at least help you when you were first diagnosed?"

I snort and chuckle. "Sorry, that was just hilarious to hear. No, they did not help out. I was no longer their responsibility, to *everyone's* relief. When I told them about it, they just said how unfortunate it was and sent me a *get well soon* gift card for ten dollars." I scoff. "Whatever. The gift card could have been for a million and I still wouldn't have cared. All I wanted was emotional support." I feel stinging behind my eyes, and I squeeze them shut. I don't like admitting to anyone just how much my relationship with my parents hurts. Luckily, I have other people in my life who help fill certain holes they've left. "My best friend's brother was doing his residency back then, specializing in neuro, and he was a huge help. Her entire family was."

"That was nice of them."

"Yes, it was." I snuggle closer into him as we watch my co-stars and me fight a ghost on TV.

Talking about my parents with him makes me wonder about his. I know they passed away, and he ended up living with his grandmother, but what exactly happened? Am I even allowed to ask? I figure if we're going to have a relationship, this is the type of stuff we'll have to talk about, right? The hard stuff? It's not just sex and mushiness?

"What happened to your parents?"

Theo shifts a little under me. He's quiet for so long I start to wonder whether he actually heard me. After a minute, though, he says, "Overdose, I think. Both of them." His voice is low and tight. "Dad was a doctor, and...well, he had a lot of access to pills. And both my parents seemed to enjoy the privilege. One night..." He takes a deep breath, steeling himself. "One night, they were out with their friends, and...I guess they enjoyed themselves a bit too much, and...I don't know. I guess...I *think* my dad passed out at the wheel or something and then ended up wrapping his car around a tree trunk that night, killing them both." He takes a deep breath. "Even as young as I was, I already suspected it. And then one day, I kind of overheard a conversation between my grandmother and a friend a couple of years later that confirmed it."

"Holy shit." My jaw drops.

Now I get the abandonment issues. And why he's such a health nut.

"Bubbe lied to me. Said it was a drunk driver." He scoffs. "I was eleven at the time, but I wasn't blind. I didn't know *exactly* what was going on, but there had been other situations in which they'd just...where they were at home and stuff, but they were *gone*, you know?"

I want to cry for him. I do. "I'm so, so sorry, Theo. I—I shouldn't have asked. I'm sorry."

He looks down at me with a frown. "No. It's important you know. I just...obviously don't love talking about it. I haven't really told many people about what happened. I don't even think Rob knows the details, to be honest." He runs the fingers of his free hand through his hair and stares up at the ceiling.

"I get the anger now. I mean, I would have understood no matter how you lost your parents, but I get why you were an angry kid. Your parents died. They lied to you about how they died. And you had to move in with your grandmother."

One side of his mouth lifts up in a sad attempt to smile. "I also had to move from a big city to the middle of nowhere. That was a big change."

"What?" I sit up a little.

"I'm actually from Boston." He smiles. "South Boston."

"You are?" I breathe. I don't know why I find this piece of information fascinating, but it's just another grain of sand in what makes Theo, and I love it.

He chuckles. "Yeah. Big Red Sox fan, too." He sighs.

I cluck my tongue at him and shake my head. "I can't believe a Red Sox man would move to Yankees territory."

He groans, laughing a little. "I know, right?" I burrow closer into his chest and kiss it.

"You don't have an accent, though."

"I was young when I moved, but I definitely pick it up quickly whenever I visit. I'll probably have to move there after I get fired tomorrow. Go back to speaking like someone straight out of *The Departed*." A sigh. "I seriously just threw my career down the toilet tonight." He sighs. "But I wouldn't take it back. I'm so over Cora and her bullying you, even though I'll never work again." He sighs deeply.

I laugh like it's the most ridiculous thing I've ever heard. "They're not going to fire you, Theo."

He looks into my eyes as if I've gone insane. "Barbara. I called one of the judges out on being a drunk and a drug user on live television. There is absolutely no way I'm going to keep my job."

"Don't worry, Theo." I take a deep breath and inhale his scent. "I've got it taken care of."

He snorts and kisses me on the head. "You should rest. Sleep." He turns off the lamp on the bedside table and lowers the volume on the TV. I close my eyes and burrow myself into him, closer still, wanting to become a permanent part of him.

"Theo?" I whisper.

"Yeah."

"Can you say, '*Pahk the cah in Hahvahd yahd,*' in a Boston accent, please?"

He bursts out laughing and kisses my temple. "No, but if you go to sleep right now, I'll tell you just how *wicked smaht* you are."

Chapter Twenty-Nine

THEO

I leave Barbara sleeping in my bed—one of the most difficult things I've ever had to do in my life—and go into the network's building early the next morning.

My meeting with Rob is soon, and I've come armed with coffee and a donut.

Barbara has taught me that little things like bringing someone food can make difficult conversations easier—at least that's how it works with her. Evidence has shown me that a quick way to her heart—or at least a quick way to appeasing her —is through her stomach. When I see the expression on Rob's face as he makes his way down the hallway toward me and his office, I pray to God they think similarly.

"Hello, friend." I smile.

"Don't," he narrows his eyes at me, taking the coffee and paper bag from my hand before unlocking his office door. He pushes it open and leads the way, dropping the food on his desk as he removes his bag and coat. "I don't even know what to say to you right now." Rob motions for me to take a seat, and I do. I realize there's no room for jokes today.

We sit quietly for a moment while Rob *glares* at me and I eye him cautiously. I know what the most likely outcome of this meeting will be, and I'm prepared for it. I'm prepared for the pink slip, for the kick in the ass out the door.

"What the hell happened last night, man? I've never seen you lose your cool like that. Have I ever seen you be a dick? Absolutely. But I would've never thought it possible for you to act that way on live television. And with a judge, no less. You're much more professional than that."

I sigh and put my head in my hands. "I know, okay? I don't know what came over me. I just— No. You know what? I *do* know what came over me. I was stressed because Barbara wasn't well, and you forced me to leave her without knowing whether she was okay or not, and then I had fucking Cora talking about how unprofessional Barbara was, and I just... *Ugh.* I couldn't take it, man. Cora's been rubbing me the wrong way all season long."

I hear Rob slurp his coffee (an irritating sound that makes me want to strangle him). "Yeah, she's definitely had it out for you from the beginning of the season, which is weird because she's never been like that. She's known for flirting with all you male dancers during judging. Maybe she feels threatened because you're one of the people that might be taking her spot?"

My head snaps up. "*She's* the one retiring? I kind of assumed Hugh would be the one. Cora doesn't strike me as the type to want to slow down or step out of the spotlight."

Rob grimaces slightly. "She's not voluntarily slowing down. The network may have *suggested* she retire and not renew her contract, if you know what I mean. The only choice we gave her was to control the narrative—either the press finds out we're not renewing her contract because we don't want her anymore, or she can say it's because she wants to take some *indefinite* time off." He shrugs.

"Of course she's going to resent anyone who goes after her job. She—wait." I think back to the other teams' performances and their results. No one has gotten near as much crap from her as we have. "Hold on. If that were the case, she'd be up everyone else's ass too. But she's been handing out eights and nines to everyone left and right. Nico and his partner even got a ten last night."

Rob pulls out the donut from the bag and takes a huge bite. "Regardless," he says, mouth ridiculously full, donut crumbs falling on his desk. "You insulted a judge who threatened to walk out if we don't fire you. Obviously, because she's already *leaving*, it didn't exactly terrify us, you know?"

"Wait, so I'm not fired?" I'm so confused.

"No, you're not. But make no mistake, you were absolutely going to be. I even pushed for it, if we're being honest. I *know* you know you deserve it. You might be my friend, but your behavior out there last night was completely unacceptable, and you know it."

He's not wrong.

"I'm...confused. How am I still here?" What the hell is happening?

"Besides the fact that you and Barbara were ahead by a fairly large margin in terms of viewers' votes, it turns out your fake girlfriend—or is she your real girlfriend now? I can't tell with you lately—is threatening to sue the network for breach of contract."

"*What?*" Barbara is not the litigious type. Not after all the legal battles she's been through this past year. No way. I'm sure that just the thought of entering into any type of legal battle right now would bring on a panic attack or something.

"I find that extremely difficult to believe," I say.

"Did you know she has epilepsy?" Rob asks, and I nod hesitantly, not sure whether she would be okay with me confirming it to someone else. "Well, it turns out that, because of that, her contract specifically states there cannot be any strobe lights while she is performing onstage. Apparently, they can trigger seizures in people with these types of disorders, and...well. She has cause and a strong case, given the fact that she almost had one, and there are several witnesses there that can confirm it."

"I don't understand. What does me getting fired have anything to do with the fact that she wants to sue the network for breach of contract over strobe lights?"

Rob stares at me like I'm the densest person in the entire universe. "What do you think, you idiot? It's because of *you* that she wants to sue. She's using the breach of contract as leverage to keep you here. I got a call from her agent—my fucking girl-friend—late last night, and she started laying into me for not following the contract. After scaring the shit out of me and our legal department until well past midnight, she told me the only way Barbara wouldn't be suing us is if you keep your job."

When the hell did Barbara find the time to contact her agent last night? Was it when I went out to buy all her favorite snacks? Jesus, she moves fast.

"We thought it would be best not to call her bluff and call Cora's instead. So...you still have your job. And Cora hasn't quit."

I make a choking sound, shocked that Barbara would be willing to go through all of that again for me. My heart squeezes in my chest just from knowing that I'm not alone in this, that she's there for me just like I want to be for her.

"Barbara's agent is terrifying, by the way. I think I might ask her to marry me." He takes another big bite and chases it with coffee.

I snort. "Because she yelled at you? That's disturbing."

He shakes his head with a smirk. "Nah. It's hot."

I laugh at him. "So, I'm definitely not fired, then?"

He sighs, I think just as relieved as I am. I don't think anyone would particularly enjoy firing their best friend. "No. But you could have easily been." He runs his fingers through his hair. "Fuck, *I* could have been fired, too. I still don't know how I wasn't."

"What? What do you mean? You didn't do anything. Did you?"

Rob shakes his head again and squeezes his eyes shut. "Someone left a note for the lighting department saying that you guys wanted a last-minute change in the whole light display. It said you wanted 'rave level' strobes in minute...whatever it was, and the note was signed by Rob Ortiz."

I shake my head, frowning. "That doesn't make any sense. Who would do that?"

"Pfft, I have no idea, man. Someone who wanted to screw me over and almost succeeded?" Rob leans back in his chair, taking a long sip of his coffee. "This season has been so weird. It's like I haven't caught a damn break since even before we aired. Between finding another partner for you because of that whole thing with Alessandra, having a recovering alcoholic fall off the wagon minutes before her first performance on live TV, and having to deal with Jess going full-on crazy on one of the other dancers just before a performance... It's been a crazy ride." He groans, rubbing his hands down his face. "I swear, after this season is over, I'm gonna take Sabrina and go somewhere remote. No cell phones, *nada*."

Rob starts listing off possible locations (all five-star luxury hotels fully equipped with functional WiFi), but I'm lost in my own thoughts because he's right. This season has been insane. Sure, there's always been the side dramas among the behind-the-scenes people—hookups and the like. But celebrities having their hearts ripped out, drunk performers, violent attacks of jealousy, and health crises? Those have never been an issue. And what about Cora? Since when is she so aggressive with me? I've gone over my relationship with her in my head a million times, and I still can't find anything that I did that might have pissed her off. And I doubt Barbara, who has had absolutely no previous contact with her whatsoever, has done anything to hurt her.

It's all so overwhelming and exhausting that it's making me doubt whether I actually want to put myself through this for another year. I need to focus on my personal life and not let myself be distracted by all this drama. Will things be better as a judge? I won't be personally involved with the day-to-day anymore, which would be a huge relief. *And* all the free time would give me the ability to work on other projects and see Bubbe more.

But as a dancer for the show...I think I'm done. I think if I don't get this judging position, I'm not renewing my contract for next season. I'll figure out what comes next when I need to, but for now, I'm just going to focus on the near future—on next week's episode and my weekend with Barbara's adoptive family.

"...and anyway, I think it would be good for us to double."

"Huh?" I'm pulled back from my thoughts, realizing that I've missed everything Rob just said. He narrows his eyes at me.

"*I said*, you and Barbara should double with me and Sabrina. You know, now that you're *actually* dating and all."

I raise my head to meet his gaze. "I—What?"

"Oh, come on. You think I'm an idiot? You didn't pull that whole alpha-male protective shit last night just for show. And no one would threaten to sue an entire network for their *fake* boyfriend. You're either really dating or on the cusp of really dating. Either way, I'd gather you caught real feelings for her now."

I smirk at him. "Yes. We're actually dating now."

"Good. If word ever got out that you were fake dating in order to get more votes, I swear to God, I'd have to retire. I can't handle any more drama."

Chapter Thirty

THEO

Hoping to run back home and slip back into bed with Barbara, I dash quickly into the first cab I see. Before I make it to Queens, unfortunately, she calls me to let me know she's on her way to her call-back. It's easy to hear the excitement in her voice—like she's walking on air. And I'm happy for her—I swear, I am—I'm just concerned about her health and wearing herself too thin. And, okay, I'm a little concerned about her losing her focus on our competition because she's distracted by other things.

But mostly it's the wearing-herself-thin thing.

"But you weren't feeling well last night," I tell her over the phone. "Shouldn't you be staying at home? Resting? That's why we canceled practice today, remember? Because you weren't feeling well."

"I'm feeling better now," she assures me. "Your bed is *very* comfortable, and I was able to recharge my batteries to about seventy percent." She chuckles, but I frown. That's not quite enough for me to be satisfied. "This is a once-in-a-lifetime opportunity, Theo. Working on this musical...you don't understand."

I sigh and let it go, trying to trust her and her decision-making abilities. "You'll just have to tell me about it later today —make me understand."

We decide to meet up later in the day for an afternoon picnic in Central Park. It's the first sunny and warm day of the season, and according to Barbara, it would be a crime not to enjoy it under the sunshine together. So, I agree to bringing the blankets and wine, and, to my horror, she commits to bringing the food.

We meet at the Bethesda fountain and walk together all the way to Sheep's Meadow, where I pick a spot on the edge, right beneath a tree. Barbara frowns at me as I shake out a blanket and lay it on the grass. "The whole point is to be *under the sun*, not the shade. It was an intense winter—I need some vitamin D."

"I'll give you some vitamin D," I say in a low voice with a smirk. She rolls her eyes at me and presses her lips together, trying hard not to laugh.

The park is full of people enjoying the sunshine and the fifty-degree temperatures. It's still cool enough to have to wear a light coat, but some just wear t-shirts and act as if it is a summer day.

"Spring is so ridiculous," I comment, shaking my head at the people around us. "Last night, it was flurrying, and less than twenty-four hours later, it's warm enough that people can lay out in the sun wearing t-shirts?" I cluck my tongue. "It's madness, I tell you."

"Wow, I don't know if I can be with someone who dislikes my favorite season so much. Seriously. You need to lay off spring." She rolls her eyes at me. "Plus, that's part of the fun. You never know what you're gonna get."

"Alright, Forrest Gump, calm down."

She gives me an annoyed look, hands on her hips, and I just

laugh, fucking giddy that I get to bicker with her like this. I grin at her and take the cooler from her hands, taking a seat, using the tree trunk as a back rest, and setting it beside me. "C'mere and stop complaining about your grumpy boyfriend." I tug on her hand, and she sits next to me. "I haven't seen you all day."

She leans over, and I take her face in my hands, kissing her deeply. "Missed you," she whispers against my mouth. I bite her lower lip before releasing her and grin.

The mind, it reels. Things have changed so much in so little time. I remember thinking how annoying I found her on the first day, how completely irritating. But now I can recognize that it was because I didn't know what to do with someone like her. My initial reaction to her, to who she is, was so dramatic I had no other way of processing it. Her outfits, her personality, her terrible jokes... I've never dated anyone like her. I love every single thing about her, and I didn't even realize it at the time.

And she's good for me, too, I think. She takes me out of my comfort zone, makes me do shit like go to the park on a Tuesday just because it's nice out, even though it means skipping practice. Make me try new foods and shows me that it's okay to have fun from time to time.

"Missed you, too," I say before kissing her again, struggling to pull away, her lips a magnet to mine. I pull back before things get too intense, already feeling the blood rush to my cock, and Barbara sits back down, crossing her legs in front of her. With a goofy grin on her face that I proudly caused, she opens the cooler and starts pulling out some cheese, a container of strawberries, some goldfish crackers, and of course, a family-sized bag of peanut M&Ms.

I start to do the mental math on how much she must've spent and feel a little guilty. She shouldn't be spending money on a picnic for me. I should be treating her. She should be focusing on her future. But I don't want her to feel self-conscious, so I don't say anything about it.

"Not bad," I tease as I carefully uncork the wine. "At least there's *one* natural ingredient in this entire lunch—that's one more than I expected. No protein, but I think we're good."

She rolls her eyes at me again and pulls a couple of paper cups out of her bag, holding them out to me so I can pour generous amounts of white wine into them. Once I'm done serving, I cork the bottle and put it back in the duffel, hiding it behind the cooler, away from the prying eyes of law enforcement.

"How was your day?" she asks, cutting a piece of cheese and popping it into her mouth.

The question is so normal, so commonplace, that I burst out laughing.

"What?" she asks self-consciously. "Do I have something on my face or something?" She draws her hands up to her mouth and chin, making sure she's fine.

"No," I chuckle. "You're fine—you're more than fine. You're perfect. I'm just still a little shocked. Being with you...it's kind of surreal." She smiles and scoots closer into me, making it possible for me to wrap my arm around her. I kiss the top of her hair and inhale.

Mmm, caramel.

"My day was okay," I finally answer. "It's perfect now, though." I feel her lips on my throat, and I close my eyes as she kisses up my neck. This thing between us...it's like alchemy, and I'm scared if we start something here, we might not be able to stop. "How was your call-back?" I ask just to get her to talk, to have to separate her lips from my skin.

She inhales as she thinks it over, leaning back slightly to look at me. "It was actually really good. They seem legitimately interested in me, which is just mind-boggling."

I frown at her. "Why would you say that? You're incredibly talented. Even as a child, you were talented."

"It's just—" She bites her lip. "The musical... I didn't want to jinx it...but Barbra Streisand is going to be taking the lead starting this summer. Working with her... I can't even describe what that would mean to me." She shakes her head, eyes glazed over as she takes a sip.

"Oh, yeah. You've mentioned you're a fan."

Barbara chokes on her wine. "*A fan?* Oh, Theo. If we're going to continue seeing each other, there's one thing you should know: Barbra Streisand is an absolute goddess, and I'm not just a *fan*. I'm a follower in the religious sense of the word."

I chuckle and kiss her on the cheek. She's so cute when she fangirls.

"I'm serious." She looks at me with widened eyes. "This isn't a joke. Barbra was there for me at my lowest. Her movies, her musicals... They're what inspired me to act, which ultimately led to my independence from my parents. She's strong, and hardworking, and a truly fine example of what an exceptional performer should be."

I purse my lips, absorbing her truth. "Okay, I get how she could be a reprieve, but I don't understand the whole independence-from-your-parents thing. What does Barbra Streisand have to do with that?"

She nestles back into my side and takes another sip of her wine. "It's complicated. She's kind of the reason why I first started acting."

"How so?"

"Well, my parents worked a lot, and I was an only child, so unless I was at school or with Liza, I was basically home alone, watching TV. I got really into musicals, and one day, I watched *Funny Girl* on TCM, and...I don't know. Something clicked. I saw Fanny Brice go from being a nobody showgirl to a star and everything she'd accomplished, and I thought, *Damn, if you work hard enough, if you're talented enough...* I don't know. It just inspired me to start acting and to do things on my own. And I liked it. It was *fun*. Plus, Fanny didn't need anyone, and I so desperately wanted that. So, I started enrolling in auditions, begging my mother to take me whenever she could—or even going by myself, sometimes. And then, one day, I went to an open casting in New York City and got asked to be part of *Phantom Fighters*. Filming was actually all the way up in the Berkshires, and my parents couldn't—*wouldn't*—leave their jobs for this, which, you know...fair enough. So, I emancipated when I was fifteen and have been living on my own since. And the rest, as they say, is history." She shrugs and takes another sip before reaching for a strawberry.

"*Fifteen?*" I breathe. "You were forced to become a grown-up at *fifteen?*"

Barbara snorts. "'Grown-up' is a relative term. When you're that young and have that much access to money, you basically hire people to do everything for you, to take on certain responsibilities that you just can't wrap your head around. Which, in the end, bit me in the ass because when everything crashed and burned, it meant I had no idea what I was doing, you know?" She offers me another strawberry, and I take a bite, thinking about what it must have been like for her. "I never learned how to be a grown-up. Until recently, anyways," she laughs.

"Still," I say, still chewing on the fruit. "It's a lot to take on."

"Yes, but it meant I was free from people who didn't want the obligation of a child." She says it so matter-of-factly that it's shocking. Like your parents having lukewarm feelings toward you is no big deal. My heart aches a little knowing how she must *really* feel—unwanted, insignificant.

I don't know who her parents think they are, but I hope I never have to meet them. I don't think I'd ever be able to control myself enough to *not* give them a piece of my mind. They don't deserve to even be associated with her—this hardworking, loving, free spirit of a woman.

"So that's what your career has always meant to you? A sort of...independence? Freedom?"

She chews on a piece of cheese while she tilts her head at me and thinks my words over. "A *tool* for it, yes—mostly. Through these latest auditions, though, I've only recently begun to realize how much fun I actually used to have. In a way, this whole losing-my-money thing ended up working out a little. It made me realize how much I actually missed acting, *performing*. And it led me to you, of course." She smiles up at me and pecks me on the lips.

She pulls back, but I follow her lips and deepen the kiss, wanting more of her—always fucking wanting more, *needing* more. My hands cup her face, and in the brief instance where our lips separate, she gasps—that sound she makes that only fuels my hunger. I pull her back to me, wanting to feel her on me. My hands slide to her waist, and I pull her onto my lap, adjusting her legs on either side of mine so that I'm in between them.

God, I love it when she straddles me.

"*Theo*," she says my name in that way that drives me crazy. I tilt my hips up as I nibble on her lip and growl, wanting her to feel just how crazy she makes me, how hard I already am. I move my hands under her coat, wrapping my arms around her, hiding my hands. "We're in the park," she whispers, looking around nervously.

To be honest, I only wanted to kiss her, but when she shifts slightly over me, a low moan breaks from my throat. I start kissing up her neck, right below her ear, where I know it drives her crazy. She says my name again, and I wish more than anything that we could just apparate to my bed—or just anywhere with some privacy, a door that locks, *anything*. For all her nerves, though, she kisses me back, rocking just the slightest bit on me, and I drag my hands down her body, down her thighs, over her tights, and then reverse course under her skirt. Suddenly, I'm met with her soft, bare skin and a strap of some kind. I separate and look down in her lap, raising the material of her skirt just a little, just enough to see.

"Holy shit, you're wearing stockings?" I whisper-yell. Does she want to kill me?

She smirks at me with that witchy look in her eyes. "That was supposed to be a surprise for later." She raises a suggestive eyebrow as I run my finger underneath one of the straps, toying with it.

"How much later? Like, *right now* later?"

Chapter Thirty-One

THEO

I'm desperate for her, dying—fucking starved. I let go of the strap with a *snap,* and she squeals a little with a laugh. My hand slips right between her legs, where I stroke her, feeling how much she wants this through the fabric of her wet panties.

She squeezes her eyes shut and presses her lips together, swallowing down a moan. "Theo, we're in public," she whispers again, taken aback, I think. "In broad daylight."

I keep stroking her where I know she likes it as I look at the crowd around us, making sure no one is watching. I grin when I see everyone is too busy playing frisbee, or sunbathing, or drinking to even take notice. I don't know where this lack of control is coming from—it's so unlike me—but I can't stop myself. I need her right here, right now.

"I just need to feel you," I confess, fully aware of how desperate I sound, how gravelly the words sound coming out of my mouth. I burrow my face in her hair and inhale. "Just be inside you," I whisper in her ear, my stomach tightening as my dick hardens even more. I kiss down her neck, to her clavicle, and pull back, meeting her gaze.

Her eyes widen, and she looks around nervously again. "I—*Here?* What if someone catches us?" She's scared, but I can feel just how much she wants this on my fingertips as I slide her lace panties to one side and drag a finger through her.

"*So fucking wet,*" I whisper against the skin of her neck.

She inhales sharply and shifts her hips over me.

"No one will catch us," I promise. "At most, people will think we're really into PDA." I kiss her neck again, suck on her collarbone, drag my teeth over it, all while touching her, my hand hidden inside the protective curtain of her coat. I don't know what's happening to me, but I know that if I'm not inside her soon I'm going to spontaneously combust. I haven't had her since this morning, and that's far too long.

Suddenly, I can't stand it any longer. "Pull your arms from your coat and wear it like a cape—it's long enough to cover us. Quick." She follows my instructions, hands shaking, her lips parted. Barbara adjusts her legs more comfortably, my finger still inside of her, pumping lightly in and out of her. "Now," I whisper in her ear, "pull me out." She moans slightly at my words, clenching around my finger, and I smile wickedly, knowing how crazy I can make her feel, too.

Barbara's hands tremble as I kiss her jaw, and she works my belt buckle open, slowly dragging the zipper of my jeans down. When her hand slips through the front of my boxers and she holds me in her hand, we both groan.

"You're so hard," she says in wonder. "I can't believe you want to do this here."

"I told you, I just want to feel you. We don't actually have to do anything." But I curl my finger inside her, and she jumps a little. "Shh," I warn her. "Don't make it look so obvious."

"*How?*" she looks down at me as if what I've just told her is insane. "How am I supposed to pretend like we're not doing anything?"

"You're an actress. Pretend," I growl and bite into her neck.

Something unleashes within her and she quickly moves to pull me out of my pants. The rush of doing something so wrong and the fact that she seems so into it makes me harder than I've ever been in my life. My hands tighten on her hips just as she rises slightly higher, scooting to position me just under her, pulling her panties aside. Pressing her forehead to mine, Barbara slowly lowers herself onto me, holding her breath. I do my best to control myself, but I can't help but release a low groan.

Fuck, I'm gonna come, and we're not even moving.

Don't come don't come don't come.

I can't even imagine what cleanup would be like in this situation.

"Oh my God," she whispers, her lips against mine. "*Theo.*" A sharp intake of breath.

"Baby, you look so hot right now." I bite her lip and barely —*just barely*—press my hips up into her. My hands travel to her ass, under the protection of her coat, and knead her there, pulling her into me. Barbara squeezes her eyes shut and presses her lips together, suppressing a whimper.

"*Gonna come,*" she whispers, her voice trembling just a little.

"Fuck yeah." I smile against her neck. I repeat the movement and press my lips to her ear. "You like being a bad girl for me, Barbara?" I thrust a little harder this time. She shivers and pants in my ear, and I smile and run my tongue lightly up her neck, knowing just how much it turns her on when I talk dirty. "What if someone catches us, huh? What if someone sees how I make you come? Sees just how bad a girl you *really* are?" I thrust up with my hips, my hands tightening on her waist. I'm pretty sure I'm gonna find bruises in the shape of my fingers on her skin tomorrow.

"Oh my God," she moans low in her throat.

"*Shh,*" I try to silence her, but I thrust back into her, and she gasps. Her arms wrap tighter around me like a vise, and I know she's about to come—it's her tell. "You gonna come on my dick?"

"*Y-y-yes,*" she whispers, and she rocks slightly on me. My hand travels to her clit, and I press down with my thumb just for a second, just once, and with that, I feel her muscles tighten and her teeth dig into my shoulder through my coat as she tries to stifle her moan.

"Holy shit." I smile victoriously as she melts in my arms. I glance at the people around us, making sure no one saw us, and grin. "See, baby? No one saw us." I lift one of my hands to the side of her neck and bring her lips to mine for a soft kiss.

She's panting, breathless. "I can't believe we just did that. What was that?"

"I don't know, but it was fucking amazing." I'm still as hard as a rock and inside her, doing my best to hold on, but I don't care. I want to tell her that I'm on the precipice, too, but I want to make this just about her.

"It *was* amazing, but... What about you?" she asks, breathless.

"Later," I kiss her deeply. "I want to lose my fucking mind with you later."

She smirks at me and kisses my forehead. "I just need to—" She lifts herself off me, and I slip out. Very carefully, she puts me back in my pants and zips me up, buckles my belt. Her face is the picture of concentration the entire time, and I just fucking beam at her, completely gone for her. Barbara adjusts her panties and slips her arms through her coat sleeves again before dismounting me. She kneels by my side and snuggles into me, eyes closed. I pull her bag to me and set it on my lap as I wait for my boner to die down.

"No one saw us, right? Lie to me if they did, please?" she asks.

I chuckle low in my throat and wrap my arm around her, kissing the top of her head. "No way. No one saw. This is New York City. Two people heavily making out in public is probably the least weird thing they're gonna see today, and that's exactly what we looked like."

She bursts out laughing and covers her face with both her hands.

"What?" I laugh. Her cheeks are flaming red.

"You're so unexpected. Even with sex." She snorts.

"Did you think I'd be boring or something?" I smirk at her.

"No, not boring. More like...controlled? Disciplined? But not in a chains-and-whips kind of way. Just in a *restrained* kind of way?" She blushes, and I laugh at her sheepish expression.

"So...boring, then." I lift an eyebrow at her.

She snorts again, flushing a deeper shade of crimson. "I guess." She rises to her knees and presses a soft kiss to my lips. "I guess I'm happy you surprised me. *More* than happy."

I laugh against her lips and kiss her, pulling back quickly before I get too excited again. "Okay, we need to go."

She pushes back at me, confused. "Where?"

"Anywhere with a door and a lock. Now," I say, getting up.

She smirks her witchy smirk at me, and I pull her to her feet. "Quick."

Chapter Thirty-Two

THEO

"So, Liza is probably going to freak out when she sees you, but please don't hold it against her. She thinks you're, like, a real celebrity or something." She smirks at me, but I can hear the nerves in her voice as she talks about her adoptive family in preparation for today. "Easter is a huge deal for them, like I said, so Catterina is gonna be all about it. They'll already have gone to mass, which is great, because that way we won't have to. I got us out of it after I told her you're Jewish." She looks at me sideways. "You *are* Jewish, right?"

"Jew-*ish*." I smile as I keep my eyes on the road. She made me rent a car this time, even though the Jetfire has been repaired and is back in action. According to Barbara, driving down the Long Island Expressway in my car would've been a surefire way to get us killed. I just rolled my eyes and agreed to it, not wanting to argue with her. She's already nervous enough as it is. "I celebrate the high holidays, but...I mean, it's not like I go to temple all the time or anything."

"Liza's mom will probably make a joke about how Jesus was Jewish, too, or something." She snorts.

"You're cute when you're nervous." I smile. She's cute when she's a lot of things. When she watches me sleep, and I pretend not to notice. When she sings show tunes in the shower after we have sex in the mornings. When she bickers with me over the silliest things. She's *especially* cute when she's boneless, melted in my arms, and looks up at me with those big hazel eyes of hers.

I grin, and my chest constricts just thinking about this morning, about waking up with my face in her hair, my arms wrapped around her. It's my favorite way to wake up, and I don't ever want it to go away.

It hasn't been long since we decided to make this official, but I already know I'll never get enough of her. Not enough of her smile, her brain, her passion for the arts, her sassy temper.

I smirk just thinking about getting to spend every day with her from now on.

"I'm not nervous," she grumbles, annoyed with me. God forbid Barbara unwillingly shows some vulnerability. "I'm just...*anxious*."

I snort and shake my head. "Which is just another word for nervous." She rolls her eyes at me and looks out the window, chewing on her bottom lip. "Hey." I reach out my right hand for her. She looks down at it and takes it. "What are you afraid of?" I ask. She looks so scared for a moment that it makes me wonder whether this really is a good idea. Not because I don't want to meet them, but because she kind of looks like she doesn't want me to.

She stares at me for a minute, and my eyes move back to the road (she's not wrong—people do drive like maniacs here). "This feels...really *real*, you know? I've—I've never introduced anyone to my parents, which is—you know, whatever. But Liza and her family...well, they're the closest thing *I* have to a family, and I really want them to like you."

"What's not to like?" I shrug.

She brings my hand to her lips and kisses my knuckles softly. "Honestly, nothing. I can't find anything wrong with you, really. Besides how judgmental you are about my eating habits."

I chuckle and move her hand to my lips, kissing her knuckles now. "That's just because I want to take care of you, not because I'm judging you." Another kiss. "It'll be fine. We'll be fine. I brought Liza's mom something Italian, just like you told me to. And I got your goddaughter and her cousins some toys, as well as flowers for Liza and Danielle. And I brushed up on sports info so I'd have stuff to talk about with Liza's brother and her husband. Did I do well?"

She grins. "*Perfect*, as usual. Very thorough."

LUNCH IS INCREDIBLE. I SWEAR, NO ONE EATS BETTER THAN Italians do, and no one cooks better than Catterina. We gorge ourselves on brightly colored spring vegetables and savory pastries, hard-boiled eggs, salami, a delicious rack of lamb with mint jelly, and top it all off with a *colomba* cake I have never tried before in my life but will never forget. We also have more chocolate eggs than I can count.

The company is amazing, too. Barbara was right that Liza would have a 'fangirl moment,' as she called it. But after a while, we were able to slip easily into having normal conversations not centered around *Celebrity Dance Battle*. Vinny and Danielle are *hilarious* and bicker almost as much as Barbara and I do, and their kids are huge balls of energy who love to bust their uncle Matt's balls—especially while they go about their Easter egg hunt in the backyard. I also get to see Barbara's softer side with Lucy, her goddaughter. My girlfriend usually always has a tough wall of sarcasm up, but seeing her there in a beautiful floral sundress, playing with the baby, stirs up some emotions inside me that I didn't know I had. They make me start to wonder whether she and I will ever have a future like that, whether we will ever get married or have kids. Does she even want them? Do I?

I already know deep down inside that I'm in this for the long haul with her. The thought of losing her, not having her, brings forward an unfamiliar ache in my chest that I never want to feel again. And having a family with her... Well, that definitely doesn't sound like a bad idea.

Things are going great, and I'm enjoying being around all these people who love her, who see just how amazing she is as a person. I like hearing about the trouble she and Liza used to get into when they were younger, like that one summer where Barbara convinced Liza to jump onto someone's yacht and lay out sunbathing all day on it without ever getting caught. I love hearing how Catterina speaks about her like a regular mother would, asking me whether I've seen her show or plays, whether I agree that she's an amazing actress or not.

I love how she's loved. She deserves it.

It's while we're having coffee after our second helping of cake that Barbara gets a call from her agent, Sabrina. She excuses herself from the table, throwing an apologetic glance in Catterina's direction, and walks out to the backyard to take the call.

I watch her walk back and forth on the lawn as a grin starts to form on her face, and she squeals in delight. "Oh my God! Thank you! Thank you!" Everyone else at the table turns to see her jump in circles with a surprised look in their eyes. My stomach turns, wondering what role she's booked. She's been on so many auditions this week, throwing our practice schedule a little off the rails. But it's okay, because our dance is going great, and I know she needs this.

"*Theo!*" she screams from the backyard. "Oh my God, I got the role for the play with Barbra!" Everyone at the table collectively gasps. Are they all aware of her obsession with Barbra Streisand, too?

"*Holy shit,*" Liza says, a hand flying to her mouth. I guess that answers my question.

"Shit!" Leo, Vinny's son says. Danielle glares at her son and reprimands him while I get up from the table and walk over to her with a small smile on my face.

"*Streisand,* Babsy?" Danielle asks, biting her lower lip.

"Yes!" She smiles, jumping in place, looking happier than I've ever seen her.

"That's amazing," I say, wrapping my arms around her. "I'm so happy for you." And I am. I really am. But isn't this the same play or musical or whatever where she's supposed to start *before* the last episode of *Celebrity Dance Battle* is filmed? Isn't this the one where she would have a scheduling conflict? Didn't we talk about this already?

"It's such a dream come true," she says into my neck, her voice breaking. "Barbra Streisand. Oh my God, Theo." I hear her sniffle, and I tense, my stomach turning over again. This is her dream. Her absolute dream. She's not gonna give it up for the possibility of making it to the final of a fucking *dance* competition. "I worked so hard to get here." She did. I know she did. I ran lines with her before, during, and after rehearsals. I heard her practicing the songs in the shower after we had sex. I kissed her goodbye before her last call-back a couple of days ago, when she couldn't even eat anything from the nerves.

I know how much she wants this.

She wants this more than the finale.

She wants this as much as I want to win the show, as much as I need the judging position.

I hold her tighter to me and force myself to smile, not wanting to ask the obvious questions that are right on the tip of my tongue: *"But what about us? What about what we agreed? Don't you care about what I want? What I need?"*

I feel like an asshole. Here she is, crying from happiness, where I can feel the relief oozing out of her, and I'm thinking about myself.

But I'm not. Not really. I'm thinking about *my* family, too. About the person dependent on me. This isn't just about me or my career. It's about who I need to take care of.

I'm so conflicted. I don't know what to say, what to do. So, I muster as much enthusiasm as I possibly can and say, "I'm so proud of you, babe." Which isn't even a lie.

Chapter Thirty-Three

BARBARA

Something's wrong. Something's majorly wrong, and we both know it.

He hasn't said anything since I got that call—not really. I watch him talk to Matt about football, his jaw tight, with as much interest as he would have if he were talking about women's shoes.

It's like he's not even trying anymore. Doesn't he know these people are like my family?

He's being rude, and that's not even who he is. I know, first-hand, that he can be a dick, but he wasn't when we first got here. He was pleasant, and nice, and sweet, and kind—the real Theo. Or at least who I thought the real Theo was.

And now... I don't even know who this guy is.

Every time I say something to him or try to participate in his conversation, he avoids my gaze, gives me one-syllable answers. I chew on my bottom lip and start freaking out, wondering what the hell went wrong.

What did I do?

At a certain point, I can't take it anymore and excuse myself from the table where we've been finishing our coffee. I walk into the kitchen, hoping to be able to eat my feelings by polishing off the rest of the *colomba*. I cut a massive piece and shove it in my mouth, not even bothering with a plate or napkin, when I hear Liza walk in behind me.

"Don't," I tell her with a mouth full of cake. "I don't want to talk about it. Mostly because I have no idea what happened."

She sighs, and we both take a seat at her mother's kitchen table. "I think this house might be cursed for new relationships during holidays. Remember that one Thanksgiving where Vinny beat the shit out of Matt?"

"This house is not cursed." I swallow. "*I'm* the one who's cursed. My life is a mess. I thought I was getting my shit together, walking around all proud of myself. New job, new boyfriend. Ooh, look at me! I'm finally acting like a grown-up and stuff. And yet, here I am, the girl with the rude boyfriend who treats her like crap."

Liza rolls her eyes at me. "Babsy, come on. Everything's gonna be okay. Whatever it is that's going on between you two, you'll talk it out and fix it. I'm sure it's nothing."

I shake my head at her and take another bite, chewing the piece in my mouth and swallowing before speaking again. "I don't know. If this is how it's gonna be... If he's going to be adorable and lovable one second and then a complete and total asshole the next... I don't need that in my life. I don't need someone so mercurial. It's disruptive, and I need to focus on getting my life together."

She rolls her eyes at me. "*Puh-lease*. It's cute how you think you could so easily walk away from him. I can tell how into him you are. You're so far gone for him it's insane."

I scoff, ignoring her little comment on the depth of my feelings. "I'm a little over people telling me I'm cute, thank you very much. I'm actually a vicious lioness."

"More like a kitten, you mean." She snorts. "Listen, just talk to him. It's really not that difficult. It's a normal part of relationships. Communication. Talking. Partnerships. You know." She pulls her brown hair over her shoulder and starts to braid it.

"That all sounds kind of terrible, if you ask me. And maybe talking isn't our forte." I take another bite because why the hell not. "We're more into bickering."

"Well, then bicker. That's kind of like communicating. Or, you know, try to *actually* communicate your feelings. It's just like with your dancing. Practice, practice, practice. I've heard it makes perfect."

AFTER THE TENSEST CAR RIDE OF MY LIFE, THEO AND I make it back to the city. "You want me to drop you off at your hotel, then?" he asks, his voice tight, as we exit the Midtown Tunnel.

"Uh, I kind of thought we'd go to your place and talk about whatever it is that's up your butt." I decide to be blunt—so sue me. I don't have the energy to beat around the bush tonight. And honestly, Liza's right. Being with a partner means being able to communicate—something that, apparently, he hasn't been capable of doing all afternoon.

He glares at me so intensely I physically flinch. It's the same look in his eyes that he had when I first met him on the street, all those weeks ago, right before he said I was, "*So weird.*"

It hurts my heart in ways I never thought it could hurt. So cold, so detached... I'm not used to this Theo anymore. The one who used to think so little of me, who thought I was some bored actress with nothing better to do with my life and didn't take anything seriously.

He just looks at me like...like the past month and a half never happened. Like we didn't just spend almost every day getting to know each other for who we really are.

"*Whatever's up my butt?* Do you mean how you basically agreed to take on a role that you know is going to conflict with the *Celebrity Dance Battle* finale? Or did you forget that they asked you to start rehearsing as soon as possible? That you told me they wanted you to start a week before the final episode of *Celebrity Dance Battle* is filmed?"

"Is *that* what this is about? You think I'm just gonna quit the show?" I raise my voice at him. I never told him I accepted the job outright! Does he not know me at all? Of course I wouldn't take it under those conditions. I would never. I would never to do that *on principle* to anyone, let alone do it to him. I know how much he needs this. I know that he's not the only one who needs for him to get this job.

"I don't know, you tell me. Were you thinking about throwing the competition instead of flat-out quitting? Slipping in the middle of the performance and then apologizing to me? That we'd lose and you'd pretend like it was an accident or something? I'd lose out on the opportunity of a lifetime to help my grandmother and my career, but you'd be fine. You'd walk out with a hundred grand and another job, and I'd be left with nothing."

My jaw drops, and my eyes water in anger. "Are you fucking kidding me, Theo?" my voice fills the car. "Are you *kidding* me right now? How can you even think that? How can you even say that?"

He laughs harshly once. "Oh, I don't know. I keep hearing about how important this role is to you. How once-in-a-lifetime it is.

'It would be a dream come true,' she tells me. You keep missing practices to go on these auditions, putting the show second. What the hell else am I supposed to think? The show isn't your first priority anymore, obviously. *I'm* not your first priority anymore." His voice chokes a bit on the last word, and I know why he's doing this. I really do. But why can't he trust me? How can he think so little of me?

I pull my eyebrows together at him and start to cry—really cry—angry tears at him. "How selfish can you be?" He flinches slightly, turning onto Eighth Avenue. "You know how hard I've been working to get my life back together, and here you are, making this about *you*? About what *you* want?"

"It's not just about me, and you know it. Being in a partnership means making these decisions together and making them based on what's best for us as a couple, as people," he says in a low voice. "It's about *us,* and it's about my family. It's not about you breaking promises you said you'd keep."

I swipe a hand over my nose and run my fingers over my cheeks, trying to clear the tears from my face, but they just keep coming.

He stops in front of my hotel, right by the valet, and then, with his eyes focused straight ahead, in a low voice, he says the worst thing he could possibly say: "You're just like your parents, and you don't even realize it. Prioritizing yourself and your work over the people you love."

It's like a punch in the stomach—it makes me want to throw up—because it's absolutely not true. I might be dedicated to my career, but I have never—*will never*—abandon the people I love for it. *Never.*

And the fact that he believes that? After everything I've told him? It's heart-wrenching. If he'd given me half a minute to explain, to tell him about something called *contract negotiations,* he'd understand.

I stare at his profile—cold and hard. I barely recognize him. And I can't be near him anymore.

"You know what, *Theodore*? Fuck you, and fuck your stupid show." I push the passenger door open and struggle to get out before slamming it as hard as I possibly can, never looking back at him.

Chapter Thirty-Four

BARBARA

I wake up the next morning—performance day—with puffy eyes and a red face. I laugh darkly at myself at how hard the makeup department is going to have to work in order to get these bags under my eyes under control.

I didn't sleep at all. Not a wink.

I spent all night crying into my pillow, freaking out over my career, and Theo, and how someone who you care about so much can get things so wrong. How they can absolutely devastate you.

Because that's what I am. Devastated that someone who I thought knew me so well could be so absolutely wrong about me.

In my limited experience, it is my belief that boyfriends are supposed to be supportive and understanding. They're supposed to be *trusting* and not total and complete assuming assholes. I mean, how could he seriously believe that I was going to leave him in the lurch?

I thought things with Theo would be different. I thought things with Theo were easy—that is, only after things weren't, of course. Sure, we wanted to kill each other a lot of the time, but I had opened myself up to him. And the fire, and the chemistry, and the love were there—at least on my end. And I don't think I've ever loved a guy before, actually. Not really. Not before him.

I never even got to tell him—*thank God.*

And now I never will.

Last night was a nightmare. I couldn't stop going over what he said, what he thought of me. How could he just believe I would abandon him? Seriously? Comparing me to my parents? It's like he knew exactly what knife to stab me with and how to twist it in the most painful way.

I run my fingers through my hair and feel a little light-headed. Scrunching my eyes shut, I balance myself with both hands on the sink.

Fuck.

This is not good. I am *not* well. I did *not* sleep. How am I going to get through today? Maybe I should go back to bed for a bit, see if I can sleep for an hour or two. I still have some time before I need to be at the studio today. I should be okay.

But I need to get up. I have other things to do, too. People to prove right and people to prove wrong. Contracts to negotiate.

Obviously, first, I need to go over the contract for the Barbra musical before I sign it. I made it very clear when I went into my first audition that there would be scheduling conflicts, so they shouldn't be surprised when I come back with that as part of my counteroffer. Rescheduling the start date was always non-nego-tiable, and it kills me that Theo automatically thought I wouldn't be finishing the show. That he thought so little of me that I would just cast him aside.

Second, I need to get a handle on my emotions, mentally prepare myself for tonight's performance. Because yesterday was Easter, Theo and I had agreed to do our dress rehearsal this morning, and I'm not about to prove him right by showing up late to this thing. I need to get it together and shower—prove to him that I'm committed. If not to him, because he's an absolute dick, then at least to the show.

I slowly walk to the shower and turn it on. Carefully, I grab the hem of my nightshirt and start pulling it off. Just then, the same cold feeling comes over my head, blinding me. My brain goes foggy and—

Chapter Thirty-Five

THEO

I CAN'T BELIEVE SHE REALLY ISN'T COMING. I CAN'T believe she's just gonna bail.

Sure, we had a fight, but does that really justify missing the show?

She wanted to skip rehearsal? *Fine.* I didn't feel like seeing her again, either, to be honest. Not today, at least. The less time spent with her the better, at this point. We need space before we talk about us again. But to not show up to perform at all? And to not even call me to let me know?

I can't believe her. I really can't believe her.

She's always gone on about how she values professionalism, and now look at her. One fight and she can't be bothered to make it to film one fucking episode—or at least let me know that she isn't coming.

I thought we were both professionals.

I know she's going to take the job, but at least have the decency to wrap things up, you know? At least until she absolutely has to start working on the musical.

I see Rob stomp over to me, looking very unhappy.

"Theodore. Where the hell is she?" He taps on his clipboard with a pen. "You guys are supposed to be on in ten minutes, and I don't see her anywhere. Our records show she hasn't even checked in with the production team."

That's because she's not here, genius. And she's not coming.

I grit my teeth together and pull my phone out of my pocket. "I don't know, Rob. Let me call her again." But I know exactly what will happen as soon as I hit *send*. The call will go straight to voicemail, just like they've all been going to all afternoon.

I wonder if she's blocked me. I wonder if she got pissed enough to just fully cut me out of her life, just like that. Gone with no warning, nothing at all.

The feeling is like a stab in the heart.

"What did she say at rehearsal this morning?" he asks. "Did she tell you she wasn't coming or something?"

"She never showed." I shrug, trying to remain unfazed when, really, I just want to angrily scream at someone—fucking *anyone*, really.

The pain of her absence is visceral, and I don't want to feel it anymore. I want it gone. I want her gone.

I spent the entire night last night running what happened yesterday over and over in my head. Admittedly, I was an asshole. I know that. I hit her where it hurt because I got scared and was a little coward. So, yeah, sure, I was an absolute dick. I should have never said that thing about her and her parents. But I at least wanted the chance to apologize, to make things right.

But to just leave me like this? Leave the show like this? It's her reputation that's on the line here, as well.

I run my fingers through my hair and groan.

God, why did I have to act like such a massive dick?

Rob's eyes widen. "What do you mean she never showed to rehearsal?" he asks slowly, menacingly, as if it were my damn fault—which I guess, it kind of is, in a way. "I have one dancer whose heels, mid-performance, literally just broke off—*both of them*—and is on the way to the hospital for possible broken ankles. And now you're telling me I've lost another fucking performance?"

I take a deep breath, about to lose it on him. I want to tell him off, to leave me the fuck alone. Can't he see that I'm fucking heartbroken over here? I'm not responsible for her. It's not my job to know where she is. I'm not in charge of what she does or where she goes. If that were true, we wouldn't be in this fight to begin with. I'm also not responsible for his day becoming a dumpster fire for him, because, guess what, so has mine, and I couldn't give a shit right now.

But I get ahold of myself because I know my problem isn't with him. It's with the woman who left me and didn't even have the decency to call.

"I can't help you right now, Rob. Sorry." More like *sorry, not sorry*. I turn and start to walk away, but he grabs me by the shoulder just in time, pulling me back.

I look down at his hand and fist my hands at my sides.

Control yourself, Theodore. The last thing you need is to beat the shit out of Rob.

So, I take a deep breath to settle myself and do my best to explain. "Listen, Rob..." I sigh. "We had a fight last night. Barbara and I. A really ugly one. And honestly, man, I don't think she's coming tonight. Apparently, she's decided to take another job that's more important to her, and she proved to me yesterday that she doesn't really give a shit about this show or me."

Rob stares at me for a beat, wide-eyed, like I've lost my goddamn mind.

And you know what? Maybe I have. Maybe I've deluded myself into thinking this was something more than it was.

My mistake.

"What the hell are you talking about? She's fucking in love with you, you idiot." He says it with such confidence, with such authority, that, for a brief second, my hopeful heart believes it.

My heart flips at the possibility of *love*, but I squash it. I remember that, when it really counted, she chose herself over me—over *us*, really. I'm just too angry to even think about that. Instead, I choose to shake my head at him, laughing humorlessly. "The only things Barbara Holt loves are herself and her career. She made that *very* evident to me last night."

Guilt courses through my body. At best, she might have been tempted to pick the musical over the show, but I most definitely pushed her over the edge by comparing her to her parents.

My fault. My fault. My fault.

Still, though.

Rob narrows his eyes at me, his hands on his hips, while he thinks my words over. "Well, what am I supposed to do now, then, Theodore? What should I tell the audience, huh? How am I going to fill up the air time? You guys have your regular performance scheduled and then a dance-off with another team. Now I have nothing."

"Honestly, Rob," I tell him, doing my best to control the edge in my voice. "I just had both the possibility of an improvement to my grandmother's care and my entire career completely flushed down the toilet by the woman I thought I loved. I couldn't give a shit about how you're supposed to fill your air time. Just pull us from the goddamn show. I'll see you tomorrow in your office for my final meeting with you. For now, I'm going the fuck home."

I pull my phone out and decide to end this thing with Barbara once and for all. Maybe she'll read it, maybe she won't—who knows if she blocked me or not. I mean, I haven't been able to get through to her all day. Regardless, I need to do this for me.

Immediately after sending the message, I block her number

and delete her contact from my phone. In a moment of complete heartbreak on the Uber ride home, I proceed to delete all the pictures I have of her and us. I pause briefly at the accidental video we made under the cherry blossom tree and decide to play it. I see how she smiled up at me, how I just beamed down at her, laughing at the ridiculousness of the situation and how much fun we were really having with each other. She looked so fucking beautiful it hurts, and even then, I looked halfway in love.

The pain is so goddamn deep it makes it hard to breathe.

I swallow the lump in my throat and delete the video, too.

Chapter Thirty-Six

BARBARA

Everything hurts.

It's the first thing I think of as I feel myself awaken for what I think isn't the first time today.

I don't open my eyes, but I take stock of my body. My muscles are sore, my forehead is throbbing, and my brain is foggy. Above all, though, my mouth hurts. The coppery taste of blood is so overpowering it makes me nauseated. I sit up quickly and lean over the side of the bed, hoping not to get vomit on the bedspread.

"Are you going to throw up again?" I hear a voice beside me, and something is dragged below my head—a trashcan? I open my eyes slowly and am met with Liza's concerned face. The room is dark, the only light on coming from the bathroom, but I can see she's pale, and her hair is a mess.

"What happened?" I ask her once I realize that I will not, in fact, be throwing up for what apparently isn't the first time. My mouth is so sore it hurts to talk. The insides of my cheeks are raw, and I definitely bit my tongue in several places.

"Housekeeping found you. I guess you had a seizure?" Ah, yes. That would explain the blood in my mouth and the rest of my symptoms. "You asked them not to call 911, so the hotel called your emergency contact instead. I came over with Vinny so he could make sure you were okay, and I've been here monitoring you ever since." Liza shrugs like it's no big deal, but I can tell she's concerned. "Don't you remember?"

"No." I softly shake my head, the room spinning a little. "But that's normal. I don't remember much after a seizure. I probably won't remember this." I inhale deeply, trying to clear my head, but it's a struggle. So much cognitive fog...and then I remember. "What about Lucy? Who's taking care of your kid?"

She shrugs. "Matt can handle her alone for one night."

I flop back onto my pillow and close my eyes only to sit up quickly again. "The show!"

Big mistake.

I lose my balance and fall back again, groaning, my head spinning for a second time, but worse than the first. I squeeze my eyes shut and bring a hand to my forehead, wincing at my own touch. "God, what the hell happened?" I *carefully* press my fingers to my forehead again and flinch.

"You, uh, hit your head against the counter on your way down, I guess. You have a pretty bad cut on your forehead..." Liza's voice shakes a little. "Thankfully, it looks like your head landed on a pile of dirty towels and clothes and not on the marble floor. It appears that you being extremely messy saved your life this time." I open my eyes and look at her and her wry smile.

"Thank you for being here," I say weakly, reaching out to grab her hand. I close my eyes again. So tired.

"Of course. You know I love you."

I want to squeeze her hand in response, but I'm finding it a bit hard for my brain to send a message to my fingers. I give up after a second. I'm too tired.

"What happened to the show? Who called Theo to let him know?"

"Well, I...no one, really. We couldn't find your phone, and when we did, it was dead. By the time we finally charged it, we couldn't get into it to call him or even your agent because we didn't have your passcode."

My eyes fly open. "So, he doesn't know? He just thinks I left him like that?"

"I'm so sorry, Barbara. But I'm sure once you explain, he'll understand. I mean, how could he not?"

"Oh my God, what time is it? What time is it?" I wail. I check the clock on the nightstand and panic. It's well past midnight.

Oh no.

"Where is it? Where's my phone?"

She hesitates but hands it to me anyway. "You should really calm down. Vinny said you need rest. I'm sure Theo will understand, Babsy. It's just a show."

"No, you don't get it," I start to cry, my head hurting even more now. "We got into a huge fight. We weren't really talking, I don't think. He said some horrible things, and—and so did I, you know? Stupid, dumb things. He's gonna think I did this on purpose. He *needed* me to do this. I was going to follow through. I was never going to leave him." I struggle to unlock my phone and search for his contact. When I try and call him, though, the call goes straight to voicemail. "Shit!" I go over to my messages to shoot him a text but see that he's already sent me one.

THEO

> I guess this is you officially ending things. Nice to know I meant so little to you that you couldn't even take thirty seconds to shoot me a text, at least. Joke's on me for trusting you, right? Never again.

"Oh my God!" I cry. "I think he blocked me. I think he's really done with me."

It hurts. And I'm not just talking about my entire body, which feels broken. No, I'm talking about him and his goddamn assumptions.

"How could he really think I wouldn't show up? Does he really think I'd be capable of just abandoning him? It doesn't matter that we fought. I would've been there," I sob. "I wouldn't have bailed. I would've been there, Liza."

She watches me with sad eyes and suddenly kicks her shoes off. Liza slips into bed with me and holds me as I spend the rest of the night sleeping and crying in her arms.

I WAKE AGAIN AROUND FIVE A.M. WITH THE STRONGEST urge to pee. I carefully push Liza away and sit up in bed, doing my best to keep my balance as I walk into the bathroom. Not wanting to disturb my best friend, I close the door behind me and turn on the light.

I look like a walking nightmare.

My hair is a mess, naturally, and I'm puffy and exhausted. But the real showstopper is that bloody shiner on my forehead, jutting out of me like I'm in the process of becoming a unicorn.

It's not pretty, I'll tell you that.

Belatedly, as I'm peeing, I see my pajama top from this morning from the corner of my eye on the bathroom floor. I look down at myself and realize that I'm wearing one of my workout tops instead.

"Oh my God," I groan. This can only mean one thing: whoever found me, found me topless, and someone had to dress me. "Great," I whisper to myself.

When I'm done, I struggle to lift myself off the toilet, but eventually, I manage. I try, unsuccessfully, to brush the knots in my hair out, but the bumps in my head make it impossible. Hurts too much.

I can't believe I really didn't feel this one coming. Usually, there's more time between my auras and my seizures. I guess I was more upset and sleep-deprived than I thought I was.

Exhausted, I turn the bathroom light off and make my way back to the bedroom, in search of my phone. I pick it up from my nightstand and cuddle up on the chair where Liza was sitting, hoping to have a message from Theo. To my disappointment, my phone is devoid of them. Heartbroken, I realize I might never get any new messages from him ever again.

For the time being, I push our relationship drama aside. I need to reach out to Sabrina and let her know what happened yesterday. I already have several missed calls and messages from her, extremely concerned. She knows about my situation, and she texted, asking if I was okay.

See, Theo? She gave me the benefit of the doubt. She knows I would never have just abandoned a project, no matter how big of a dick my costar was.

Angry tears resurface, but I do my best to push them back. I can't handle the disappointment right now. I need to focus.

Sabrina. I need to text Sabrina.

Hey. I'm so sorry to worry you. Yes, I had a seizure yesterday. Pretty bad one, apparently. Please inform the network as well. I'm sure they must be pissed. I can get a doctor's note, if needed. I'm still in the hotel but, as I evidently am no longer a participant of the show, will need to check out tomorrow morning. Not sure where I'm going yet, but I'll let you know.

Not two minutes later, I get a reply from her.

I'm really sorry to hear that. I know you'd been doing better lately. Consider the network notified. Let me know if you need anything at all.

Rob says feel better. ;)

I smirk. So, I guess that's going well, if they're together—awake—at five a.m.

I set my phone down on the armchair and look out my hotel window. Pulling my knees into my chest, I think about what my next steps should be. Given everything, if I'm feeling better, I won't need to talk to the people from the musical about changing my start date. So, there's that. I can just put Theo and *Celebrity Dance Battle* behind me and move on.

The ache in my heart is back, and I absentmindedly rub the space on my chest over it.

I made it through four episodes of the show, which means I made a hundred grand total. After subtracting Sabrina's ten percent commission and whatever taxes I would owe from it, I still have enough to make a significant dent in my debt.

With this money, my new role in the play, *and* my incoming

residuals, I should be able to pay more than what the payment schedule the financial managers set up for me is. Slowly, but surely, I will dig myself out of this hole.

Even if I dig myself out of it alone.

Chapter Thirty-Seven

THEO

I'm miserable.

I'm so fucking miserable I don't even know what to do with myself.

The past forty-eight hours have felt like a nightmare I haven't been able to wake up from, where I've not only lost the only girl I've ever truly loved, but also my career and any hopes of providing my grandmother with the care she deserves.

Because I owe it to Bubbe, I will not be renewing my contract with the show—not that they'd offer it to me anyway after everything that's happened. I'll be moving to the middle of fucking nowhere in upstate New York to take care of her until she passes. I'll live the next few months a jobless, single, pathetic guy who fucked up everything good that was going on in his life.

I press my back against the wall, squeezing my eyes shut as I wait for Rob to make it to our meeting. I know he had a late night last night from his text's timestamp, but he's ten minutes late to a one p.m. meeting, and I'm starting to get antsy.

I just want to get this over with. I want to leave *Celebrity Dance Battle* and Barbara behind, take some time off while I take care of my family, and then figure out what comes next in my life. Maybe I can choose a quiet life for myself, you know? Maybe I'll open up a small dance studio somewhere in Massachusetts near where I used to live with my parents and just teach kids how to dance.

My stomach turns over, and I groan because, even though I do like kids, that sounds like an absolute nightmare to me. I feel like I'm too competitive in nature for that life.

But what else am I supposed to do?

I sigh in relief as I hear footsteps coming down the hall. Though I'm kind of dreading this meeting, I'm happy for its distraction from my now-constant dwelling on my misgivings about how I handled things with Barbara. I feel like I'm about to lose my damn mind, and I just need a break—even if the break itself is unpleasant in its own way.

I turn to see Rob walking toward me, bags under his eyes, exhaustion written plainly on his face. Jesus Christ, what the hell happened to him?

"Business or pleasure?" I ask in a teasing voice when he reaches me.

He sighs deeply, clearly exhausted, and pulls his keys out of his pocket to unlock his door. "Both, actually. Business kept me up late. Pleasure kept me up later," he says with a smirk.

I chuckle in spite of everything, because at least he's happy. And I should be happy for him. I need to learn how to be happy for other people, because their accomplishments and successes don't mean my failure.

We sit down in our usual seats, just like any other meeting we've had this season, except I don't bring him coffee or donuts this time. I'm not trying to kiss his ass today. Although, I should have brought something to soften the blow of my... Resignation? Can you call it that when you're pretty sure the offer to renew your contract isn't going to come up anyway?

For the purpose of this meeting, I'm just gonna call it a *mutual parting of ways.*

How diplomatic of me.

"You know," he starts, "these meetings of ours are really starting to annoy the hell out of me. They're always so early and about shit I *really* don't want to be dealing with."

I laugh once—a pathetic, resigned, hard laugh. "Sorry, man. I don't mean to inconvenience you. I won't be doing it much longer. Although, it *is* one in the afternoon, so I don't know what you're referring to when you say *early.*"

"One p.m. after a night of near-debauchery is the same as saying five a.m any other day. You could've at least brought me coffee one last time, for old times' sake." He smirks at me, but his eyes are tight. He's been expecting this. He knows what I'm about to say. "So, you're not coming back, then?"

"Come on, Rob. You weren't going to ask me back, anyway. We both know that. Not after the whole Cora thing and especially not after last night." I hate that I'll be leaving the show after so long on questionable terms. I value my reputation as a professional, and I messed it up.

"Last night wasn't anyone's fault." He frowns at me. "You can't be so hard on yourself, man."

I don't want to get into how I don't know *exactly* whose fault it is—whether it was me for pushing Barbara away, or whether it was her for just disappearing like that after an argument—but I know for a fact that it's definitely someone's.

"No," I say, just because I don't want to talk about it, "but I haven't exactly been the network's favorite person, lately, have I?"

Rob narrows his eyes at me and purses his lips, thinking it over. "No. No, you haven't." I shrug and smile sadly at him.

I am fully aware that I can be difficult, and I'm sure they didn't mind that much when it was the only thing they had to deal with. And even though I'm sure that the fake-dating thing wasn't something they were excited about, at least the network was able to benefit from it.

But then, the way I got involved when the Jess-and-Shawn drama broke out and *causing* all the drama with both Cora and Barbara... That's the type of stuff they don't want to deal with. It's not the "good" kind of drama that draws in more audiences. It's the kind that drains away at their time and resources.

"So, you're just gonna, what? Go back to Butt-fuck, Nowhere and let your career die?" He exhales, frustrated. "I know you're doing the noble thing, okay? I just really wanted this for you and your Bubbe. You deserved that spot. The audiences grew to really love you this season. Plus, I think you would've made a great judge. You certainly have the experience and knowledge for it. And you wouldn't have let any bias affect your scoring."

"I appreciate everything that you're saying, really, but... They loved Barbara and me together—not Theodore Wallace," I clarify, raising a finger at him.

"Yes and no. They loved you together, it's true. But to be honest, you as a person have grown to be more popular with our audience. Seeing a more personal side of you really intrigued them. You would've been the perfect guy for the job—much better than Cora."

"Oh, well, I definitely know *that*." I snort. "It's not too difficult to do it better than her."

He chuckles slightly and runs a hand down his face. "Not to sound overly mushy here or anything, but I'm kind of going to miss you, buddy. I mean, who the hell else is going to cause trouble and make me come in early to my office after creating some sort of drama the day before?"

"Again, it's not early," I laugh. "And I don't know. Maybe Nico? When he's your judge?" I smirk at Rob, knowing he's secretly dreading having to deal with him on a more executive level now. "I just hope you don't get slammed with any public controversies involving him."

"Oh, God," he groans. "Can you imagine that self-centered, wannabe-Calvin-Klein model as a judge? I feel like he's a sexual harassment scandal waiting to happen. Plus, he already tries to make everything about him. Hugh is gonna hate him. It's gonna be an absolute nightmare."

I scoff. "Rob, you know you don't have to pick him, right? You can pick literally anyone else."

"I kind of have to pick him, at this point. I've lost all of my best dancers this season over freak accidents or crazy dramas. The only people remaining are newbies and him, really. Realistically, of the dancers left, he's the most popular one. The most liked. It's a no-brainer in terms of who's going to bring in more viewers and make the current audience happy." He looks me straight in the eye for a beat. "I would've given it to you in a heartbeat, bro."

"You said that already, but thanks." I shrug and take a deep breath, staring out Rob's office window, watching the people below us. Every pedestrian seems to walk with purpose, determination. They know where they are going. Me, however... Totally lost.

I don't belong here anymore.

"Listen, Rob. Shit happens. I messed up, I let people down and people let me down, and now I suddenly find myself unable to recognize my life anymore. But it's okay. If there's something I've learned from Barbara, it's that you can always rebuild yourself no matter what—you just need to have the determination and an indomitable will to do so." And that's one of the things I'm grateful to her for. She taught me what it looks like to be able to rebuild your life and yourself. I just hope I don't ever put myself in a position where I have to hurt the people who love me in order to do it.

Rob nods pensively at me and smiles. "I'm sorry you two had a fight, but I'm sure you'll fix it." I try to swallow the knot in my throat that's suddenly appeared, making it quite difficult for me to breathe. The ache in my chest is back, and I want it gone.

I don't want to feel this way—like I've lost everything, but more importantly her. I can find another career, look for another job. I can't find another Barbara.

I feel like such a fucking failure right now.

"How is she, by the way?" he asks, pulling me from my dark hole. "I know you're in a fight, but do you know how she's doing? Is she feeling better?"

I tilt my head at him in confusion. "What do you mean?" I ask because he seems to be looking for an answer that's more detailed than, "*She's fine.*"

"Well, Sabrina told me why she couldn't make it last night. I know that Barbara's pretty private about all of it, but I just want to make sure that she's okay."

My back tenses, and suddenly, I feel like someone's injected cold water in my veins. I feel my stomach drop in realization, and a cold sweat breaks out on the back of my neck.

I am the world's biggest fucking idiot. I am an asshole. A jackass.

The feeling of absolute and total dread courses through my body, and suddenly, I want to throw up the green juice I had this morning, because I know—*I just fucking know*—what happened. "Oh God," I mutter under my breath, absolutely horrified with myself. "What happened?" I need him to confirm my stupidity. Leaning forward in my chair, lightheaded, I ask him again, "What happened to her?" Except my voice sounds distant this time, like it isn't even mine.

Rob widens his eyes at me and leans back in his chair. "You don't know?"

"No! No, I don't know! We were in a fight—we *are* in a fight! I don't know what we are. Just tell me!" I can hear the desperation in my voice, but I don't give a shit. I'm pretty sure I'm about to throw up.

Rob looks taken aback by my reaction. "Buddy, she had a seizure yesterday. She wasn't able to warn the network in time—obviously, since no one knew where she was last night—but she texted Sabrina early this morning about it, and she told me. The network isn't happy, but..."

I block Rob's voice out as a ringing in my ears starts.

I fucked up. I fucked up. I fucked up. I fucked up.

She's never going to forgive me.

"...and so we're not going to be—"

"I need to go." I sit up fast in my seat, my breath coming in pants. "I—I need to go see her. See if she's okay."

"Theodore, I—"

"Sorry, Rob, I can't do this right now. I have to go see her. I have to go to her hotel. I have to go apologize."

He checks his watch as I gather my things. "She's probably gone by now, dude. It's one-thirty."

"Gone?" I ask, almost yelling.

"She's probably checked out by now." Rob looks almost as anxious as I feel.

"What do you mean, 'checked out'? Where the hell did she go?"

No, no, no, no, no.

Bile rises in my throat, and my hands start to shake. I can't believe what an idiot I am. I was a presumptuous ass, and now she's hurt, and I wasn't there for her when she needed me.

I need to find her.

"Well, seeing as she is no longer a contestant on the show,

she would've been made to check out this morning. I don't know where she went. I'm sorry. Can't you just call her? Or go to her place?"

"She doesn't have a place to live!" I practically wail. "I have no idea where she is now. And I can't call her. I can't have this conversation with her over the phone—and that's assuming she'd even pick up."

I dig my hands into my hair and look up at the ceiling in desperation. I've never disliked myself more. I've never been so disappointed in my actions.

I should've known better.

Rob frowns and looks at me in concern. I don't think he's ever seen me like this before. I don't think I've ever felt this way before. "Want me to call Sabrina?" he asks, his voice hopeful. "See if I can get it out of her?"

I start pacing in the small, confined space of his office, trying to figure out my next move. I can't call her because she deserves better than that. And I don't want to have Rob call Sabrina, because I don't want to give her the chance to refuse giving me the info and alerting Barbara that I'm looking for her—not if she doesn't want to see me.

The only way I'm going to be able to get through to her is if I have the element of surprise.

But how do I find out where she is?

"Did she leave a forwarding address or something?" I ask him.

Rob hesitates for a minute before opening up his laptop. "Let me check her contract. Maybe there's something there."

While he brings his computer to life and searches through his files, my mind starts to work. If she had a seizure yesterday, she's going to be in need of rest; she'll need someone to take care of her. Kicking myself for not being the one to do so, I think over what her options would be. She wouldn't ask her parents for help—obviously—but she'd reach out to her best friend, Liza.

Though I'm pretty sure she would do anything for Barbara, I doubt Liza's apartment would be the best thing for her recovery. From what I've heard, Lucy is still very much a crying baby in need of constant attention—not something that's very conducive for proper rest.

The best option for her would be Catterina, out in Long Island. I know for a fact that that woman loves Barbara almost as much as her own children. She would definitely be able to provide her with the care and attention that Barbara deserves. Plus, I'm pretty sure she'd even have her own room. And didn't Barbara mention that's where she'd been living before the show started?

"Holy shit, I know where she is," I tell Rob. "I have to go. I have to go find her."

"How do you—" But I don't let him finish that sentence because I'm out the door faster than the weather changes during springtime.

I want to run to her—no, fucking *fly* to her. To beg for her forgiveness, of course. But mostly to make sure that she's okay, that nothing more serious happened.

But first, I'm gonna need a couple things.

Chapter Thirty-Eight

BARBARA

AFTER HELPING ME PACK UP MY THINGS AND CHECK OUT OF the hotel, Vinny and Liza drive me all the way to Sag Harbor to Liza's mom's house—where I'm stuck for the time being. Until the money from the show is deposited into my account and I officially sign the contract for the musical, I can't really find my own place. Which honestly isn't bad at all, if I'm being honest.

I'm tucked in bed in the guest bedroom—*my* bedroom, I guess—at Catterina's house, where she's been nothing but attentive since my arrival. She's always been caring and generous with me, but I'd go on to describe her as more of a guardian angel now. Every couple of hours, she comes by to make sure I'm comfortable, that I've had something to eat. She brings me water and extra blankets—really anything to make me feel better.

I feel loved with her—*cared for*—and I wonder briefly if this is what it feels like to have a mother. Someone who doesn't just care whether you live or die, but who takes on so many roles just to be there for you in any way they can.

And I need that right now (I don't like to admit it, but I do), practically and emotionally. Practically, because there are just things that I can't physically do a couple of days after a seizure, things that my body just can't handle. Emotionally, because I'm so fucking tired of doing this all on my own.

I guess it's just nice to feel supported.

Especially after feeling absolutely *not* by Theo. Who, by the way, still hasn't called me and still hasn't unblocked my number. Not that I've called him again or anything. Not like I've been super pathetic and checked my phone every time I've woken up from my dozing.

I hear a floorboard creak, steps coming down the hall, and my eyes fly open. The bedroom door opens with a squeak, and Catterina's head pops in.

"Hey." I smile at her.

"I brought you some more chamomile, love," she says with a gentle smile. "Are you feeling any better? Any stronger?"

"Thank you." I reach out to take the cup, but she just sets it on the nightstand. "And yes, I suppose I do feel a bit better. I'm just tired, really. But I'll be fine in a couple of days." I reach for the tea and carefully take a sip. The hot water burns my upper lip a little, but the tea is comforting in the way only chamomile can be. "Catterina, I don't know how to thank you enough for everything that you're doing for me. Really. I'm not used to...*this*."

She's known me long enough to know exactly what I mean and why I'm saying it.

"Of course." She nods, looking away. "I'm always here for you, darling. You know I consider you as one of my own, right?"

Suddenly, there's a tightness in my throat and a stinging in my eyes. I've been so dense and stupid about so many things in my life, including my relationship with this family, with her. I've always considered Liza more of a sister to me than a friend, but I never stopped to think about my relationship with her brother and mother, too. Vinny has always been there for me—especially throughout my diagnosis—and there has never been one instance where Catterina hasn't made me feel at home in this house. Even when Liza's dad, Pietro, was still alive, I always felt like I had a protector in him.

How stupid do I have to be to not realize that I've had a family all along? *A real one.* One that reciprocates my feelings. One that wants me as much as I want them.

To Catterina's horror, I start tearing up. I settle my tea back on the table before wrapping my arms around her. Crying into her neck, I thank her once more for her help, knowing it won't be the last time she'll offer it.

She rubs my back in gentle circles, and we remain quiet for a few minutes, respecting the moment for what it is.

After some time, she pushes me back and wipes her eyes with the back of her hand. She clears her throat and pushes her hair back before asking, "Are you up for some visitors?"

"Visitors?" I ask as she stands. It can't be Liza, since she literally left only a couple of hours ago. "Who?"

Catterina gets up and wiggles her eyebrows, smiling hesitantly. "I'll send him up."

Oh God.

MY STOMACH TURNS, AND A KNOT FORMS IN MY THROAT. I don't think I'm ready for this. I really don't.

"But—" I start to complain, except she's already out the door, not giving me time to protest.

"Fuck," I mutter under my breath. I can't even imagine what I must look like right now. I mean, when was the last time I showered? Two days ago? Three? What about my hair? And my breath?

I put my hand in front of my mouth and exhale, scrunching my nose at my breath. Hoping to alleviate some of the afternoon morning breath I seem to be suffering from, I do my best to chug the hot tea.

I hear a small knock coming from the other side of the bedroom door, and I sit further up, smoothing my pajama shirt over my chest before saying, "Come in." I was going for a cool-as-a-cucumber voice, but I got a high timber instead.

"Hey," Theo says, hesitantly stepping into the bedroom. His smile is wary, and his eyes look sad, but he's here, holding a glass vase of ranunculus flowers in one hand and a bag of peanut M&Ms in the other. "Jesus Christ, your forehead," he says, his voice laced with concern. "Are you—are you okay?" He squeezes his eyes shut, shaking his head. "God, that's such a stupid question. How are you feeling?" he asks, closing the door behind him.

I take him in, head to toe, and it takes me a second before I can answer that.

"You know, it's really not fair of you to show up like this."

He sighs heavily, eyebrows pulled together, and sets the vase beside my teacup. "I—I'm sorry, I should go. You're right. I should give you space before we talk. I just heard about what happened and wanted to—"

A slow, sad smile starts to spread on my lips. "I meant it's not fair because you look *really* good, and I don't have to look at myself in the mirror to know I look like crap."

And he does look really good. He's not in his signature Steve-Jobs-meets-athlete gear—black track pants, black zip-up hoodie, black sneakers. Nope, he's in a long-sleeved navy-blue tee that makes his eyes pop and highlights his broad shoulders—makes them look absolutely delectable. He's also wearing dark-blue jeans, the ones that hang from his hips in the best possible way. His hair is disheveled just how I like it, in the way that it sometimes looks after I've run my fingers through it multiple times.

Even in my weakened state, I can appreciate how freaking hot he looks right now.

Damn him.

Theo chuckles a little at my comment and takes a seat next to me on the edge of the mattress. "You look beautiful, Barbara. You always do." He raises his hand as if to touch my face but drops it onto his lap instead.

I roll my eyes at him and scoff. "Is that the best you can do? I'm beautiful? You *hurt* me," my voice breaks a little. "You really hurt me, Theo."

His eyes flash with concern, and he swallows loudly. "I know. And I want you to know that I swear I'm not here to grovel," he says, his eyes tired but sincere. "Not yet, at least. I just came here to make sure you're okay." He hesitates for a bit. "Although, I'll be honest, I'm ready to start begging for forgiveness the second you feel better. Right now, however, I just want to be here for you. My first priority is making sure you're okay. The begging-for-forgiveness part comes after—when you're ready."

I take his hand from his lap and hold it between both of mine. I don't care that I'm supposed to be super mad at him. I miss him, and I want him close right now.

He brings our hands to his lips and kisses mine—first one, then the other—all while holding my gaze with his gorgeous blue eyes.

"That's a big shiner you got there, champ. You wanna tell me about it?" He nips at one of my knuckles, and I smile.

"It looks worse than it is. The theory is I hit my head on the bathroom counter on the way down." Theo winces and shakes his head. "Vinny said it's probably just a concussion, but nothing too serious. And I didn't need stitches or anything, so I'm good."

His mouth twists like he's in pain, and his eyes crinkle at the corners. "I only just found out this morning." He squeezes his eyes shut. "I would've been there earlier. Even if I was mad, even if you were mad, I would've been there."

"I know." Because despite him acting like an ass, Theo is the kind of guy who, if he cares about you, will stand by your side no matter what. He's loyal, strong, and would never leave someone behind.

"I brought you ranunculus," he says in a soft voice.

"I can see that." I look to my left to really take in the arrangement. The vase is comprised only of ranunculus, but in an array of different shades of pink.

It's beautiful.

"I remember you telling me on our first fake date how much you love them, what they mean to you. And I know you hate me right now, and I know I was total jerk, but I promise that, if you ever find it in your heart to forgive me, I will make sure to have at least one vase filled with them in your house at all times whenever they're in season."

I nod and look out the window, doing my best to avoid eye contact with him. I know he's waiting for me to say something, but I wouldn't know where to start. *Thanks for the flowers? I miss you like hell?*

"I'm sorry I didn't trust you," he says finally. "I'm sorry I, once again, made the assumption that you were flaky. Because of course you're not. You've shown me time and time again that if there's anyone who's loyal and committed, it's you. Whether it's to the people you care about or to your job. I should have never assumed you had skipped out on the show. I should have realized earlier that something was wrong." His face is dripping in guilt, and for the first time, I notice the dark circles under his eyes, the scruff. I don't think I've ever seen Theo without a perfectly shaven face.

"I'm sorry I freaked out about the play. I was supposed to be your biggest cheerleader—not the one to bring you down. I am so proud of everything you've accomplished—I swear—and I just let my past and *my* problems affect our relationship. I don't want you to feel like I want to hold you back, because I swear all I want to see you do is succeed and be happy. I want you to know that, despite my behavior these past couple of days, your dreams are my dreams. That no matter what you decide to do, I'll be here to support them—whatever they may be."

I feel my lips tremble, and I swear I'm doing my best to keep it together, but the exhaustion is breaking through, and it's getting harder and harder to hold on. "You should've known I wasn't just going to leave you hanging, Theo. You should have known I would've figured something out," my voice breaks, and the tears start falling.

He reaches out to cup my face and wipe my tears with his thumbs. "I know, baby." His voice sounds tortured, repentant. "And I figured it out way too late." He places the softest kiss on my forehead, next to my bruise, and leans back.

"I should've trusted you, and I didn't. I put all my shit on you—all my insecurities—and you didn't deserve that. That's all on me. I'm sorry that I ever said that thing about your parents. I've never met them, but from what you've told me, you're nothing like them, and I can't believe that I even thought that for one second. Saying you were like them... That was a low blow on my part."

He rubs his eyes with his thumbs, pausing. "But above all, Barbara," he continues after a beat, "I'm sorry I wasn't here for you sooner. I'm sorry I wasn't the one to pick you up and take care of you. I respect that you're independent and strong, but please know that helping you and taking care of you will never be a burden to me. If you let me, I promise you that taking care of you when you need me would be a privilege. Because that's what being with you feels like. Like a damn privilege."

He takes a deep breath to steady himself before saying, "I was selfish and scared, and you don't deserve that. I'm so fucking sorry."

He hangs his head as if in defeat, and his breath comes in pants, hands squeezing mine tight in his, cold and clammy from nerves.

I put a hand on his cheek, and he holds it against his face, looking up to gaze into my eyes with a sad half-smile. "God, I'm so sorry. Please forgive me."

"What about *Celebrity Dance Battle?* Will you go back next season? I know I cost you the judge role." I grimace because, although I know it wasn't my fault, I still feel guilty for having cost us our loss. "It's my fault you're out of a job."

"I don't give a damn about *Celebrity Dance Battle,* to be honest," he growls, his navy eyes fierce. "Not anymore."

I know that deep down that's not true, but I don't feel like debating it right now. There's a much more pressing matter to discuss.

"But what about Bubbe?" I feel a pang in my chest as I realize what I've cost a woman who was nothing but nice and welcoming to me. She deserves better.

He exhales and watches me with guarded eyes. "I'm going to take time off and be with her, take care of her in her own home. As for my career... I have no idea what the hell I'm going to do from now on, but I know that I want to figure it out with you." He swallows hard and kisses my hand again. "Is that okay? Can we figure things out together? Can we be partners again?"

I sniff and nod my head. "Yes, of course we can."

He wraps his arms around me, holding me tight. I feel his

nose in my hair, and I laugh because I know he's inhaling my scent. Pulling me in tighter, he places a tender, slow kiss on my neck, and I melt.

I love Theodore Wallace.

"I love you, too."

Chapter Thirty-Nine

BARBARA

THE NEXT FEW DAYS ARE A BLUR, BUT EVENTUALLY, SLOWLY, the cognitive fog starts to lift, my bruise starts to fade, and my cut starts to heal. I'm exhausted most of the time, but it's fine. After adjusting my meds a bit, my doctors are confident that we're on the right track to finding what the best dosage is for me.

That's the thing with epilepsy. There's no set prescription for it, like when you get bronchitis or something and are prescribed a set dosage of a Z-pack and some steroids. Nope, it's all trial and error. All about figuring out what side effects you can handle, how your organs react to the chemicals, and whether it affects your state of mind.

It ain't easy, but it's how it gets done.

Theo's been great since our whole discussion. I'm living at his place now while he makes arrangements to move upstate and I save up some money to get my own place—something I'll finally be able to do with the new show.

Though he'll be gone, I'll get to go visit him during my days off, and he can come down to the city to see me. He still doesn't know what's next for him professionally, but one thing's for sure, and that's that we want to stay together and figure things out as a couple.

Sometimes I feel bad that I seem to be (finally) getting my life together when I basically caused the demise of his career. Of course it wasn't on purpose, and he says he doesn't blame me at all, but I can't help the guilt. I love him, and I want what's best for him, and I know that if it hadn't been for my seizure, we would've at least made it to the finals.

By Friday, I'm feeling well enough to go into Manhattan by myself to finalize the deal with the play people. Contracts need to be signed, people need to be met, schedules need to be hammered out—you know, the usual.

Theo is adamantly against me going on my own, but I told him I'm going to have to get back to my real life soon. It's always scary to get back on the horse after a seizure. You're left wondering whether the adjustment in medication will work or not—is this when it's really going to start working? Or am I going to be triggered by something while I'm all alone walking down the street? How bad will it be? Will I hit my head? Or will someone catch me in time? And yes, it's all very scary stuff. But you have to keep on living your life, because it could always be worse, even if it could always be better.

In light of me needing to go back to having some sense of normalcy, Rosie and I make plans to see each other on Sunday night. We decide to meet up for a late-ish dinner at the network building since she needs to wrap up final wardrobe details, and I need to pick up some things Theo and I left in the dance studio.

Seeing the familiar polished wood floor and the mirrored room causes a bittersweet ache in my chest. On the one hand, I'm kind of relieved that the competition is over—it was exhausting and took a physical toll on me. On the other hand, it will always hold a special place in my heart because it's where I first met Theo, where I first got to know him, and where I met so many cool people like Rosie, who I hope stay in my life.

It's a place that will always mean the world to me.

After spotting Theo's favorite black hoodie and my pink rhinestone cat ears in the corner and stuffing them in my bag, I start to head out toward the fitting rooms to meet Rosie. A noise coming from one of the studios stops me in my tracks, though. A moan? A groan?

Holy shit, is someone having sex in one of the studios?

Gross.

Although, calling it gross would absolutely be the pot calling the kettle black, because Theo and I *may or may not* have partaken in some late-night activities in his studio a couple of weeks ago.

(It's the mirrors.)

I would love to get the hell out of here, but in order to go where I need to go, I would need to walk right by the studio in question. And I *really* don't want to see anyone in the throes of passion.

Sighing in frustration, I resolve to walk by as quietly as possible with a hand over my eyes. I don't want the trauma of having to make eye contact with some stranger while they're—

"Nico," I hear a woman moan. *Ugh.* I practically gag.

Of course it's Nico. Of course Nico would be hooking up with someone right now.

I shake my head and continue to walk down the hall, almost past the door when—

"Cora, you're so beautiful," Nico grunts.

What.

The.

Fuck.

I drop my hands, uncovering my eyes, and have to do everything in my power not to freak out and start screaming. There are just so many things wrong with this situation.

This can't be. It's not possible.

Am I going insane? My head injury must be worse than I thought. This can't be a real thing.

I bite my lip, mulling over what the right thing to do here is. I mean, she's a *judge*! And sure, she's retiring, but she's not retired *yet*. It's a huge conflict of interest!

And no offense to Cora—I'm sure she was a lovely lady when she was younger—but the age difference between these two is...*substantial,* to say the least. Their relationship is highly suspect at this point.

Maybe that's why we were getting such terrible scores.

Oh. My. God.

"Fucking Nico," I mutter under my breath. My hands fly to my mouth, and I tense, dropping to my knees, hiding behind a trashcan, hoping they didn't hear me.

I wait a couple of seconds and listen for any signs that I've been caught, but the only noises I can make out are sucking and moaning ones.

Gross.

He must've been colluding with Cora this entire time! She's been helping him with judging, inflating his numbers and deflating ours. And what about all the other incidents and dramas that happened this season? Was that them, too? Were Theo's instincts about Nico sleeping with his former partner to get back at him correct?

Holy crap.

Okay, what should I do?

What should I do? What should I do? What should I do?

I bite my lip and slowly rise to peek into his studio through the tiny window in the door. Wow, okay, they are *heavily* making out on a yoga mat, and Cora seems to keep trying to lift

Nico's shirt off. He fights her a little until giving in, and she gasps in wonder at his body.

I mean, it really is a fantastic body, despite everything. *Go Cora?*

I squeeze my eyes shut and sigh quietly because I'm about to do something really sleazy. I know that if I do this, though, it will definitely help keep Nico from becoming a judge.

I pull out my phone, open the camera app, set it to video, and hit record. I don't quite know how long I should record for—I figure about twenty seconds would be enough for the network to get the gist of it—but when Cora says, "I told you if we worked together, we'd be able to pull it off," I know I'm going to have to keep going for much longer.

She continues, "I've been having so much fun watching the network pay for not renewing my contract. And planning all these sabotages and scores with you..." She shivers. "So exciting."

"Yes," Nico laughs. "Tomorrow is going to be amazing. We just need to wait until the damn stylist leaves so we can start ripping some seams on the other people's costumes, and then we're done. One step closer to the finals."

Holy shit.

I stop the recording and quietly—*oh so quietly*—tiptoe all the way back to the fitting rooms. When I see Rosie putting the costumes away, I don't hesitate.

"Girl, you better take those home with you *tonight*, and make sure they never leave your hands until they are physically on every single performer."

She gives me a look like I've lost my damn mind—and honestly, I think this whole thing might have blown it up—so I show her the video and tell her everything. I tell her about Cora and Nico hooking up, I tell her about their evil plan, and I tell her they're about to set her up to take the fall for messing up the costumes—all in hushed tones, of course. Nico and Cora are still in the building.

By the end of the story, we're both wide-eyed, absolutely shocked by what has happened.

"I think they also did all that other sketchy stuff that's been happening around here. First, it was the whole thing with Alessandra, Theo's old partner. Then came Ronnie falling off the wagon from a bottle that she just so happened to have found on-site. After that, the Jess-and-Shawn thing, the strobe lights, the *two* heels that came off at last week's performance... I mean, you're the one with more experience on the show, obviously, but it's been crazy, hasn't it? More than usual?"

"Yes." Rosie brings her hands to her head and makes an explosive sound. "Mind. Blown."

"*I know, right?*"

"What are you going to do with the video, though? Leak it to the press?" She looks nervously down at my phone, as if it were an actual bomb.

I think for a minute on what the best way to handle this is. Obviously, the fact that they've been playing everyone like this has been extremely unfair—especially to Theo. Nico didn't deserve to be a judge before, and he certainly doesn't deserve it now. There's no way I'm going to let him get away with it.

"I don't know. Leaking it to the press won't really ensure that Nico and Cora will face the consequences of their actions— not really. Honestly, the network is capable of just brushing it off or even just letting them go. Or worse, who knows whether the network would choose to do damage control and *still* hire him? I've seen crazier things happen in showbiz."

"Isn't that what we want, though? To get them fired?"

"Yes...and no. I think I know exactly how to play this to benefit us all. In the meantime, I'd watch over everyone's costumes like a hawk from now on."

Chapter Forty

THEO

"Babe, where are you?" I ask Barbara over the phone. I've been waiting for her at her favorite place in the Theater District for almost half an hour now. "I thought we were meeting up for lunch before I go back home to start packing." I'm supposed to head up to my grandmother's old house tomorrow morning and start making it *senior friendly*. In addition to that, I have to start looking for a nurse or something who can help me during the daytime. I really need to find someone to watch her during the day so I can run errands and teach at a dance studio a couple of hours a week. Like I said, teaching dance to kids doesn't sound like career goals, but honestly, it will be a good way to get me out of the house and have some money —albeit very little of it—coming in.

"I'm, uh...not sure that's what we said. Did we agree to meet for lunch? Are you sure?" she stutters.

Concern floods my system, shooting through my veins. Is she confused again? I thought she was getting better. I thought we were past this phase. She did come in pretty late last night— barely spoke to me from how exhausted she was.

"Are you okay? Where are you? Do you need me to come get you?" Maybe it's the meds that have her confused. They did increase the dosages, and let me tell you, those meds are scary *as fuck*. I made the mistake of Googling the different types of medications she takes and dove deep into a dark hole of their side effects. It's much easier to process all the scary ones when they're being spoken out loud in a very fast, very cheerful voice in a commercial, but when you're *reading* them alone on your computer? Shit is scary.

First, it starts with the annoying dumb stuff: headaches, vomiting, diarrhea. Then, it gets weird: hair loss, rash, extreme weight gain, but then also maybe extreme weight loss? Then, it gets scary: suicidal thoughts, stroke, liver failure, kidney failure, heart attack, death.

Oh, yeah, super chill, *here's a pill that's supposed to help you but also might kill you.*

Not scary at all. Nope.

It's not easy knowing all these things now, but it's only a fraction of what she has to deal with on a daily basis.

"Babe?" I ask again because she's gone quiet, and I need to know she's okay.

"What? Huh? No, yeah, I'm fine. I'm just here with Rosie and completely lost track of time." She sounds distracted, her voice far off. "Can we reschedule to tonight? Maybe have dinner together at home?"

Home.

I love the way she says the word. It's already ours. Even when I'm gone, it'll still be *home*. Wherever she is: *home*.

All of a sudden, I realize something odd about what she just said. "Wait, what are you doing with Rosie? Today's filming day. Shouldn't she be freaking out, putting finishing touches on everyone's outfits?"

"Uh... Did I say I was with Rosie?" Her voice is uncertain.

Okay, she's either lying about something, or she's still suffering from some cog fog. *Or* she's lying about not having any more cog fog.

"Yes," I say, waving at the waiter for the check.

"I meant Sabrina," she says quickly. "I'm with Sabrina. You know, going over contracts and stuff."

"Are you sure you're okay?" I say into the phone. I'm trying really hard to not be suspicious, to trust her like she asked me to. But after seeing her in that condition and knowing how out of it she's been lately, it's a bit hard to let go.

"Yes, I— Theo I have to go. But let's talk later tonight when I get home, okay?" She hangs up, and I stare down at my phone in my hand. What the hell happened? My mind instinctively goes into overthinking mode, but I bring it to a halt.

I'm choosing to trust her and her decisions. If she says she's fine, then she's fine. Sure, she sounded a little sketchy, vacillating between who she was *really* with, but maybe it really is just the cognitive fog.

This sucks.

I check the time on my phone and figure I can easily stop by and visit Rob at work before he needs to get into executive-producer mode. I haven't seen him in a while, which is definitely a bit disorienting. I know I'm supposed to sound all macho here, but I'm allowed to miss my guy friends, okay?

I leave a ten-dollar bill on the table and walk out into another warm afternoon. Seriously, shouldn't the temperatures be kind of consistent already? If I could, I'd write a Yelp review about this season. Or at least write Mother Nature a letter...

Dear Mother Nature,

Spring is absolute bullshit. I never know how I'm supposed to dress—and if you say the word "layering," I swear to God I'm gonna lose my mind. Dudes do not do "layering."

As with any other season, would you mind keeping the temperature progression of spring consistent? Where summer goes from warm to hot as balls, fall goes from hot to cold, and winter goes from freezing my butt off to kinda cold, I would really appreciate it if spring could just go from plain old cold to warm. It would be much appreciated—and less infuriating.

Sincerely,

Theodore Wallace

I STICK MY HEAD IN ROB'S OFFICE, ONLY TO REALIZE THAT he's not there. Usually, on performance days, he goes in for a couple of hours before he heads out to check on performers and stage set-up. When I run into his assistant, Lawrence, he tells me he's lost his boss as well.

Weird. Lawrence can usually pinpoint his exact location.

I dial Rob's number and wait. It rings once before he sends my call to voicemail. "What the fuck?" I say under my breath. Annoyed, I dial again and again, with the exact same results, until he picks up on the fifth call.

"Hey, buddy, what's up?" he answers in an overly friendly tone.

"Don't you, '*Hey, buddy, what's up?*' me. Why are you dodging my calls? Is it because I'm not a part of the show anymore, so I'm not as important?" It's only a half-joke.

"You called? Huh. That's odd. I haven't seen any missed calls." He's never this cheerful before filming—it's hella suspicious.

"Okay, you and I both know you've been sending my calls to

voicemail. What's going on here?" If he tells me one more time that he's not dodging my calls...

"Buddy, I *swear*. I'm not—"

"Rob, Jesus Christ." I'm furious now, walking around the building hallways, searching for him. "What's going on? Where are you?"

"I'm at the office."

Oh, hell no.

"That's hilarious. I didn't know you were invisible now, because I was just there and didn't see you," I deadpan.

There may as well be crickets on the other end of the line. "Listen, man. I'd love to tell you all about it, but I can't right now. I have to—"

"Rob?" A female voice on the other end of the line grabs my attention. Is that...? "Rob, do you have a towel?" It's the sound of my girlfriend. In the background. Asking my best friend for a towel.

"Rob," I start in a very calm voice. "What *the fuck* is my girl-friend doing with you, and why is she asking for a towel?" Not that I'd ever believe that those two would screw around behind my back—knowing Barbara, there's probably some ridiculous explanation behind it—but the fact that they both lied about where they've been? Avoiding me? Not cool.

"We're...doing something for you. And you're just going to have to trust us."

"Is that Theo?" I hear Barbara whisper-yell.

"Please tell her that she is the loudest whisperer ever." I pinch the bridge of my nose between my thumb and forefinger, squeezing my eyes shut in frustration.

A heavy sigh. "Yes, Barbara. He wants to know what we're doing."

"Well, he can't!" she says from a distance. Suddenly, there's a rustling sound, and her voice is in my ear, clear as a summer's day. "You can't, Theo. Not yet. We're still trying to figure out logistics here."

I grunt. "Logistics for what, Barbara? And since when do you and Rob get into hijinks like a pair of besties from a kid TV show?"

"*Theo*," she says in that tone of hers. I can just see her rolling her eyes at me.

"*Barbara*," I match her tone.

"What did we say about trust?"

I groan and run a hand down my face. "This is stupid. I don't like you guys hiding stuff from me."

"You don't want to get your hands dirty on this one—trust me. This is all for your own good, and you are so going to thank us for it."

I tap my feet as I think it over. "Fine," I mutter finally. "Just know that I'm extremely concerned about this collusion of yours."

"Don't worry about it," I hear Rob say in the background. "Hey, by the way, we need you to come in for tonight. For the show, I mean. Not to perform or anything," he says quickly, nervously. "You know, sit in the audience. Front row seats, VIP treatment, et cetera."

I scoff. "Um, no. I'm not going back to *Celebrity Dance Battle* again, thanks. I'm busy."

"Except you're not," Barbara counters. "You're free. Because you and I made plans to have dinner tonight, and this is me canceling. Or moving the dinner to a different location. You pick. Either way, this isn't something you can get out of."

Fuck.

"Is there a particular reason why I need to go tonight?"

"Yes!" they say in unison. From the background, I hear Rob say, "Come dressed in, like, a suit or something. NO TRACK PANTS! VIPs are always dressed really fancy. You can pick up the tickets at the entrance and...you know, have fun."

I hesitate. "Fine. One last *Celebrity Dance Battle* for old times' sake."

"Amazing!" I hear her clap enthusiastically. "I'll meet you there, okay? It's gonna be so much fun!"

Chapter Forty-One

THEO

When I pick up the tickets from the door and make my way to my seat, I realize for the first time that I have never seen the stage from this point of view. Not ever, not once—even after all these years. I've always been either performing onstage or behind the big black curtain, watching.

It's surreal to be here like this after all this time.

I first got the job on *Celebrity Dance Battle* eight years ago, straight out of Julliard. At the time, I wasn't looking for anything like it. I was exploring different forms of dance and considering going on tour with a company and everything. But the tour got canceled, and the stars aligned, and somehow, I found myself auditioning one summer morning in front of ten different people for "the role of a lifetime," as they called it. Call me pretentious, but I never considered it as such, to be honest. It was a job that I enjoyed doing, that's for sure, but I didn't see it as my dream.

Now, though, I realize just how much I truly enjoyed it and how much I'm going to miss it. I've always been the team grump, but I've grown to care for the people on the cast and crew. It will be difficult not seeing most of them ever again. I think one of the things I enjoyed most about it was the competition aspect of it. It was exhilarating to go up against people and compete. Real ballroom dancing competitions don't last that long and definitely do not have the budget for costumes, music, or lighting that *Celebrity Dance Battle* offers.

The other amazing thing I took for granted was getting to meet a lot of interesting people—and I don't just mean the celebrities. I mean the young kids who came in to make the show possible. I got to see them grow and evolve into their own. After a couple of years went by, I became sort of a mentor to some of the younger members of the cast. Imparting my knowledge on a younger group of individuals was actually quite fulfilling.

I'm surprised by how much I'm gonna miss it.

Will teaching and mentoring children be as fulfilling as well? I truly hope so, because I've scheduled a meeting with the head of a dance studio near my Bubbe's house for the day after tomorrow to talk about me taking over some classes starting next month.

"Ladies and gentlemen, please take your seats," the voice over the speaker says. *"The show will begin in five minutes."*

Five minutes? Where's Barbara? I pull my phone out to text her but see that she's already written.

BARBARA

Running late. Don't worry about me. Be there ASAP.

I sigh and silence my phone before slipping it into my pocket. Where could she be? She said she and Rob were working on something for me, but I can't imagine what those two could scrounge up together.

I pass the time by making a mental list of all the things I

need to pack as soon as I get home. I don't intend to leave for a long time this first trip, but I may as well start transporting some of my stuff there. I'm still not sure what I should do with my apartment. Earlier today, I decided I might offer it up to Barbara, ask her to help cover rent as soon as she can.

The overhead lights start dimming, and the voice on the speaker asks all members of the audience to take their seats. There's a hustle and bustle coming from behind me as people settle down, but no other people make it to my section. Barbara and I are the only ones in the VIP area, and she hasn't even arrived yet.

I hear the distant voice of the director say, "And we're on in three, two, one," and the lights come up, and Troy comes out in all his spiky-haired glory.

"Welcome, welcome, ladies and gentlemen, to the season semi-finals! We have a fantastic show for you tonight with some new surprises!" The crowd starts cheering, and an opening musical number comes on to introduce the show. I notice it's mostly dancers in training or first-year members of the cast. It's tradition that newbs be the only ones to participate in them.

Jesus, did I used to be that young?

When the performance is over, Troy refers back to the surprises the show has in store for us after the first commercial break. The feed cuts, and the lights come back on. I take advantage of the short break to check my phone again.

Nothing.

I decide to type out another quick message:

THEO

Are you okay? The show just started.

"We're back in ten seconds, people," someone announces, and the crew moves quickly into their places.

"And we're back from our first commercial break, ready to

tell you the big news that has shaken our show. Are you guys ready?" Troy smiles that big fake smile of his and places a hand to his ear, and the crowd goes wild. "*I caaaan'tttt heaaarrr youuuu!*" The audience screams louder still, and I wince. This is crazy. "Ha-ha-ha," Troy fake-laughs. "Well, we just wanted to make a couple of announcements tonight. First off," he starts, walking from one side of the stage to the other. "One of our favorite dancers, Nico De León, has had to drop out of the competition due to personal reasons." The crowd gasps, and honestly, so do I. What could possibly have made Nico willingly drop out of the running before the finals? "But not to worry, his former partner will be dancing later tonight with one of our newest dancers." The audience seems a bit stunned but claps nonetheless.

"But the truly big news of the night is that, sadly, one of our judges has decided to retire." The crowd *awwws* in disappointment.

Oh wow, they're going to announce Cora's retirement tonight? That's really unexpected. I thought they'd wait until after the finale, release some sort of statement through the media.

Where the hell is Barbara? She's missing this entire wild adventure. If it weren't for the fact that it's being recorded and I can use it as evidence, I don't think she'd ever believe this happening.

"Yes! After several years of service, the lovely Cora Lyon has left us to take some time off for growth and personal development," Troy continues with a fake sad face, but of course, I know it's all bullshit. I know why she's *really* leaving. She's—

Wait.

Did he just say, "...*has* taken time off"? As in the present tense?

"But we, as a family, could not be happier for her and this

opportunity to reinvent herself, aren't we?" I turn to look at the judges' table as the crowd starts cheering and see Hugh's and Bex's very *un*happy-for-her expressions on their faces.

"Holy shit," I say under my breath. Did she just up and quit? Did they fire her? When did this happen?

I'm not used to not being in the know. It sucks.

Nico and Cora are both gone. Wow. We totally would've beaten the damn competition with them gone.

Oh well. You can't turn back time.

"But of course," Troy's voice pulls me back to the present, "we can't just let the lovely Bex and Hugh take on all the judging responsibility! We needed to pick a new judge—one who you'd love just as much as we do!"

I'm absolutely gutted. I knew they were going to pick someone to take on the role, but I never expected it to be this quickly or for it to be someone who wasn't Nico. If not either of us, then who? All of a sudden, there's nothing I want more than to be able to get out of here and go home. Which is *exactly* what I intend to do as soon as Barbara gets here.

"Do you want to know who it is?" I hear Troy trying to rile up the crowd as I pull out my phone again.

THEO

Hey, not feeling well. Going to head out. See you at home?

I slip my phone back in my pocket as I hear Troy's overly friendly voice say, "Here to introduce your new judge is someone who you might recognize, too." The crowd cheers as I gather up my coat and scarf before leaving my seat. "Miss Barbara Holt, everybody!" The crowd starts cheering as I watch my girlfriend practically glide onstage wearing the sexiest red dress I've ever seen in my life.

What is she doing? Why didn't she tell me about this?

"Barbara, so good to have you back!" Troy says.

"So good to *be* back, Troy." And she says it with a genuine smile, her beautiful golden hair hanging low on her back.

"Last time you were here, you were doing very well in the competition until you had to retire for personal reasons, correct?"

"Yes, Troy. But I'm not here to talk about me." She dodges the question beautifully, not wanting to put the focus on *why* she couldn't perform. "I'm here to talk about your newest judge." Her smile is broad and hopeful, and I'm so very, very confused. Did they pay her to come out and announce it? Is that why she asked me to come by?

"You may have guessed it after seeing me onstage, but to clarify it for you...it's Theodore Wallace!" She looks in my direction and flashes me that witchy grin I love so much from her.

I drop my coat in shock and do my best to stand up straight when I see the cameras point at me.

"*Ah*-mazing!" Troy exclaims. "Theodore, come right up here, please, and introduce yourself."

It takes me a minute to process what is happening. I feel like I'm having an out-of-body experience, like this isn't even my life.

Is this for real?

The audience cheers and claps loudly as a PA pulls me by the hand and pushes my shocked butt up the stairs onto the stage. I slowly walk toward Barbara and Troy, doing my best to not appear as in a daze as I feel.

"Theodore, my friend! So exciting to have you back—and on a permanent basis now!"

My eyes widen, and I'm frozen to the spot. Barbara reaches out and grabs my hand, squeezing it in hers, grounding me so I can be present in this moment.

This is obviously what she and Rob were planning all day

today, but how the hell were they able to manage it? And what the hell happened to Nico and Cora?

"I can't believe it either," I finally manage to say, because it's true. Looking down into Barbara's eyes, I smile and say, "It's like a dream come true."

I start to turn these things over in my head, but right now, I couldn't care less. I don't know how this happened, but I know for a fact that she did this for me. She worked together with Rob to help make this happen. So, I pull her into my arms and hold her as tightly as I can, for as long as I can manage without it becoming weird on national television. Before I release her, I whisper, "I love you so much, Barbara. I don't deserve you," in her ear. She squeezes me tightly once, and we separate, keeping her hand in mine.

"Love you, too," she mouths at me. I grin like a goofy idiot, staring out into the audience, marveling at this turn of events.

"Well, it's so good to see you this happy. Now, it's time for you to head to the judges' table, where you'll be seated from now on."

Epilogue

BARBARA

FIVE MONTHS LATER

"This heat is killing me," I say, fanning myself. "Is it supposed to be this hot in mid-September?" I step over a tree root and almost lose my balance. Theo's hand shoots out to catch me just in time.

"Yes," he laughs. "And it's not even that hot out. Two weeks ago, it was almost a hundred degrees. My weather app says it's only eighty-two now."

"Eighty-two is still hot," I grumble.

He smirks at me and pulls me in for a kiss, and even though it's disgustingly hot and sticky out, he still gives me the shivers. "Relax," he says against my mouth, foreheads pressed together, lips brushing against each other. "The whole point of this picnic is to unwind and just be together." He nips at my lower lip, and suddenly, I'm digging my fingers into his hair, pushing myself against him, and kissing him back.

After a few breathless moments, he gently pushes me back and chokes out a laugh. "Jesus, now I'm hot."

"Told you. Summer limits certain activities." I smirk at him, and he gives me a final kiss on the cheek before pulling me back to our tree—the one where we shared our first picnic together.

"No X-rated play at the park allowed in the summertime, for example," I grumble.

"Technically, there's no X-rated play allowed at the park *ever*, but yeah, I know what you mean. It would be difficult to pull off." I shoot him a look, but he doesn't see me. "Okay, here we are. Let's sit."

He takes the cotton blanket from my hands and spreads it under the tree, making sure it's even and not bunched. He sets the cooler down and takes a seat, pulling me down as he goes.

I pull my hair up into a bun, feeling a drop of sweat run down my back.

Gross.

"I hate summer," I mutter grumpily.

"I'm sorry," he says with a smile. Theo pulls me into him and kisses me deeply. "Fall is right around the corner. You'll be happy then."

I know fall is every girl's favorite season, but honestly, "I'd rather have winter." Snow, snow sports, cozy fires...so much better than summer.

"Well, then it's a good thing that the filming location for the *Phantom Fighters* reunion movie will be in a winter wonderland, isn't it?"

I look up at him with a giddy smile. "The location is *sick*." We got the official news today—reunion shows and movies are in, and *Phantom Fighters* will officially be back to continue the trend. Filming is supposed to begin in late November, and I couldn't be more excited. *Celebrity Dance Battle* will be on hiatus by then, so Theo will be able to come with me. I'll spend workdays filming while he skis, and then we'll spend romantic nights by the fire after work—getting *very* X-rated.

"I'm so excited to see the cast and crew again. You have no idea."

"Oh, I think I have an idea." He grins. "You talk about it all the time," he says, but he doesn't say it unkindly.

The play is going amazingly. Reviews are strong, and working with Barbra feels like a dream I never want to wake up from (similar to how I feel whenever I'm with Theo), but I'm taking a small break from it to work on this project. *Phantom Fighters* was where I was born and grew as an actress, and being part of this project feels like coming full circle.

"I'm so happy Rosie is coming, too. I'm so excited for her to be in charge of my wardrobe again."

"Just like old times," he muses, playing with my hair.

"Well, not *exactly* like old times. You're a big-time judge on a super-cool dance show now."

He snorts and blushes, still not used to his success. Even weeks after the show ended and the official contracts were drawn and signed for the new season, Theo still couldn't compute what was going on or how we managed to pull it off.

"It was really simple," I told him. "I just went to the other person in your life who knew you deserved this above anyone else—and actually had the power to make it happen."

If we had gone to the press, there's no telling what would have happened. The network PR people could've brushed it off, or Cora and Nico could've been fired and someone else would've been picked. Whereas, going to Rob felt like the equivalent of starting a controlled forest fire in order to make sure things didn't get out of hand. With the video, Rob obviously had enough cause to fire Cora and Nico, who were definitely not happy. After receiving several lawsuit threats from both of them, Rob made sure they knew he had evidence and was not afraid to use it. They could either go quietly, or *the network* would press charges against *them*.

It was all quite beautiful, really.

After that, it was just a question of convincing the higher-ups to ignore the whole whoever-makes-it-to-the-final-gets-the-judge-position thing. It was a no-brainer that Theo was the perfect man for the job—he always had been. But what really convinced the network was how much the audiences had grown to love him. How much they genuinely enjoyed his presence on TV.

Almost as much as *I* enjoyed his presence.

With that, he got a *major* deal with the network and had more than enough cash to move his Bubbe back home. He got her the best care available and is able to visit several times a week with his flexible schedule. The difference in Bubbe's state of mind and consciousness has been remarkable. I truly never thought it would be possible. She still sundowns sometimes, but it's less often. More importantly, though, she's so much happier being home, getting to live the rest of her life where she wants to be.

Theo twirls a strand of my hair, winding it tightly around his finger, and tugs on it a bit. I squeal a little, but he laughs before kissing me again, holding my face between his hands. "I love you," he whispers again, and another goofy grin is plastered all over my face.

That happens a lot in front of him.

"Should we eat, then?" His voice is eager.

I roll my eyes, knowing what to expect. It was his turn to pack the picnic this time, and every time he does, it's full of healthy snacks like fruits, and veggies, and hummus. Which is... fine, but not great.

I pop open the cooler and am happily surprised to find a massive bag of peanut M&Ms (which is good, since I think the one I have stowed in my bag has probably melted by now, and this one's been on ice), kettle chips, a bottle of chilled champagne, and other very yummy, very delicious-looking snacks—

none of which a health-nut like Theo would ever willingly consume unless his girlfriend was making him.

I raise an eyebrow at him. "What is this?" I ask, shocked. "This is *not* your usual packed picnic basket, sir."

He smiles his sexy half-smile, but there's a bit of concern or anxiety behind his eyes. "This is a special one for you—for us," he corrects. "I brought all your favorite things, because—" Theo reaches into his pocket and gets to his knees, pulling a velvet box from his pocket.

"Oh my God—*what?*" I squeal. Nestled in a light-blue velvet material is the most beautiful engagement ring I've ever seen in my life—a champagne, vintage cushion cut diamond in a delicate gold setting with smaller diamonds on either side.

So unique, so romantic...

"Barbara..." Theo takes a breath. "You drive me crazy. We bicker and disagree on so many things, but I honestly love you so much more for it. You bring much-needed balance into my life and challenge me in the best possible ways every day. Despite our differences—which I love"—a small smile—"we have the same core values, which is pivotal for sharing a life together. And I can't imagine spending one second without you in it, can't imagine ever loving anyone as much as I love you." He pauses to steady himself, and I think I'm still unattractively staring at him, slack-jawed. "Barbara," he says in a lower voice, "will you marry me? Be my partner *for life* this time?"

I scream and launch myself into his arms, throwing us off balance, causing us to roll back onto the blanket. "Yes! Yes!" I straddle him and kiss him as he laughs against my lips. He gently pushes against me, blushing slightly, as we realize that we're being watched by neighboring parkgoers. Some shout their congratulations, and another tries to start a slow clap but stops once no one follows along.

Laughing, I manage to sit back into a more ladylike position.

Theo's smile is wide and bright as he reaches over to grab the ring I knocked out of his hands. He takes my hand in his, and with his beautiful navy eyes on me, he slides the ring on my finger, where it'll stay until the day I die.

THE END

Thanks so much for reading Barbara and Theo's story! I hope you enjoyed reading their story as much as I enjoyed writing it. If you did, please drop me a review and follow me on Instagram to stay up to date on all future releases and cat pictures.

Want to read Liza's story? Make sure to read Book 1 in the Seasons of Love Series by clicking here.

Acknowledgments

I can't start thanking anyone without first mentioning my husband, the man who helps me through every single one of my writer's blocks or talks things through with me if I write myself into a corner. Barbara's story would have been completely different had it not been for him. Because epilepsy is something that personally affects me, it was difficult to write about it without bumming the reader out or making light of something that affects so many people in different ways. It came to a point where I doubted even making her have the condition, but K pushed me because he knew I wanted to write about someone who could represent people like me. And I'm so damn glad he did.

Because of what this book specifically means to me, I would also like to take the opportunity to thank my doctor and everyone at NYU Langone Epilepsy Center for all that they have done for me and countless others. Everyone on my provider team has been extraordinary, and I truly could not have dreamed of better care. I know that I am truly blessed; that not everyone is as lucky as I was.

The circumstances under which I found myself under their care were not happy ones, but they brought so many life lessons with them that I can't help but be a little thankful for it. When I came to them, I was also young, rebellious, and not taking care of myself. They taught my immature self that things could be better, it's true, but they could also always be worse—and for that I should be thankful.

I want to thank my dad for being by my side through the worst of it all and being the complete opposite of what Barbara's parents were. My mom, for also having to deal with an angry teenager who just couldn't understand why there were things she couldn't do that seemed so normal for everyone else. Simple things like staying up late or sleeping over at friends' houses. I didn't get that—it took me a while to understand—and for that I'm sorry.

Also, the rest of my family for almost completely coming around and supporting me and my dream.

I want to thank the Arthur Murray Dance Studio in Boston for their kick ass advice, dance lessons, and help during my research process. Kristen, Harrison, Bjorn, Danni, Rob, and the whole team. You guys are amazing and have me officially hooked! Though I'm pretty much a sucker for any sport that will require me to wear cute outfits and shoes.

To my besties AZ and EG, always my biggest support systems. Love you and miss you loads.

To Barbara, for letting me use her namesake—hope I made you proud—and my CJBC peeps. You guys crack me up.

And to Massachusetts—I f-ing love it here!

Also by
CAROLINE FRANK

Seasons of Love Series (Open-Door Romantic Comedy):

Fall Into You (Book 1)

Shall We Dance? (Book 2)

Happily Ever Disaster (Novella - Book 2.5)

Second Chance Snowmance (Book 3) **Coming Soon!**

Standalone Women's Contemporary (Open-Door):

In For a Penny

CAROLINE FRANK

Caroline Frank is an indie author and self-proclaimed shoe addict. She currently resides in Massachusetts with her husband and two crazy cats, Señor Kitty and Salem.

She spends her days reading, crocheting, crafting, writing, and biking. Her favorite things include the first sip of a Coke on a hot day, crocheting, and using self-deprecating humor to get through the day.

Though she always planned to eventually take over the world, she thinks writing fun stories every day is pretty freaking awesome and plans to continue to do so for the foreseeable future.

www.ingramcontent.com/pod-product-compliance
Lightning Source LLC
Chambersburg PA
CBHW050924220726
48290CB00018B/1527